... well-known Indian writer. For the ... he has been working full-time to realise his ... dream of retelling the great tales of Indian myth ... legend. He has completed the third and fourth books of the Ramayana, *Demons of Chitrakut* and *Armies of Hanuman*, and is currently finishing the last three books, *Lair of Rakshasas*, *Lord of Lanka* and *King of Ayodhya*.

Ashok lives in Bombay, India.

Find out more about Ashok K. Banker and other Orbit authors by registering for the free monthly newsletter at www.orbitbooks.co.uk

By Ashok K. Banker

The Ramayana

Prince of Ayodhya
Siege of Mithila

Look out for

Demons of Chitrakut

Ashok K. Banker

SIEGE OF MITHILA

BOOK TWO OF THE RAMAYANA

www.orbitbooks.co.uk

An *Orbit* Book

First published in Great Britain by Orbit 2003

ISBN 1 84149 198 5

Typeset by Hewer Text Ltd, Edinburgh
Printed and bound in Great Britain by
Mackays of Chatham plc, Chatham, Kent

Orbit
An imprint of
Time Warner Books UK
Brettenham House
Lancaster Place
London WC2E 7EN

Ganesa, lead well this army of words

For Sanjeev Shankar,
marg-saathi from Mahapalika Marg to Mithila.
And beyond.

ACKNOWLEDGEMENTS

Hugs and kisses all around for:

Liz Williams, science fiction novelist and author of *Ghost Sister, Empire of Bones, The Poison Master* and *Nine Layers of Sky*. And for Charles, who will be missed.

Shawna McCarthy and Danny Baror, two of the finest literary agents in the business. They launched me on the first stage of this epic journey.

Tim Holman, who continues to exhibit the kind of understanding, patience and editorial wisdom that would have rightly earned him seer-mage status in ancient Arya. Pranaam, Guru-dev!

The people at Orbit and Time Warner Books UK, for putting their muscle and their hearts behind this series: Gabriella Nemeth, desk editor; Ben Sharpe, editor; Jessica Williamson, publicity and marketing; Nicola Hill, export manager; Bella Pagan, editorial assistant; all the printing, production, distribution, sales and marketing guys who work backstage to keep the music rolling.

A special thanks to the bookshop buyers and staff who actually take the time and effort to read and recommend good books – and I don't just mean this one! – to potential readers. You are the lifeblood of this field. Keep on reading, and selling!

With a special thank you to fellow authors Meg Chittenden (*More Than you Know*, Berkley), Cecilia Dart-Thornton (*The Bitterbynde Trilogy*) and Juliet E. McKenna (*The Tales of Einarinn*) for taking time off from busy writing schedules to offer valuable advice and encouragement.

Special hugs for my wife Bithika, my son Ayush, and daughter Yashka. None of this would be possible without any of you. You complete me.

And last but certainly not least of all, thank you, constant reader, whomever you may be, for joining me on this long adventure from Ayodhya to Mithila, and beyond.

Om Bhur Bhuvah Swah:
Tat Savitur Varenyam
Bhargo Devasya Dhimahi
Dhiyo yo nah prachodayat

Maha-mantra Gayatri
(whispered into the ears
of newborn infants at
their naming ceremony)

PRARAMBH

———

AGAINST A
DARK BACKGROUND

I

'*Rama . . .*'

He twisted on the straw pallet, battling nightmares. A merciless giant tightened her grip on his heart, squeezing harder . . . harder . . .

He thrashed, his naked torso flayed by invisible lashes. Sweat beaded on his muscled limbs, dripping through the crushed darbha blades on to the mud floor of the hut, staining it the dark vermilion hue of heart-blood.

Beside him, Lakshman slept deeply, too deeply, unnaturally still, curled like a Sanskrit symbol. His chest barely rose and fell, his body's rhythm slowed to the verge of stasis.

'*Rama . . .*'

Softly, like a gandharva whispering a coy secret.

Rama moaned, burying his face within the darbha pallet. Reeds of straw scratched his face, pricking his tightly shut eyelids. He fought invisible phantoms. Lakshman slept on, his breath ragged, heartbeat irregular, on the knife edge between dreams and eternal dreamlessness.

Still softly, but with a sense of growing urgency.

'*Rama . . .*'

He grew still, then utterly motionless, remaining that way for a long frozen moment. A vein pulsed steadily on his neck, the only sign of life. Beside him, Lakshman's breathing stopped too, his fluttering pupils slowing behind his eyelids, growing deathly still.

Rama opened his eyes. They glowed icy blue, their inhuman light reflected off the curved glass of a lantern suspended from the thatched roof.

Slowly, like a swan rising up from the surface of a lake, he got to his feet. On the floor, Lakshman resumed breathing with a harsh intake of breath.

Rama went to the open doorway of the hut, stood limned against the faintly lighter darkness of the doorway a moment, then stepped outside.

The ashram lay quietly asleep. At the far end of the sprawling compound, in the northernmost hut, brahma-charya acolytes tended the sacred yagna fire, keeping the chain of mantra recitation unbroken. Except for them, Siddh-ashrama was deserted and still, the rest of its hundred and six male occupants deeply asleep. They all dreamed the same shared nightmare that Lakshman was now dreaming. In an hour or two, the compound would swell with the noises of a hundred brahmins, sadhus, rishis and brahmacharyas, going about the daily chores of a forest retreat. But for now, it may as well have been a graveyard.

Not a soul saw Rama emerge from the southernmost hut, pause a moment as if listening to some unheard voice, then turn to walk away from the ashram, through the vegetable grove and bamboo thicket that lay behind; and then, several hundred yards later, enter the deep, forbidding Vatsa jungle. The darkness parted like black velvet folds, enveloping the slender form, then closed around him. No sign remained of his passing.

In the hut, Lakshman's breathing resumed a natural sleep pattern. His pupils began swirling behind closed lids again. He descended into the arms of familiar nightmares.

She was waiting for him in the darkness beneath a peepal tree. Silvery moonlight shrouded her like an enormous gauze veil. Her hair and eyes were raven black, her skin the shade of chalk. She stood amongst the wild peepal tendrils, singing softly in the still, silent jungle. A pair of lions nuzzled at her hand, feeding docilely on the savouries she held in her palm. He looked closely and saw that they were tiny squirming beings, perhaps an inch high apiece. He could hear them screaming tinnily. She fed them into the whiskered mouths of the lions. The beasts licked spots of blood off her milky fair hands.

She was naked, clothed only in the moonlight. There was something about that which disturbed him; it disturbed him more than the other things, but he could not understand why for several moments. Then it came to him: Holi purnima was eight nights ago. The moon couldn't possibly be this bright and full tonight. It bothered him more than anything else about this dreamlike scenario.

She raised her head, as if noticing him only now, and smiled. Her teeth were as white as the pearls gifted to his father last winter by southern fishermen, pearls gleaned from the depths of the Banglar ocean. They gleamed dangerously in the moonlight. The lions parted their jaws sleepily, mirroring her smile. Their fangs were flecked with blood. In the maw of one, Rama could see the half-chewed bodies of those little beings – what were they? – still wriggling feebly. The lion growled softly and snapped its jaws shut, jerking its head as it swallowed down the remnants. Her tongue was black as coal, Rama saw. Her teeth, despite their pearly whiteness, were jagged and misshapen. It was a terrible smile, filled with the dark promise of certain destruction. A smile foretelling the end of all creation.

She gestured, calling to him.

He took a step forward. Then stopped.

She smiled.

'Do not fear me. If I wished to harm you, the lions would know. They know everything that has been, and everything that will be.'

In perfect unison, the lions lowered themselves to the ground, resting their great heads on their paws, whiskers frisking her bare feet. He saw that each lion was old, beyond the measure of human reckoning. Almost as old as time itself.

'Yes,' she said. 'And almost as old as I. For we three are one. Now come. There is something I wish you to see.'

He remained where he was for another moment. Then he looked up at the moon pointedly.

She laughed. A tinkling laugh, like the tiny silver bells of a woman's anklet. Her belly shook, and a bright orange bird with yard-long yellow and green plumage emerged beak-first from her navel. It flew up screaming and was lost in the treetops. A chilli-green feather drifted down slowly, bobbing.

'Do you fear the moon? You, Rama Chandra? He Who Has The Face Of The Moon Himself?'

He waited.

She inclined her head, exposing the delicate line of her long slender neck to the wash of moonlight. 'This is true. It should not be a full moon tonight. Awamas is almost upon us. Yet I wished to have light by which to see you more clearly. Does it trouble you? I should change it back if it pleases you.'

She raised her hand, prepared to reduce the moon to a sliver. He shook his head slowly. Then he shrugged.

She lowered her hand, then held it out to him, beckoning again. 'Come then. You have nothing to fear from me. I do not hate all men. Only those who . . . but that does not concern us, here and now. Come.'

When he still didn't respond, she lost her smile. Her eyes, so dark in the shadows of the peepal boughs, flashed. Their light was the light of distant stars that have long since burned to white dust yet remain suspended in the trap of time and space for millennia uncounted; it was like looking into the heart of the heart of the sun at noonday.

'Who are you?' he asked.

She remained motionless. The lion to her left began to growl softly, its tail stiffening in warning. Rama saw her eyes sparkle softly, dangerously, in the shadows, glinting with a cold colourless light, like a fire trapped in obsidian ovals. A raven, jet black to the point of blueness, emerged tail-first from her navel, walked up her belly, and perched on her left breast, regarding Rama sullenly. Then, as the fire in her eyes died down, the raven rose without flapping its wings and shot directly upwards like an arrow aimed at the belly of the sky. The lion ceased growling and began swirling its tail slowly in lazy circles. It lowered its jowls to its paws again, eyes half-hidden by the wrinkled folds around them.

She replied, 'What do you wish to know? My name? I have more names than there are words in any tongue. Some have been forgotten aeons before you people were created, some will not be spoken for aeons yet.'

He did not say anything. She tossed her head, her hair glinting with flame-bright sparkles. 'The people of Eric the Norseman named me Frejya. The Inuits of the land that is always clothed in ice call me Sedna. In the land of Nippon, I am known as Amateras of the Sun. In Greece, Demeter of the Corn. In Egypt, they know me as Isis of the River. In times past and future, I have been and will be known as

Tara, Coatlicue, Ishtar, Artemis and Shakti. These are but a few of my infinite names. Which would you like to call me?'

When he did not answer, she went on, 'I am the life-bestower, nourisher, lover, comforter and, finally, life-taker. I am the mother-goddess who resides in dark caves and sits on pink lotuses surrounded by birds and beasts, spinning the web of life or kneading the earth with life-giving sap. Sometimes I am a man, for what else is a man but a woman who has altered her form to suit a different purpose? My friend here is portrayed as one lion or two, but also as a swan, a cow, or a pack of dogs. You see him as lions, and you see me as you see me now, because that is how you choose to see us. He is the masculine to my feminine, the completion of my circle and my first creation. Together we are I. I am all things to all beings.'

He spoke softly, neither apologetic nor arrogant. He knew that the first would elicit a loss of respect while the latter would entail a loss of his life. He said simply, 'Devi, lead me where you will.'

She smiled again at last, this time revealing flawless pearl-white teeth dazzling to behold in the darkness. She stepped forward and raised her arm, now bedecked in a diaphanous garment of a fashion he had never seen before. He walked the few yards to her side and allowed her to take his arm, gripping it with both her hands as she walked him deeper into the forest. Without looking back, he knew that the lions did not follow. He had passed their scrutiny.

In the northernmost hut of Siddh-ashrama, Brahmarishi Vishwamitra was seated in the lotus posture. On the stoop of the hut two pre-pubescent brahmacharya acolytes sat chanting slokas alternately, maintaining a chain of recitation that had not ceased since the ashram's inception, over a thousand years ago. They would be relieved in a few hours, at dawn, but for now their entire concentration was on the recitation. Not a syllable must be dropped or mispronounced.

Within the single room of the hut, a room bare of furnishings or adornments as befitted a holy man, the brahmarishi himself was neither asleep nor awake. He was in that yogic state of suspended animation known as yoganidra. The sleep of meditation; not truly a sleep, but a trance-like condition conducive to higher contemplation. His flowing white beard and tresses were evidence of his five millennia of intense tapas – literally, the heat generated by self-sacrifice. In this exalted state, he barely needed to draw breath, able to sustain his bodily needs by a mere wisp of air drawn every few hours, perhaps a sip of water taken once every day. Even that was voluntary. He could have remained without nourishment indefinitely if he chose to do so; indeed, he had only recently roused himself from a two-hundred-and-forty-year penitential trance, necessary for achieving the spiritual goal he had set himself.

In times past, he had meditated thus in deep jungles, on icebound mountaintops, in flowing rivers in spate, even at the bottom of the ocean once. Nothing could break his yoganidra. The faint blue glow of brahman shakti surrounded and protected him from all risks, physical, mental and spiritual. He had no need to chant mantras or slokas aloud; he had long since mastered the art of achieving silent, perfect harmony with the cosmic reverberations of supreme Om itself, the heartbeat of all creation.

Yet now, for only the second time in two hundred and forty years and a week, his concentration broke. It was by choice that it happened, yet that was no less a rarity. For it took a crisis of cosmic magnitude to rouse a seer-mage of Vishwamitra's stature from even a single night's meditation. His eyes opened, the blue light of brahman flickering like cerulean lightning within their deep-set orbs. His lips parted, drawing a single minimal breath.

There was nobody to see his awakening. The two young acolytes outside on the stoop continued their recitation, unaware of the mighty forces swirling around the ashram this night.

Yet if anyone had been there to look into Vishwamitra's opening eyes, they would have seen, for a fraction of an instant, a tiny reflected image on both his pupils. The kind of image that one might expect to see if the seer-mage had been staring at a particular object.

It was the image of Rama entering the Vatsa jungle alone.

The brahmarishi spoke a single word, barely audible even in the stillness of the ashram. Against the sound of the rote incantation of the brahmacharyas, the word was an unseen drop in a rain-washed pool. Yet its echoes filled the universe.

'*Rama . . .*'

Sita.

Whisper-smooth, silken-soft, feather-gentle. The voice caressed her as sensually as a peacock-feather fan. The erotic undertone was unmistakable: the speaker wanted her.

She blinked herself awake, thinking it was another of those strange disturbing dreams that left her oddly aroused and unable to sleep. She sometimes had them after listening to Sakuntala-daiimaa's scarier stories – although she was the one who always coaxed and cajoled the ageing wet nurse to tell those gruesome tales. Never again, she swore now, shivering even though the winter chill had all but fled since Holi. No more scary stories after dark.

She reached up slowly, touching her face and upper body, making sure she really was awake and not dreaming. She could still feel the spot on the nape of her neck where he had breathed her name. She had felt the warmth of his breath before he spoke, as if he had been nuzzling her and had then whispered into her ear. She turned her head on the pillow, convinced that there would be a dark shadow looming beside the bed. A towering hulk of a man looking down at her from the darkness of a thick black cloak. And a cowl around his head that bulged impossibly wide to either side, a cowl pulled so low across his face that she could see nothing but his yellow eyes, gleaming like hot ingots in a goldsmith's furnace.

But the corner by the bedstead was empty. As was the rest of the room. Of course it's empty! What else did you expect? She smiled sleepily at the folly of her thoughts. A man? In her bedchambers? In the thick of night? Impossible! Her father was ferociously possessive of his daughters, and none of the four jewels in his crown – as he called them proudly – was more precious than his eldest. At the time of her birth, Raja Janak had instituted a special division of female kshatriyas, dubbing them rani-rakshaks to remind them that they were exactly that, queen-protectors. They were oath-sworn to guard her with her life. They monitored her every action, rising or asleep, and checked every visitor and would-be visitor. Even now, she knew, they would be patrolling her palace in the traditional Mithila ring-formation, at all times within sight and sound of her presence. All she need do was whisper aloud, and they would be beside her, ready to give their lives in her service.

Especially Nakhudi. The amazonian chief of the clan would sooner die than allow a man to get within ten paces of her princess. Her queen, as she always calls me, even though I'm a long way from being crowned. Yes, Nakhudi would surely be outside the door of her chamber, only a few yards away.

At that thought, the last vestiges of trepidation faded away and she tossed her head carelessly, scornful now of her brief nervousness. A bad dream, that was all it was.

She sat up and was enveloped by the gossamer folds of the insect netting. Pushing the net away, she swung her feet out of bed. The red-tiled floor was deliciously cold against her sleep-warm soles, a sensation she loved. A gentle night breeze nudged the tied drapes of the open veranda, whispering softly. The princess gardens fronted the four-sectioned palace in which she and her sisters resided, keeping at bay the animal fetors and other cosmopolitan odours of the city. The breeze carried in only the sweet natural scents of the gardens, its blossoms just starting to bloom in this first blush of spring. She could make out the individual scents of her favourites, name each species and sub-species as authoritatively as Sadanand, the royal gardener. But right now she was content to simply breathe in the aromatic fragrances. A celebration of the new season. Before it ended, she would no longer be simply a princess, or even a crown princess. She would be a wife.

The thought made her want to laugh out loud. She rose to her feet, walking around her bed towards the enticing scented breezes of the veranda. I, married? A wife? Some day a mother? The thought was ludicrous. She had laughed aloud when her father had told her solemnly that she was to be married this season. He had not approved of her laughter, although he was a good enough father to understand it. But his understanding had been tinged with sadness when she was done guffawing and he had continued speaking. Alas, he had said, I am about to lose my most beloved daughter, and laughter is not the response that rises most naturally to my senses. That had stopped her. She had lost the churlish grin at once and caught his hand. Then don't make me do this, she had said with all the earnestness of a sixteen-year-old. Don't make me marry just yet, if ever. And he had smiled sadly and said, It's that *if ever* that makes me certain you must be married now.

Now, she stood before the open veranda, basking in the aromatic night breeze. The flimsy fabric of her nightgown swirled and billowed around her. The delicate teasing

breeze made even the diaphanous silk seem to melt away.
The silver bells on her anklets tinkled delicately.

The wind grew bolder, more insouciant, daring to caress
her sleep-delicate skin sensuously. Her nightgown teased
her lightly, dancing in the wind, reminding her of the
expert oiled fingers of Irawali, her personal masseuse. It
brought to mind the divinely relaxing rose-scented bath
she always took after her oil massages, and she shut her
eyes, surrendering to the sensual pleasure of the memory.
She smelled the moist perfume of the bathwater, felt the
steam rising languidly from the large round marble tub,
the soft warm waves lapping at her tingling skin . . .

You arouse me beyond endurance.

Her eyes flew open, her body tensing as she fell into the
dragon crouch that Nakhudi had taught her so well in
their daily training sessions.

Nakhudi's guttural Jat accent spoke quietly in her
memory: queen's first duty, survive. The dragon crouch
reduced her targetable area by two thirds, confusing
potential assassins and removing her vulnerable upper
body from the sweep of any handheld weapon. Now
she could dart forward like a lizard, slash at her attackers'
vital organs or knock them off their feet and open their
throats.

Gone was the odour of scented bath and rose petals.
Instead, an alien stench assaulted her nostrils: sharper,
pungent, penetrating. It reeked of something ancient and
corrupt, of dank dungeons and moulding corpses, of
mausoleums and tombs that had not seen the light of
day for centuries.

She scanned the chamber urgently, seeing everything,
missing nothing. Seeking. Scouring.

The chamber was empty.

No attackers, no assassins. Just the drapes dancing in

the wind, undulating like a drunken gypsy naachwaali in a lotus-lust frenzy. And that fetor, like . . . like . . . What was it? It was like a Nilgiri stag in musth. Like the stench of a wildcat carcass rotting in nightsoil, remembered from when she was eight and out hunting with her father. Like the smell of her monthly blood-nights, but deeper, more acrid and sour.

Still in the dragon crouch, she moved through the room with the speed of a panther in sight of prey, snatching up the nearest weapon at hand – a curved sword from a brass suit of armour once worn by an illustrious ancestor – and completed a full circuit of the chamber in seconds. The four-footed crouch was impossible to maintain for long stretches but perfect for a quick sweep; it kept her out of the eye-level of any aggressor and enabled her to move lithely and swiftly, turning on four points rather than two.

Nothing, no one. Chamber empty and sterile of risk.

Your beauty past compare, your body a perfect poem composed by Mother Prithvi herself in a paroxysm of divine inspiration.

She whirled, feeling violated. She had been enjoying the breeze, surrendering to the languid relaxation of half-sleep, clad for the privacy of the bedchamber. Not preening for the eyes of some uninvited watcher. She was Rajkumari Sita Vaidehi Janaki, crown princess of Mithila. Her body, her beauty, were for her future husband's eyes alone, a husband she would choose of her own volition, not for this alien presence who dared not even show himself, the coward.

That is easily remedied, my love. Would you like to gaze upon me? To appreciate the masculine perfection of my body as I have admired your feminine secrets? It would be only fair.

A gust of heat below her left ear, like a sigh released

reluctantly. She spun, sword flashing in the moonlit dimness, slashed at empty shadows.

Nothing would give me greater pleasure than to reveal myself before you, in all my masculine splendour. Soon, I vow, you will look upon me and we will join together in a glorious union. The god of love himself could not orchestrate a more perfect joining.

She lunged out with the sword, guided by her instincts rather than her eyes. Yes, I want to see your body, she wanted to shout, so I can sink this needle-sharp blade into your flesh and free your life's blood. She wanted to silence the voice that seemed to be everywhere and nowhere, inside her and beside her left shoulder, On the veranda outside and inside her wardrobe across the room, all at once. To stop the arrogant presumptuousness of this invader.

'Show yourself, you craven,' she said aloud, her voice merging with the loud thrumming of the drapes in the gale-strength wind that billowed now through the chamber. 'I'll kill you before you lay a finger on me.'

And yet, before long, you will beg me to lay my hands on you and give you the gift of my seed. It is our fate, my sweet one. It is our karma.

'It's your karma to die at my hands,' she spat. 'Show yourself if you have an ounce of manhood. Show yourself and face me like a man.'

Girl. Still you do not understand. See then for yourself. See and believe.

A blinding flash of crimson light scorched her vision and she was transported.

3

The rain struck her with the fury of a monsoon storm, lashing her face and scantily covered body like a nine-tailed whip. She resisted the urge to cry out, not wanting to give her oppressor the satisfaction. But her foot slipped on the wet slimy stone floor and she fell to her knees hard. She grasped the wall before her, struggling for a handhold on the slippery blackstone, and found a rectangular slit.

The rain battered her relentlessly, unpleasantly warm and smelling oddly acidic. She tried to avoid swallowing any, but it ran into her eyes incessantly, stinging like brine. A knee-high stream rushed around her feet, pushing her to the right. The rainwash was being sucked down a gaping hole with the force of a swollen river in spate. She recognised it for a siege bore, a funnel-shaped pit in the floor of the rampart designed for pouring boiling oil on invading armies.

She used a pranayam breathing rhythm to calm herself, slowing her heartbeat from a Holi-dance drumbeat to a measured yagna chant-measure. She felt the moment of panic dissipate with each successive breath.

A thundering sound rumbled low and deep, coming from all around her. She recognised it for the sound of the ocean and knew at once that she was on the rampart of an island fortress. The toxic scent in the air, the warm rain, the faint odour of ash and something that smelled like smelting iron confirmed that the mountains were volcanic, and recently active. The fortress ran along a volcanic ridge, and rose and fell with its gradient. Moss-coated crenellations in the wall told her additionally that this keep had not suffered a siege for a very long time. Not for decades, centuries even.

Suddenly the rain felt as cold as ice, chilling her to the bone.

She knew of only one such island fortress in the sub-continent. And that one was not situated in any Arya nation, or any kingdom friendly to the Arya nations.

The rain had lessened sufficiently for her to venture a glance upwards. The sky seemed to loom just inches above her head, as besmirched as a rust-blackened tin roof that somebody had neglected to clean. Purple-blue clouds boiled and seethed like smoke from a dozen separate fires clashing and colliding. As they parted, the light grew, revealing an ominous and bleak sky. She blinked at the unexpected light. The stormclouds dispersed quickly, their fury spent. The rain died. The sucking, gurgling sound of the rainwash going down the numerous siege bores faded away at last, permitting a new sound to reach her ears.

It was coming from somewhere far below. Slowly, as she listened and attuned her senses, she realised that it was not new. The sound had been there from the instant she had appeared on this rampart, but she had mistaken it for some effect of the rain and wind. Only now could she discern it as a sound caused by living beings. Once she listened for it, it was unmistakable. She knew that sound. As a warrior-princess of one of the seven greatest Arya nations, it was a sound she was bred to recognise, respect and fear.

It was the sound of an army assembling for battle.

She moved instinctively to her left, the ground sloping upwards. At the end three broad steps were cut into the rock. She climbed the last one and found herself on a promontory that seemed to lunge for the belly of a looming thundercloud. Jagged spokes of crumbling blackstone and rusting iron fused together like the spokes of a giant crown slashing the empty air. She approached the outer edge cautiously, her breath catching in her throat as a gust of wind pushed at her like an invisible hand. The terrible sound grew louder as she reached the lip of the precipice. She looked down.

'Devi, protect us!'

The exclamation was torn from her lips and shredded by the wind.

An army of Asuras lay assembled, far below the thousand-foot-high fortress. Seen from this height, in this murky monsoon light, they seemed little more than ants swarming across a forest floor. Yet the sheer numbers awed her. It was a living carpet of bestial species, covering every square yard of the island-kingdom. Their distinctive shapes and movements were unmistakable even when seen from this great height.

Scores of different species of Asuras moved in ragged lines interrupted by inter-species and inter-rank scuffles and brawls. Rakshasas, nagas, uragas, pisacas, danavs, daityas, gandharvas, vetaals, and other species she couldn't name were pouring out of the fortress atop which she stood.

Roars of outrage, shrieks of fury, ululating cries of anger rose and fell as the belligerent beasts brushed against their alien compatriots. Bellowed commands overrode all other cries, issued by larger, distinctly marked rakshasas who stood on wooden riggings, wielding ten-yard-long whips with knife-tipped ends. She searched her childhood

memories of daiimaa tales, seeking the name of those
larger rakshasas. It came to her with an ease that surprised
her: kumbha-rakshasas.

The kumbha-rakshasas were a giant sub-species of
rakshasas; in the complex hierarchy of the Asura races,
rakshasas reigned supreme, while kumbha-rakshasas
reigned over their fellow rakshasas as well as all other
Asuras. There were similar distinctions between the other
demonaic species as well, she saw, a kind of grotesque
mirroring of the caste divisions of the Arya peoples. The
kumbha-rakshasas towered above the other Asura castes,
working their whips ceaselessly to administer control and
direction. The brutal, slashing sounds of their whip-blades
cutting through carapace and flesh and bone added to the
chaotic mêlée. The other species howled in fury at this
brutal treatment but continued to move in their sullen
lines.

Yet as she watched in fascination, she understood that it
wasn't just the size of the kumbha-rakshasas that held
their fellows in check: the other species combined easily
outnumbered their cruel captains and Asuras were notorious for their inability to accept order and discipline.
Those hulking, snarling beasts down there would sooner
feed on the kumbha-rakshasas than obey them. A few
hundred ten-yard-tall demons with blade-tipped whips
were hardly enough to keep a million ferocious beasts
submissive. So why were the Asuras so obedient? The
answer lay right before her eyes.

Only once before had all the Asura species been united,
and on that unforgettable occasion, it was said, the three
worlds of heaven, earth and hell had trembled with fear.
For that host had dared to invade nothing less than
Swargalok itself, the plane of the devas. And the Asuras
had won that war, led by the self-declared king of the

rakshasas. This sight could only mean one thing: the Asura species had been reunited for a fresh assault on one of the two higher worlds. And only one being could be responsible.

The clouds lifted, buffeted onwards by the gale-force winds high above, and suddenly her opinions were confirmed by a panoramic vista as breathtaking as it was awful.

Moored off the shores of the island, stretching out into the open ocean as far as she could see, was the largest fleet of warships ever assembled. At least, it must be the largest, for she had never heard of such numbers before, let alone seen such an armada with her own eyes. The Arya nations were not sea-faring people; the few forays their ancestors had ventured upon the watery deserts of the oceans had not been auspicious. The belief had set in, once mere uneasy superstition, now rock-hard conviction, that they were not meant to cross the large saltwaters of the world. Just as every civilised deva-devout Arya believed in the sacred cleansing powers of the holy River Ganga, so also did they believe in the unholy destructive power of the deserts of brine.

And like a terrible prophecy fulfilled, here was living proof that the oceans could bring death and destruction to mortal civilisation. A fleet of Asura warships such as even myth or legend had never described before, assembled here off the shores of this desolate island-kingdom. The sight chilled and seared her soul both at once, causing her to drop to her knees and grip the slippery rim of the promontory in anguish.

Her body pressed to the cold wet stone of the promontory, she peered down intently, seeing the clear pattern in the bestial chaos.

The Asuras were being driven to the ships. Endless

hordes of different species were emerging from the bowels of the fortress, clambering up the mushy wet black soil and being directed to the dozens of piers that lined the rocky shores. As ships were filled to capacity, they moved away, travelling around the curve of the island, out of Sita's line of sight. From their careful orchestrated movements she had the impression that they were being lined up on the far side of the island, some kind of holding point where they were to wait before proceeding to their final destination. But which destination was that?

Suddenly, the answer was obvious.

She rose to her feet with a start, the keening wind pushing at her roughly, trying to shove her over the edge. She stood her ground, turning this way, then that, scanning the sky, the ocean, the lie of the winding fortress, judging distances, geographical positions by knowledge and instinct rather than scientific estimation. There were no stars or constellations to tell her for sure, yet she knew where she was with a cold, unshakeable certainty.

Lanka. The island-kingdom the self-declared king of rakshasas had stolen from his brother Kubera, a volcanic island off the southernmost tip of the sub-continent, which, through his perverse use of brahman sorcery, the lord of rakshasas had turned into a portal to Narak, the hellish underworld. Domain of the king of the Asura races and every foul scum that walked, crept, swam, crawled upon or flew above the mortal plane of Prithvi.

She had heard the stories, the terrible nightmarish tales. But she had never understood. Not completely. Not even when her own father and uncles and other survivors of the Last Asura War had narrated their terrible experiences. Because she was a child of peace, born in an age where demons and monsters were things of the past, things to be forgotten.

And yet here she was, on the mythical island that was the gateway to the underworld itself. Stronghold of the rakshasa king who had once sworn to dominate the three planes of mortals, devas and Asuras. Whose original given name was long forgotten in the foggy swamps of race-memory, and who was eternally known by the name given to him by the devas. Three syllables which carried an entire compendium of meaning. He Who Makes The Universe Cry Out In Terror.

Ravana.

Girl. At last you begin to see. Now realise also the futility of resistance. I am the Beginning and the End of Everything. Soon I shall be at your threshold, in the flesh. And you shall learn to use that magnificent body for better things than battlecraft.

'NEVER!' she screamed, turning, slashing with her sword. Determined to fight to the death rather than yield an inch.

But her blade met only empty air. There was nobody there. And in a flash of blinding crimson light, she was transported again.

Nakhudi burst into the bedchamber, hissing like a clutch of angry cobras. Her enormous frame filled the space by the bedside as she tore away the mosquito netting, seeking out her mistress, seeking to protect.

The bed was empty. She grunted in frustration, raising her large head, her curled locks glistening darkly in the moonlight.

'Here, Nakhu.'

The amazonian bodyguard was across the bed and by the veranda door in a flash. She squatted beside Sita, her powerful thighs bunching like a young elephant's legs, her several sheathed weapons catching the direct moonlight from the low-hanging half-moon and glittering like jewellery. She reached tentatively for her mistress.

'Rajkumari?'

'I'm fine, Nakhu. I just had a bad dream, that's all.' Sita gestured sheepishly. 'I fell out of bed, I guess.'

The protectoress scanned the face of her princess anxiously. A noise came from the open doorway as Sita's other bodyguards followed in Nakhudi's wake. Nakhudi waved them away impatiently. They took in the scene, bowed apologetically, and retreated, shutting the doors to the rajkumari's chambers.

Nakhudi turned back to Sita.

'When I heard you cry out—' Her voice was low and gruff. She shook her head, clenching her fist. 'I thought perhaps dakus . . .'

Sita almost smiled. Dakus? Forest bandits would hardly attempt a raid on the royal palace of Mithila. Nakhudi's heart was larger than her intellect.

'It was a very bad dream. I must have cried out.'

The bodyguard exclaimed in her native tongue and her large hand shot out with the speed of a cobra lunging. Yet her grasp was as gentle as a mother holding her babe. She raised Sita's hand to the moonlight.

'A bad dream that bleeds?'

Sita followed Nakhudi's gaze, looking at the sword still clutched in her hand.

The tip of the blade was smeared with blood.

4

Kartikeya was minding the herd when he saw the smoke. It rose slowly, lazily, at first, like wisps of ganja smoke from the pipes his father and uncles smoked in the evenings and on feast days. For a moment, lulled by the calm of the early hour and the memory of the warm khatiya he had left only moments ago to tend to his morning chores, he thought it *was* ganja smoke. He imagined he could smell the sickly-sweet odour of the drug roasting, feel the intoxicating lightheadedness that came just from inhaling that exuded smoke.

He had never smoked a pipe directly, but all his brothers had and they took pleasure in ragging him because just being around other smokers was enough to make him fly higher than a patang on kite feast day. It was one of the natural hazards of being the youngest in a large rakshak kshatriya family and an even larger clan. Their taunting nettled him, making him eager for the day when he would be permitted to sit with the older men and smoke as they did. But truth be told, just inhaling their second-hand smoke was sufficient to make him relax enough to spin wild, extravagant daydreams. As he was doing now, sitting on a flattish rock at the top of the knoll, as his family's herd grazed on the slope below.

They were dreams of growing up to become as big and

strong as the other men in the clan, as proficient a warrior as the kshatriya code demanded. Of some day leaving the village and setting out for other places, other worlds. Not just Dujh, the town over the hills, but perhaps to ride on one of the giant sailing vessels that docked in the bay below the town, thence to travel to foreign shores. Or even to go the other way, up the cart path that led out of Dhuj, past numerous tiny hamlets and villages like his own, thence to journey to the raj-marg that led to other Arya nations, the fantastic rich kingdoms of legend that his father and uncles were always talking about – Kosala, Videha, Banglar. To see the famed capital cities of those faraway nations, walk the gold-paved streets of Ayodhya, Mithila, Kolkat. Perhaps join a rakshak troop guarding mighty Mithila Bridge or Gandahar Pass, or any of the strategic points that kshatriyas were trained and caste-sworn to protect and maintain. Ah, those were fine dreams indeed for a cowherd in a remote sleepy hamlet too small to even have a proper name or a court-ordained pan-chayat. Ganja dreams.

Perhaps that was why he was so slow to respond to the sight of the smoke. It was only after several moments had passed and the wisps had turned into plumes and then into large roiling black gouts that he realised his error. He leaped up, startling the animals browsing closest, and stared at the distant hilltops. He rubbed his eyes and stared again. There was no mistaking it this time: those dark forbidding clouds rising up from over the hills were very real, and very ominous.

Dhuj was burning.

Kartikeya took to his feet. He sprinted through the flock, calling out impatiently in his singsong voice, using his stick to poke and shove the beasts aside. He slipped on a pile of hot and slick manure and had to grip the horns of the nearest animal to keep his balance. She protested loudly and indignantly, and that set the lot of them lowing raggedly.

He all but threw himself down the hillside, loping with large ungainly strides as he left the outskirts of the herd and gained open ground.

As he neared the gauthan, he heard the excited yells of other cowherds calling out and saw their white dhotis flashing luminously in the dull, gloamy light of dawn. They had all seen the smoke and were running home. By the time he reached his hut, his brothers were already streaming out of the narrow doorway, some still hurriedly knotting their langots in the tight fashion that all rakshak kshatriyas – perhaps all kshatriyas, for all he knew – favoured for combat. As was the clan custom, they were naked apart from the langots, their only other clothing their swords and maces. There had been no time to oil their bodies in the rakshak manner, the better to slip through the enemy's grasp in close-quarter fighting, which itself conveyed to Kartikeya how urgently they took the threat. One of his middle brothers, Jayashankar, had already yoked the bulls to the cart and brought it around, large wooden-spoked wheels rumbling on the brick ground. His brothers poured out of the hut and clambered aboard grimly as he stopped, breathless and minus his stick, which had snapped and which he had discarded along the way.

'Fire!' he said.

Nobody paid attention to him. He watched wide-eyed as his sisters and mother emerged from the hut, each one armed and with garments girded at the loins in the martial fashion of rakshak women at war. His mother called out to him to move out of the way to let the cart pass. He was shocked to see her without her enormous nose ring, and bereft of all her customary jewellery. That brought the magnitude of the crisis home to him like nothing else.

'Come on, Kattu,' his youngest sister said, swatting his head as she pushed him back the way he'd come. 'We have to go back and get the herd. They'll make a good protective circle around the houses.'

He looked around, bewildered, and saw that all the other houses in the gauthan were similarly occupied – men and boys clambering aboard carts, riding off up the mud track which led to the town, while the women and girls prepared for an attack. But where was the enemy? Who were they preparing to fight?

'Protective circle,' he repeated numbly. 'Protective against what? The fire?'

'Kattu, take care of your sisters and your maa,' his oldest brother, Vinayak, called out. 'You are now the oldest male in the village.'

He was the *only* male in the village, he saw, casting a bewildered glance around at the unexpected chaos that had shattered the customary routine. Even old Panchamchacha, who must be all of seven decades, was perched precariously on the back of one overcrowded cart. The front cart, his own family's, was goading the bullocks into a run with the urgency of a cart race. The carts trundled noisily and surprisingly quickly up the path to the bay town. Whenever possible, rakshaks always rode, believing that the energy conserved was better utilised in the first crucial moments of martial contact.

'Come on!' his sister cried impatiently, tugging at his arm. She ran toward the hill. 'There isn't time!'

He followed her awkwardly, still trying to catch up with this sudden rush of events. To their right, as they ran up the grassy slope, the dozen or so carts filled with armed men and boys rattled and rolled noisily away, the road winding around the steep rise to take a gentler gradient towards the town. They dropped out of sight a moment later as he topped the first knoll and went down the other side.

Ahead, his sister was a pale streak of muscled flesh limned against the green of the pasture slopes. Over another two hills and they would reach the pasture where he had left their herd grazing.

'What happened?' he asked, shouting to her as he struggled to catch up. She had long legs and was the best runner of them all, except only for their second eldest brother.

'Asuras landed at Dhuj,' she called back, and disappeared over the next rise.

He stopped then, dead in his tracks, as if he had run into a tree, as he had once when much younger. Sat down with a whoosh of expelled air, right on the dew-damp grass. A small, sharp stone dug into his left buttock. He sat there and breathed with his mouth open and eyes staring blindly, gasping. A fat black wasp came buzzing around his head, then veered off westwards, toward the burning town. The entire western horizon was glowing reddish-orange now, as if Surya Deva had suddenly decided to reverse his normal route and ride his solar chariot from west to east this day.

His sister came back a moment later, looking exasperated. 'What happened?' she yelled. 'Come on, Kattu! Get up! There isn't time!'

He shook his head, not looking at her. Buried his face in his hands and rocked himself forward and backward, like a brahmin boy reciting his rote-learning.

'Kartik,' she said in a less harsh tone, dropping to her knees beside him. 'I know how you feel. We all feel that way. But this is not the time to let fear freeze you like a rabbit before a cobra. We must fight. Get up and come. We have to get the herd back before they reach the gauthan.'

When he still didn't move, she bent down and put her arm around him, hugging him tight, lending him some of her warmth, although the winter chill had all but fled from the air by now. 'Kattu, Kartik, Kartikeya,' she said into his ear, her breath redolent of betelnut leaf, which he knew she ought not have been chewing this early in the day. Maa would be mad if she found out. 'We're rakshaks. We have to do our duty. Rise now and fulfil your dharma.'

He looked at her for a long moment, then clenched his teeth tight. He knew she was right. He knew he had no choice. It was the rakshak way, to form a barrier with their bodies, their flesh, their lives, to prevent the enemy from progressing further. In the Last Asura War, thousands of their clan had thrown their lives away merely to buy precious moments for other divisions to regroup, or re-fresh themselves, or even, simply, to buy time. That was why their kind always built their settlements near bay towns, near bridges, passes, outside cities. To raise the first alarm and provide the first line of defence.

When he rose finally, his knees trembled like a sapling in a sea gale. She caught his arm and helped him stay upright. He nodded to her, then realised she wasn't looking at him.

'I'll manage,' he said. She looked at him closely, then let him go. He began walking towards the west, towards that angry red sky and the billowing dark clouds.

They topped the rise together and froze, mesmerised by the sight on the other side.

The entire hillside seethed with movement, a living carpet. In the garish red light of the burning town of Dhuj, an Asura army was racing across the hillsides. Not marching or proceeding. Running. If you could call the progress of those carapaced, many-legged, bestial night-mares running.

They swarmed across the rolling slopes like an infestation of killer ants. The very green of the lush hills was churned up into black sods by their passing. Their numbers were beyond counting. Kartikeya looked right and left, and for as far as his keen eyes could discern, they covered the land entirely. Far to the right, over the ridge, where the town road was, and where the carts would have reached by now, he could faintly make out the sound of clashing weapons and cries of combat. His brothers and father and uncles had met the wave and clashed. Which meant that Dhuj itself had been overrun and put to flame.

He stared at the oncoming masses, the bristling feelers, horns, antlers, snouts, hoods and other alien forms, racing like a horde of death incarnate across the familiar pastures over which he had roamed his entire childhood, illuminated by the garish glow of a burning town that only hours ago had been the foremost docking bay of the Arya nations, and had no words to describe what he felt.

He turned to meet his sister's eyes. He saw that she had reached the same conclusion he had – there was no point trying to outrun this insane, headlong wave of carnage. Already, as the first Asuras reached the confused herd, he saw the animals being cut down like so many stalks of straw before a thresh-knife. His family's entire fortune was decimated in scant seconds. In another few moments, the hordes would be upon them.

He looked around for something, anything, to defend himself with. He remembered his stick, discarded in the haste to reach home to warn his family. Then he grinned, thinking of the futility of waving that flimsy wooden rod at these monstrosities sprung from the slipstream between legend and myth. Shouting curses would be more effective than using a cowherd's stick!

His sister caught his grin and returned it. They hugged one last time, and he was glad that she was here with him to make this last stand. It was meet to have your own blood and kin beside you when the end came. Bonded in death, bound together for eternity.

They laughed together, laughed at the snarling, slobbering avatars of death that roared up towards them like a black wave, wielding their defiant laughter as boldly as steel weapons.

The wave of invading Asuras passed over them, then through them, shattering their fragile bodies like wine flagons crushed by stampeding elephants. One moment they stood there laughing defiantly, the next they were reduced to twin puffs of bloodspray and bone-fragment.

The creatures roared on, crushing the puny human remains underfoot, surging relentlessly onward towards the tiny ten-hut hamlet where the rest of Kartikeya's clan awaited their own tryst with Yama.

Dhuj lay burning behind them.

Ahead lay the breadth and span of the land of the holy rivers, the nations of Arya, and the entire civilised mortal world.

SOMETHING WICKED THIS WAY COMES

I

Lakshman woke in the darkness before dawn, clammy with cold sweat. He reached for his sword and found his rig instead. The bow was in his hand, an arrow aligned, the cord drawn to firing tautness, before he realised where he was.

A dream. Just another dream.

He loosened the cord. Regained his breathing rhythm, slowing his pulse. As his senses attuned themselves to the here and now, he grew aware of the smells of the hut and the ashram, the sounds of the night. It was pitch dark here. No torches burned at night in Siddh-ashrama, no quads of palace guards or PFs patrolled the perimeter. Once the cookfires were doused, the lamps extinguished, the stars and moon were all that remained to light one's way. It was a world apart from the pomp and majesty of Ayodhya. A world of meditation and tapasya, not luxury and indulgence.

And yet he had come to relish it: the tranquil days filled with the sonorous chanting of brahmacharya acolytes, the peaceful nights filled with rich forest smells, insect calls, animal sounds. After the bloody violence of the Bhayanak-van, it was a welcome retreat. A quiet space in which to re-arm the soul.

And yet.

Already he felt a gnawing restlessness, a strange, anti-climactic unease. A sense of something yet to be done, a task unfulfilled.

Between battles.

It was a phrase his mother had used to describe his father after Maharaja Dasaratha had sustained a deep gash in a friendly chariot-fight at a holiday tournament. It could as well be used to describe any Arya raj-kshatriya, that sub-caste of warrior-kings whose lives were dedicated to the art of combat. Like a weapon of war forged from molten steel, a raj-kshatriya was designed to fight, to kill. However long a sword might lie at rest, it was but a moment's work to knock off the superficial plating of rust and mildew, wash it clean in a cauldron of boiling oil. And lo and behold, it was ready to sing its song of rage and sorrow once more. A raj-kshatriya was like that sword: even at rest, he did not become a man of peace. He simply remained, in Third Queen Sumitra's words, between battles. Waiting.

A light rain was pattering down on the plantain-leaf roof of the small hut when Lakshman stepped outside. The clearing before the hut was sprinkled with early spring buds and a light growth of darbha grass. Even in the dull light from the eastern sky, the new buds were visible, as varied as daubs of Holi colour on a child's face.

Lakshman stepped off the mud stoop of the hut and on to the grass. It was damp from the unseasonal drizzle and felt wonderful, cooling and soothing his bare feet. He walked slowly across the clearing, into the rear groves.

In moments, he was out of sight of the ashram clearing and surrounded by tall bowed trees, shur-shurring softly in the gentle dawn breeze like a hundred silk saris being rustled at once.

The rain became steadily heavier, growing into a more

determined shower. He brushed past a papaya frond bowing with collected rainwater and it spilled its cool contents on to his bare shoulder. He was in the midst of a papaya patch, the thick, squat trees barely as high as his head, their large palm-like fronds acting as natural cups for the rainwater. He bent his mouth to a frond and sipped tentatively. It tasted sweet as night's dew collected from a lotus leaf. He drank greedily, slaking his morning thirst. Some spilled down his chin and ran down his neck, mingling with the rain. The aftertaste was faintly redolent of the odour of unripe papaya.

The rain had awoken the natural fragrances of the forest. Lakshman could smell the rich mineral scent of damp soil, the mulchy smell of wet bark, the sweet perfume of nightqueen blossom only just starting to shut its buds against the onset of day, the papayas ripening in the grove around him, the market mélange of vegetable smells from the large plot where the rishis of Siddh-ashrama grew their produce – and cutting keenly through it all, the unmistakable cloying musk of a golden deer in musth.

He frowned. The last smell was out of place. It was too early in the season for deer to go into heat. It intrigued him, almost made him want to return to the hut to find his bow and arrow and go on the hunt – or at least play at hunting, since the taking of life and eating of meat were expressly forbidden at Siddh-ashrama.

Already, the sky was growing light enough for him to see the greenish bulges of the papaya fruits, the first tinges of muted saffron only just beginning to appear in their swollen centres. A dozen yards away, the jungle proper loomed darkly. The oak, peepal and banyan trees of the Vatsa woods were still shrouded in night-dense darkness. The rain had passed and left behind a peculiar light. It cast dreamlike shadows, suffusing the air with a deep ultra-marine luminescence. Drops of rainwater clung to the tips of leaves like jewels on the earlobes of court danseuses. The air swirled and swarmed with motes of multiple hues, like a rainbow trying to come into being. If it was possible to see an indra-dhanush from the inside out, this was what it would look like.

He smelled her before he saw her, the odour of musk dense and cloying in the still air.

She stood in a gap at the far edge of the patch of papaya trees, just within the dark shadows of the jungle. She was almost completely obscured by the trunk of a banyan tree. Her ears were the only thing that moved, twitching with that peculiar restlessness that was her own way of watching. She seemed to exude a delicate glow, her ochre fur gleaming in the watery dawn light, and her eyes were wild with the heat of her condition.

For a moment, he was transfixed. Just before leaving Ayodhya, Rama had caught a doe in the groves on the north bank of the Sarayu. Later that Holi morning, he had saved the same doe from poachers and taken Lakshman back to the spot only to find the wounded doe gone. Now Lakshman felt a curious certainty that this was that very doe. Except that he couldn't see any sign of an arrow wound. It would be a miracle if she had survived such a wound at all, let alone recovered without a trace of a scar. And it would have been fantastic for her to have then made the long journey south to Siddh-ashrama. No, it couldn't be the same doe. What was he thinking?

Yet there was something in her eyes, her eager, watchful stance, that made him remember Rama intensely. As if she knew he was searching for his brother and was trying to tell him something.

'What is it, doe-eyed one?' he said softly, keeping very

still so as not to startle her. 'Do you know something I don't?'

She stood rock-still, in that familiar frozen posture prey animals assumed when they sensed a predator. He lowered himself to his haunches slowly, coming down to her height, careful not to show his teeth, humming very softly to calm her.

'Have you seen my brother Rama?' he asked, almost singing the name. 'Rama Rama oh. Oh Rama Rama.'

The deer watched him through wide almond-shaped eyes. Her pupils were dilated, very large in their beds of white. Her ears flickered once, then were still again.

The wind changed. Somewhere in the thicket behind her, high above, a langur shrieked and was answered by its simian companions. A family of red-tailed parrots, clustered on a branch until the rain passed, shot up into the air and were silhouetted against the lightening sky, thin red and green chalk streaks on an ash-grey slate.

The doe skittered, twisting round and round as if chasing her own tail, her ears twitching madly. She spun for a moment like a temple dev-daasi whirling in a paroxysm of religious ecstasy. Her musky odour increased.

She came to an abrupt halt facing the thicket of dark-enshrouded banyan and peepal trees that marked the start of the forest. Lakshman tried to follow her gaze, to see what had startled her. The langurs resumed their screeching and chittering in the trees above, passing on a primordial panic alarm, and the doe bolted.

She was gone in a flash, a golden shadow rippling through the woods, a pari fleeing back to her fairy realm. Her musky perfume lingered a moment longer, then was lost in the smells of rain and forest.

Lakshman remained crouched on his haunches, peering

into the darkness of the trees. The wind changed again abruptly, bringing the scent to him a fraction of an instant before his eyes found the beast.

It was standing in the dense shade of an enormous banyan tree, the high vaulting boughs too thickly interwoven to allow the dull light of dawn to pass through easily. He saw its eyes first, bright as diamonds gleaming against the dark background of the jungle. The rest of it was all but invisible, but the eyes were riveting, yellow orbs of fire smouldering in a bed of coals.

The tiger stepped out of the shadows, becoming visible in stages. Its striped flanks seemed to go on for ever. The lithe, slow steps it took, the deep impressions its pugs made in the soft loamy ground, and the sheer size of the animal took his breath away. It was a beautiful young male, very large for its age.

Lakshman's throat felt parched despite the water he had just drunk. There were many tiger pelts in his father's palace in Ayodhya. None were as large as this creature.

The tiger's eyes watched him intently, its throat issuing a low growling sound that was its way of throwing down a challenge. He understand at once that it was angry at having been deprived of the doe, which it must have been stalking for a while. A nocturnal creature, it had probably not fed this night, and soon the heat of the sun would drive it back to its deep forest lair, to sleep empty-stomached until nightfall. It was on the hunt, and since it had lost its chosen prey, this two-legged one would have to do instead.

It came slowly, one outstretched paw at a time. Ten yards from him, then nine . . . seven . . . In moments it was within springing distance. It stopped, crouching down, its powerful shoulder muscles bunching, the golden black-striped fur creasing as it gathered all its strength for the leap.

At the very last instant, a voice spoke out, unexpectedly loud over the stillness of the thicket.

'Shantam.'

The single word acted as a mantra on the crouched tiger. One moment it was coiled to unleash its ferocious destructive energy upon its two-legged prey; the next it relaxed its powerful muscles and sank to the ground, purring like any house cat.

Lakshman rose to his feet as Brahmarishi Vishwamitra strode past him, approaching the tiger with fearless familiarity.

The seer-mage bent and stroked the animal's head. Its ears twitched appreciatively and it rolled over, offering up the pale fur of its belly. Vishwamitra chuckled in his deep, gravelly voice, his long white beard rippling with his amusement.

'You want to play, do you? I would love to play with you awhile, my friend. But there is much work to be done. Your workday is ending, while ours has barely begun. The good rajkumar here and I, we have a journey to make today with our companions. A long journey.'

The tiger mewled.

Vishwamitra smiled. 'Yes, certainly. When I return I shall play with you. Now, run along and give your brothers and sisters my regards. Go on now, it's almost sunrise, and your mother will worry.'

The tiger snorted twice, issued a last sulky growl, and rose to its feet, padding away quickly. In moments, it had blended with the shadows of the forest and was gone.

Vishwamitra turned to face Lakshman.

'Rajkumar Lakshmana, the animals of Siddh-ashrama live in harmony with humans. They mean you no harm.'

Lakshman bowed his head, putting his palms together respectfully to offer the first greetings of the day to his new guru.

'Pranaam, Guru-dev. The tiger was clearly hostile to me. When it sought to assault me, I was left with no choice but to prepare to defend myself.'

The brahmarishi inclined his head slightly, acknowledging Lakshman's explanation. 'What you say is true. But remember that in this place we are the outsiders. Perhaps you were a little too quick to invoke the power of the maha-mantras Bala and Atibala. Certainly the tiger sensed your great strength and saw you as a hostile intruder. Even though it knew your enhanced abilities would result in its destruction, still it sought to defend its habitat and its dignity.'

Lakshman was silent as he pondered the brahmarishi's words.

He *had* been very quick to challenge the tiger. It was almost as if . . . well, as if he wanted the fight. He recalled his earlier restlessness on awakening. *Between battles.* As if he needed to pit himself against a foe, any foe. If rakshasas and giant demonesses weren't on hand, then a tiger would do. But if this was so, then he hadn't been consciously aware of it.

'Forgive me, Guru-dev,' he said quietly.

Vishwamitra walked over to Lakshman and squeezed his shoulder. The strength in the seer's hands surprised Lakshman. 'Feel not ashamed, Sumitra-putra. You are young yet and it is barely eight days since you received these potent infusions. It takes even great warriors many years to learn the intricacies of their usage. Why, it took a raj-kshatriya such as myself several hundred years to achieve mastery of my martial abilities. Of course,' he added, 'that was before I set down my sword and bow to take up this life of spiritual penance. And yet, those same qualities of yogic self-control stand me in good stead even today. The greatest battle is the one a warrior wages with his own animal impulses.'

Lakshman glanced up at the brahmarishi's face. It was the first time he had heard the sage speak of his historic past. Every Arya child learned of Raja Vishwamitra's stirring exploits as a warrior-king, as well as of his transformation into a seer through centuries of tapasya. Like any other kshatriya graced with the presence of such a great warrior, Lakshman had a hundred questions he wanted to ask the brahmarishi.

But before he could speak another word, a flash of blinding light seared his vision. He flung his hand up to cover his eyes, taking a step back from the source of the effulgence. Still, his warrior's instinct demanded he try to discern what was going on, to defend himself against any possible assault. He sensed Vishwamitra standing his ground and staring directly at the blinding illumination.

As suddenly as it had appeared, the light faded away, leaving behind only a searing memory burned in Lakshman's mind's eye.

He lowered his hands and saw the lone figure of his brother Rama, standing in the midst of the papaya grove.

2

Kausalya woke from a light doze to find Dasaratha's eyes open. The maharaja was lying on his back, hands clasped on his chest, head fallen to the right, eyes fixed on the thin slice of indigo sky visible through the window at the far end of the vaulting bedchamber. She observed him calmly for a moment, marshalling her emotions.

She knew what she should be thinking, that her husband had departed the mortal realm for more elevated pastures, that at least he had passed away peacefully in the night without further suffering, but she stoically refused to entertain such thoughts. It was as if a part of her believed firmly that by thinking such thoughts she would give them credence and substance. An Arya wife did not think ill of her husband and children, whatever the circumstances or provocation. Yet it was more than mere tradition and upbringing. It was a deep-rooted, intensely felt inner conviction. If life gave you thorns, you made do with thorns. You didn't brood on their nature, the colour, the species, the length, the sharpness . . . instead, you plucked them out, tossed them aside, and kept walking, on bloody feet if you had to.

She had acquired that attitude from her mother. Indeed, those very words – *make do with thorns* – still echoed in her memory in that familiar soft voice. Her mother had passed away the year before Kausalya was married, a tragic piece of timing. But her voice and its lessons, learned in childhood while those strong, deeply lined hands plaited her oiled locks or massaged turmeric paste into her supple young limbs, had carried her through fifteen years of marital turmoil, neglect and loneliness, seven of those years spent without even her growing son, pride of her loins, jewel of her heart, to bring comfort and joy. So much had been denied her. Yet still, that resilient Kausalya, daughter of pride, mother of fortitude and silent will, refused to yield to the samay chakra's cruel turns and twists. And so she rose from her seat thinking not that Dasaratha was dead and lying glassy-eyed but that he was simply awake and gazing.

The muted rustle of her sari – she had laid aside the ritual silks of her queenly station the day after Dasaratha had taken to his sickbed, and donned simple homespun saris instead – attracted his attention. He blinked once, and turned his head slightly, adjusting his frame of view to encompass her. Her heart raced as the enormity of the moment dawned on her. Dasa was awake. Alive and awake. It was only then that she realised how close she had come to growing resigned these past eight days. How the muted whispers of acceptance around the palace had begun to seep into her resolve, melting it like a glacier thawed over centuries by the unrelenting heat of the sun. On this occasion, those thorns of life had dug deep enough to draw out more than blood; they had almost drained her of hope. And hope, as her mother had said so often, was the real food of mortal existence; food of the soul.

He turned his head slightly as she approached, eyes startling in their clarity. The rheumy, glassy look of the feverish nights was gone, so was the glazed, slack-jawed looseness. He had lost weight during this latest bout and it showed on his face. It gave him the appearance of weary determination; a warrior who had fought yet another unwinnable battle and had survived. Not won, for neither this new battle nor the war itself was winnable by any mortal, but survived. He had lived to fight another day. And she was blessed to be here to see the miracle with her own eyes.

'Kausalye.' He used the affectionate 'e' suffix that was the closest to a nickname he had ever permitted himself. That was all he said; simply her name. It was enough.

She dropped to her knees by his bedside, burying her face in his arms, clinging to his shoulder. His skin felt cool and dry to her touch, no longer fiery with fever or clammy from sick-sweat. She kissed his forearm, his hand, his wrist.

'I will propitiate the devi,' she said. 'I will offer a hundred rams as thanks for your recovery.'

He made a small choked sound. She looked up, alarmed, then realised it was an approximation of a laugh, the best he could manage in his weakened condition.

'Spare the rams, Kausalye. Just get me something to eat and drink.'

She looked up at him. If she needed proof positive, here it was. 'Are you sure?'

'Sure?' he echoed. 'Of course I'm sure. If I'm alive, I must eat and drink, mustn't I? Unless I have died and this is Swarga-lok and you've been given the ultimate penalty of nursing me eternally. In which case, I'll eat one of those rams you were planning to sacrifice. Roasted, preferably, with plenty of stuffing!'

She smiled, warmed by his attempt at humour. It spoke more eloquently than any assurance of well-being. 'It would be a pleasure, not a penalty.'

He smiled a wan smile. 'Ever the dutiful and noble

Kausalya. Don't you at least occasionally feel ill towards anybody? Think dark, terrible thoughts? Wish destruction and holocaust on those who have hurt you and caused you misery?'

She thought of the night she had first known he was in the clutches of Kaikeyi. Not the first night he had spent in her arms, for she had accepted Kaikeyi's presence by then – not liked it, but accepted it nevertheless – but the first time she had learned of how deeply he was besotted with his voluptuous second queen. She had learned it from Sumitra, who had broken the news to her as gently as possible, confirming what Kausalya had dismissed till then as idle palace gossip and court chatter. She remembered the darkness that had come over her then. The wave of black rage that had risen like an ocean deva bent on destruction, the pounding fury in her heart. She had forgotten all her mother's lessons at that moment. Forgotten all the wisdom she had acquired through diligent study and practice. She had been at that moment a pure avatar of the devi, lightning-bolt in one hand, trident in the other, lion at her knee, and all she knew was man-hatred and woman-rage.

And then the infant Rama had called out, shattering the tense silence of her bedchamber. He was barely a year old then, only just weaned. She had gone to the bed, thrown herself there by his side, and bared her breast to him, teasing his curled lips with her forefinger, drawing him to her breast. He had found the hot nipple and paused, turning his head to stare up at her, his silent wide eyes asking the question his wordless mouth could not frame, and she had smiled down at him, caressed his downy soft head, and moved it back towards her breast again. He had drunk then, sucking happily, greedily, as he was permitted this rare return to a familiar luxury, and she had felt the ache in her right breast as the veins of milk, still full and bountiful in their gift of life, began to convey their precious nectar.

Sumitra had leaned over her, wiping the tears that flowed down Kausalya's face, drenching Rama's swaddle clothes, and said quietly, words that Kausalya would remember for ever, 'At least we have the loyalty of our sons.'

Kausalya blinked away the moistness that threatened to creep into her eyes now and looked at Dasaratha. She was stroking his hirsute arm gently, the way she had stroked Rama's infant head that fateful day. He was staring up at her with an inscrutable expression that mirrored the fixed watchfulness of his infant son in her memory, and in that instant she saw how much he regretted, how much he wished he could undo, how time and past errors of judgement had eaten into the heart of his ego and denuded his former arrogance. This was her Dasaratha again; not Kaikeyi's Dasaratha, that stranger she had stood by during official functions and court rituals over the years; but her Dasaratha, the prince of Ayodhya she had wed long years ago, the prince she had loved, the king she had watched with pride and admiration, the man to whom she had given her maidenhood and all else, the father of her child, the keeper of her honour.

'We choose,' she said. 'We choose to walk in light or darkness. I chose my path a long time ago. I have never looked back since.'

He stared at her mutely for a long moment. Then he turned his head away, towards the window again. The first blush of dawn was visible through its carved arches, above the delicate boughs of the flower grove. His voice was soft and young, more like his son's clear, quiet tones than his own customary gruffness. Her Dasaratha was speaking now.

'Some of us walk in darkness without knowing we do. We see with black eyes and black hearts. And only when we have gone too deep into the jungle do we realise our mistake. But by then it's too late to turn back, impossible to find our way home.'

She felt his despair and ached for it. This was her curse, not just to bear her given burden, but to feel profound empathy for the pain of others as well, including the one who had caused her own pain. 'It's never too late to come home,' she said.

He looked at her again. She saw the colours of the dawn reflected in his eyes, the yellowish cast of first light on his wasted features.

'Do you think so? Can a black heart change its path this late in the day?'

She touched his chest gently, proprietorially. 'The path was always there. If the heart could but see it.'

'And the consequences of past actions? Our karma?'

She shrugged. 'What we have done even the devas can't undo. But what we have yet to do, even the Asuras cannot prevent us from doing. If you wish to walk the path of light, you can do so even now.'

His eyes filled with tears, and his hand gripped her arm with shocking strength. Not the strength of youth and vigour he had once possessed with pride, but the strength of desperation. 'I'm so afraid, Kausalya.'

Her eyes widened. She knew it must cost him dearly to make such an admission. Even had they not been through such vicissitudes in their relationship, it would still be very hard for him to entrust her with such insight. It made her love for him swell even more. She put her other hand over his, gripping him as tightly as he gripped her.

'You will not walk alone, Dasa. I'm with you to the end.'

He shook his head. 'It's not the walk to death I fear, Kausalye. It's the walk back to righteousness. I fear that I've done too much damage to repair. That I haven't enough time for reparation. That you, my sons, our people, will all suffer the consequences of my mistakes.'

For a moment she was unable to fathom his meaning; then she understood. He was speaking not just as a husband, but as a king. 'You have raised four fine sons. They will walk the path of righteousness for you.'

He half rose, face filled with an emotion she had never seen there before, a peculiar mingling of fear and shame and desperation. 'That is what I fear most! You remember the dream I spoke of yesterday, or the day before, before I slept?'

She didn't have the heart to tell him that it had been eight days ago, not one or two. 'The one about killing the youth in the jungle, the son of the two blind paupers?'

'The ones who cursed me,' he said, then gasped in a deep breath. 'I had more dreams. Terrible, awful dreams. I dreamed that the youth turned and looked up at me as he lay dying, and he was our son, Rama.'

She blinked several times, unprepared for this fresh assault. There were things she was not prepared to deal with yet, if ever. 'Nothing will happen to our son,' she said. 'It was but a dream. Our son, all your sons, will do you proud, Dasa. They will carry on the work you began, and accomplish greater things than you ever dreamed.'

He shook his head, tears rolling down his face. Their hands remained entwined, but his grip had lost its strength. It felt too much like her mother's hand as she lay dying in that dark and shadowy sickroom in another kingdom, another palace, another lifetime almost, it seemed now. And the Dasaratha who spoke next was the ageing and ailing, broken and defeated Dasaratha.

'I fear the crimes of my karma will be visited upon my sons. And the cost will be more than they can bear to pay.' He twisted his head in anguish, hand limp in her grasp and growing clammy with sweat. 'I fear I have done more wrongs than rights, that the tally of my karma will not make up for the sacred duty I have been unable to fulfil, that all my life's sins will be visited upon Rama and Bharat and Shatrugan and Lakshman like a plague of vengeance. I see the signs already, in the intrusion of the rakshasa, the seer taking away Rama and Lakshman, the resurgence of Ravana and his hordes . . . I tell you, Kausalya, all this is my karma coming back to haunt me. It is the sum of my past misdeeds.'

He choked on his own emotions, and she had to offer him a few sips of water before he could continue. 'You don't know half the things I've done, the things I've said. My promises to Kaikeyi . . . the two boons . . .'

He turned his face away, unable to go on. The nascent light cast a pallor on his face, making it seem deathlike in its agony. 'Kausalya, I tell you, it is the beginning of the end of all we love and hold dear . . . It is the day of our reckoning, and the price of my past misdeeds will bury us all alive like a juggernaut. . . what have I done! Deva!'

He buried his face in his hands and shook, weeping.

Enough. This was too much. It was no way for a maharaja to behave.

'Dasa!'

He stared at her, startled by her loudness.

'Are you dead yet?'

He blinked, taken aback. 'What? Dead? No, of course not, but. . .'

She emphasised each word as she spoke, giving him time to understand it implicitly. 'Then rise. Awaken. Live. Prepare your sons for ascension, meet your people and give them confidence and assurance, ensure the sustenance and survival of all that you love and cherish. Do what you can, what you must.'

He stared at her as she continued.

'What's done is done. We cannot change our past karma. But what we do now, this moment, and every moment hereafter, is in our hands. Do it! Change what needs changing. You have already shown you can do it by coming to me on the morning of Holi feastday. By repairing the broken wings of our lost love.'

He looked at her uncertainly. 'Did I succeed?'

'You know you did. I would still be here by your side even if you had never apologised or asked my forgiveness. It is my duty as a wife. But I would not have opened my arms to you that day, nor shared my bed. In the act of loving you, I was forgiving you. Surely you knew that?'

'Yes,' he said. There was an acceptance in his tone that reassured her. His arm gained strength, his skin stopped exuding sweat. 'I made you suffer for fifteen years; you took me back in fifteen counts.'

'Fool,' she said, softly this time. 'Foolish, foolish Dasaratha. I never let you go in the first place.'

He stared at her, then nodded abruptly, trying to cover his surprise without success. 'I knew that.'

'Then know this too. It may not be as easy to repair all else the way you repaired our bond. It will be very difficult indeed, but it is possible. You can walk the road of light again. The devas have seen fit to let you live. Use the time wisely. Set your affairs right, put your house in order.'

He was silent for a long time. They sat that way, the light from the arched window growing steadily until it seemed the devas were issuing a benediction over her words and his resolve. She said no more. He needed only prompting, not advice. His was the folly of the wise man who had been momentarily blinded by the gaudy brilliance of his own excessive thoughtfulness. It required only a gentle nudge to bring him back to his true path.

Finally, he sat up, wincing and squinting. He put his left hand over her two hands and his own, then tightened his grip again and met her eyes squarely.

'With you by my side, I will not falter now.'

And gently, like the first light falling on the opening blossoms of flowers outside, he kissed her brow, smudging her sindhoor ever so slightly. Outside, the light brightened into the first rosy flush of sunrise.

3

The doe shuddered in the darkness of the peepal thicket. Vines and creepers swayed in the rising wind, brushing her flanks. She bared her teeth and snapped at them. Her musk, the precious kasturi that mortals sought for its use in the making of perfumes and attars, continued to ooze, filling the forest with the rich, pungent odour of her condition.

The tiger was not long in coming. Despite its brush with the strange mortal, it had not lost the scent of the doe. That musky effusion was unmissable even in the midst of the rich scents of the recent rainfall. He found her within moments, skulking around an enormous peepal with vines as wildly profuse as a rishi's matted locks, and came upon her from behind.

The doe was ready. She turned to face the tiger just before he leapt. His eyes narrowed, fixing her in the formidable death-stare that froze virtually any herbivore in its tracks, even frightening the ponderous bigfoot. This was his jungle, and he knew it. The doe ought to have been transfixed, staying motionless as the raja of the jungle leapt upon her, crushing her underfoot and ripping open her vitals, feeding on her steaming innards as life still fluttered within her tremulous breast.

Instead, the doe bared her teeth at the tiger and grinned.

The tiger froze.

The doe clacked her teeth. It was a strange action, unfamiliar to her kind, and the large teeth snapped together with a bone-jarring impact. Those white teeth were meant to tug at leaves and yank at stalks, not rip flesh and crack bone. But there was no mistaking the doe's message. She was ready to fight.

The tiger paused, wondering at the folly of this pathetic herbivore. He had once attacked a doe protecting two young; that one had kicked viciously at his belly, trying to use her hoofs to tear his soft underbody open. He had dodged her with a simple side-step, snatched her by the neck and ripped her head off in one smooth motion. She had died still kicking. What did this foolish musth-deluded creature hope to achieve? A quicker death perhaps? Or a much slower, much more painful one?

He was already skittish from the encounter with the mortal. There had been something odd about that young two-legged human. That blue glow in his eyes. That aura of power. He was glad when the ancient one had stopped the fight. Mortals were dangerous beasts, by far the most dangerous of all. He had seen what havoc they could wreak with their fires and sharp slivers carved from tree trunks, and those shining metal claws they used in combat with one another. And the way they slaughtered one another but left the bodies to rot. Killing without feeding. Yes, mortals were dangerous and strange.

But he understood the doe. She was half out of her mind with her musth, desperate to be covered by a buck, to receive his seed while still in heat. It was probably her first heat, judging from her youthful appearance. Although there was something about her eyes and stance that was odd, almost un-deerlike. He dismissed these thoughts with the same careless ease with which he might swat away a swarm of bees. She was food, that was all. And she didn't know enough to respect the approach of a life-taker. Foolish dumb thing. Soon she would face Yamraj, lord of death, and she would understand everything. By then, her mortal body would be in his eager belly, providing him with days of much-needed nourishment.

He sprang.

His leap was a short one, barely three yards. Yet he landed not on a bundle of squealing, terror-stricken doe-flesh, but on the forest floor, in a flurry of dust and rotted vines.

He swung around, seeking his prey. How could she possibly have moved so fast? He hadn't taken his eyes off her for even an instant. Where was she? He turned a full circle, coming back to where he'd started, then turned again, unable to understand what had happened. His growls of frustration filled the jungle, sending small creatures skittering away in terror, causing a family of young langurs in the branches above to cling to each other fearfully.

He turned a third time, saliva dripping from his open jaws, and glimpsed a flash of movement on the trunk of the large peepal. He crouched, shoulders bunching instinctively. At first he took it for another cat, a panther perhaps. There was a large pack in this part of the jungle, and they preferred to stay in the trees.

But it wasn't a panther.

It was the doe.

She was on the tree.

And she was . . . different.

Her rear end and skin colouring were still doe-like, speckled and lightly furred. But her upper half was completely different now, a form he knew all too well. Shaggy fur, an enormous head, bulging eyes with feline slitted pupils so much like his own, a double set of eyelids that shut horizontally as well as vertically, and that mouthful of teeth. What teeth! Even he was impressed by them. Their needle-sharpness and size put even his own magnificent bone-daggers to shame. What couldn't he do if he had teeth like that! He could tear through the hide of a rhinoceros, those half-blind, short-tempered brutes. Or even bring down a bigfoot.

He raised his head, staring appreciatively at the creature that clung to the peepal tree, gazing down at him with a manic feral grin. He was too used to being the predator of this territory, quite unused to being the prey. He was distracted by the peculiar combination of species, neither wholly deer nor wholly rakshasi.

That was his mistake.

Supanakha didn't bother to finish changing completely. Her lower half was still that of a doe, although even as the tiger stared up at her in wonderment, her flanks were widening, bones snapping and crackling as they expanded and changed shape before his amazed eyes. She leapt while her rear limbs were still hoofed.

She brought the tiger down before he could brace himself. He lost his balance and tumbled over on the forest floor, snarling in shocked anger at being attacked by a creature he had been stalking just a moment ago. For that brief instant, his belly was exposed to her.

She ripped him open from throat to groin, doing to him exactly what he had intended to do to her.

His roar of anguish and fury echoed through the jungle. Then she held his flailing paws down, his fast-fading power no match for her rakshasi strength, dipped her head and ate greedily. It had been a long, long time since she had eaten tiger. It was as good as she remembered it.

* * *

Later, she slaked her thirst at a large, newly formed rain puddle. A nest of new-born cobras seethed and slithered in a rabbit hole nearby, their eggshells still slimy. She put her foot, now fully re-formed in its hoary taloned rakshasi bulk, into the nest and watched them lunge instinctively, seeking to stab and inject her with the venom they had yet to develop. She picked them up with the same foot and made them an after-dinner sweet dish.

Her cousin arrived without warning. One moment she was licking her lipless mouth, washing the snake ichor and tiger blood from her chin and neck with splashes of water from the puddle, the next moment he was before her, obscuring her entire view.

Cousin.

She grinned happily up at him. 'I thought you had forgotten about me. I called upon you last night.'

I thought I made myself clear the last time we spoke. I assumed you were capable of following my orders without needing to be watched over like a child-novice. Obviously I was wrong.

Her grin faded. She swiped at her chin, smearing fluids across her chest-fur. She stood, unable as ever to decide which of his many heads to address. Most of them looked angry and grim. Except for a pair on the left side, which looked distracted, as if they were taking care of other business even while dealing with her. She knew he could be in many places at once, and that just one head was sufficient to control his actions and speech in any one spot. But which one was in charge here and now? It was impossible to tell for sure, because most of the time the central head was the one that spoke directly, although the others all whispered and muttered to each other and to the central one constantly. It was like speaking to a council of ten men who were always bickering, each one of them capable of turning brutally violent at any moment.

Tiger got your tongue, Supanakha?

'I . . . I don't know what you mean. I did exactly as you asked. I followed the two princes of Ayodhya all the way, watched them invade Bhayanak-van and destroy all our cousins, including Tataka, which was a sight to see, I have to tell you. And I never interfered once! Not once! I did exactly as you told me to, Vijay!'

He swiped at her with almost careless ease. The impact was bone-shattering. She flew across the clearing, smashing against the trunk of a peepal with enough force to crack the two-hundred-year-old tree. She slid to the ground, tumbling on to her belly, dust filling her mouth, mingling with the blood. She spat out three jagged teeth, her jaw feeling as if it was filled with shards of glass.

Don't use that name with me, foolish hag. And don't play games with me either. You were to observe, not interfere. I thought I made that clear.

She cried out through her mouthful of agony, spraying blood and splinters of teeth. 'But I didn't interfere!'

A flash of brilliant crimson light exploded in her brain. She cringed, raising her taloned claws before her face. Then, slowly, she lowered her paws, taking in the changed surroundings.

He had transported her to the spot of the ambush. Where she had intercepted and killed the kshatriyas last night. The stench of death was still thick in the air, mingling with the scents of the recent rainfall. Her bellyful of tiger flesh threatened to expel itself. Her entire body screamed with fear.

A horde of crows and vultures rose squawking and screeching into the air, startled by the sudden appearance of the two rakshasas.

Ravana's ten heads turned and scanned the underbrush. Above him, the sky was a light greyish blue shot through with streaks of saffron and vermilion from the rising sun.

He walked over to the foot of a huge boulder, the very boulder on which she had waited before the ambush, his bulging upper body silhouetted against the brightening sky. He kicked at an object lying on the ground. The object flew across the dusty path on which she now sat and struck her chest. She tried to catch it but it slipped and fell, bouncing on the ground, mud adhering to its sticky wounds. It was a severed human head, the eyes badly gouged by the birds. It still wore a battered helmet with the lightning-shaped sigil of the Vajra kshatriyas.

4

*Has your memory been refreshed sufficiently? Or do you
need a few more taps on your skull to get it fully functional?*

'Master,' she said, scrambling to her feet, keeping her
eyes down and her head obsequiously low. 'I saw this
group of kshatriyas leaving the main party back at the
ashram. They were clearly on their way back to Ayodhya.
I was afraid they would bring reinforcements. I thought it
was important to kill them and prevent word of the
princes and seer reaching Ayodhya.'

*Supanakha, the last time we spoke, in the groves of
Ananga-ashram, I distinctly recall telling you to only
observe the princes and the mage, not interfere with them.
Don't you consider killing a dozen men to be a violation of
that order?*

'I meant you no disrespect,' she cried, pleading now. 'I
thought you would be pleased. I called upon you all last
night. I had a plan.'

*The only plan is the one I made for the invasion of the
mortal realms. I'm not interested in your puerile plots or
your feeble excuses. You disappoint me greatly, cousin.
What am I to do with you now?*

She fell to her knees, then stretched out fully on the
ground, her hands extended towards his cloven leather-

strapped lower limbs, prostrating herself in the most abject of postures. It was something she had never done before in all her five hundred years.

'My Lord, great one, ruler of all the three worlds and supreme commander of heaven, earth and hell! I beg your forgiveness. I will do any penance you prescribe. Don't kill me. Please. I am a good fighter. I will be of use to you in your war against the mortals. I beseech you, let me live and repair the damage I have done.'

She kept her head down for what seemed like an eternity, the gritty rain-dampened mud of the path coating her muzzle and filling her battered mouth. Blood and spittle oozed from her injured jaw to the ground in a steady drip. She waited, expecting at any moment to feel his powerful cloven foot stamping down on her neck, snapping her spine and crushing her to death.

When his voice spoke within her mind, it sounded almost amused. It was not the reaction she had expected.

Yes, that's quite true. You do deserve to suffer for your misdemeanour. Disobedience cannot go unpunished in a martial race. It breeds insolence. But I might be able to turn your stupidity into something less damaging to our cause. Perhaps even to our advantage.

She waited, not daring to breathe, let alone speak.

Rise, cousin.

She did so slowly, shivering with fear and shock. She still didn't believe he was going to let her live.

He was smiling.

At least, the central head was smiling. A few of the others were engaged in other matters, but two of them, one on either side, were clearly sharing in the central head's pleasure.

Your foolish impulsiveness has inadvertently provided

*an opportunity to play another deception on our mortal
opponents.*

He gestured at a corpse that lay beneath a bush nearby.
The body rose stiffly up into the air as if hauled upright by
invisible wires. Supanakha recognised it as the corpse of
the leader of the Vajra kshatriya party. A man who wore
the sigil and helm of the great grey wolf as his chosen
totem. The order of Bheriya.

Ravana gestured, one of his heads mouthing mantras
she could barely hear for all the cross-talk buzzing between the others. With the startling abruptness of great
sorcery, the corpse came to life.

The soldier who had once been Bheriya opened his eyes.

He looked at his resurrector, then at Supanakha. He did
not seem alarmed at the sight of the two rakshasas, or at
the unmistakable and terrifying fact that he was facing the
king of Asuras himself, Ravana, the Lord of Lanka. In fact,
Supanakha noted through her mingled emotions and
mangled thoughts, the mortal seemed oddly emotionless.
She was familiar with this phenomenon. It was an unavoidable consequence of re-animation. You could restore
a body to life, but something remained absent. The mortals called it aatma, the share of brahman that was allotted
to each living being at the moment of birth. Not that she
believed in such mortal superstition. But the kshatriya
seemed alive in every way except that which mattered
most.

*Yes, he will do quite well for our purpose. Now, pay
heed, cousin. You have used up the last of my patience. I
will tolerate no further lapses. Am I clear?*

'My Lord,' she replied, trembling. 'If I fail you once
more, I shall take my own life.'

He laughed.

Death would be a small price to pay for failing me. You

*well know that there are fools imprisoned in the lowest
level of Narak who offended me in some trivial way a
thousand years ago. Go down and take a look at them
sometime, then you might begin to understand the true
consequences of failing me.*

She shuddered. Her cousin's appetite for inflicting pain
was infinite. It was for good reason that the devas, outraged at his capacity for ingenious brutality, had erased his
given name from memory and renamed him Ravana, He
Who Makes The Universe Scream.

*This mortal shall continue to Ayodhya. I have repaired
his body but left a few wounds to substantiate his story of
being attacked en route. He will return to Dasaratha and
relate the message that I am putting into his mind now. As
you know, twice-lifers can be very good slaves. He will do
my bidding without hesitation, and no matter what he's
called upon to do, he will have no fear for his own life and
limb. After all, he is already dead!*

The demon lord's laughter filled the air.

Supanakha's face twitched; she was unsure whether to
smile in acknowledgement of her cousin's humour, or to
remain impassive. She chose the latter. It was best not to
show any emotion before the Lord of Lanka. One never
knew what might anger him. But she couldn't help offering
a small comment, speaking as meekly as she could manage.

'A brilliant plan, Lanka-naresh. But might the Ayodhyans not recognise him as a twice-lifer? After all, the seer-
mage they call Guru Vashishta is no less a master of the art
of brahman. Won't he be able to see that this man is
nothing more than a walking corpse?'

His smile disappeared.

*Do you take me for a fool such as yourself? Just
a moment ago, when we were in the jungle behind*

Siddh-ashrama, within half a mile's reach of Vishwamitra and his two new chhelas, would he not have sensed my presence? Or eight nights ago, when I appeared to you out of a tree in the fruit grove beside Ananga-ashrama, did he sense my presence then? No brahmin will be able to tell this twice-lifer apart from any other living mortal. He will seem as alive and normal as their own sons!

She cringed, bowing her head so low she was bent over double. 'Forgive me, my lord. I don't understand. What mantra could achieve such a powerful deception?'

No mantra in living knowledge can do that. Nay, I will infuse him with the one thing that will make him indistinguishable from any living mortal. I shall give him an aatma.

Supanakha's face revealed her surprise. She quickly wiped the expression off.

Yes, that's right, cousin. A soul. It is something few brahmarishis can achieve. But as you know, my millennia of penance and prayer compelled the devas to grant me great power. Just as the seer-mage Vishwamitra reanimated the boy-prince Lakshman and sued the Lord of Death for the return of his aatma, so also shall I give this mortal a soul.

The voice turned crafty, revelling in its own brilliance. The faces turned to one another, leering and grimacing with pleasure and arrogant glee.

But it shall not be his own soul. No, cousin. I shall infuse this body with the soul of a man who will be more suited to my plans. A great assassin, as well as a great actor. . . . But first, I must help you realise the folly of disobedience, my sweet doe.

And as she watched in dull, glazed terror, as transfixed as a frozen doe before a pouncing tiger, he unclasped the leather thongs crisscrossing his chest and began to undulate. In pairs, his second set of arms emerged from their binding, just below the first pair and just as muscular and powerful. Then the third pair. Then the fourth.

By the time the tenth pair emerged, almost at his waistline, she was beyond fear. All she could do was lie back and await the execution of his punishment.

The wilderness echoed with her screams for a long time.

5

'Brother!'

Lakshman rushed forward to embrace Rama. His brother's body felt hot and sweaty, as if he had just run a full yojana without pause. Lakshman looked at Rama's face. He looked no different. The same straight features, the classically handsome Suryavansha profile, hair as dark as a raven's wing, coal-black eyes, smouldering as if capable of bursting into flame at any moment, neither too widely set nor too closely, focused as if gazing at a point a thousand yards distant. It was their father who'd once said that Rama had the look of a perpetual archer: always focused on the eye of a target that only he could see.

'Brother?' Lakshman said again, questioning this time. 'Are you all right? I woke to find you gone. Where were you all morning?'

Rama's hand gripped Lakshman's shoulder. Lakshman felt as though a python had coiled itself around his bicep, squeezing tightly enough to make his every nerve scream yet barely aware of its own strength.

'I'm all right, Luck,' Rama said softly. He released Lakshman's shoulder gently.

Lakshman stepped back. He glanced at the brahmarishi, who was watching them both intently, his narrow eyes slitted with concentration. In the growing morning light, Vishwamitra's uncut white hair, bushy brows and long beard glowed with dazzling brightness, each strand illuminated by the slanting first rays of the rising sun. Set against that stark backdrop of whiteness, the seer's eyes seemed as closely and deeply set as the eyes of the tiger as they gleamed from within the shadows of the peepal boughs.

Vishwamitra came forward, stopping a few yards from Rama and Lakshman.

'Rajkumar Rama,' Vishwamitra said. 'Where do you appear from so unexpectedly, clothed in effulgence like the ancestor and founder of your dynasty, Surya-deva himself?'

'Pranaam, Guru-dev,' Rama said, folding his hands in a namaskar.

Lakshman couldn't help noticing that while Rama's voice and gesture were respectful, there was something in his manner that made him seem different somehow. Almost verging on insolence. But that was unthinkable. Anyone else, perhaps. Despite the pride with which all Aryas regarded the guru-shishya tradition, it wasn't unheard of to have a rare disagreement or two. But to think of Rama as being part of such a disagreement? Acting insolent to a guru? Impossible!

Yet there was something in the seer's tone as well. A coolness that was unlike the warm affection Vishwamitra had displayed these past few days. Especially since yesterday, after the successful completion of the yagna, the brahmarishi had been almost paternal in his manner towards both of them. Certainly he'd never spoken as brusquely to Rama as he did now.

'A good shishya would greet his guru before venturing on any other task, young Rama. Surely Guru Vashishta schooled you in this primary fact of the guru-shishya relationship?'

Rama bowed his head cursorily, enough to satisfy protocol, yet too little to suggest genuine humility. 'Maha-dev, the first thing I have done today is greet you. Pray, grant me the gift of your ashirwaad that I may see this day through by the grace of your divine blessings.'

'My blessings are ever yours, young prince. For you earn them by your deeds and words, not by simply calling yourself my pupil. But why do you deign to ask for my ashirwaad now? Did you not think to ask me earlier when you ventured alone into the solitude of the dense Vatsa woods at an hour well before dawn? Had I not expressly forbidden both of you from leaving the boundaries of Siddh-ashrama without my permission?'

Lakshman glanced at the brahmarishi, startled. He had assumed that the seer was as unaware of Rama's whereabouts as he had been. He berated himself silently; he should have known better. Of course the brahmarishi knew where Rama was all along. Why else were seers called seers?

Rama kept his head lowered slightly, his tone immaculately polite. 'Guru-dev, as you possess perfect awareness of most things that occur on this mortal realm, so also you must know that I did not leave of my own volition. I was called away by a power so great that I had no choice but to go where it took me.'

'Rama, oh Rama,' said the seer sadly. 'Do not speak so naïvely. I have already spent many words praising your remarkable maturity and inborn wisdom. Son of Kausalya, you know as well as I that even the most powerful force on earth can only command us. It is up to us to choose whether to obey that command or not. Even the great wheel of time that turns the universe itself does not deprive us of free will. We each have the power to choose everything we do or say. You went because you chose to go. Is it not so?'

'Yes,' Rama said. 'But maha-dev—'

'Enough!'

The seer raised his hand, showing Rama his out-stretched palm in the formal gesture of conclusion.

'I will not stand here and debate issues that even a first-year shishya at any ashram knows fully well. My duties demand I return to Siddh-ashrama. Today, we proceed northwards to Mithila, thence to the snowbound slopes of mighty Himavat, where I shall resume my bhor tapasya. If you and your brother still serve me, you will prepare to depart for Mithila the moment your morning ablutions are done. I shall be in my hut until then.'

And with those words, the brahmarishi turned and walked away, striding swiftly back towards the ashram compound.

Vajra Captain Bejoo was praying when he heard his name being called.

He paused in the act of touching the idol, the tips of his fingers reaching out to the small oblong-shaped black rock which represented his patron deity Shani.

It was the last stage of the daily prayer ritual he had followed every day of his life since attaining manhood. He had poured the customary offering of mustard oil over the rock, sprinkled freshly plucked spring flowers and placed a garland of herb leaves around the deity. All that remained was to break the coconut. Before the ritual he had picked a desiccated coconut from the mound that lay at the temple threshold, and stripped away the tough strands of fibre, exposing the kernel.

Now, he had only to smash the kernel on the granite floor of the temple while reciting the Shani mantra, thereby sanctifying the coconut. Then he could partake of the coconut milk and the thick flesh which would have become sacred food blessed by the deva. By drinking the milk and eating the flesh, Bejoo would have partaken of the god's essence, gaining not just his blessing but also his strength and courage in battle.

Shani, whom the Greek envoys to the Arya nations called Saturn, was the patron deity of charioteers. And for Bejoo, captain of a Vajra unit built chiefly on the swift striking ability of chariots, it was unthinkable to start a day without completing this simple but vital ritual. He had performed it on battlefields far from home, with malarial fever searing his brain, with the cries of his wounded and dying men filling the forest for miles around, with the screams and shrieks of charging Asuras ringing in his ears, through the worst of times and the best of times. He would not miss it today, not for some foolish soldier who didn't know well enough to wait until his commander was done with his morning prayers.

What could be so urgent anyway? They were in Siddhashrama, the most peaceful sanctuary in all the seven Arya nations, under the protection of the seer-mage Vishwamitra. There was no general alarm, no other indication that they were under attack or in any kind of danger. So why was this fool persisting in calling out Bejoo's name when he could see he was in the temple?

As if on cue, the voice rang out again, much closer this time.

'Bejoo,' the man said. 'Captain, you must listen to me.'

Bejoo resisted the urge to tell the man to go drown himself in the nearest well. It wouldn't do to lose his famously short temper when saying his prayers.

He took a deep breath, forcing himself to ignore the annoying voice, and raised the coconut kernel above his head.

'Bejoo, it's Bheriya. In the name of our friendship, I beg you, listen to me.'

Bejoo lowered his hands slowly. He placed the coconut on the mandap before the deity. Prostrating himself once again, he touched his forehead to the edge of the mandap then rose to his feet, keeping his hands joined and his eyes shut, and slowly backed away. When he was at least three yards away, he allowed himself to turn. His hand reached out and struck the temple bell with a instinct born of sheer habit, even though he hadn't actually finished his ritual. He came down the steps of the Shani temple and looked around.

There was nobody in sight.

'Bheriya?' he called out, puzzled and irritated now. 'Where in the three worlds are you, man?'

There was no reply. He frowned, on the verge of losing his temper. Why the devil had Bheriya come back here anyway? He should have been in Ayodhya by now, Bejoo's message duly delivered to Maharaja Dasaratha, and then, if he had no other duties, he should have gone home to his new bride, trying to make little Bheriyas to carry his name!

'Bejoo, listen to me.'

Bejoo swung around. The Shani temple was a small one, located in a thicket of neem and other assorted herb trees. It was where the rishis of the ashram grew the medicinal herbs and conducted their Ayurvedic research into new cures for various ailments. It was here that they grew the world-famous herbs that were said to cure the diabetic condition, among other miraculous natural herbal cures. Bejoo was alone here this morning; all the other residents of the ashram were busy packing their wagons in preparation for the journey to Mithila. Even his own men were engaged in their morning exercises, on his own orders. He scanned the neat rows of neem trees stretching away in all directions for several hundred yards, but couldn't see hide nor hair of any living soul.

'What are you up to, Bheriya? Playing hide-and-seek with me? We're too old for games. Show yourself, man.'

'Bejoo.' The voice came from behind him this time. Bejoo swung around, startled. He stared into the shadowy recesses of the stone temple. How could Bheriya have got past him and into the temple? This was the only way in, and the steps on which he stood were barely a yard wide. Even the wind-god Vayu couldn't have got past Bejoo without his sensing it.

'Bejoo, please. Time is short. Don't worry that you can't see me. Just listen. I have something very important to tell you.'

Bejoo ran his fingers through his thinning hair. Baldness was a bane of his family's male lineage. He was comparatively lucky. His father and grandfather had been bald as marble statues by the time they hit thirty. He still had some of his hair intact. He felt the hackles on the back of his neck prickle as he looked warily around the deserted Shani temple.

'Bheriya, I don't know what you're up to, but this is no time or place to be playing childish pranks.'

'Bejoo! In the name of Shani-deva, heed my words. The Lord of Lanka has stolen my body and infused it with another man's aatma. The Bheriya that is making his way to Ayodhya even as we speak is not me. He is a twice-lifer serving the king of Asuras. His mission is to spread false information at the court of Maharaja Dasaratha and distract the maharaja and his generals from the coming invasion.'

Bejoo reached for his sword, then remembered belatedly that he never wore it to temple. He cursed himself for not keeping it by the temple steps. Living at Siddh-ashrama for eight days had made him soft.

'Bheriya, I still don't understand how you're perpetuating this foolhardy prank. But Holi is over, and the time for spring-day jokes is past. Show yourself now, son, and let's not have this kind of crazy talk.'

The temple bells rang.

Bejoo started, almost losing his footing and tumbling backwards down the narrow steps. Recovering, he caught the crumbling wall and stared up at the two pillars at the top of the stairs. Several bells of different sizes and heights hung between them. All the bells were ringing before his very eyes, their loud brassy peals deafeningly loud. He could actually see them slowing down then swinging out abruptly, just as if someone were ringing each of them one by one, reaching the end of the row, then starting over with the first one again.

But there was nobody standing beneath the bells!

Bejoo raced up the steps. He never paused to think that any force that could ring temple bells without visible physical means might also be capable of doing him bodily harm. He was a Vajra kshatriya. It was his job to make forays into the heart of enemy territory and probe the enemy's weaknesses and strengths. Suffering bodily harm was a part of his job description.

He reached the top of the steps in a fraction of a second. He now stood directly below the swinging bells. He reached up, moving his hands this way, then that, feeling for strings or any other means of trickery. But the air around the bells was empty. They were suspended from an iron rod fixed between the pillars, not fixed in the ceiling itself, which precluded the possibility of hidden devices. In any case, he doubted very much that the rishis of Siddh-ashrama would rig their Shani temple with cheap con-juror's devices.

And yet the bells rang on.

Bejoo sank to his knees. He turned his gaze to the mandap at the far end of the temple, folding his hands and invoking his patron deity's name again. 'Om Shani Namah,' he said. 'Protect and preserve us, my lord.'

The bells stopped pealing. When the voice spoke again it seemed to come from right beside Bejoo.

'Have no fear, Bejoo. I am in the spirit world now, but I am still Bheriya. I would never do anything to cause you harm. I have come only to help you.'

Bejoo reached out and touched the empty space where the voice seemed be coming from. His fingers met only air.

He hesitated, taking the final leap of faith that was needed for him to accept the fact that he was speaking to a ghost. 'If you're in the spirit world, Bheriya, then that would mean that you're . . .'

'Dead. Yes, Bejoo. We were ambushed last night, at the foot of the South Cliff. It was a rakshasi, a very powerful one. She tore into us like a whirlwind.'

Bejoo nodded. He was accustomed to news of sudden death. Although hearing of Bheriya's unexpected demise was more than a little unsettling for reasons beyond professional regret, he kept his reaction to himself. He would deal with that later. 'And what you just told me, about Ravana using your body to infiltrate Ayodhya . . .' He paused. 'What did you say exactly?' He hadn't paid much attention the first time around. Now, his head throbbed with concentration as he tried to catch every syllable spoken by the disembodied aatma of his erstwhile lieutenant.

Bheriya said slowly, 'My re-animated body is possessed

by a malevolent aatma who does Ravana's bidding. He is
on his way to Ayodhya right now, carrying false information designed to distract our king and his generals and
point them away from the real threat that approaches.'

'And this threat is . . . ?'

'A full-scale Asura invasion.'

Bejoo swallowed. 'If what you say is true, then I should
ride back to Ayodhya at once, intercept this imposter and
warn our king and the army in time to prepare for the
invasion. That is why you . . .' He searched for the
appropriate word. Knowing how best to address spirits
was not part of his martial experience. 'Why you returned,' he said at last. 'You wished to warn me to take
action to prevent this from happening. Isn't it? Bheriya?'

But there was no reply. Just the stony silence of the
temple and the usual early-morning sounds of birds and
insects in the grove outside. And the faint whistling of
wind through a crack in the temple wall somewhere.

Bejoo rose slowly to his feet. 'Bheriya?'

He walked around the temple, calling out his former
lieutenant's name several times.

He felt foolish. Had he imagined the whole thing? Had
he finally grown senile, succumbed to his old war injuries?

The only sound he heard in response was the faint
whistling of wind.

He stopped dead in his tracks. Wind? There was no
wind here. It was as still as a becalmed warship in a dead
strait.

He sought out the sound of the whistling. It was coming
from the deity of Shani itself.

Bejoo swallowed nervously as he folded his hands once
more and knelt before the deva's symbolic stone effigy. As
he bowed his head, he could hear the faint disembodied
voice coming from somewhere in the region of the idol. It

sounded like words called out down a long narrow underground passage.

'. . . no time . . . return to the afterworld now . . . speak . . . again . . . later.'

'Bheriya? If what you say is true then I must leave for Ayodhya at once. This is more important than my mission to protect the rajkumars, isn't it?'

He immediatedly felt foolish. Although he had accepted the unlikely premise that he was in communication with Bheriya's ghost, surely he was expecting too much in asking questions of the spirit.

'Do you agree, Bheriya? Is there anything else I should know before leaving for Ayodhya?'

There was a long silence, during which Bheriya felt progressively more uneasy and foolish as he waited with his head bowed, listening carefully. 'Bheriya?'

After what seemed like several more minutes, he was on the verge of giving up and leaving the temple to start preparations for the trip to Ayodhya. But just at the instant when he was about to rise to his feet again, the voice returned, fainter than ever and obviously fading.

'Bejoo . . . don't go . . . Ayodhya . . . Rama and Lakshman in danger . . . accompany them . . . Mithila.'

Bejoo waited, not daring to speak lest he miss any part of Bheriya's message. Finally, he heard three words, spoken a little louder than the preceding ones, punctuated at the end by a long, painful sigh, like a man drawing his last breath, then the temple fell silent.

Bejoo raised his head, his eyes meeting the black stone representing Shani. The deva's effigy glistened, flower petals sticking randomly to the surface of the smoothly carved stone, the three thick horizontal saffron lines on the forehead of the effigy slightly blurred by the daily pouring of oil by devotees.

He looked at the coconut kernel that he had yet to break. He should complete the ritual and consume the sacred food, sharing it with his men to ensure a safe and successful journey today. But somehow, his heart was no longer in the ritual. A cold sense of foreboding had begun to spread through his being, chilling him to his core.

Bheriya's message rang in his ears like the echoes of the now-silent temple bells. A twice-lifer possessed by a malevolent soul was on his way to Ayodhya, carrying deceit that could disarm Ayodhya's defence against an imminent invasion. Bejoo couldn't understand how a solitary man – let alone a walking corpse – could achieve such an ambitious task, but he knew better than to underestimate the power of the Lord of Lanka. His job was not to analyse the situation, simply to report. Which he felt he must do at once, before any damage was done. Ride back to Ayodhya like the wind, speak his message into the king's ear discreetly, trust that Maharaja Dasaratha would believe his story of messages from a ghost and walking-dead imposters. Expose and dispatch the twice-lifer quickly and help the kingdom concentrate on its real challenge – preparing for the impending invasion.

Just that last thought chilled him further: an all-out Asura invasion on the Arya nations? It was true then, what the seer-mage Vishwamitra had spoken of back in the sabha hall of Ayodhya just nine days ago. Ravana's army was ready to invade. When? Within days? Weeks? Months? Bheriya hadn't said, but Bejoo had the impression it would be soon. Perhaps a day or two, at most a week.

So his path of action seemed quite logical and clear. Return to Ayodhya. Expose the imposter. Help prepare the kingdom for the coming invasion.

But Bheriya's last words had been equally clear. The

aatma of his former lieutenant – the man he had come to think of as a surrogate son, the son Bejoo had never had but had yearned for all his life – had not advised him to do any of these things. On the contrary, the ghost had clearly said he must *not* return to Ayodhya. Bheriya had warned of danger to the rajkumars Rama and Lakshman, whose protection was Bejoo's sworn duty until their safe return home. And at the very end, the words that Bheriya had managed to convey through the idol of Shani-deva itself – another portentous omen, if Bejoo needed one – were the cause of his current confusion and deep unease.

Bheriya's last words had been: 'Go to Mithila.'

6

Manthara allowed herself a tiny flicker of amusement. She waved the trident over the images flickering in the unholy fire, the blood-encrusted tines blackening in the flames. The image of Kausalya and Dasaratha embracing in the maharaja's sick-chamber wavered then blurred to obscurity.

Manthara closed the spell of maya, the mesmerising art of illusion, with an invocation to her master. Once again, she thanked the Lord of Lanka's immense mastery of brahman that had cloaked her furtive activities from even the consciousness of the powerful Guru Vashishta. She knew that the ancient seer sensed the use of brahman in the vicinity – no mantra could mask that – but he was unable to pinpoint Manthara as the source of the flow. Nor was he even suspicious of the ageing deformed wet nurse. Which was because Manthara wasn't the source – she was merely the channel the Dark Lord used to achieve his ends.

Manthara mused on what she had just seen.

It made her want to vomit.

Kausalya thought she could rouse Dasaratha out of his stupor and talk him into performing miracles overnight.

Her faith in him had even convinced the maharaja that it was possible.

But both of them were about to be thrown off their cloudy perch and brought crashing down to earthy reality again.

It was time to start the final act of this drama. And this time, she, Manthara, would be the heroine of her own epic poem. Not relegated to the sidelines as a mere bit player in the chorus, or typecast as a villainous shrew on account of her birth deformity and misshapen form. No. In the playhouse of the Lord of Lanka, maya was supreme. You could be anything you chose to be. Even a deva, if it pleased you. For what was a deva, she mused, if not the highest caste of all, a caste of proto-brahmins who had arrogantly granted themselves supreme elevation above all others? Yes, she could be a deva if she pleased.

Manthara rose with difficulty and went to the far wall of the secret room. A mantra muttered, a quick gesture, and the wall melted away to provide a portal through which she passed. She had no need to bend over to pass through – her hunchback gave her a natural stoop, compelling her to go through life in a perpetual posture of apparent servitude. It had been the source of great humiliation in her childhood; now, it was the mark that proclaimed her uniqueness among a race of tall, sculpted Arya women.

Ravana had brought this to her attention at the outset of their relationship, when she had only just begun to worship the dark Asura lord in a desperate adolescent search for a deity that could hear her angry, fervent pleas for justice and reparation.

Manthara, he had said to her that fateful day, your body is stooped because your mind towers above all others. The devas feared that if they let your physical body reflect the stature of your mind and soul, you would overshadow all other Arya women. Out of jealousy, the devi recast you in this form, bending your spine in the womb of your mother.

Yes, my lord, she said silently as she emerged into her own private chambers, sealing the portal to the secret chamber. She passed out of the traditional pooja room which she maintained for the sake of appearances and into her bedchamber. You spoke truly. And now the time approaches for me to seek redressal for my unfair treatment at the hands of the devas. Soon I will have power enough to bend the spines of all these wretched Aryas who walk so proudly tall and straight; bend them . . . and break them.

The serving girl started as Manthara emerged from the bedchamber.

'Mistress!' she said, dropping the gold drinking vessel she was holding. Manthara cursed and gestured. The vessel froze in mid-air. She gestured again and it rose up and hovered inches before the astonished serving girl.

'You were stealing from me,' Manthara said.

The girl stared at the drinking vessel suspended in mid-air, her fingers instinctively clasped together in a namaskar to the gods. She swallowed, terror making her voice tremble. 'No, milady! I was only admiring the craftsmanship.'

The gold vessel leaped forward, striking the girl on the forehead with a dull ringing. She gasped and fell back several steps. The vessel followed her, hovering overhead like a cobra stalking its prey. 'Forgive me, mistress! Yes, I did have impure thoughts! But I would have resisted them. I would never actually steal from you. Forgive me, my lady!'

Manthara gestured impatiently. The drinking vessel flew back to the nightstand beside her bed and came to rest there, making only the tiniest click as it came into contact with solid wood. She shuffled forward, her uneven legs – one was longer than the other – giving her a lurching gait that still made children laugh and sneer when she went by, and struck the serving girl hard on her cheek.

The girl cried out and fell to her knees, fat tears pushing their way out of her large green eyes and spilling down the front of her blouseless garment, rolling down the swelling curves of her bare breasts. She clutched Manthara's feet, kissing them fervently.

'I beg you, mistress, do not kill me. I will serve you in any way you desire. Please, only let me live!'

'Get up, harlot,' Manthara said quietly. She was perfectly calm. The slap had been only routine discipline. It would not do to let the girl think she could steal from Manthara. Already, she knew more than Manthara would have liked. It was only the special warding mantra that ensured her silence about the dark, unlawful deeds she had witnessed over the years that kept her alive. The day she crossed the line, she would become just another pile of solid fuel for Manthara's fire ritual in the secret chamber.

Until then, Manthara had use for her.

Especially today.

The girl rose to her feet, blubbering foolishly. Manthara slapped her again, not hard, just enough to make her stop crying and pay attention.

'Stand straight, don't slouch,' Manthara barked. 'What are you? Hunchbacked? Stand like an Arya!'

The serving girl looked dumbfounded at this unexpected criticism, coming from the most severely deformed hunchback in Ayodhya. She stood straight, thrusting her exquisitely formed bust forward. Her pallo had slipped off, leaving her naked from the neck down to her abdomen.

Manthara poked at her firm belly, then at her ripe high

breasts with intense scrutiny. The girl visibly resisted the urge to giggle, tickled by the prodding and pressing. When Manthara's claw-like fingers brushed her nipples, she stopped giggling and sighed instead. The aureoles turned rosy pink and the nipples swelled to their fullest.

'Mistress,' she whispered. 'Do you wish me to please you? I have much experience in the art of love, and am proficient in loving both men and women. If you wish, I could—'

'I wish you to stand still and shut your maggoty mouth,' Manthara snapped. She walked around the girl, continuing her examination with almost clinical detachment. She grimaced at the girl's offer; how could humans take pleasure from rubbing sweaty bodies against one another, and the violent exchange of bodily fluids? It was a notion repellent to Manthara, and a mystery that she had always found inscrutable.

She told the girl to strip. Wide-eyed and flushed now, the girl did as she was ordered. Manthara finished her examination and nodded to the girl. 'Be very still now. Whatever happens, you must not move or speak a word until I command it. Understood?'

The girl nodded vigorously, eager to please.

Manthara began the incantation. The words came easily, passing through her like water through a sieve. The Lord of Lanka had infused her brain with the mantras at their last communion, along with the details of the action he wished her to take. All Manthara had to do now was let the mantras speak themselves.

When she had finished, several moments later, the serving girl was gone.

In her place stood the living effigy of Second Queen Kaikeyi.

Manthara stood the girl before a full-length mirror and

showed her her new form. The girl gasped in Kaikeyi's husky tones, touching her naked body in disbelief. She was fleshier now, as befitted a woman who had borne a son and packed a lifetime of carousing and gluttony into the last fifteen self-indulgent years.

'Mistress,' she said in awed amazement. 'Your power is boundless!'

'Shut up,' Manthara said absently. She was deciding which garment the girl should wear in her new avatar. If she was to appear to be Rani Kaikeyi, she must wear Kaikeyi's jewellery and saris. Kaikeyi had her own individually designed saris, gold-inlaid and embroidered so heavily as to weigh more than entire jewellery sets worn by the other titled queens. The girl must wear one of those trademark saris or the guise would be incomplete. And jewellery. Nobody could mistake the jangle of Kaikeyi stalking the corridors and hallways of the palace. Kaikeyi appearing in public without her trademark five or ten kilos of solid gold jewellery would be as noticeable as a plucked peacock.

'Come with me,' she said, going to the door.

The serving girl hesitated at the doorway of Manthara's chambers.

'Mistress?'

Manthara looked back, frowning impatiently. 'Come on! I haven't got all day!'

'But I'm not clothed! The guards . . .'

'The guards have seen more happenings on a feast night in these corridors than you've dreamed of in your wretched lifetime. Come on, now. We have to go to Rani Kaikeyi's palace to get you dressed.'

The girl stared stupidly through Kaikeyi's light brown eyes. 'But what about Rani Kaikeyi? Won't she object? And what will she say when she sees me like this?'

Manthara cursed the girl's parentage, her clan, and her ancestors back to the beginning of time. 'Rani Kaikeyi is asleep. She has slept eight days and nights and will sleep eight more days and nights if it so pleases me. What did you think? That I would have two Rani Kaikeyis running around the palace? Do you take me for a fool? Enough talk now, you stupid she-goat. Come on!'

The girl went, still blushing furiously as they walked down the winding corridors. Once they were actually underway, however, she began to change her tune, relishing the amused – and amazed – glances and stares from the guards, other serving girls, daiimaas, and other palace staff that they passed en route. The realisation that they were seeing not her, an ordinary serving girl, but Rani Kaikeyi, Second Queen of Ayodhya, gave her a new boldness. She began to strut and roll her hips, deliberately flaunting her nakedness, brushing against the guards, showing off her fleshy nudity.

Manthara gritted her teeth and let the girl have her foolish thrills; she didn't want to attract further attention by seeming to chastise her mistress publicly. At best, the bemused spectators would assume that the Second Queen had been consuming more soma than she could hold, and was in an unusually carefree mood because of the maharaja's recovery. News of this last event had already spread through the entire palace, she knew, in the time it had taken her to recast the serving girl in Kaikeyi's physical form. The crowds waiting eagerly outside the palace gates for word of their king's condition – some camped for the past eight nights – were cheering hoarsely and asking for their liege to show himself on one of the balconies facing Raghuvamsha Avenue so they could worship their godlike ruler and praise the devas for aiding his recovery. In the flurry of excitement, Kaikeyi's brief naked walk would hardly be noticed. The Second Queen had done wilder, more wanton things in her time.

The serving girl had already gone far ahead, her absorption in her newfound role making her forget that the hunchbacked daiimaa she served was physically impaired and unable to walk as fast. Manthara wasn't bothered. She was used to falling behind. She used the time to daydream of the sweet revenge she would wreak on the House Suryavansha this day and the next. Already, she knew, the armies of Ravana had begun landing on the western shores of the subcontinent. As the Arya nations went about their foolish rituals and so-called civilised activities, the greatest host of Asuras ever assembled was swarming across the land. That was one bit of news these sickeningly self-righteous Ayodhyans had no clue of; and by the time they learned it, it would be much too late to defend themselves.

And in the event that they would still seek to defend and put up a futile resistance – for the Aryas were proud to the point of death – the Lord of Lanka had planned a careful strategy to sabotage their defences and disable their armies. The plan Manthara was now executing was a part of that larger plan of sabotage. And this time she would not fail in her given task. Too much was at stake for her.

She shuffled down the corridor, her stunted torso and twisted gait turning the simple act of walking into an awkward, angry series of contortions. Her bent shadow was magnified a dozenfold by the early-morning sunlight streaming in through the corridor windows. Her crooked shadow loomed across an old portrait of Maharaja Dasaratha, painted back when he was a young warrior-prince, casting a pall across his handsome features.

7

Lakshman turned to Rama. 'Brother, what happened? Where did you go at night? Why did you speak thus to the brahmarishi? He took grave offence at your tone and your argument.'

Rama's face was expressionless, his tone quiet. 'I meant no offence. He would have been angered no matter what I said or did.'

Lakshman shook his head. 'I still don't understand.'

Rama put his hand on his brother's shoulder. 'Come, let us finish our acamana first. Then we shall go to Guru-dev together. All will become clear to you then.'

Lakshman's mind was filled with a dozen questions. But he knew better than to press the point. In any case, it was already growing late, the rising sun filling the grove with warm sunlight. Soon the appropriate time for performing their morning rituals would pass. He followed Rama without question or argument.

There was no river near Siddh-ashrama. Instead, a large catchment pond on the eastern side served the needs of the ashramites. The elder rishis had finished their ablutions earlier but a steady flow of young acolytes came and went as Rama and Lakshman performed their morning prayers, offering thanks to their ancestor Surya for his life-giving sunshine, reciting the maha-mantra Gayatri, along with other rituals.

When they were done, their faces and bodies cleansed, they took a little sacred food as nourishment – papaya from the same grove, served on large velvet-soft banana leaves. As soon as courtesy permitted, Rama and Lakshman rose from their places, thanking the brahmins politely, and headed for the brahmarishi's hut. Everywhere, white-clad brahmacharyas, saffron-clad rishis and red-ochre-clad maharishis were busy preparing for the north-ward journey, yoking bullocks to carts, tying their meagre belongings into small bundles. There was very little chaos or noise. Everyone greeted Rama and Lakshman warmly and with great respect. The role of the two princes in the successful completion of the yagna had earned them the undying love and gratitude of the entire hermitage.

As they neared the brahmarishi's hut, Lakshman heard a loud voice calling Rama's name. He turned and saw Vajra Captain Bejoo coming towards them, his stocky, muscular, leather-clad form a stark contrast to the billowing dhotis and ang-vastras of the brahmins. Rama waited with evident impatience as the kshatriya commander approached.

'Rajkumars,' Bejoo said, saluting them. 'I have something very disturbing to tell you. We must speak privately at once.'

'Privately?' Rama asked. He gestured at the ashram. 'We have no secrets here, Bejoo-chacha.'

Bejoo rubbed his bristling chin uncertainly. 'Even so, it would give me some satisfaction if we could discuss my . . . ah, news . . . in not so public a place.'

'I think I know what your news is,' Rama said quietly.

Bejoo stared at him. 'Mayhap so, Rajkumar Rama. But it is not the news alone, but also the manner in which it was conveyed to me that is most disturbing. You recall my lieutenant Bheriya, whom I dispatched—'

'Bejoo,' said Rama. 'It doesn't matter how you learned about it, what matters is that you were informed of the invasion too. You wish to tell us that the Lord of Lanka has landed his armies on the shores of the sub-continent and they are already swarming across the land, headed for the Arya nations, is that not so?'

Bejoo's ruddy complexion paled by at least two shades, a difficult task since the Vajra kshatriya's florid face was sunburned from constant exposure almost to the point of charcoal duskiness. He swore on his patron deity Shani and spat to one side, an act that drew disapproving frowns from passing brahmacharyas. After brahmanical study and Vedic learning, the only other preoccupation of the ashramites was the cleanliness of their sanctified environs.

'My prince, I don't know how you are aware of this news, or when you came by it—'

'Only a little while ago, Captain,' Rama said quickly.

'Well, then if you know about the invasion, you also know the urgency of the situation. If our sources of information are correct, then the invaders will be at the gates of Ayodhya within two days. Why, by tomorrow past-noon itself they might enter the outer limits of the Kosala nation and wreak their havoc on our fellow citizens! We must act at once! We must inform Ayodhya.'

'Captain,' Rama said calmly. 'I know the urgency of the situation. That is why I am about to ask Brahmarishi Vishwamitra's permission to return to Ayodhya at once. If you will wait but a few more moments, Lakshman and I shall gain our guru's ashirwaad and join you on the road home.'

Bejoo grimaced. 'With all due respect to the brahmarishi, rajkumar, your first duty is as a son of Kosala and a prince of Ayodhya. I have some measure of brahmins and their love for pontification. Why wait precious moments debating the spiritual facets of the crisis? Let us go *now*. I have already given word to my Vajra that we shall ride at once. Shani willing, we can be at Ayodhya before sunfall. Any delay could cost precious lives.'

Rama's voice was firm.

'My first duty is to fulfil my dharma, Captain. And dharma decrees that our oath to the brahmarishi supercede all other concerns. We cannot leave without our guru's blessings. Have patience for a few more moments.'

Without waiting for Bejoo's response, Rama nodded to the Vajra captain and walked the last few dozen yards to the brahmarishi's hut. Lakshman, who had held his silence until now, followed him and caught hold of his arm. 'An Asura invasion? When did this happen, brother? Why didn't you tell me?'

An odd look came over Rama's face. It was the same expression Lakshman had seen on the evening after the Bhayanak-van battle, when he had tried to learn what had happened after he had been knocked unconscious. The question that had provoked the response then had been Lakshman's puzzled demand as to how he could have been knocked senseless during the battle without sustaining a single visible injury. Rama's face had looked exactly like this then.

'You were about to find out in another moment, Lakshman. This is the same matter that we were on our way to discuss with the brahmarishi. The fact that Bejoo learned about it somehow as well doesn't change anything.'

Lakshman searched Rama's face closely, trying to hold back his own surge of anger. 'Is that what you learned during your trip to the jungle last night? You heard somehow of this invasion?'

Rama's face closed over, growing expressionless once more. 'Among other things.'

He put his hands on Lakshman's shoulders and squeezed hard. 'Let us go to the seer now. Bejoo was right about one thing, time is precious.'

Lakshman nodded. 'Let's go.'

Bejoo watched the princes walk away. He had to exert a great deal of effort to stop himself yelling out, roaring with fury. Kshatriyas were not renowned for their self-control; some sub-castes firmly believed that too much self-restraint bred weakness. The only thing that held him back was the knowledge that causing a commotion would only delay things further, by drawing the attention of the brahmarishi, who disapproved of vulgar kshatriya out-bursts. Bejoo's men and Bejoo himself had not taken a drop of soma or sniffed a whiff of ganja in the eight long days they had been stationed with the rajkumars and their new guru. In this place of brahmins, kshatriyas were the subordinate caste, disobeying the ashram's austere rules at the price of their own moksh.

As far as Bejoo was concerned, even moksh could go take a long walk off a tall cliff. What good was salvation when demon hordes were invading your motherland? He wanted nothing more than to climb on to his horse and ride back to Kosala this very minute, stopping only when he reached the capital city, Ayodhya. If he had harboured any doubts after the encounter with Bheriya's aatma in the Shani temple, they were dispelled now. His supernatural encounter could conceivably have been some kind of Asura trickery – although he didn't think so – but if Rama had learned the same news, then it was indisputable. The invasion that the Arya nations had feared had begun.

The fact that twenty-two years had elapsed since the last Asura intrusion made it that much harder to face. It was a little more than one generation since Aryas had begun to sleep soundly of nights, believing that the Asura menace had been contained finally in that terrible last campaign. Even the PFs, the regiments who were the last survivors of those terrible assaults, believed that the Asuras were still mulling over their ignominious losses in their island-fortress of Lanka, as their Dark Lord fumed and seethed with impotent rage. But now, it seemed, exactly the opposite was true: the Asuras had been rebuilding their armies, and building ships all this while. And now, those ships and those armies *were on Arya land*. There was no time to waste touching the feet of brahmins; it was time to raise one's head, wield a sword and shout an impassioned invocation to the gods of war.

Bejoo's mission was to accompany the rajkumars and bring them home safely. Prime Minister Sumantra himself had issued that order, acting on the wishes of Maharaja Dasaratha. If not for that given directive, Bejoo would already be on his way back to Ayodhya, riding like Marut, the wind-deva. Instead, he had to stand around here and wait 'a few more moments'.

And as he knew from long experience with brahmins, a few more moments never turned out to mean just that.

Still, he smothered his impotent impatience and waited sullenly for his wards to complete their business. As he waited, he clenched and unclenched his ham-sized fists angrily, a short, dark man with a barrel chest, and a face that lived up to the name of his totem, the black bear. Brahmacharyas scurried around him, careful to avoid touching his leather garb and polluting themselves spiritually.

Brahmarishi Vishwamitra stood on the small patch of grass-strewn ground before his hut, dispensing a few last sandeshes to the senior-most maharishis and rishis of the hermitage concerning the trip to Mithila.

As Rama and Lakshman waited silently for the seer to finish, Vishwamitra repeated their planned schedule for the benefit of his rishis – the intention was to reach the River Shona by nightfall and camp there for the night, in the morning to proceed to the sacred mother-river Ganga, perform the customary rituals there, then continue to Mithila. It was possible they would reach Mithila by next nightfall, tomorrow evening. If not, then the following day. As always, the brahmarishi would go on foot along with his new acolytes, leading the procession.

Lakshman felt a brief twinge of guilt as he heard their names mentioned, knowing now that Rama and he wished to go their separate way to Ayodhya. But he could hardly interrupt and correct the brahmarishi.

The sage discussed a few more minor matters with his rishis, then the entire congregation chanted in unison, 'Sadhu, sadhu,' with palms joined and held high above their heads, retreating backwards to avoid showing their backs to their guru. A few of the more senior rishis remained, waiting until their spiritual leader was ready to begin the long journey.

Vishwamitra saw the rajkumars and smiled, beckoning them forward. They performed the ritual obeisance as he blessed them warmly. Lakshman noted that the seer's spate of barely concealed hostility seemed to have dissipated. Then again, perhaps he had misread the sage's earlier state of mind.

'Long life, Rajkumar Rama, Rajkumar Lakshman. May your every deed be siddh from this day on, for you have served Siddh-ashrama nobly, risking your very lives and limbs these past eight days. Truly, you have brought great honour to your family and your dynasty.'

The rishis chanted again, 'Sadhu, sadhu.'

'Guru-dev,' Rama said after he had regained his feet. 'I pray that you are content with our service.'

'You know it well, young Rama. I am more than content, I am proud of the choice I made. I could have approached any maharaja of the seven nations, asking him for his champion to rid the Bhayanak-van of the menace of Tataka and safeguard my yagna. Yet I knew that you alone, Rama Chandra, were destined for that noble task. As were you, Lakshmana, destined to accompany your brother on his great mission. I am vindicated in my choice.'

'Then, Guru-dev,' Rama said respectfully, 'I have a boon to ask of you.'

Vishwamitra stroked his beard thoughtfully. 'Speak it then, rajkumar. All that you ask shall be granted to you today. You have earned the right to demand any boon of me. If it is within my power to dispense, you shall have your heart's desire.'

'Maha-dev,' Rama said, 'grant my brother and me leave to return home to Ayodhya.'

The brahmarishi replied without hesitation.

'Rama, you do not need my leave to return home. Ayodhya is where you must go. You are to be crowned king-in-waiting in a few days. Your people need you to be there at that auspicious occasion, to take the reins of statehood from your illustrious father and continue the glorious lineage of your Suryavansha ancestors. Dharma demands that you must be there in time for that auspicious occasion.'

Lakshman's heart skipped a beat. Could it be this easy? Were they to be allowed to leave without any debate or discussion? Surely it wasn't possible? Let it be so, he prayed.

Rama seemed to be as stunned as Lakshman at the guru's quick acquiescence. 'Then I shall take your leave, maha-dev. My brother and I shall return to Ayodhya at once, to take up arms and defend our nation against the oncoming Asura assault that threatens our civilisation. With your ashirwaad, brahmarishi, we shall return to fight for our lives and our homeland. Pray, grant us your divine blessing.'

Vishwamitra smiled, his lined face still wreathed in a gentle expression. 'You shall have my ashirwaad, Rama. And you shall have much else besides. But first, stay and hear my words. I know of the vision you have been given in the dark hours of this morning. I feel your eagerness to return home to do your duty to your family and your nation. If that is your wish, I will not stop you. You are free to go as you please. But you must know one thing before you go.'

And the brahmarishi paused and leaned forward, directing the full force of his intense ice-blue gaze upon Rama.

'If you go back to Ayodhya, you will be doing exactly what the Lord of Lanka wishes of you.'

8

It took Rama only a second to find his voice, yet it seemed as though aeons passed in that second. The morning sunlight, so comforting on his bare shoulders, suddenly lost its warmth. The air, balmy on this early spring day, began to feel cold, tinged with the frosty bite of the distant Himalayas. Insects that had shurred busily and birds that had chirped melodiously all seemed to fall silent. The very ether that he occupied seemed to want to push him out of existence, to fill the space his being occupied.

'Maha-dev,' he said, his voice unexpectedly steady despite the turmoil he felt within himself. 'I do not fathom your meaning. How could my returning to Ayodhya possibly please Ravana?'

Vishwamitra nodded sagely. 'It would and it must. You see, Rama, this is a test by the devas. They are subtly coercing you to return to Ayodhya. To do the logical thing. Protect your family, your home, your kingdom.'

Rama stared blankly at the seer. It was as if the brahmarishi was speaking some foreign language. He could hear the seer, understand his every word, but he could not fathom the meaning behind the literal meaning of what he was saying.

'But, maha-dev, what other choice do I have?' A

thought occurred to him. 'Unless you mean to say that there is no invasion? That I was misinformed?'

Vishwamitra shook his head sadly. 'Alas, no. Your visitation this morning was no trick. Nor was your nightmare vision, young Lakshman. Nor the occult encounter our Vajra Captain Bejoo had a little while ago. The forces of Lanka have indeed landed on the shores of this great subcontinent, and even as we speak they are swarming across the desolate deserts of Kutchha. Before this day has ended, they will reach the first true major settlements of the Arya nations and begin wreaking a terrible vengeance.'

'Then what else can I possibly do?' Rama asked. 'How can I not return home to protect my home and my loved ones?'

The sage sighed. He spread his hands. Vishwamitra was a large-boned, handsomely proportioned man, his every limb shaped as perfectly as a well-designed weapon of war. His palms were flat and deeply scored with more lines than Rama had seen on any person before. He raised one hand, then the other, holding them at chest level, like scales of an invisible balance.

'That is one choice, certainly, Rama. The natural choice. The one which the devas expect you to make. That is why you were given the gift of that divine visitation this morning. That privilege is granted to but a few fortunate mortals and almost as few immortals. Do you see my point? You were being subtly influenced in favour of this choice. The nightmare vision of your brother Lakshman ensured that he would not argue against your decision, as indeed he will not. And the further sandesh from your Vajra captain, whose lifelong scepticism of all things supernatural was so miraculously overcome in a single encounter with a disembodied voice, cemented the decision. See for yourself then. Forces around you are pressing you to make this one choice and one choice alone.'

The brahmarishi let his right hand fall significantly, as if a five-kilo weight had been dropped on that side of the balance.

'On this other side is your second choice. There are no divine visions certifying this one, no Vajra captains trying to underline its importance; indeed, there is no influence bearing upon you to choose this path at all. You may almost ask the question, "Why this?" And you would be perfectly justified in asking it.'

'But maha-dev,' Lakshman asked, 'what is the second choice? We already know the first choice is to return home to Ayodhya. What would be our alternative?'

'Well asked, young Lakshman. After all, though I address my words to your brother Rama, you are as much a part of his karma at this moment. The second choice of which I speak is simply the path you were to take originally.'

And the brahmarishi let his left hand drop, but only slightly, as if a mere kilo weight had been put there, not nearly enough to outweigh the five kilos on the right side.

'To travel to Mithila?' Rama asked slowly, looking baffled. 'To attend the swayamvara and marriage you spoke of yesterday? But . . . what would be the point?'

The seer-mage smiled. 'Now, Rama, you ask the real question. Not what the other choice is, but *why*?'

The word hung between them like a bee hovering in mid-air, droning. *Why?*

The brahmarishi dropped his hands and said simply, 'Because I have asked you to come.'

There was complete silence for several instants. Rama could hear the stubborn lowing of a bullock at the far end of the ashram, a good hundred yards away, and the muted grunts and coaxing of the young brahmacharyas struggling to move the difficult animal. From the sound, he could even recognise the bullock; it was a surly beast, given to moods and fits. But the chanting of the Gayatri mantra in its right ear would get it moving again. In the brief silence that followed, he guessed that one of the cleverer acolytes must be doing just that. After an instant, he heard the bullock snorting appreciatively and then the jangling of its bells as it began heaving the laden cart up the path again.

'Maha-dev,' Rama said softly, 'you said earlier that we are free to return to Ayodhya. You agree that the defence of our homes and loved ones is of paramount importance. Then what possible purpose could we serve by travelling in another direction altogether, into the heart of the Videha kingdom, to the capital city Mithila, fifty yojanas away from our home and duty?'

Vishwamitra raised his hands in a shrug. 'What purpose did you serve by leaving your homes and loved ones in the first place and travelling with me into the heart of the Bhayanak-van? What purpose did you serve by risking your lives by facing Tataka and her bestial brood? What purpose did you serve by fighting Mareech and Subahu and ensuring the sanctity of my yagna?'

'That was our dharma, Guru-dev,' Rama said. 'You came to our father's palace and demanded as dakshina that we accompany you. All of Ayodhya agreed that it was our dharma to do so.'

The seer-mage nodded slowly, looking at Rama. The weight of years seemed to press down heavily on his lined features, as if a great burden of sadness had descended upon him all at once. 'And it is your dharma to accompany me now to Mithila.'

Rama blinked several times. He felt as though the question that had hung between them like a bee had darted forward and stung him between the eyes. He felt the pain of the answer to that question piercing his brain now, sending a wave of agony through his entire being.

'Maha-dev,' he said, 'you know we live to serve you. Until you release us of our oath, we are your shishyas. If you insist we accompany you to Mithila, we have no power to resist you. We will obey without question. But pray, grant me the answer to one why. Why is it so important that we come with you to Mithila?'

Vishwamitra looked up for a moment. The vivid blue of the sky cancelled out the blueness of his own eyes, just as fragments of ice floating in the clear cold waters of the Sarayu became invisible. Rama was seized by an almost painful conviction that he would never see the Sarayu again, that his beloved river, his beloved home, were all floating away downstream like those fragments of winter ice, far out of his futile mortal reach.

'Rama, that question can only be answered by coming to Mithila.'

The seer put out a hand, touching Rama's shoulder gently. 'And now it is time for us to depart on our long journey. I shall leave you for a few moments as I assemble my acolytes for one final prayer. You may use these moments to arrive at your final decision. Remember that I do not bind you to this choice: dharma binds you. You are free to return to Ayodhya at any moment you desire, just as you were free to refuse to accompany me into the Bhayanak-van eight mornings ago. The choice is now in your hands. Choose which route you will.'

Bejoo saw the brahmarishi coming around the hut, accompanied by an entourage of white-haired, white-bearded rishis. He pointedly pretended to be looking the other way until the brahmins had gone by, neither wishing to give offence by ignoring the ritual greeting nor keen to indulge in formalities he had always considered a waste of time and energy.

They passed by several yards from him, engaged in discussing something amongst themselves. He waited until they had gone, then strode quickly around the periphery of the hut. He saw the rajkumars standing below the banyan tree before the brahmarishi's hut, looking as if they had both been struck by lightning. Bejoo's stomach cramped suddenly, only partly because he hadn't eaten anything that morning, and he had a sinking feeling that his worst fears were about to be realised.

'Rajkumar?' he said, coming up to Rama. 'If your leave-taking is finished, we should mount and ride at once. Ayodhya is a long way yet, and the Asura hordes will not halt to ask *their* guru for ashirwaad.'

Rama's face was a portrait of inscrutability. He looked like a man who had just seen the future and recognised it for what it truly was: a battlefield across which one had to fight one's way one precious yard at a time. It took Bejoo a moment to realise that whatever the brahmarishi had just said, it had had a profound effect on the prince. Gone was the boy who had left Ayodhya a mere eight days ago; in his place was the man he was destined to become, a man soon to become king, and on whom the heavy weight of king-ship appeared to have fallen already.

'Rajkumar?' Bejoo repeated gruffly, trying to find a balance between his natural rough vulgarity and a more suitable tone. 'What is it? What did the brahmin say to make you look thus?'

Lakshman answered. His own face was as grim and forlorn as Rama's, but the delicacy of Rani Sumitra's features lent softness to the younger prince's expression. Bejoo saw that in his own way, he was as devastated as Rama. But while Rama's emotions were as inscrutable as craggy, granite-faced Mount Himavat during a winter ice-storm, Lakshman's feelings showed as lucidly as the mirrored surface of a lotus pond.

'Guru-dev says we are free to return to Ayodhya any time, but it is our dharma to go with him to Mithila.'

Bejoo paused for two beats of his heart, absorbing the words, making certain he had not missed any hidden meaning. These brahmins were so maddeningly fond of their open and hidden meanings that one never knew for sure whether the words being said were the real message or simply the paan-leaf in which it was concealed. Layers within layers, wrapped in coded symbols to which only they held the mysterious key. But he could find no ambiguity in this sandesh; its meaning seemed to be entirely straightforward.

He grinned, relieved. 'Is that all? So go get your rigs and swords and let us ride to Ayodhya!'

Rama walked away, going to the banyan tree. This tree was the mother-tree of all the others in the environs of the ashram, a massive creation over three hundred and forty years of age. Its roots had long since begun to push their way out of the earth, wrestling with one another for space in the crumbling topsoil. Gnarled clumps of root had broken free in places, like the hirsute toes of a giant rishi who had stood three centuries on one foot in meditation. Rama put a foot on a knot of roots and stared towards the east, where the rising sun had begun to reveal itself through the densely growing firs on the eastern hills. Patterned sunlight lit up his profile. He seemed oblivious to the conversation, buried like the banyan in timeless contemplation.

Lakshman answered for both of them. 'Bejoo-chacha, Captain. You don't understand. We must do as the guru desires. It is our dharma to follow him to the ends of the earth if he so commands.'

Bejoo stared at Lakshman in disbelief. This was exactly what he had always warned his young recruits about. Prayer and rituals were all very well, but if you came too close to brahmins, they sucked your very manhood out of you, leaving you a shell good enough only for wearing whitecloth and chanting mantras all day and night long.

'What do you mean, dharma?' he said now. 'It's your dharma to protect your home, isn't it? What about that dharma then?'

Lakshman put a hand to his forehead, rubbing the skin between his eyes slowly, as if trying to wipe away some invisible blemish. 'Bejoo, you don't understand. We are oathsworn to serve Brahmarishi Vishwamitra. To disobey his desires would be to dishonour the code of the kshatriyas and disgrace the name of Ayodhya itself.'

Bejoo snorted. 'Horseshit and cowdung! An Arya's duty – Shani mind me – any *mortal's* duty is first to protect his family and home. Even Lawmaker Manu never said to put brahmins before family. They are our conduits to Swargalok, I don't deny that. But what good is heaven if we can't defend earth? Dharma cannot demand that you sacrifice your heritage and blood-links to follow a brahmin. Besides, what brahmin, what *guru*, would demand such a sacrifice? You completed your given mission, you rid the Bhayanak-van of the Asura scourge. That feat will be retold millennia hence. What more could anyone ask of two young princes, two young sons?'

Bejoo reached out a hand, clutching Lakshman's arm. He directed his words to Rama's profile as well. 'Argue no more. I am not a man of words, rajkumars. I was raised on simple precepts. To love, to protect, to procreate. If a kshatriya cannot perform these simple duties, then what else matters? Come with me, young sons of Ayodhya.

Come with me and defend your homes before it is too late!'

Silence met his words. Lakshman continued rubbing the spot between his eyes. When he took his hand away, Bejoo saw that the spot had turned red and raw, like a tilak applied after a pooja. The younger prince's eyes were misted by pain and confusion. They met Bejoo's gaze then turned away, unable to answer the plea in his eyes. Lakshman spoke to Rama, his voice rich with emotion.

'Rama, my brother. I leave our fate in your hands. I know that what Brahmarishi says is beyond questioning. It is his right to demand that we serve him until he feels the guru-dakshina is fully paid. Until he releases us from our oaths, we have no independent volition. It is our dharma to follow him where he wills. But listen to what Bejoo-chacha says as well. He speaks simple, honest sense. What good is dharma if we do not defend our homes? What use is a code that demands the sacrifice of all we hold dear? If the Lord of Lanka overruns our city and our kingdom, to what will we return to proclaim the fulfilment of our oaths? Who will praise our dutiful obedience of the brahmarishi's wishes? Will anyone be left alive to celebrate our triumphs and our deeds?'

Lakshman paused to wipe a single tear from his right eye. 'I do not tell you what we must do. I only ask that you consider both sides of the argument. That you choose. Whatever you choose for yourself, I shall follow that path as well. For I am linked to you as closely as breath to air. Where you go, there shall I go as well. If it is our dharma to follow the brahmarishi, it is my brotherly love that makes me follow you. Choose wisely, Rama, for on your choice will hinge the most fateful decision of our lives.'

9

First Queen Kausalya greeted Guru Vashishta with a sincere namaskar, joining her palms together and bowing her bindi-dotted forehead dutifully.

The seer-mage acknowledged her gesture of respect with an upraised palm, the customary response of a venerated brahmin.

The guru was alone in his private yoga chamber in the maharaja's palace. There were chambers such as this one set aside in every apartment in the vast palaces of Ayodhya, to allow each member of the royal family his or her own space to meditate in tranquil solitude, but the guru's yoga chamber was unique because it wasn't merely a room in his apartment, it *was* his apartment. The guru's real home was a modest hut in his ashram in the forest north of Ayodhya, where he schooled the sons and daughters of Arya in all the science and arts of Vedic knowledge. When in the capital city, he was mostly occupied with the numerous matters of state and policy on which the maharaja and the rajya sabha of the kingdom of Kosala consulted him routinely. His rare private hours were spent in this chamber, engaged in profound meditation.

He was seated in the lotus position, feet crossed over his thighs, hands outstretched, wrists resting lightly on his knees, right hand clutching a prayer-bead necklace, his fingers continuing to count off the red beads as he mentally recited the sacred mantras even as he addressed the queen. His eyes were half closed in that unmistakable look that signified a deep meditative trance. The sage's long, bony limbs and leanness of flesh were proud emblems of the gruelling penance that had earned him his stature as a brahmarishi, highest of all brahmins. The hard lines of his beard-enshrouded face conveyed the immense spiritual power the guru had acquired from his millennia of transcendental devotional meditation.

Kausalya meditated too, so she knew how hard it was to achieve that level of transcendence. She couldn't begin to fathom how the sage could maintain it while carrying on a conversation with her. Yet she could see him managing both these disparate tasks with the ease of a Mithila bowman firing arrows while astride a charging stallion. Her admiration almost made her forget the purpose of her visit. Almost, but not quite: her news was much too thrilling to forget.

'Guru-dev,' she said, 'I am pleased to bring you good news. Maharaja Dasaratha's health is improved for the first time since his collapse nine days ago. Since last evening, he has begun walking about my chambers and seems to be regaining some of his strength. Perhaps more important than these signs of physical recovery is the fact that he is speaking coherently and intelligently once again. All of us are greatly encouraged by his recovery. I wished to share our joy with you and invite you to visit him in his sick-chamber.'

She looked around the bare chamber briefly. 'I apologise for interrupting your trance. I am aware that you have been meditating for the past eight days and left instructions you were not to be disturbed. But I felt certain you would want to hear this happy news. If I have offended you, please forgive me.'

She pressed her hands together once more. 'Forgive my lapse, Guru-dev.'

Guru Vashishta's face creased in an indulgent smile. His eyes focused on her gradually, taking a moment to return to the world of the here and now. 'Good Kausalya,' he said warmly, 'you owe me no apology. It is for your husband's recovery that I have undertaken this penitential fast and meditation. How could I possibly be disturbed by news that my spiritual efforts have borne such heartening results? May you be blessed with a long and happy marriage for bringing me this joyous communication.'

Kausalya bowed her head at once, touching her forehead to the guru's folded feet. 'May your words be heard by mighty Brahma himself.'

Vashishta touched her head and recited a verse from the Upanishads, the great repository of knowledge, wisdom and prayer created and collated by the seven great seer-mages of whom Vashishta was one; its hallowed contents had taken millennia of tapasya and meditation to create and compile.

The sloka was one Kausalya had never heard before. As best as she could tell, it was an invocation to warriors fighting in a just and righteous cause. Not quite the kind of verse she would have expected a seer-mage to speak to a queen-mother, but being Kausalya, she accepted the benediction gratefully, keeping her head bowed, eyes closed and palms together.

Vashishta ended with the ritual term signifying the close of any such invocation: 'Swaha.'

When Kausalya raised her face to the guru, her eyes were brimming with tears. 'I am truly fortunate to have your blessings, great one.'

'You are fortunate on account of your own spotless existence, mother of Rama. You have lived your entire life with a nobility truly worthy of your race. Women and men such as you embody the true meaning of the word Arya. Noble One, it means in our beautiful deva-given tongue of Sanskrit, and truly you have lived your life nobly. Even without my blessings, you shall ever be watched over and loved by all the devas, including the great creator Brahma himself. Now, pray tell me, why do you shed these tears? Are they out of joy for your beloved liege's recovery? Or are they on account of your anxiety for your son Rama?'

Kausalya struggled to regain control of her emotions. She dabbed at her eyes with the corner of her pallo. 'Your wisdom is infinite, Guru-dev. What can I tell you that you do not already know? You have named both the causes of my outpouring of emotion. My heart is as much filled with joy for my husband's recovery as it is pierced with anxiety for my only child. It has been nine long days, great one. And not a word has reached us yet of the outcome of Rama and Lakshman's mission. The great Vishwamitra promised he would return with them safe and sound in time for the day of Rama's coronation as prince-heir. That happy day is only six days away now. And still there is no news or sign of their return.'

The guru nodded sagely. He stopped counting his beads and wound the necklace around his wrist. 'And yet six days remain. You need not fear on their account, good Kausalya. I can assure you that your son Rama and Sumitra-putra Lakshman are both safe and well at Brahmarishi Vishwamitra's Siddh-ashrama. Well is that sacred sanctuary named, for their mission was siddh.'

'They were successful?' Fresh tears flowed freely down Kausalya's face. Her finely formed features, still retaining the beauty that had made princes and kings across the nine

Arya kingdoms sigh with desire in her youth, grew radiant with happiness. 'They are alive and well? Neither of them suffered any injury during their terrible mission?'

Guru Vashishta paused a moment before replying. The pause was uncharacteristic of him. The great seer always spoke with the eloquent ease of an actor who had not only mastered his own dialogue but had written his own part. Yet he seemed to search for a phrase before answering Kausalya's eager questions. 'They are both well. Your son Rama achieved a great victory over Tataka. And both of them showed great courage and prowess in the battle against the dread demoness's army of vile offspring. They shall return as champions to Ayodhya in time for the coronation. That auspicious day is also the day of Rama's naming, his sixteenth navami. And proudly will he stand before his creator and be declared a man not just in age but in achievements.'

Kausalya's lips parted with amazement as she repeated the guru's last words. 'A man. My Rama will return a man.'

'And he will be crowned king. This is his destiny and he well deserves it. These things I have seen through the flow of brahman that pervades the entire universe, by the grace of the devas who have granted me this ability as a boon for my long bhor tapasya.'

Kausalya bowed her head again, preparing to touch her forehead once more to the guru's feet. But Vashishta stopped her this time; catching her shoulders and raising her upright, he brought her to her feet, rising with her. The seer towered over the First Queen, although, like most Arya kshatriya women, she was as tall as any average man.

'Do not thank me, good Kausalya. It is I who should thank you instead. For bearing such a great son, and for raising him so well.'

The guru's voice softened, his penetrating gaze growing gentler. 'For too long you have endured the negligence of Dasaratha and the malicious will of Kaikeyi silently. Pay heed to what I say now, Kausalya. For this is the most important advice I shall ever give you in this lifetime.'

Kausalya's eyes widened.

The guru's word was akin to law. Perhaps because of this, he gave advice so rarely that the court scribes kept detailed records of each of his dispensations in a special bank of scrolls named Vashishta-Puran. It was said that a newly crowned king could find enough wisdom in that book to see him through fifty reigns. After all, it had been just about that long that Guru Vashishta had been acting as spiritual guide and mentor to the Suryavansha dynasty. Kausalya showed her respect for the guru's gift of wisdom by wiping her tears quickly and listening raptly.

'There shall be challenges ahead in the days to come, good Kausalya. Great challenges that shall test your mettle to the limit. I know you will weather these challenges and emerge triumphant. But in the hope that I may lighten your heavy burden somewhat, I offer you this word of gentle direction. Remember that your son Rama Chandra is as much a child of dharma as he is a child of your body. I have been guru to the royal family of the kingdom of Kosala, and its throne here at Ayodhya, for nigh on eight hundred years. Not once in all that time have I seen a prince or princess with as much promise as your son. Truly he is blessed by the devas with great qualities.'

Kausalya's fair complexion, as white as a lily's petals, coloured with a blush of pleasure and pride. She touched her mangalsutra instinctively, the black-bead necklace that every legitimate wife wore to indicate her married status to society at large, silently mouthing an invocation to Durga, the avatar of the Mother Goddess Sri to whom she prayed daily for the well-being of her family.

The guru nodded approvingly and continued. 'Yet great prowess is tempered with great responsibility. The head that wears a crown must bear its weight as well. Remember this when trying times approach, Kausalya, and you and your son will weather the storm that gathers above Ayodhya.'

Why does he not include Dasaratha? Why does he only mention Rama and me? The thought flashed through her mind as fleetingly as lightning glimpsed in a distant monsoon cloud.

Aloud she said, 'Great One, I do not fathom your meaning. Are you warning me of some danger that will befall us? When will this crisis descend?'

Again, that uncharacteristic trepidation passed over Guru Vashishta's ancient features. It lasted a fraction of a second but this time Kausalya was watching him closely and she caught the expression.

'In a kingdom as vast and powerful as this great land, danger is a part of life. Whatever the crisis, rest assured that you and your son will face it and triumph in the end, good Kausalya. Now, I must go to visit the maharaja. I wish to see his face with my own eyes.'

Kausalya hesitated. She wanted to ask the sage many more questions. But she was aware how precious and rare this whole encounter had been. She was too good a person to impose any further on the great guru's patience.

It was Vashishta himself who sensed her hesitation and paused. 'I see a question lingering in your eyes, good Kausalya Go ahead then, ask. You have earned that much at least with your diligence and patience.'

She bowed her head gratefully. 'Guru-dev, some days past, on the night of Rama's departure, you called the royal family together in the Seal Room to discuss an urgent matter. All of us were in attendance, apart from Second Queen Kaikeyi, whom you requested be kept apart for reasons best known to you alone.'

His voice was gentle and patient. 'Indeed, Kausalya. You were present at the meeting. You recall that discussion as well as I do.'

'Yes, Guru-dev. But after the meeting you retired to this yoga chamber with instructions you were not to be disturbed. And only today, eight days after that last encounter, do I have the opportunity to be graced with your venerated presence once again.'

She gestured mildly, trying to explain herself more eloquently. 'What I mean to say, great guru, is that a statement you made at that secret meeting has been troubling me all these past days. Could I ask you what you meant by that statement?'

Vashishta nodded. 'You may, good queen.'

Kausalya breathed out slowly. 'Then pray tell me, Guru-dev, when you said that the threat to our kingdom would come from Maharaja Dasaratha himself, what did you mean? All of us have debated and sought to understand your meaning, but we are as perplexed today as we were that night. How could Dasaratha, the protector and saviour of the mortal realm and the Arya civilisation, he who risked his own life and immortal aatma by battling the Asuras in the Last War, how could he cause any danger to his own beloved kingdom? Or to his own family? Pray tell me, for I cannot believe that my husband can do or say anything that will cause harm to the kingdom of Kosala. You are infinitely wise and omniscient, maha-dev. What was the real meaning of that statement you made?'

Vashishta was silent for a moment. This time, the silence

was deliberate and it weighed heavily in the air, giving the guru's next words greater significance.

'Karma, my good queen. The only thing that can outweigh the scales of character and bring the noblest of mortals to his knees. If dharma is one side of the scale of a man's character, then karma is the other side of that same scale. Maharaja Dasaratha need not commit any new deed or speak any new word that will cause harm to his kingdom and family. It is his past misdeeds and misspoken words that threaten us all. In due course, you shall see the truth of my prophecy revealed clearly. I can say no more at this time, for it would endanger the balance of the scales. The wheel of time, the great samay chakra that governs all our lives, gods and mortals and Asuras alike, shall reveal all in due course. There is the answer to your question. Now, I take your leave to go visit the king in his sickchamber and hasten his recovery.'

But before the guru could take another step, a serving girl rushed in, agitation writ large on her face. 'Guru-dev, Maharani, pardon the intrusion. The maharaja and Third Queen Sumitra . . .'

'Yes,' Kausalya asked curiously. 'What about them?'

The serving girl wrung her hands in distress, tears spilling down her cheeks. 'Something . . . something terrible has happened. Please, come quickly.'

10

The sun was barely over the treetops when they set out for Mithila.

Shortly before leaving, the brahmins of Siddh-ashrama assembled in the open field before the main hermitage. Brahmarishi Vishwamitra led the congregation in a final chanting of mantras, asking the devas to watch over the hermitage, its surrounding forest and flower groves, and the animals that roved freely. Rama saw several species of animals watching from the edge of the woods. The animals of Siddh-ashrama lived without fear of humans; they had never known violence or aggression from their two-legged friends.

The seer-mage ended the prayer with a mantra praying for their safe journey and speedy return. The entire congregation prostrated themselves before him, then stood and came forward singly to accept the simple prasadam of desiccated coconut from his blessed hands, bowing their heads for the guru's ashirwaad.

The adoration on the faces of the ashramites was striking; some of them had come to the ashram as infants, brought by their parents to be raised in the holy ancient ways, and had only heard of the great founder of the hermitage. Even the oldest sadhus and rishis had not seen Vishwamitra in the flesh before. After all, Rama recalled,

narishi had been cloistered in a grotto deep in the
or over two hundred and forty years, performing
the nse transcendental meditation that brahmins called
bhor tapasya. He had only interrupted his long penance in
response to the petitions of the rishis of the ashram, who
were troubled by the rakshasas who had begun disturbing
their holy rituals. And few brahmins, even those as devout
as the residents of Siddh-ashrama, lived anywhere close to
Vishwamitra's five thousand years.

Rama himself felt little reaction to any of this. He felt
little of anything. After the debate over which choice to
make, he had reached a point beyond emotion, a point
where he felt he was walking on a road so unfamiliar that
he hardly knew whether it led upward or downward, over
a bottomless pit or into a vale of flowers. He knew only
that he had chosen, and that he must now see that choice
through to its end, whatever that end might be. There was
a phrase his mother had always used when speaking of
life-choices: as you choose, thus must you act. He had
chosen. It was no longer his job to judge whether that
choice was the right one or the wrong one. His only to act
and fulfil the promise made by his choosing.

After the distribution of prasadam, which Rama and
Lakshman as well as the Vajra kshatriyas accepted from
the seer-mage, Vishwamitra then led the congregation in a
mantra offering thanks to the rajkumars Rama and Lakshman for cleansing the Bhayanak-van, breeding ground for
the yaksi Tataka and her demonaic offspring, and protecting their sacred yagna from Tataka's vengeful sons Mareech and Subahu.

'It is thanks to the courage and battle prowess of these
two noble kshatriyas that our great yagna was successful,'
the brahmarishi concluded. 'They have upheld the code of
the kshatriya and fulfilled the oath they swore unto me

before their father. They are true keepers of the sacred flame of dharma. We shall chant their names aloud at sunrise and sunset when we perform our ritual offerings.'

Rama sensed Lakshman's numbness. His brother had accepted his decision without argument or debate, folding his hands respectfully, as befitted a younger sibling – even though he might be only days younger – and pledging acquiescence. Unlike Bejoo, who had ranted and raved on for several minutes, refusing to accept Rama's words.

Rama turned his head a fraction, and glimpsed Captain Bejoo, watching from the cart path where he stood at the head of his Vajra.

The look of open fury on the Vajra captain's face said all that needed to be said. He would not, indeed could not, hide his feelings. But he was sworn to protect the rajkumars wherever they might go, and to return with them alive, or not return at all. He would do his duty no matter how it rankled. In his own way, he was fulfilling his own dharma as well.

The ritual over, the congregation dispersed and moved with an orderliness born of centuries of monastic discipline towards the row of bullock-carts waiting on the dirt track. Rama watched as the Vajra commander mounted his horse and issued a crisp order to his charioteers. The Vajra chariots rode around the line of bullock-carts and brahmins, disappearing up ahead in a cloud of dust. Having heard Bejoo giving his unit their orders the previous evening, Rama knew that the chariot would scout about a mile ahead, making sure the path was clear of obstacles.

The Vajra elephants were the next to receive their marching orders. They trundled forward, trumpeting happily at being on the move again, their armoured saddles polished to a glitter. They would walk at the head of the brahmin procession, a quarter- to a half-mile before the humans, a formidable defence against any unexpected trouble. If he couldn't fulfil the latter part of his orders by delivering the rajkumars home swiftly, Bejoo was making sure he fulfilled the first part – to protect them vigilantly.

As the elephants trundled by, the ground trembling beneath their tonnage, the lead bull – named Himavat after the tallest peak in the northern range, the father-mountain of the great Himalayas – trumpeted a friendly greeting to Lakshman, whose gift for befriending voiceless beasts had only been enhanced in the benign environs of Siddh-ashrama. Despite the momentous events that had marked this day already, Rama was compelled to smile at how eagerly the towering bigfoot rolled his trunk upwards into a salute to both of them. The royal elephants of Ayodhya could hardly have mustered a better salute to their maharaja during the annual parade.

He nudged Lakshman, admonishing his brother for not responding to the elephant's innocent greeting. Lakshman glanced up at Rama. Rama met his brother's eyes and held them firmly with his own strong gaze.

'As you choose, thus must you act, Lakshman,' he said quietly, knowing that his brother understood the full implications and meaning of the phrase. 'Once decided, there is no place for regret or remorse.'

Lakshman stared at him a moment, as if battling with some great turmoil within himself. Then he nodded briefly, once, turned and waved to the elephant. Himavat trumpeted again, louder than ever, to show his delight. A pair of maharishis standing nearest to the bigfoot covered their ears, blasted into temporary deafness by the volume of the pachyderm's joy.

Himavat's fellow bigfoot echoed their response. The

entire clearing filled with the powerful sounds of their effusion. In the distant depths of the Vatsa woods, their wilder brothers blew their own trumpeting responses.

While the elephants moved up to the front, the horse section of the Vajra unit turned around in the opposite direction, riding to the very end of the entourage, where they took up a defensive rearguard position. Now, the procession was ready to set off. Rama noted that it was already two hours since sunrise. They were running a little later than the brahmarishi had desired.

A breathless young acolyte, his oiled pigtail bouncing atop his shaven pate, came running up to inform the rajkumars that the seer-mage was awaiting their presence at the head of the procession. Rama and Lakshman acknowledged the acolyte's message. The young brahmin-in-training executed a deep bow and a namaskar while retreating backwards to avoid showing them his back. When he was the requisite three yards distant, he turned and sprinted back to join his fellow novices, who were waiting eagerly to ask him about his close personal encounter with the heroes of Bhayanak-van.

Rama and Lakshaman began walking across the grassy field to the front of the long, winding line of carts and brahmins. They passed rows of carts filled with white-haired, white-bearded rishis reciting their mantras while counting off the red beads on their prayer necklaces. Younger brahmins waited on foot, herding the cattle that would provide the only nourishment the brahmins would partake of during their journey: cow's milk. The rajkumars passed the line of young acolytes, smiling and waving at their excited admirers. The boy who had brought the message waved familiarly at them, showing off for his associates.

'He reminds me of Dumma,' Rama said to Lakshman

when they were out of hearing range. Though he avoided staring directly, nevertheless he was watching Lakshman closely. His younger brother had ever been more prone to emotional sensitivity, and Rama was concerned that he might not be able to bear the strain of the crushing burden they had been given.

He was relieved when Lakshman managed a reluctant grin. 'Dumma and his flying fruits!'

Rama smiled as well, remembering the young brahma-charya running after them on the riverbank, tossing fruits to them as they glided downriver on a raft.

'And his falling dhoti!'

Lakshman laughed involuntarily. 'You think we'll see him at Mithila?'

'We might. Brahmarishi Vishwamitra said that this annual congregation is a big thing. Every brahmin in both kingdoms should be there. You know how much Chacha Janak loves a good philosophical debate.'

He was referring to the neighbouring kingdoms of Kosala and Videha, of which Ayodhya and Mithila were the capital cities. The Chandravansha dynasty that ruled Videha from the moonwood throne at Mithila was related to the Suryavansha dynasty to which Rama and Laksh-man were heirs. Maharaja Janak, king of Videha, was a distant cousin, affectionately referred to as 'chacha' by Rama and his brothers, although he wasn't actually their uncle by blood, only distantly related by marriage through their father.

Lakshman said impishly, 'And you think we'll see Rajkumari Sita at Mithila too?' He glanced mischievously at his brother as he said it.

'Isn't it Rajkumari Urmila you really want to see?' Rama said, grinning back good-naturedly.

He and Lakshman had been teasing each other – and

their brothers Bharat and Shatrugan – about Sita and her sisters for as long as he could remember. It was inevitable, given that their mothers and daiimaas were always talking about how fitting it would be for the four princes of Ayodhya to wed the four princesses of Mithila when they came of age.

It didn't hurt that Rama and Lakshman both had soft spots for Sita and Urmila respectively.

Lakshman spied a flock of birds flying overhead and shielded his eyes from the rising sun as he tried to identify them. 'Are those gurung?' he asked. He failed to notice a hummock and stumbled briefly.

Rama caught his arm. 'Don't fall down and muddy your face, brother. You want to look your best for Urmila, don't you?'

Lakshman shrugged off Rama's hand, recovering smoothly. And you're probably looking forward to continuing your game of hide-and-seek in the armoury with Sita again!'

He was referring to the time when they were seven, just before they had been sent for the traditional seven years of schooling at Guru Vashishta's gurukul. That had been their last visit to Mithila, and during a game of hide-and-seek, Rama and Sita had vanished. They were found long after the game was over, in the armoury of all places – strictly off bounds for children and games – sitting cross-legged at the foot of the great Shiva Bow. Sita had a small cut on her shoulder which Rama was dressing with a swatch torn from his ang-vastra. Both refused to explain what had happened and their brothers and sisters had teased them both mercilessly.

A week later, after their return to Ayodhya, Rama and his brothers were sent to the gurukul, where they spent the next seven years studying the Vedic sciences and arts.

'What did actually happen in the armoury that day?' Lakshman asked Rama now. It was a question he had asked several times over the years. He had yet to get a satisfactory answer from his brother.

Once again, Rama failed to answer. Instead, he smiled mysteriously back at his brother. 'Maybe you should try asking Sita herself when we meet her,' he suggested, smiling a challenge.

Lakshman grinned back. 'Maybe I will at that.'

An unspoken message passed between them then. It was a tacit acceptance that they had chosen their path now, and that it would serve no purpose to brood on what might have been and could have been. For better or worse, their feet were set on this road, and they would see it through.

As you choose, thus must you act.' Lakshman held out a hand.

Rama took it and gripped it hard, willing the gesture to say all that he could not speak aloud.

They walked the last few yards in a warm silence bred by years of brotherhood.

Brahmarishi Vishwamitra was waiting for them at the head of the procession. He stood a good half-yard taller than either of the two rajkumars – or any of the rishis and brahmacharyas – and his hand rested lightly on the knotted grip of his wildwood staff. He looked every inch the powerful warrior-king-turned-seer-mage of whom so many bards had composed songs of praise, his leonine features silhouetted against the early-morning sun, his flowing white hair and beard a proud emblem of his centuries of penance and meditation, while his lean, muscled back and limbs still bore the numerous scars of his former life.

'Rajkumars, walk with me,' he said simply.

Turning, he raised his staff to catch the attention of his fellow brahmins. A murmur of excitement rippled down the length of the procession.

Vishwamitra faced northwards again and struck his staff on the dust of the cart-path, speaking a brief Upanisad mantra aloud. Rama blinked as blue and gold sparks shot out from the ground where the staff landed. Despite all the amazing things they had witnessed over the past several days, the brahmarishi's easy mastery of the power of brahman never ceased to impress him. The sage seemed to be a living reservoir of brahmanic energy.

Vishwamitra began walking forward with long, powerful strides. Rama and Lakshman matched his pace, walking in perfect step a yard behind and slightly to the right of him. Ahead of them, the Vajra elephants trumpeted as their mahouts urged them forward with gentle verbal requests, and the procession began ambling down the cart-track towards Mithila.

II

Third Queen Sumitra was in the rear hall of the sick-chamber when Kaikeyi came to visit the maharaja.

Immediately after Kausalya had left them, saying she was going to speak to Guru Vashishta, Dasaratha had turned to Sumitra with a familiar glint in his eyes. For a moment, she had experienced a small frisson of excitement and disbelief, thinking he was going to ask her to . . . well, to come to bed. After all, Dasaratha was famed for his great appetites. Despite having three titled wives and three hundred and fifty numbered concubines, he had always seemed to be in a perpetual state of desire, except for the past year or so, when his mysterious ailment had kept him in bed sick rather than in the arms of his wives or mistresses.

But he was barely recovered, and she had read him wrong, she realised at once. All he wanted was breakfast. She had been pleased – and secretly relieved – and had risen at once to fetch him some fruits. But Dasaratha had caught her slender wrist, her tiny hand almost invisible in his large fist, and caressed her palm affectionately, trying to seduce her into getting him a thali full of hot fried samosas, jalebis and rabadi.

She had smiled and pulled her hand away, admonishing him for being naughty. She understood at once why he had said no to Kausalya when the First Queen had offered to peel some fruit before she left to visit the guru. If Dasa had asked Kausalya for a deep-fried, sugar-saturated break-fast, she would have shaken her head firmly, and that would have been that. So he had waited till she left, then tried to talk meek and mild Sumitra into giving him what he wanted.

His ruse had almost worked. Sumitra had been so tempted to give in to him. After all, here he was feeling well enough to actually demand something to eat. Not simply lying in bed, half delirious with searing fever as he had been for the past week. But she knew she couldn't do it. The vaids had specifically forbidden fried foods and sweets, and Kausalya, probably anticipating just such a situation, had left her with firm instructions not to give in to the maharaja's whims. And Sumitra always heeded Kausalya's words.

So she had talked the maharaja out of his craving for his favourite breakfast, and had got him to agree that a bowl of her specially blended fruit punch would be a fine alternative. Dasaratha had been grumpy at first, which was understandable. He had turned away and said that in that case, he would do without breakfast. She sympathised with him. After all, it was less than a day since he had been feeling well enough to sit up, walk about the chamber and feel anything akin to a healthy human craving. And he was a man, nay, a king, accustomed to having his way in all things. Naturally he found it difficult to accept that he couldn't indulge a simple desire for a little breakfast. But he knew as well as she did that Kausalya and the vaids were right: it was his years of excessive self-indulgence that had eroded his body and quickened the course of the canker eating him up within.

And she knew Dasaratha's weaknesses. On so many

previous occasions she had seen how quickly a little breakfast or between-meal snack could grow into a kingly feast. Dasaratha's penchant for overeating was matched only by his amorous appetites. So Sumitra had hardened her heart, a difficult task for someone so gentle and caring, and had coaxed him into agreeing to the fruit punch.

Which was why she was here now, in the rear of the large bedchamber, preparing the punch. Kausalya had made the maids put in a heavy drape to separate this alcove where herbs, medicines, fruits and other assorted items needed for the king's treatment were kept handy. This way, she and Sumitra could just step back here and fetch some fruit or grind one of the several powders or pastes that the vaids had prescribed for the maharaja's treatment. It saved sending maids running in the middle of the night, and enabled Kausalya to mix the potions and medications herself; anyone could mix a batch of jhadi-buti, Kausalya had said to Sumitra, but only a loving wife could add a prayer for Dasaratha's quick recovery.

Sumitra agreed wholeheartedly. That was why she had stepped back here to make the punch herself. She could as easily have asked Susama-daiimaa, the palace's master chef, to prepare it. She was as distraught at the king's condition as the other citizens of the city, and as eager to serve him – which was precisely why Sumitra preferred to do it herself. Left to Susama-daiimaa, the fruit punch would turn into a harvest bounty!

Sumitra finished whipping the mixture of assorted fruit juices, freshly squeezed by her own hands and blended in exact proportions, then added in a treacly mixture of beaten yoghurt and honey before churning the whole concoction in a pot with a wooden ladle.

When the mixture was creamy smooth, she pulled out the ladle, touching the tip of her little finger daintily to the dripping end, and tasted it. It was perfect. She smiled with satisfaction, poured the mixture into an earthen bowl, and put it on a wooden tray. She considered adding the usual spices. Dasaratha loved his fruit punch heavily spiced. Then again, he also loved it heavily spiked! She recalled the vaids warning her that excessive spices would do him almost as much harm as soma wine. She sighed wistfully and settled for sprinkling a pinchful of black salt over the top of the concoction. There, now it was fit for a king!

She had picked up the tray and was about to return to the main chamber when she heard the sound of tinkling anklets and heavy gold bangles. She paused, her hand holding the edge of the drapes that hid the alcove, her pretty face creased by a frown. No serving girl would wear jewellery in the maharaja's sick-chamber. Even Kausalya and Sumitra had removed all but the most basic of their ritual ornaments since Dasaratha had taken ill on Holi night. It wasn't seemly to parade around in full 'battle armour', as Kausalya jokingly called it, and besides, it was impractical taking care of a sick man with bracelets jangling and necklaces flashing gaudily. Sumitra could think of only one woman arrogant enough to continue wearing so much jewellery in her sick king's presence. She listened for a moment, and when a voice spoke, her suspicion was confirmed.

Second Queen Kaikeyi's voice was pitched unusually low, its strident, commanding tone reined in by a veneer of apparent concern.

'Dasa, my love,' Sumitra heard her say. 'I would have come to you before, but I was engaged in a pentitential fast.'

The gruffness in the maharaja's voice was more elo-quent than a glimpse of his face. 'You look thin. How long have you been fasting?'

Sumitra inclined her head to one side, holding her breath. At this angle she could peek through the tiny gap where the drapes almost met the wall. She saw Kaikeyi, dressed in a rich silk-brocaded sari, her hair freshly washed and left to dry, her face almost completely scrubbed clean of powders and creams. Sumitra blinked in disbelief. Kaikeyi did look a lot thinner. And much better overall. *She looks ten years younger! Even fasting for a week can't make that much of a difference!*

Kaikeyi sighed. 'Ever since you took to your sickbed, my beloved, I haven't touched a morsel.'

Dasaratha sat up. 'But that's over eight days, Kaikeyi!'

She pressed her palms to her chest, sliding them slowly down the length of her body, over her hips, right down to the middle of her thighs, moulding the silken folds tightly to her body, demonstrating wordlessly that this was what eight days of fasting had resulted in.

Dasaratha's eyes followed her hands downwards, then he reached out as if to touch her and feel for himself the dramatic change in his second wife's contours. At the last moment he hesitated and drew his hand back.

'You must have lost ten kilos! You look twenty years younger, my queen! Not that you looked old or over-weight before . . .' He cleared his throat awkwardly. 'What I mean is, you were always beautiful but now you have a certain glow on your skin that's almost . . . ethereal.'

Kaikeyi tilted her head, letting her hair fall forward, obscuring the right side of her face, the effect lending her a sensual coyness. Her voice was husky and caressing. 'Perhaps I should always fast then. That way I would always be beautiful for you.'

He chuckled softly. 'You wouldn't last long that way, my love. Surely you must have taken some nourishment this past week?' He added hastily: 'I don't mean to distrust your word, but you seem able to move about quite well despite the lack of food. After eight days, even our palace brahmins start to faint and keel over!'

'I was nourished by my desire to see you well once more. The devas fed me all the spiritual energy I needed. And once I heard that my tapasya had pleased them and my boon had been granted, I came to see with my own eyes.'

Unexpectedly, Kaikeyi's eyes filled with tears. 'My lord, you don't know how I have suffered these past eight days! And now, when I see you well again, looking so much stronger and more vigorous, I am convinced that the devas have truly blessed me. I cried to them daily, if you do not spare my Dasa, then no Arya woman will ever respect the vows of marriage again. They will think that the devas do not heed the pleas of a wife for her ailing husband. Grant me this one boon, spare my Dasa. And every Arya wife will bless her marriage and adore the devas eternally. And today, I see with my own eyes that my suffering was not in vain. My prayers were answered! You have been returned to me, my love!'

She leaned over him suddenly, her hair falling like a dark shower over his chest and face. Dasaratha jerked back, startled, but there was nowhere to go. His head pressed against the pillows and bolsters on which he had been propped up. Kaikeyi moved her face closer to his, and before Sumitra fully realised what was happening, the Second Queen had grasped the maharaja in her embrace and was showering him with passionate kisses.

At first Dasaratha resisted, his body turning stiff with surprise and shock. But as Kaikeyi's slender and shapely body, barely concealed by the low-slung sari, began to undulate against him, he seemed to melt helplessly.

Stop her, Sumitra wanted to yell, tell her to get off you!

How can you just let her do that to you after all the things she said and did on Holi day?

But the maharaja seemed to have lost all resolve and willpower. The moment the Second Queen embraced him, he turned into a boneless mass. After a moment, Sumitra saw with dismay, he even began to respond to her passion. She distinctly heard the maharaja sigh and arch his body upwards, bending like a longbow to mould himself to Kikeyi's caresses.

That was as much as Sumitra could bear to see.

She flung the drapes aside and emerged from the alcove into the chamber, making as much noise as she could muster. She walked around the enormous eight-legged bed and put the tray down on a table.

Then she put her hand on her hip and pretended to notice Kaikeyi for the first time.

'Oh, Kaikeyi, it's you? I didn't recognise you at first. Why, you look almost as slim as a serving girl! What have you been surviving on? Wine and song?'

For a moment, there was no response. The two-headed beast on the bed remained as motionless as a sand python coiled around its prey. Then Kaikeyi raised her head and turned to look at Sumitra. The moment her eyes met Sumitra's, the Third Queen's bravado and fury took flight like a flock of pigeons startled off a veranda. For a fraction of a second, just one disorienting instant, Sumitra thought she saw the woman straddling her husband as an enormous serpent. Kaikeyi's eyes flashed with a yellow glow shot through with a deep red sparkle, and her lips parted to reveal the tip of a flickering forked tongue.

'Ssssssumitra,' the serpent sang.

Sumitra's eyes widened, her hands flew to her face, smothering a gasp. She took a step back. The back of her knee struck the table, spilling fruit punch on her sari.

She hardly noticed. She shut her eyes tight for a moment, then opened them again.

The Second Queen smiled up at her balefully.

'Sumitra,' Kaikeyi said softly. 'So nice to see you again.'

Sumitra raised a hand to her quivering mouth. She was seeing things. Surely the Second Queen's tongue hadn't really been forked? And her eyes? That must have been a trick of the light!

Kaikeyi went on, unmindful of Sumitra's lack of response. 'How is your handsome son Lakshman? Have you heard yet? Such a tragedy to see a beautiful young boy's life cut short so abruptly. My heart goes out to you.'

Sumitra found her voice. 'What do you mean? What's happened to Lakshman? What have you heard?'

Kaikeyi smiled cryptically in response.

Sumitra forced herself to stay calm. 'Dasaratha? My lord? What is she talking about? Have you heard something of Lakshman and Rama?'

But Dasaratha remained silent and motionless, pinned beneath Kaikeyi's body, his face still obscured by her long flowing tresses. The Second Queen's hair reached down to her thighs, and even though she had raised her head to speak to Sumitra, it fanned out over the pillow like a black shroud enclosing Dasaratha.

Sumitra was struck by a sudden premonition. She wanted to cry out for help to Bharat and Shatrugan, run to Kausalya, Guru Vashishta, Prime Minister Sumantra, the guards, the servants, anybody. She didn't want to be alone in this bedchamber with Kaikeyi, but she didn't want to leave Dasaratha alone with her either.

Mustering all her courage, she demanded fiercely of Kaikeyi: 'What have you done to our husband? Get off him! Can't you see he's still recovering? This is no way to behave with a sick man!'

The Second Queen opened her mouth and her tongue emerged from between jagged splinter-sharp fangs. The forked purplish-black tongue flashed out half a foot in the air and vibrated, flicking spittle. The sound was exactly like a cobra hissing.

Sumitra gasped and took another step back. The table keeled over, the earthen mug of punch smashing noisily on the stone floor. Sticky liquid lapped at her bare feet.

Kaikeyi's serpentine eyes glowed with a deep reptilian lust that was as sexual as it was predatory. She spoke again sibilantly.

'It was good of you to do your wifely duty and take care of my Dasa for me. But now he's in my hands again. You should run along and join your sister-queen Kausalya. You might want to buy a few dozen white saris apiece, the both of you. For all you know, you might be in mourning a lot sooner than you realise.'

Kaikeyi turned her head to look at Dasaratha. Then she reached down and picked him up as easily as a mother raising her child to her breast. Through her frozen shock, Sumitra glimpsed Dasaratha's face emerge from the curtain of raven-black tresses. His eyes were glazed and empty, like those of a rabbit mesmerised by a snake. He wasn't aware of anything that was being said or done. Kaikeyi cradled the maharaja's face between her blouse-encased breasts, her taloned hands stroking him possessively.

'As for the good king here, I think all he needs to complete his recovery is the attention of a woman who knows how to satisfy his appetites. Fruit punch? I don't think so, my dear. It's Kaikeyi flesh he needs now. I have his cure right here and ready.'

And she opened her jaws, revealing two enormous serpentine fangs, each as long as a short dagger. The fangs were ivory white, and glistened in the sunlight streaming in from the windows. As Sumitra watched in horror and disbelief, a viscous white fluid rolled slowly down one fang, formed a drop at the very tip, and then dropped off. It landed on Dasaratha's crisp white cotton kurta, which Kausalya and Sumitra had helped him don just this morning. The spot where the venom fell turned yellowish at once, sullying the purity of the white cloth.

With one final heart-chilling hiss, Kaikeyi raised her head and fell on Dasaratha with the fury of a predator in heat. Her mouth closed over Dasaratha's neck.

Like a lamp being blown out abruptly in a gust of wind, Sumitra's entire field of vision blinked out, and mercifully for her she saw no more.

12

Manthara allowed herself a tiny flicker of amusement as she sat before her chaukat, enjoying the havoc she had wrought. The image of Sumitra fainting on to the floor of the maharaja's sick-chamber wavered then blurred to obscurity.

Everything had gone just as she had planned.

Rani Sumitra would awaken in moments to find herself and Dasaratha alone once more in the bedchamber. The maharaja would seem to be unconscious, then found to be comatose. A half-consumed mug of the same fruit punch that lay spilled on the floor – it would be taken from the residue in the pot in the rear room – would be lying by the maharaja's outstretched hand. Drops of the concoction would be on his lips and chin, and staining his kurta.

On closer examination, the punch would be found to be faintly malodorous, redolent of an intoxicating herb some-times favoured by tantriks to bring long deep sleep fol-lowed by startlingly vivid hallucinations. The finely shredded herb closely resembled the expensive spice kesar which was loved by the maharaja but was forbidden by the vaids in his present condition. Everyone would assume that docile, malleable Sumitra had given in to Dasaratha's coaxing but mistakenly added the drug instead.

Sumitra's head would be cloudy and confused. She

would babble incoherently about bizarre images of Kaikeyi visiting the room and turning into a giant serpent. On further investigation, it would be found that Kaikeyi had not left her private chambers for the past eight days. The guards at the entrance to the maharaja's chambers as well as the guards outside Kaikeyi's own chambers would confirm this.

None of them would even think of mentioning the serving girl, one of several who constantly ran to and fro on various errands, who had entered the maharaja's sick room around the time of the incident. Sumitra would be adamant that she had seen Kaikeyi and nobody but Kaikeyi.

The blame for accidentally sending the maharaja's delicate physiology into a toxic coma would fall wholly on Sumitra's slender shoulders. Meanwhile, the maharaja would sleep on in his drug-induced coma for days.

Manthara nodded, satisfied that she had achieved her goal without any risk of detection. She gestured with her trident. The fire died out instantly. She rose slowly to her feet, her hunchback compelling her to lean on the trident for support. She shuffled out of the secret chamber, concealing the entrance to the unholy prayer room with a rare mantra taught to her by her mentor.

She took a moment to check on Kaikeyi, once her ward and now nominally her mistress – although Manthara's true master was none but Ravana himself.

The Second Queen lay sprawled bonelessly on her bed, looking much as Sumitra had seen her a moment earlier. With one major difference. The Second Queen's eyes were glazed and unfocused, her gaze turned inwards. That was the result of the drug that Manthara had kept her on these past days. Kaikeyi wasn't even aware of her addiction or drugged state. She thought she was simply fasting and praying for Dasaratha's recovery. When the time was right, Manthara would administer a dose of a harsh antidote that would cleanse Kaikeyi's system of all traces of the drug, and the Second Queen would regain her senses, attributing her fuzzy memory of the past eight days to the unfamiliar rigours of extreme fasting.

Manthara left the Second Queen tossing and turning, lost in her hallucinatory world, and returned to her own chambers to find her personal serving girl waiting breathlessly. The effect of the mantra had worn off, leaving the girl with her own form and appearance once more, albeit dressed still in Rani Kaikeyi's garments and jewels. The girl's face was flushed and her well-filled blouse heaved as she tried to contain her excitement.

'I did it, mistress! Everything went just as you said. The maharaja and the Third Queen never recognised me. They believed I was Rani Kaikeyi!'

Manthara spoke coldly. 'Did you do what I ordered? To the maharaja?'

The serving girl nodded. A blush crept across her pale complexion as she recalled her illicit encounter with her king. 'I . . . kissed him.' She covered her mouth with her hand, as if ashamed of what she had done.

Manthara wasn't interested in the girl's embarrassment. All she was concerned with was whether the drug had been adminstered to Dasaratha. She had applied a specially prepared lip paint to the girl's mouth herself before uttering the mantra that would cause Dasaratha to mistake her for Second Queen Kaikeyi and Sumitra to see her as Kaikeyi as well as a giant serpentine version of the Second Queen. All the girl had actually done was kiss the maharaja, passing on the drug. The toxic venom would do the rest, putting him into a deep coma that would resemble the effect of the forbidden herb. The girl herself had already been given an antidote that made her immune to the drug.

The girl babbled on about how thrilling her adventure had been and how scared she had been when the Third Queen had come into the room and challenged her. But she had retained her presence of mind and spoken the very words Manthara had made her memorise earlier. She boasted that even performers of the royal Sanskrit Manch could hardly have done better.

Manthara cut her off curtly, paid her handsomely for her chore, made her strip off the rani's clothes and don her own cheap garment, then dismissed her, giving her the rest of the day off. She watched the slender slip of a girl race out excitedly, undoubtedly heading straight for the city bazaar to spend her ill-won reward on some frivolous new vastra that was currently in fashion. Before the day was through, she would probably end up in a tavern room with some muscled lout who would use her, then decamp with most of her rupees; the girl had deplorable judgement in men. Manthara had already forgotten the serving girl by the time she left the chamber. She wasn't worried about the wench telling anyone else about these illicit chores she performed for Manthara-daiimaa. A special mantra ensured that if she even tried, she would choke to death on her own tongue.

Manthara mused on the next stage of her strategy. There was much work yet to be done. She had no time to gloat on the successful completion of this morning's mission.

The day of her master's arrival was at hand. She had already received word of the twice-lifer he was sending with his false message. The imposter would arrive at any moment, setting another sequence of shrewdly planned events into motion. She marvelled at her lord's brilliant strategems.

Her role in the whole scheme was a small but critical one. It would take great daring to pull it off. She might even run the risk of being exposed at last. And she knew the consequences of that. Ever since the incident with Kala-Nemi and the encounter in the city dungeons, Guru Vashishta was alert as an owl. It would take only one small slip for him to catch her. And once caught, she would be shown no mercy, either by the mortals she had betrayed so treacherously or by the king of Asuras, who despised failure.

She gathered her resolve, her wizened face crinkling like a crushed parchment. She vowed to herself that she would not fail this time. The Lord of Lanka would find no fault with her efforts on his behalf. She would prove to him once and for all that a single mortal spy in the heart of Ayodhya could accomplish far more than an entire legion of marauding demons. She would wreak havoc in the next few days like a canker in the heart of the mightiest Arya kingdom in existence. And then finally, her lord would grant her the reward he had promised her so long ago.

She rubbed her twisted hands together, her arthritic nerves screaming in pain. She grimaced, displaying yellowed and blackened teeth. Soon, she promised herself. Soon she would be rid of this wretched cage of flesh and bone.

'Ayodhya the unconquerable?' she snarled to herself. Soon enough that would change. It would become instead Ayodhya destroyed.

13

Brahmarishi Vishwamitra was in a fine mood this morning. Outwardly, he was the image of stoic concentration, seemingly intent only on maintaining the stiff pace he had set the procession. As his powerful long strides covered the dirt track, even the brahmins in their carts had to click tongues and coax lazy bullocks and oxen to keep up with the brahmarishi's rapid progress.

Ahead, the Vajra elephants also had to keep up the pace to avoid being overtaken by the seer-mage and his entourage. The mahouts urged their bigfoot on with words of praise and shouts of encouragement. The bigfoot, happy to be mobile after eight days of inactivity, complied enthusiastically, putting their enormous wrinkled heads down and traipsing as smartly as horses on a marching field. Only occasionally did one of them emit a brief bleating call and was allowed by his mahout to swerve off-track for a moment, where he relieved himself quickly and copiously before hurrying to regain his place in the rank.

As the sun god Surya climbed the eastern sky in his burnished chariot of gold, the procession wound its way northwards, making excellent time. The brahmarishi had warned them all that he intended to reach Mithila by the next evening, covering the three-day journey in two days.

But it was only after a few hours of the rapid pace that everyone realised just how much effort that entailed. They would not stop for the noon meal, instead taking minimal nourishment while on the move, nor would the brahmins be able to take their habitual two hours of afternoon aaram. There would be no napping or resting on this trip.

Still, such was the general air of excitement and anticipation that not a single member of the entourage voiced a word of complaint or protest. Even the young acolytes, some barely seven years of age and not yet sprouting all their permanent teeth, marched along cheerfully, chanting rhymes they had learned at the gurukul, reciting the Sanskrit and Prakrit alphabets, then the ten Vedic numerals, ending with the venerated and mystical Shunya, or zero – that masterful invention of the Vedic mathematician Aryabhatta, who had devised the decimal system of counting now followed universally throughout the Arya nations. The younger ones counted on their fingers as they recited, sticking their thumbs up into the air triumphantly when they yelled out the final 'Shunya!'

Their gurus smiled proudly at the lisping eagerness of the little shishyas, while chatting quietly about the seminars and debates they would participate in at the annual philosophical convocation in Mithila. A general mood of cheerful anticipation filled the travellers with all the energy they needed to maintain the seer's yojana-an-hour pace without a grimace of complaint.

But the brahmarishi paid little heed to these things. His mind was preoccupied with other matters. Foremost on his mind was the outcome of the mission he had begun that fateful Holi day when he had entered the city of Ayodhya and demanded Rajkumar Rama as his guru-dakshina. The consequences of that event were yet to be fully realised, and even his supremely transcendent buddhi was not complacent enough to take those consequences for granted. He briefly weighed what had been accomplished in these past nine days. It was not inconsiderable.

The demoness Tataka, a plague on the mortal realm of Prithvi for millennia, had been destroyed at last, and with her had vanished the canker that had been breeding in the Southwoods. All her monstrous miscreations, those wretched genetically engineered hybrids, were destroyed as well. The Bhayanak-van, that section of the Southwoods that had come to be known as the Forest of Fear, had been cleansed by the purifying breath of Agni, the lord of fire.

Even now, the wind occasionally brought the scent of scorched woods and a few flakes of crumbly grey ash. The Southwood fires had ceased burning only yesterday, coinciding with the end of Vishwamitra's seven-day yagna, another auspicious omen. In a few seasons, the scorched earth of the Forest of Fear would be ready once more to bring forth new life. When the time was right, he would set his brahmacharyas to planting good fresh stock: oaks, pines, ashwood, banyan, peepal, acacia, neem, palas, teak. And plenty of fruit and flower groves. A new forest would rise in the place of that long-dreaded maze of terror, a forest of hope and new beginnings. The cleansing of Bhayanak-van had been accomplished in the week of Holi, the festival of spring and fertility. The seeding of Asha-van, the Forest of Hope, would be done in Holi too, a full year hence. A generation from today, children would play fearlessly in the groves, travellers rove freely through the woods, and sadhus and rishis would build ashrams and gurukuls in the Asha-van.

Even before that, the very absence of the Bhayanak-van would open up a whole new world of possibilities for the Arya nations.

For millennia the Bhayanak-van had impeded the southward progress of the early Arya clans, until its mythic stature had thwarted even the now-mighty Arya nations. Now, that dark wall had been kicked down and ground into ash. Henceforth, the route down the subcontinent would be unbarred. The Aryas would be free to journey to the rich fertile plains of the Deccan, explore the lush vales and pleasing hill ranges of the south, and travel all the way to the tapering point of land where the two great oceans met.

Vishwamitra's craggy face darkened momentarily as he thought of that southernmost tip of the subcontinent. It was off that wild and wanton shore where the oceans clashed angrily that the island of Lanka was situated. The very thought of Lanka set his teeth on edge.

That little island-nation represented a threat far greater than a hundred Bhayanak-vans. Its lord and master, Ravana, king of the Asura races, was a thousandfold as dangerous as Tataka. And yet, until Lanka was cleared of its demon hordes, the subcontinent might as well be one enormous Bhayanak-van. A wall had been breached, but the fortress remained, as unassailable and formidable as ever. If Ayodhya was unconquerable – literally, a-yodha, or the city that was beyond war – then Lanka was its twin in that respect. Even the devas had not dared to invade Lanka.

Ravana himself had won that fabled island-fortress through treachery and deceit, by attacking his own brother Kubera, lord of wealth, in his peaceful Himalayan retreat, overrunning Kubera's pacifist yaksi city with brutal violence, and had spared the demi-god's life only on pain of ransom. The ransom being dominion of Lanka as well as numerous other precious possessions of Kubera – the airship *Pushpak*, Kubera's harem of ten thousand wives, and much else. A direct assault on Lanka was beyond the contemplation of any mortal army. And yet, as long as Lanka remained in the grasp of the demon lord, the Arya nations could not hope to explore and settle the subcontinent safely. It was a dilemma that had vexed Vishwamitra for a long time and still he could find no solution.

Just then a cloud passed across the sun, darkening the day. Vishwamitra sensed the rajkumars glancing up, shielding their eyes against the brightness of the sky. Conversation petered out momentarily in the procession as the brahmacharyas and rishis looked up too, some wondering aloud if there was a possibility of rain. Then the cloud passed by, the warm, nourishing rays of Surya shone down again, and all was as before.

Lanka was like that cloud, Vishwamitra thought. Lurking off the southernmost tip of the Asian continent like a brooding monsoon cloud in an otherwise clear sky, capable at any moment of occluding the life-giving sun, casting a dark pall across the entire earth. Ravana had dared to invade Swarga-lok a millennium and a half ago, and the devas still hung their heads in bitter shame at the demon lord's triumph at that encounter. When even the gods feared to confront him, how could mere mortals hope to defeat him?

And yet, it was these mere mortals who *must* defeat him. For Vishwamitra knew what he had chosen not to say to the people of Ayodhya, nor to their maharaja. In exchange for quitting the realm of the devas, Ravana had demanded that henceforth none of their number would ever challenge him again. Indra's eyes had flashed like hot coals at that insolent demand. The king of the gods was not accustomed to defeat, let alone terms and conditions. Yet he had no choice. To refuse Ravana at that moment was to allow the demon lord the run of the upper realm. By swallowing that ego-choking condition, the king of heaven had bound every single deva and devi in the universe. No god or goddess could ever challenge Ravana directly or cause him harm in any fashion. Centuries later, the humiliation of that acquiescence still made Indra gnash his teeth in impotent rage. Yet, as gods, he and his fellows had no choice but to honour their agreement eternally.

And so it was that the seven seers, governed by their most senior member, Narada the Wise, had perceived that the only opposition to Ravana could come from mortals now. Impossible as it seemed, it was from this middle realm, Martya, and more specifically the planet of earth on this realm, that the only opposition to the demon lord could now arise.

We must confront him, the brahmarishi thought fiercely, we must stand and repel his Asura hordes, must fight to the bitter end for the continued safety of humankind and for the sake of Prithvi herself. If Ravana was allowed to extend his rule over Prithvi too, all existence would be darkened by the shadow of his reign. Like a giant rock hurtling through space could with a single glancing blow plunge an entire planet into years of darkness and death, Ravana's rising shadow would blacken all of Prithvi for an immeasurable period.

That must not come to pass.

Vishwamitra clenched his wildwood staff tighter, the intensity of his grip grinding the knob of holy thread wound around the top of the staff. His face hardened, resembling that of a warrior-king striding into battle rather than a seer leading his brahmins to a spiritual conference. His step quickened, increasing to a speed that soon had the whole entourage struggling to keep up. Conversation died out, the acolytes ceased chanting, and even the elephants shook their heads in protest as they struggled to maintain the rigorous new pace.

Even the senior rishis paused in the ritual recitation of their mantras and stuck their bald pates out of the shade of their bullock-carts, wondering what fierce contemplation had overtaken the brahmarishi. After all, this was a man who could endure a bhor tapasya of centuries without needing food or water to sustain himself, taking his nourishment from the very flow of brahman itself. If he was entering yoganidra, a trance-like state of intense transcendental meditation, they would all fall by the way-side long before he even grew aware of their discomfort.

Already, the sage was striding at the amazing speed of almost two yojanas an hour, brisk enough to have even the bullocks lowing in complaint. Yet nobody dared invoke the wrath of the brahmarishi by interrupting his deep concentration. In times past, acolytes had been reduced to piles of smouldering ashes for merely speaking when a sage was engaged in such contemplation.

Yet if they didn't act quickly, their hearts would burst with the effort of keeping pace with him.

14

It was Rama who took the initiative.

Sizing up the problem, the young prince consulted with his brother silently through an exchange of looks and gestures, then reached a decision. He quickened his pace to bring himself almost level with the brahmarishi. Almost, but not quite: it was not acceptable for a shishya to walk abreast of his guru.

Joining his hands together and keeping his head lowered, he spoke reverentially.

'Guru-dev, I humbly request permission to address you.'

Vishwamitra blinked once, his flaring nostrils inhaling his first breath in many minutes. His mastery of yoga enabled him to accomplish physical feats that other humans would find impossible; he had been so absorbed in his contemplation that he had neglected to breathe for close to half an hour. He inclined his head very slightly to address Rama without slowing his pace.

'Permission granted, rajkumar.'

'Guru-dev, my brother and I are fortified by the power of the maha-mantras Bala and Atibala. We could maintain this pace for a week without tiring. But I fear that our companions will not be able to do so as well. Already the younger shishyas are in danger of falling and being trodden under the hoofs of bullocks and the wheels of carts.'

Vishwamitra blinked again, only now becoming aware of the speed at which he was walking. He had unwittingly continued to step even faster while Rama spoke. At the rate he was accelerating, he would soon be covering ground at much more than two yojanas an hour!

The brahmarishi exhaled slowly, wondering at his own folly. It took only a tiny exertion of his will to slow his yard-long strides, reducing his speed gradually lest he cause an accident in the procession behind. The brahmins of Siddh-ashrama released a unanimous sigh of relief as the brahmarishi slowed to the previous pace of a yojana an hour. They wiped their bald pates, shiny with sweat from the unexpected race to keep up with their guru.

One of the smaller acolytes issued a great sigh of relief and exclaimed loudly, 'Om Hari Swaha!'

It was the typical invocation that was a brahmin's instinctive response to almost anything, but the gawky seven-year-old had a strong lisp due to most of his milk teeth having fallen out and tended to run his words together, so it came out sounding more like a meaningless 'Omharithwaaa!'

At the head of the procession, Vishwamitra heard the lisped and muddled exclamation and chuckled.

At the sound, the mood of the entire company lightened at once. Smiles wreathed the faces of the company, old and young alike. Their wariness of the sage's legendary temper turned into relief. It was the first time their honoured guru had been heard expressing laughter in centuries! The scribes of the ashram were already searching for words to describe the exact quality of his brief emission of amusement.

Rama exchanged a glance with Lakshman. His brother winked, complimenting him on his tactful handling of the situation. Rama had just started to fall back to his brother's side when the brahmarishi spoke again.

'Come, rajkumars. Walk abreast of me. I would speak with you both.'

They looked at each other again, eyebrows raised. It was unheard of for a guru to ask his shishyas to walk abreast. But then again, their relationship with the sage wasn't exactly a typical guru-shishya one.

They complied with the sage's command, still keeping to his right. Vishwamitra acknowledged their presence with a glance that almost bordered on a smile, a striking contrast to the brahmarishi's usual granite impassivity. Both brothers smiled back as one.

He's in a good mood now, Rama thought, *but what was on his mind a few moments ago?*

He would give anything to be able to fathom the depths of the seer's thoughts. What was it like to have lived five thousand years, and to have been chosen by mighty Brahma, Lord of Creation himself, to live eternally as one of the seven seers who mediated between the celestial devas and earth-bound mortals? A fortnight ago, Rama would have believed it impossible to understand the thoughts of such a personage. Now, he felt curiosity and a tingling sense of anticipation. *It has something to do with me, I know that. But what?*

'Rajkumars Rama and Lakshman, by your great valour in the battle of Bhayanak-van, you have earned the right to a prashan-uttar dialogue. I invite you to pose any queries you may have about the experiences of the past few days. Or any other matter that may be on your mind.'

Lakshman was the first to speak, hardly able to contain his excitement at the unexpected invitation. Prashan-uttar was an honour reserved only for the most senior of shishyas. By inviting them to ask their queries of him, the seer-mage was acknowledging their knowledge and urging them to proceed to the next level of their education.

Lakshman asked eagerly, 'Guru-dev, back in Ayodhya you said that once we killed Tataka and her band of demons, the Southwoods would be freed of Ravana's evil influence. But how do we know that Ravana is even aware of what we accomplished?'

Vishwamitra smiled indulgently. 'He knows. Nary a cut bleeds on one of his precious wildlings but he feels the ichor ooze.'

Lakshman wasn't sure he had understood the sage's meaning. But you didn't just ask a seer-mage to explain his statements. Often the phrasing of a guru's answer was as significant as the answer itself. Like the legendary tale of the guru who had sworn a lifelong vow of silence, and whose disciples were compelled to deduce his likely answers to their philological and practical problems. The result was that every one of his disciples grew every bit as wise as their guru, able to dispense advice as sage as their teacher might have done.

The moral of the story, which Lakshman and his brothers had learned while at Guru Vashishta's gurukul, was that a guru was only a mentor who pointed out the right path; it was up to the shishya to decide how best to travel that path, or whether to travel it at all.

Lakshman was still mulling over the meaning of the cryptic reply when the sound of hoofbeats approached rapidly from behind. It was Bejoo, his face set in a grim expression. Sweat limned the Vajra captain's swarthy face and stocky torso.

Bejoo slowed his horse to a clip-clopping trot to avoid overtaking the brahmarishi. Lakshman took the opportunity to reach out and caress the mare, who nodded appreciatively at his touch.

'Brahmarishi maha-dev, I ask your leave to speak.'

Vishwamitra answered without looking back or

slowing his pace. 'Briefly then, kshatriya. The rajkumars and I are engaged in prashan-uttar at present.'

Lakshman couldn't help noticing the way the Vajra commander's face creased at the brahmarishi's words. The leader of the maharaja's own elite fighting squad was not accustomed to being called 'kshatriya' and talked to as if he was merely a brahmacharya in the seer's ashram.

With a visible effort, Bejoo swallowed his feelings and said stiffly, 'Guruji, this road we are on will take us through the hills.'

'Indeed, kshatriya. Any shishya in my gurukul knows that. What is your point?'

'Swami, the hills are notorious breeding grounds for bandit gangs, wild predatory beasts and all manner of other perils. A procession such as this would look like an easy mark for any aggressor.'

'That is why the devas saw fit to grace us with your presence, kshatriya. Surely your Vajra can deal with these aggressors should we chance upon any?'

Lakshman saw Bejoo pass a hand across his face, gathering sweat and flicking it away impatiently.

'Guruji, my Vajra is under orders to protect the rajkumars Rama and Lakshman, not—'The Vajra captain bit back his next words and finished with 'Not the inhabitants of Siddh-ashrama.'

'Then protect your wards and I will protect mine,' the brahmarishi said crisply. 'Now, if that is all, I wish to resume our prashan-uttar session. You may leave us, Captain.'

Bejoo stared briefly but intensely at the back of the brahmarishi's head, then turned his horse without another word and rode back the way he had come. The sound of his pounding hoofs faded away.

Lakshman tried to forget about the interruption and turned his mind back to the brahmarishi's last cryptic response. He wiped a trickle of sweat with the tip of his ang-vastra. His rig creaked faintly as he raised his hand to his temple, the leather already soaked with the sweat flowing down his back. Beside him, Rama was sweating just as freely.

An idea occurred to Lakshman. He voiced his thoughts cautiously. 'Guru-dev, am I correct in discerning your answer as implying that the Lord of Lanka's well-being is directly linked to that of his minions? Thus, for instance, when we killed Tataka and her hybrids, we inflicted hurt on Ravana himself?'

The seer's voice brimmed with pleasure. 'Well done, young Lakshman! Indeed, it is just as you say. To wound his minions is to wound Ravana himself. For the Lord of Lanka derives all his Asura hordes from the depths of Narak, the third and lowest realm. He pays for their deliverance with his own immortal aatma. Thus, with every rakshasa or pisaca or other vile demon he frees and enlists in his barbarous armies he mortgages a part of himself to Yamaraj, Lord of the Underworld.'

Lakshman said excitedly, 'But in that case, if we were to destroy his Asuras, might we not destroy Ravana himself?'

He sensed Rama nodding vigorously beside him, liking the logical leap. Lakshman held his breath, awed by the simple elegance of his conclusion. He waited to see if the brahmarishi agreed with his extrapolation.

The brahmarishi replied warmly.

'Guru Vashishta has schooled you well in the shastras and vedas, Rajkumar Lakshman. Your conclusion is brilliantly realised. However, the problem at hand defies all logical deduction. The Lord of Lanka was granted eternal life by mighty Brahma himself in recognition of Ravana's millennia-long bhor tapasya. Even the extinction of every last Asura in all the three worlds would not destroy the demon king. It would cause him great agony, no doubt, but Ravana is an emperor of pain, both inflicted as well as self-endured. This is his most formidable quality, his infinite capacity to cause and to endure suffering. He could surely endure the agony of a million deaths without succumbing.'

Sensing Lakshman's disappointment, the sage went on quickly, 'Also, like most innovative theories, your strategem is easier conceived than executed. Even if by some superhuman feat you succeed in decimating Ravana's vast forces, that would not end his reign. Because for every Asura you slay, Ravana would free a dozen more from Narak to take its place, and could continue doing so eternally. Therefore that fight itself is unwinnable.'

'But there must be some way to defeat him, Guru-dev.' Lakshman struggled to keep his voice respectful and steady, a difficult task when he felt so close to the answer. 'After all, by your own admission the yaksi Tataka was virtually impossible to defeat. Yet Rama brought her down with the shakti of the maha-mantras which you so graciously granted to us.'

The seer-mage glanced briefly at Lakshman, his eyes glinting in the noon sunlight. His heavy brow overhung his features, casting a shadow across his lower face. It lent him a forbidding look that wasn't much relieved by the lightness of his tone. 'Even Bala and Atibala are no match for Ravana's power. Every being, mortal or immortal, makes its own karma. It was Tataka's time to be banished from existence. And your brother's hand was the one chosen to string the arrow that took her life.'

Vishwamitra continued gently, 'Why, had it been your karma to loose the arrow, that is what would have come to pass. You fought every bit as bravely and fiercely as Rama, but a fateful blow knocked you unconscious at that crucial moment, preventing you from joining in the battle against the giantess. Do you think that was simply a coincidence? Nay, young Lakshman. Even the most casually incidental of events hews to the mystic pattern woven by the cosmic wheel of time. When it is Ravana's time to die, then die he will. But until that fated day, nothing may pierce his invulnerability.'

Lakshman's breath caught in his throat. For every waking hour over the past eight days, he had thought of nothing other than that final battle in the Bhayanak-van. Unable to remember anything beyond the fight with the hybrids, he had struggled guiltily to come to terms with his loss of consciousness. Yet he hadn't dared broach that topic; it was too sensitive for him to talk about. By discussing it so openly, the seer had given him a great infusion of relief. He understood exactly what the brah-marishi was saying: Don't feel guilty, Lakshman. You fought well. It was just Rama's karma to kill Tataka, and yours not to face her. It was the one argument that could enable Lakshman to free himself of the great weight that had been riding on his shoulders.

He sent up a silent prayer of relief to the devas. This was why the gurus were honoured and respected even by monarchs and emperors: their wisdom extended beyond Vedic science and spiritual knowledge to encompass even the subtle nuances of human psychology as well.

Rama spoke into the brief silence that followed. 'But Guru-dev, if Ravana is immortal, how can he die?'

Vishwamitra smiled, his craggy features barely softened by the grim upturning of his thin lips. 'Such is the mystery of karma and dharma. The deeds we do in this physical existence, our karma, weigh against the duties we ought to fulfil, our dharma, and in the judgement hall of the devas these two accumulations of deeds and duties are measured on the scales of infinite justice. Even those who are immortal may be recalled from one life to be granted another. In this way they live for ever, yet forsake the physical accretions of the former life.'

Lakshman frowned. He had never heard the concept of karma and dharma described in quite that way before. Again, he had to wrestle a moment to glean the sage's full meaning. He posed the next query, straining to keep his voice from rising with excitement.

'Guru-dev, in that case, it would not be amiss to say that while the devas may not permit Ravana's death, they may recall him from his present physical form and transubstantiate him into another another body of similar qualities as the one he now possesses. In this fashion, he would retain his immortality by continuing to live indefinitely, yet this particular body, the one he now inhabits, would be to all intents and purposes destroyed. So the Ravana we speak of would be dead, although the essence of Ravana himself, his immortal aatma and his entire consciousness as well all his knowledge and awareness gleaned in this and previous lifetimes, would continue.'

Rama frowned. 'But Lakshman, if he continues to live, even if it's in a different body, he could still go on with his evil ways. Only his body would change, not his intentions or evil nature.'

'But think about it, brother! If we were to somehow – and I admit it seems impossible – if we were to somehow decimate every last living Asura in the world, and at that very moment, before Ravana is able to call up more Asuras from the underworld to rebuild his army, we destroy his present physical form, there will be an instant when neither Ravana or his demonaic hordes will exist in the mortal realm. In that instant Yamraj, Lord of the Underworld, could seal shut the passage to Narak through which Ravana derives more Asura reinforcements. And if the devas delay the transposition of Ravana to a new physical body, then for a while, at least, the earth will be free of his evil! Don't you see? It's the closest we'll ever come to completely destroying that wart on the hindside of humanity!'

Rama's eyebrows shot up at the phrasing of Lakshman's last comment. But it was the seer-mage's response that took Lakshman by surprise. Brahmarishi Vishwamitra turned to the young prince and stared at him as if he was seeing him for the very first time.

'A truly beautiful answer, rajkumar. Truly beautiful.'

Lakshman's face shone with pleasure. He joined his hands and bowed his head. 'Maha-dev, it is only by your grace.'

Vishwamitra nodded sagely. 'Your mind is as swift as your bow-finger. I have been grappling for centuries with this complex conundrum. While I do not feel you have solved the problem entirely – there are still lapses of logic to be scrutinised – I believe you have opened up a pathway that may eventually lead to the final solution. Well done, young Lakshman. Very well done indeed!'

Lakshman felt a flush of pride. Rama put his arm around his brother, over the top of Lakshman's rig, and hugged him briefly, tightly. His hand was slippery on Lakshman's sweat-drenched shoulders. Lakshman nodded, grinning inanely with joy.

He felt happier than he had when he solved a particular demanding mathematical problem posed by Guru Vashishta during their last year at the gurukul. That had been a theoretical problem with no urgent practical outcome. This was the problem that plagued the whole world right now! To think that he could have opened up a pathway that had escaped even the great Vishwamitra's attention for centuries was enough to send a paroxysm of pleasure rippling through his entire being. He was so excited, he barely heard the brahmarishi's next words.

'Truly inspiring, young Lakshman. Rightly has it been said that each one of us has a place in the great scheme of things. Rama's seems to be the place of the one who takes up arms against evil and vanquishes it despite impossible odds. If there is one kshatriya alive who holds great promise, it is your brother, my good Lakshman.'

The sage went on, 'And your role seems to be not only to shield him with your sword as he fulfils his dharma, but also to guide him mentally. For he who acts must often-times not pause to think too deeply at the moment of action. Your nimble mathematical mind can do the think-ing for him at those crucial moments.

'Thus you will be as two hands of one archer, one guiding the bow's aim after a thorough examination and analysis of the mathematics of distance, wind, atmo-spheric pressure and other vital factors, while the other provides the great strength and perfect timing required to release the missile at precisely the correct instant. Both hands must act together in unison or the target will be lost.

'And truly, I have rarely seen two warriors as harmo-niously fitted to each other as you and Rama. If there is one warrior who can accomplish this seemingly impossible task, it is the both of you.'

The seer's voice bore no trace of amusement at his last paradoxical statement. Lakshman blinked, moved. He's serious. He means that Rama and I together are as great as any of the greatest kshatriya heroes that ever lived. But he can't possibly mean what he just said. 'Guru-dev, which impossible task do you refer to?'

The sage's next words were deceptively calm, as if he were merely discussing what they might eat for their evening repast when they broke journey for the night.

'Rajkumar Lakshman, I think you already understand which impossible task I mean. It is the issue we have been debating in this prashan-uttar session all this while.'

As Lakshman groped for the appropriate words, the brahmarishi went on in a voice as cold and hard as uncut granite: 'Ravana-vinaashe.'

Killing Ravana.

15

Senapati Dheeraj Kumar watched from his position atop the first gate of Ayodhya city as a tiny cloud of dust appeared in the distance, growing slowly larger. Beside him stood a gatewatch guard with a conch shell, ready to sound the alarm on the general's order.

While the soldiers around him were dressed in the traditional white and red of the gatewatch, the senapati – literally 'lord of the army' – wore a distinctive saffron-and-black uniform with the Sanskrit letters corresponding to P and F ornately embroidered in gold on the sleeves of his ang-vastra. His distinguished aquiline Arya features were creased with age, yet his power and strength were still unmistakable. A long-undefeated champion of the wrestling square, the general's passion for physical sports had enabled him to stay fit even two decades after his last military engagement.

Many of his former colleagues in the PF battalion he commanded, the Purana Wafadars – so named because they were veterans of the Last Asura War – had either succumbed to old war injuries or retired from active duty. There were more young faces – mostly sons and daughters of their veteran parents – in his ranks now than actual veterans. Like many old soldiers, he had achieved the dubious distinction of outliving those he had once held dear, including almost all his gurukul colleagues, army peers, a wife and two sons, and even many of his much younger subordinates.

This gradual erosion and eventual isolation had left Dheeraj Kumar more thoughtful and introspective in his later years. Although not so introspective that he would contemplate retiring from active duty: if anything, the senapati was more determined than ever to serve king and country. Graciously, the devas had seen fit to grant him perfect health and good strength even in his septuagenarian years. Dheeraj Kumar wasn't an overly religious man – like any good kshatriya he believed that his first duty was to protect and serve, leaving the praying to the brahmins – but he had come to the conclusion that if Yamaraj, lord of death, had spared him while laying waste so many others around him, there must be a good reason. The great senapatis of the armies of the devas, Kartikeya and his elephant-headed brother Ganesa, must have a battle plan for him, he felt. He was content to attend to routine duties until that great plan was revealed to him.

He watched now as the visitor approached down the length of the raj-marg. His bushy white brows knitted together as the dustcloud slowly resolved into the unmistakable silhouette of a two-horse Vajra chariot riding at full-out speed. The chariot was alone.

The senapati, renowned as much for his brilliant grasp of military strategy as for his physical prowess, liked to play a little game at such times. His presence at the first gate was not exactly the most desirable posting for a general of his age and experience. Yet he himself had volunteered for the task, knowing that if there was the slightest risk of any mass intrusion this was the place it could best be stemmed. Most of the time, he had only to scrutinise the commonfolk visiting or leaving the capital city on trade, leisure or personal work. Not much of a challenge for the most decorated veteran of the worst war in Arya history.

So he whiled away the long days by postulating different invasion scenarios and theorising how best he would deal with them if they actually happened. The sight of the approaching chariot had sparked off one such scenario in his agile mind.

Ayodhya was accessible by only two main routes, the south raj-marg and the north raj-marg. The city's first gate faced the southern approach, flanked by the raging white waters of the Sarayu on the left and an almost sheer rise to the right. Any invading force would either have to come upriver on the Sarayu, which was almost impossible given the furious white-rapid flow of the river at this point, climb down the crumbling sheer bank of the cliff – exposing themselves pitifully during the difficult descent – or simply march, walk and ride up the raj-marg. If any invading commander was actually arrogant enough to dare such an attempt, the senapati mused, he would be sighted long before he reached the city proper, spotted by the ever-alert rakshak kshatriyas posted at Mithila Bridge or any of the hundred other vantage points which led to the capital of the kingdom of Kosala. The rakshaks would ride with the speed of Vayu the wind god, whom they worshipped as the deity of their order, bringing the news to the first gate precious minutes or even hours before the invaders.

The city's response would be immediate. All seven gates would be shut and barred, the enormous drawbridges pulled up in moments by the use of well-oiled winch pulleys, leaving yawning thirty-yard gaps between each of the city's seven concentric walls. Moats filled with a profusion of deadly creatures occupied those gaps. The seven walls were a daunting ten yards high, running in oval circuits around the city, manned at every yard by Ayodhya's best archers and javelin-throwers.

To get to the city proper, the invading force would have to breach all seven walls or gates, crossing those twenty-yard-deep moats while contending with the crocodiles, sharks, poisonous water-serpents and piranha that teemed in the dark waters. If they got that far, they would have almost the entire army of Kosala – a staggering three-quarters of a million foot-soldiers, a third of that number armoured and mounted on horseback, and as many archers and bigfoot. Just the elephant division was enough to withstand an army of a million enemies on its own, and had done so in the Last Asura War on an open battlefield. In these closer quarters, fighting to defend their own home turf, the bigfoot and their valiant mahouts could probably fend off an army twice that size.

But long before any invasion actually got that far, the foolishly ambitious enemy commander would have to contend with the approach to the first gate. That half-yojana stretch of open dirt road unfolding in an almost perfect straight line, so designed by the great Vishwakarma, architect of the Ikshwaku nation that had first settled these parts, to provide a clear view of any approaching enemy.

Senapati Dheeraj Kumar, standing atop the battlements on the first wall, now conceived a fiendishly clever plan. What if the enemy, emboldened by the rakshasa Kala-Nemi's success in infiltrating the city and getting within striking distance of the maharaja, now sent not one soldier in disguise but an entire group of them! After all, the war council would take place in a day or two, and sizeable contingents of kshatriyas would arrive from the other Arya nations accompanied by their generals, prime ministers, and perhaps even their maharajas. If the Asuras managed to slip in disguised as any one of those groups, they would be able to pass through all the city's defences and gain access to the most powerful group of Arya leaders in the world. They might not be able to kill them all, but they would surely do great damage before succumbing to Ayodhya's security forces.

There was only one problem with that plan: it had been anticipated. Along with any number of other possible and even seemingly impossible scenarios. It was part of a military technique the senapati himself had developed. He termed it drishti-shastra, the science of vision. He had liked the word drishti enough to name his first-born with it. Despite his formidable history, the general was a man who believed in looking ahead to the future at all times, and being prepared for it.

As the fast-riding Vajra chariot closed the distance to the first gate, he shook his head slowly. The chariot was solitary. Which negated his scenario. He was only partly relieved. After almost nine days of inactivity following the shock of that first intrusion, he craved some actual contact with the enemy.

He used a curt gesture to order the alarm-crier to call down, and shouted to his lieutenant standing ready down below by the first gate machinery. The description of the approaching visitor – 'chariot, single, Vajra' – had already been communicated swiftly through pre-set hand signals all the way to the royal palace in the time it took the chariot to approach.

'Send the rajkumars up,' Dheeraj Kumar said.

Immediately, two robust young men in full battle armour began to climb the iron stakes set on the inside of the first gate. They breasted the top of the wall quickly and easily. The stockier of the two was slightly ahead of his partner. Both saluted the general smartly.

The senapati nodded approvingly. 'Rajkumar Bharat,' he said shortly.

Bharat grinned, nudging his brother. Shatrugan didn't seem to mind. 'Next time,' he promised.

The senapati indicated the chariot, now less than half a mile from the gate and approaching rapidly.

'What do you see?'

Both Bharat and Shatrugan replied together, their responses overlapping, 'A chariot!'

Shatrugan added quickly: 'A Vajra chariot.' He nudged his brother to underline his one-upmanship.

'What else?'

They shielded their eyes from the noonday sun, peering intently. The chariot was a hundred yards from the gate now and closing fast. As the driver reined in the pair of horses, both boys offered their observations.

'Driven by a Vajra kshatriya no more than twenty years of age, a first lieutenant from his colours,' Bharat said.

'He's been travelling for a long time, at least two days,' Shatrugan said.

Bharat said, 'The two colours of the mud coating the sides and underbelly of the chariot and the riggings show that he must have passed through the Southwoods. That particular black soil could only come from there.'

'And by the state of the horses,' Shatrugan said, 'he hasn't stopped to rest or nourish them for at least a day. Which means his mission is urgent and important.'

'He's been attacked sometime during the course of the journey. Those wounds on his person and rips in his vastras are not severe but they are undressed and untended, as they would have been had he suffered them before starting his journey. I say that he was attacked because he would not break a mission of such urgency to pick a fight.'

Senapati Dheeraj Kumar raised his eyebrows, glancing briefly at the rajkumars. 'Is that all?'

Both boys squinted intently at the man they had just been describing. The Vajra kshatriya had dismounted from his chariot, patted his horses to calm them, and was now striding to the first gate. He stopped at the edge of the moat, and before the gatewatch guard could challenge him, he raised his hands to indicate that he was unarmed. Looking up, his eyes scanned the alert and watchful faces on the rampart and settled on the senapati with an expression close to relief. His fatigue was unmistakable but he seemed to have no serious injuries.

Shatrugan added in a mischievous tone: 'Oh, and he's recently been married.'

Bharat turned to stare at his brother. 'How can you tell that? Sure, he's wearing a yagna thread around his wrist, but that could be from any yagna ceremony. Not necessarily a marriage! How can you be sure he's married?'

Shatrugan grinned back. 'Because we attended his marriage. The day before Holi. Bejoo-chacha asked us personally to put in an appearance.'

To the senapati, Shatrugan added, 'His name is Bheriya, first lieutenant to Vajra Captain Bejoo, commander of the maharaja's personal Vajra.'

'Damn!' Bharat slapped his own thigh with a firmly muscled fist. 'Of course! I should have remembered that!'

The senapati nodded approvingly, ignoring Bharat's outburst. 'Well done, rajkumars. Keen eyes and sharp minds are a kshatriya's best weapons. Now, I hand over the task of inspection to both of you equally.'

The two princes looked at each other, their playful rivalry forgotten at once. Over the past few days they had involved themselves in every aspect of Ayodhya's security and defence, from joining in army training exercises to saddling elephants, putting in stints as weaponsmiths, attending classes in military strategy and philosophy, interviewing veterans on their personal experiences, and anything else they could find to occupy the time. It was difficult enough being forced to wait here impotently for news of their brothers, not knowing if Rama and Lakshman's mission to the Southwoods had ended in failure or triumph, and the hectic schedule of activity the senapati had drawn up for them had helped them get through without yielding to frustration or anxiety. This was their third tour of duty on the city walls and they had enjoyed an unexciting morning, forced to wait behind the barred first gate and merely watch and listen as the senapati or his associates challenged visitors and checked their credentials before permitting or denying them access to the city. Now, finally, they were being given a chance to actually do something!

Shatrugan took the lead by mutual consent.

Stepping to the rampart, which shielded and protected his torso and lower body while allowing him to speak freely to the kshatriya standing on the raj-marg below, he raised a hand as he had seen the senapati do a dozen times since sunrise.

'Identify yourself and state your business.'

The kshatriya performed an Arya salute. 'Rajkumar Shatrugan? It is I, Bheriya, second-in-command of the maharaja's Vajra. I carry a message of great urgency from my commander Captain Bejoo to Maharaja Dasaratha.'

Bharat spoke next. 'The city is on high alert. You will have to prove your identity before you are permitted to pass. Is there anyone who will vouch for you?'

The man inclined his head at Dheeraj Kumar. 'Senapati Dheeraj Kumar knows me well. He was my guru of military strategy during my training. Senapatiji, I request you to acknowledge me.'

The senapati replied formally: 'So acknowledged.'

'Very well, kshatriya,' Shatrugan said. 'You may hand over your message to us and be on your way. We shall see that it reaches the maharaja speedily.'

The kshatriya shook his head slowly. 'I beg your pardon, rajkumar, but my message is verbal, not scrolled. And my captain's orders were to deliver it in person to the maharaja and none other. It is a matter of Kosala's national security.'

Bharat and Shatrugan exchanged a glance.

Bharat said, 'Be that as it may, nobody is permitted to visit the maharaja.' He didn't add that Dasaratha was recovering and unable to receive visitors. It wasn't relevant to the situation. 'You will have to deliver your message verbally to either Rajkumar Shatrugan or myself and trust us to make certain it reaches the maharaja's ears. As fellow kshatriyas and citizens of Kosala, we shall ensure its secure and swift passage.'

The man looked up unhappily, his grimy, blood-streaked face wan with exhaustion. 'Once again I beg your pardon, rajkumar, but I would defy my captain's orders by doing what you ask. His instructions were explicitly clear. My message must be delivered to the maharaja in person and spoken only in his presence.' He indicated the sun shining down harshly. 'Already precious time is wasting. As you can see, I almost killed these two fine Kambhoja stallions to get here as fast as possible. Pray, do not delay my business further. You have my word as an Arya and as a kshatriya that my message is of grave importance to the well-being of the entire kingdom as well as the city of Ayodhya itself. I beg you, let me pass within the gates and address the maharaja directly.'

Shatrugan leaned over and spoke softly to Bharat, keeping his voice pitched just loud enough for the senapati to hear as well. 'I say we let him pass. He has been acknowledged and identified. We can search his person and subject him to the scrutiny of Guru Vashishta before taking him before Father. There's no point prolonging this conversation further. If his message really is that urgent, Father needs to hear it fast.'

Bharat nodded, agreeing. 'And he is awake and alert again. Yes, he should hear this man's message quickly.'

Both rajkumars glanced briefly at the senapati. Although he had left the entire exchange to them, he was still the superior officer on duty.

'With your permission, Senapati, we wish to permit the visitor to proceed to the seventh gate for further verification prior to his being granted an audience with the maharaja.'

Senapati Dheeraj Kumar was impressed. The rajkumars were doing their job admirably enough, but it wasn't their ability to handle the gatewatch task that impressed him. It was the fact that they had both avoided making any mention of their brothers thus far. Both Shatrugan and Bharat knew that Captain Bejoo's Vajra had been dispatched to accompany the rajkumars on their Southwoods mission. This lieutenant would surely know how that mission had transpired. Yet neither prince broke protocol to ask the personal questions that must certainly be burning in their minds at this moment: How are our brothers? Are Rama and Lakshman alive and well? They were too well disciplined.

He nodded curtly at them. 'I concur. However, before you proceed, I have a query of my own for the visitor.'

They bowed their heads at once, acknowledging his privilege. 'Of course, Senapati.'

Dheeraj Kumar stepped forward to show himself over the rampart. He addressed the visitor directly.

'Kshatriya, on your last mission, you were stationed with the rajkumars Rama and Lakshman, is that right?'

'Indeed, sire. It was my privilege.'

'In that case, tell me when you last saw them and in what state they both were.'

Beside him, he felt Bharat and Shatrugan growing alert and tense as they awaited the kshatriya's reply. This was the moment of truth. Were Rama and Lakshman all right? Every citizen in Ayodhya had waited nine days to know the answer.

The Vajra kshatriya looked up at the senapati silently, then down at the ground, at his sandals worn threadbare and on the verge of falling apart, at the moat that still separated him from the first gate. The water level was a good ten yards below his feet, but the surface teemed with various predators hopeful of receiving an unexpected addition to their natural diet. An eager gharial's long, swordlike snout scratched the side of the moat's stone-lined wall, snapping eagerly up at the kshatriya. Bheriya stared down at the gharial as if he wished he could leap straight into its gaping mouth.

'Kshatriya,' Dheeraj Kumar called out. 'Did you not hear my question? What of the rajkumars Rama and Lakshman? What news do you have of them?'

With obvious reluctance, the Vajra lieutenant raised his head and looked up at the senapati. His face, lined with exhaustion, grime and dried blood, looked pleadingly at the general. 'Sire, I regret that I am unable to answer your question.'

Shatrugan clutched Bharat's arm reflexively. The heftier prince had leaned forward at the visitor's response, as if he wanted to leap down off the wall, over the moat, and on to the kshatriya himself. To beat the answer out of that stubborn man, Dheeraj Kumar guessed. But privately, he admired the Vajra lieutenant's steadfastness. The man was only doing his job.

Still, that didn't stop Dheeraj Kumar from steeling his voice when he spoke again. 'You will answer my question or return with your task unfulfilled. The choice is yours, kshatriya.'

The man looked stricken. He joined his hands together. 'I beg of you, Senapati. Grant me my audience with the maharaja and your query shall be answered as well. My lips are sealed here because the information you seek is part of the message I am entrusted with passing on solely to the maharaja. I cannot violate my orders by speaking even that portion of the message here.'

Bharat and Shatrugan looked at each other. Senapati Dheeraj Kumar saw the expression on their faces and understood exactly what they were thinking. Even though the Vajra lieutenant hadn't answered his question directly, his refusal itself was reply enough. Had the rajkumars been safe and sound, there would have been no need for secrecy. If news of their condition was part of the secret message, that could only mean one thing.

Rama and Lakshman were either seriously injured, or dead.

16

Sumitra swam up out of a nightmarish vision of a giant cobra attacking her sons. In her dream, the twins were still mere infants, peacefully asleep in their cribs, gaining a few scant hours of rest from their perennial squabbling. Even in his sleep, Lakshman still hitched in his breath resentfully at irregular intervals – he had lost the last bout to Shatrugan. Both boys had their thumbs securely stuck in their mouths, and each clutched a separate corner of the same favourite blanket in his tiny fist. Lying facing away from one another, the blanket tugged taut between them, they resembled each other so perfectly, even down to their grumpy expressions, that even Sumitra could only tell them apart by Lakshman's irregular breathing.

She was lying right beside them, her fingers gently brushing away curls of hair from their chubby faces, when the cobra appeared. It reared up from behind the bed, its enormous hood fanning out and casting the entire room into shadow. Its black eyes glinted demonically as it hissed, the long, sharply forked tongue flicking out to spatter droplets of venom all over the blanket. It grew impossibly huge in size, looming over them all, its hooded head bursting through the roof of the chamber, rising above the chamber, the palace, the city itself, so awe-inspiring in its power and deadly beauty that she knew it could be none other than Takshak himself, king of the cobras.

But its face was the face of the Second Queen.

Kaikeyi looked directly into Sumitra's eyes and issued a sibilant cry that was as deafening as a squalling ocean battering against the sides of a storm-tossed ship.

'SSSSUMITRA! NEXT IT'LL BE THE TURN OF YOUR SONSSSSSS!'

Sumitra woke up screaming.

Kausalya's gentle hand caught her in time before she could fall out of bed. 'Hush, Sumitra,' the First Queen said softly. 'There's no danger here. You're safe.'

Sumitra sat up, her chest heaving, sari unwound, hair over her face. She looked around the chamber, assuring herself that it had been just a nightmare. Her breathing gradually slowed enough to permit speech. 'It was Kaikeyi again. This time she was after Lakshman and Shatrugan.'

'It was just a bad dream. You're still in shock.'

Sumitra looked around wild-eyed, still needing confirmation that the chamber was clear. Kausalya and she were alone in the room. A maid appeared at the doorway, looking in inquisitively. Kausalya waved her away, then picked up something from the bedside table. She turned back with a drinking vessel in her hands and brought it slowly to Sumitra's lips. 'Here, drink some water.'

Sumitra took a sip, still shivering from the memory of the dream.

'Enough,' she said, sitting up further. She caught Kausalya's wrist, spilling a little water. 'Kausalya, tell me. Were you able to catch the shrew? Did you and Guru Vashishta confront her and tell her that I saw it all?'

Kausalya moved the vessel to her other hand and put it back on the bedside table. 'We confronted her. We told her all that you described to the guru and me. About your seeing her in the maharaja's room, straddling him, biting him . . .'

'Like a snake! A giant she-snake with huge fangs!' Sumitra held up two fingers inverted before her own lips to show how large the fangs had been. 'And she wasn't just biting him. She was poisoning him. I saw the venom dripping, Kausalya. It stained his ang-vastra. The mark must still be there. And devi help us, I think she put her fangs into his neck. Devi alone knows what the venom would have done to him in his sickly state.'

Kausalya looked down at the space between them, smoothing the ruffled bedcover. 'Sumitra, Kaikeyi was in her own bedchamber, deep in meditation. She hasn't left her chamber for the past nine days. I had placed my own guards on double watch at the hallway to her apartments; they confirmed that the Second Queen hasn't come out from her rooms even once in all that time.'

Sumitra stared at her. 'What do you mean? I saw her, Kausalya. I saw her right there in the sick-chamber!'

Kausalya looked up, her face gentle but apologetic. 'Sumitra, she couldn't have been in the maharaja's sick-room. Even the maharaja's palace guards confirm it. Nobody saw Kaikeyi leave her rooms or enter Dasaratha's chambers.'

'Nobody except me, you mean?' Sumitra got out of bed, pushing away the sheet with which Kausalya had covered her while she had slept. She went to the window, looking out. The thick drapes were tightly drawn, but the spring sunshine shone brightly through the cracks. She guessed from the angle of light that it was past noon. She had slept the whole morning away.

Behind her, Kausalya said cautiously: 'We spoke to all the palace staff, Sumitra. There's nobody else to corroborate your story. And the guruji himself met with

Kaikeyi. He says she's so thin and weakened from her nine days of fasting, she couldn't possibly have done all you said she did. Even if she did somehow pull it off, she certainly wasn't hissing or lunging about like a serpent. He says she was barely conscious. He ended up trying to convince her to take some nourishment.'

Sumitra turned back to Kausalya, her eyes flashing. 'So what does that mean? That I made up the whole story? Kausalya, when you found me lying unconscious on the floor of the sick-chamber and revived me, I told you and the guruji everything that had happened. Why would I make up a story like that?'

Kausalya began folding the bedclothes with a slow, deliberate manner that made Sumitra's heart sink. 'Sumitra, nobody's saying you made up the story. It's just that we can't find any proof to support your version. Please, don't get upset again. I know you must have been through a terrible experience. But the guruji feels—'

'What? What does he feel?' Sumitra realised how angry and resentful she sounded and felt instantly ashamed. Harsh words and angry looks didn't come easily to her. They were Kaikeyi's weapons. But she couldn't believe that the nightmare scene she had witnessed in the maharaja's sick-chamber was being dismissed as . . . as what exactly?

Kausalya stood and came to her. She took Sumitra's wrists in her hands, massaging the pulse points gently, trying to soothe her. 'There was a stain on the maharaja's ang-vastra. The guru identified it. I saw it too. In the exact spot you said it would be found.'

Kausalya pointed to a spot on her own midriff, just below her ribs. 'There.'

A surge of hope leapt in Sumitra's heart. 'Then you have proof! The venom from her fangs, it dripped and fell on to his ang-vastra. There's no way that venom could have come there except if what I saw is true! You have proof!'

Kausalya looked at her silently, continuing to stroke Sumitra's wrists. 'That's what I thought too when I saw the spot. But then the guru identified the cause of the stain.' She stopped stroking and touched Sumitra's cheek gently. 'It was the fruit punch you had prepared for him, Sumitra. A drop spilt on his ang-vastra, that's all.'

Sumitra wanted to scream again. The nightmare had been more bearable than this reality. At least she could wake up from the nightmare. What did all this mean? That her senses had tricked her? That she had slipped and fallen and struck her head and imagined the whole bizarre scenario? Or that Kaikeyi was behind this too, manipulating everything to cover her tracks?

Sumitra pictured Guru Vashishta's grim face and changed her mind immediately. Whatever the extent of Kaikeyi's witchery, she couldn't possibly have come face to face with the sage and deceived him as well. That was simply impossible.

But then what was the truth? What had really happened in that sick-chamber?

Sumitra took a deep breath. 'Kausalya, at least tell me this much. If the whole thing was just some kind of nightmare hallucination, then Dasa must be well, mustn't he? Nothing happened to him because, as you say, nothing happened at all.'

'Bhagini,' Kausalya said, using the affectionate term the two queens shared, meaning literally she-with-whom-I-share-all. 'There's something else I have to tell you. Come sit here for a minute.'

They sat on the edge of the bed again, this time on the side facing the window. The afternoon sunshine leaked through the cracks and crevices in the drapes, creating a peculiar sense of being neither wholly indoors nor out-doors. Like a prison cell with a large barred window, Sumitra thought. Now, why did I think such a thing?

Kausalya said softly, 'Guru Vashishta smelled a strange odour in the fruit punch spilled on the floor and in the stain on the maharaja's ang-vastra.'

Her deep brown eyes watched Sumitra closely, search-ing for a reaction. 'He recognised it at once as the juice of the vinaashe root.'

'Poisonroot?' Sumitra said, not understanding at first. 'But that's impossible! Why would anyone put poisonroot in Dasa's punch?' She clapped her hands to her face, horrified. 'Devi! If he drank vinaashe root, then—'

Kausalya shook her head reassuringly. 'The maharaja is going to be all right. Guru Vashishta and I entered the sick-chamber not an instant too soon. The guru sent for the antidote right away. We were able to revive the maharaja. Fortunately, he didn't imbibe too much of the drug. The vaids say that given his condition, the drug might well have put him into a permanent coma. Or worse.'

She added slowly: 'If we had arrived even a few minutes later, the maharaja might not be with us today.'

Sumitra stared up at the woman who was not just her senior in the family hierarchy but also her dearest friend. At that instant, despite her dishevelled and distraught state, Sumitra herself still looked more like a young girl than the mother of two fifteen-year-old sons. Her large light-brown eyes glistened wetly in her delicately shaped face. Her innocent mind struggled to comprehend the implications of Kausalya's shocking revelation.

'But how could the vinaashe root have got into his punch, Kausalya? I made it myself with my own hands. I know how poisonroot smells – how it stinks! I would have known at once if it was mixed with the other herbs. Besides, if you and Guru Vashishta say that Kaikeyi wasn't in the sick-chamber, then nobody else was there either. There was only the maharaja and myself.'

Kausalya looked down at her silently, still holding Sumitra's hands. Her beautiful almond-shaped eyes brimmed with an emotion that was part sympathy and part sorrow. Sumitra stared at her, suddenly understanding the full significance of Kausalya's words.

'Devi spare us,' Sumitra said, choking on the realisation. 'You believe that I put the poisonroot in his punch? That I tried to poison him?'

Kausalya shook her head. 'No, Sumitra. I know how much you love Dasaratha. You would give your life for him. Why, after he deserted me for Kaikeyi, I turned bitter and angry. It was all I could manage to keep from actually wishing him ill. I wanted to curse him, Sumitra! I hated him for what he had done to me.'

The First Queen shook her head, trying to banish those bitter years of neglect and betrayal. 'But you, Sumitra? He neglected you as much as he did me. Yet I saw how you took it. I used to cry on your lap, you remember? You used to comfort me like a little mother! You couldn't bring yourself to hate him even then. I know you can't hate him now, when he's weak and ailing and so full of regret.'

Kausalya paused to wipe the tears from her cheeks.

Sumitra waited, knowing there was more.

After a short pause, Kausalya went on, 'But as I've said already, the guards confirm that nobody else went in or out of the sick-chamber between the time that I left to go see the guru and the time that the guru and I returned together. You admitted it yourself, only you and Dasaratha were there together. Alone.'

And a giant anthropomorphic serpent with Kaikeyi's

face, Sumitra thought silently. But I can't prove that. Just as I can't prove that I didn't do what everybody thinks I did in that chamber, even though I know I didn't do it.

Kausalya went on, her hesitation making it clear that she didn't enjoy saying what she was about to say, but that it had to be said anyway. 'The guru thinks that perhaps you were distraught with anxiety for Dasaratha's condition. That perhaps the maharaja, in one of his sudden fits of delirium, begged you to give him something to sleep peacefully and make the transition to the afterlife without further suffering. We all know how you can't bear to watch another person suffering, Sumitra. So maybe . . . and I don't believe this myself, mind you . . . but perhaps it's possible that you ground up some vinaashe root with your herbs and you mixed it into his fruit punch and then gave him a sip. And as you watched him fall unconscious, you were overcome with guilt and shock at what you'd done, and fainted dead away.'

Kausalya stopped, her face reflecting her pain at saying these things. She searched Sumitra's face for some confirmation or denial of what she'd just said.

Sumitra finished for her: 'And then my mind, unable to accept what I had just done, conjured up a wildly fanciful tale of Kaikeyi turning into a giant serpent and stinging the maharaja into his coma.'

Kausalya's eyes widened. She started to say something, then stopped as Sumitra motioned her to wait.

Sumitra's voice was low but steady. She was over her upheaval and fear now. Not a woman given easily to anger, she was beyond that hot state of fury. She was cold as Himalayan ice. 'Because it's easier for me to believe that Kaikeyi turned into a snake and attacked Dasaratha than to accept that I poisoned him.'

Kausalya stared at her silently, uncertain whether to speak yet or wait.

Sumitra said, 'That is what you believe, isn't it, Kausalya? That's the explanation that you and the guru came up with after reviewing all the facts of the situation. That half-delirious, agonised Dasaratha cajoled and convinced docile little Sumitra into drugging his punch. And now her fragile feminine mind can't deal with the monstrosity of such a deed. That more or less sums it up, doesn't it?'

Kausalya nodded unhappily. 'Something like that. But Sumitra, we understand, we know you didn't mean to do it. We've all been under a great strain of late.'

Suddenly Sumitra felt very tired, as if she hadn't slept in weeks. In a way that was partly true: since Holi she had napped only a few hours each day, spending all her time in the maharaja's sickroom tending to his needs. Shouldn't have bothered, she thought bitterly. Should have just mixed up a good batch of poisonroot fruit punch and poured it down his throat nine days ago, would have saved us all a lot of grief and heartache.

She giggled at the absurdity of the thought.

Kausalya looked at her with new concern.

Sumitra shook her head. 'Don't worry, I'm not turning hysterical. It's just so bizarre, it's almost funny.' But once she had said it, she didn't feel like laughing.

A thought occurred to her. 'Tell me, Kausalya, this scenario you and the guru came up with to explain this morning's events, does Dasaratha corroborate your version?'

Kausalya shook her head slowly. 'He doesn't remember anything. Only that you offered to make him some of your famous fruit punch and he tried to convince you to give him something else, but he can't remember what that other thing was exactly.'

She hesitated before adding: 'He doesn't know about our theory, of course. It would only make him feel worse.' Her tone had a plea in it.

'Of course,' Sumitra agreed without rancour. 'I won't say a word to him. How is he now?'

'He's all right, just a little shaken. He had only just begun to recover this morning, you know. This incident—'

'Yes, I understand.' Sumitra stood up. 'What do you and the guru mean to do now? Arrest me? Imprison me in my chambers? Throw me into the dungeons?'

Kausalya looked horrified. 'Never! We love you, Sumitra. You know that. I never said that I believe this is what actually happened. It's just—'

'The only explanation that fits all the facts,' Sumitra finished wearily. 'Yes, I know. In that case, Kausalya, if you don't mind, I'd like to bathe and change my clothes and say my prayers. I would have done it in the morning, but somehow in all the mêlée, I just don't seem to have found the time. If you'll excuse me.'

Kausalya stood up. 'Of course. I'll be with the maharaja. Maybe, after you've finished, you should rest a while longer. You look like you need it. You've been under a great deal of strain these past nine days.'

Sumitra nodded and added silently: I have a feeling there's going to be a lot more strain in the days to come.

Kausalya went to the doorway. 'If there's anything you need . . . if you need to talk about this some more . . .'

'I'll come to you. Of course. Good day, Kausalya.'

Kausalya paused a moment longer at the threshold. Their eyes met for an instant and something passed between the two women. Something that was part regret and part confusion. And all sadness.

The First Queen turned and made her way down the

corridor. Sumitra watched her go, feeling as if she had just lost her best friend in the whole wide world.

She shut the door, latched it, leaned her head against the softly scented pinewood, and began to cry.

17

They ran into trouble in the late afternoon.

The sun was behind them now, beating relentlessly down on their backs, searing the nape of Rama's neck. From the cool touch of the rig against his bare back, he knew that the leather was soaked through with sweat. So was his ang-vastra, reduced now to a limp rope-like garland hanging around his neck and wound around his arms to keep it out of the way. They had been travelling for over eight hours without pause, he estimated. A little after noon, the brahmarishi had exhorted them to eat some fruit and salt and drink some water, but Vishwamitra himself had not taken a morsel. In fact, Rama realised, in the nine days they had been together, he couldn't recall ever seeing the seer-mage eat a full meal. Small wonder then that not a single one of the three-hundred-strong brahmin procession had uttered a word of protest at either the relentless pace, the searing heat, or the lack of a rest. Old and young alike, the brahmins and brahmacharyas of Siddh-ashrama had followed their guru stoically. There was no more chanting or recitation – there wasn't enough energy for that – but the entourage had trudged on without protest or complaint for the better part of the day.

Around noon, they had left behind the rolling grassy plains where wild horse, elephant and rhino roamed freely and entire clans of lumbering hippopotami rolled cumbrously in mud-pools, and the path had begun undulating constantly, seemingly unable to stay flat any longer, while thickets of wildbrush, sage, bamboo and bizarre profusions of lavishly multi-hued wildflowers bounded it on either side. The path widened steadily and the ruts continued to deepen as they went northwards, a considerable improvement over the narrow grassy dirt-track that had led them out of Siddh-ashrama. It never actually became a proper road, at least not one that any Arya cartographer would officially label a 'marg', but clearly this part of the route saw fairly regular traffic.

The trees bordering the path provided some welcome shade and the air grew slightly cooler as they toiled steadily to a higher level above sea. Rama spied flashes of movement in the depths of the woods they passed by and several times glimpsed the tip of a busy tail or the glint of dark feral eyes. But no animals troubled them. Even the most ferocious predators shied away from a procession of over three hundred humans travelling with elephants, horses and bullocks. Even the occasional lowing of the bullocks or whinnying of horses from the rear of the line was perfunctory, like little animal exclamations rather than nervous complaints. After a while, the road seemed to rise and fall in waves like an ocean. The swells grew higher each time, until they could see nothing of the land ahead until they reached the top of the next rise.

They crested yet another of these rolling swells and were rewarded by a dramatic change in view.

Brahmarishi Vishwamitra came gradually to a halt, raising his staff high above his head to let the procession know that he intended to stop.

'*Slow!*' his strong booming voice called out.

The message rippled down the line as noisily as the

quintet of parrots flying squawking overhead, their long green and red tails flashing brightly against the ocean-blue sky. A few of the older rishis had begun to doze sitting upright in their carts. They came awake at once. The younger acolytes peered around the rear of the bullocks, trying to see what had warranted the unexpected halt. With a series of creaking, clanking, lowing and tongue-clicking sounds, the pilgrim procession ground to a halt.

The same little lisper who had amused the company earlier emitted an unselfconscious yawn, stretched mightily, and repeated his now-famous phrase: 'Omharithwaaa!' bringing a brief smile to the faces of everyone except Rama and Lakshman, whose attention was focused on the brahmarishi.

Vishwamitra hefted the staff and used it to point ahead, explaining the decision that lay before them.

They were in an overgrown meadow bordered by bamboo thickets. Up ahead, Rama saw, the cart-track they were following curved sharply right and wound its way eastwards for as far as he could see. About a hundred yards further ahead, just about where the Vajra bigfoot had stopped on seeing the main procession halt, a thin, sketchy line wound its way through the brush, wavering upwards into the lower slopes of what seemed to be a range of rolling hills of varying heights. The path, if it could be called that, disappeared into the dense woods of the hills. The hillside was cloaked with densely growing trees all the way up its height, which seemed to rise to at least three hundred yards.

'Rajkumars, heed me,' the seer-mage said, using his staff to point ahead. 'Those hills lie just below the southern-most boundary of the Videha nation. If we were to follow that narrow winding path up through those hills, in less than a mile we would be able to look down on the River

Shona. The river marks the southern border of Videha. The capital city, Mithila, is less than a day's journey from there.'

He pointed to the left. 'The boundaries of Kosala are four yojanas in that direction, at the point where the Shona curves northwards. Its west bank then marks Kosala's easternmost border and its east bank marks Videha's westernmost border. Do you follow me thus far?'

Both Lakshman and Rama agreed they did. This was basic geography of the Arya nations and they had studied it well at Guru Vashishta's gurukul.

The seer-mage nodded and raised his staff to point to the far right. 'Twenty yojanas in that direction the Videha nation rubs shoulders with the kingdom of Banglar, the easternmost Arya nation and the blessed place whence hails Rajkumar Rama's noble mother Kausalya-maa.'

Vishwamitra then pointed ahead again, tracing the main cart-path's winding line upwards to the right. 'There lies our marg. The nameless dirt path on which we stand travels two yojanas north-east then goes due north for another yojana and a half before turning north-west until it reaches the River Shona. The river runs weak and shallow there and can be crossed easily on foot. We shall breach it and continue north-west across open fields, passing through the town of Visala and continuing until we reach the sacred Ganga. On the blessed banks of that great river we shall spend the night. From the Ganga's north bank, it is perhaps ten yojanas to Mithila city.'

The sage lowered his staff. 'Do you have any questions, rajkumars?'

Rama spoke for both Lakshman and himself. 'Guru-dev, why not go up the hill and down the other side? We would reach the River Shona in an hour or less and Mithila city is less than ten yojanas thence. We would cover a third of that journey before this day ends, break for the night at a spot of your choosing and arrive in Mithila well before noon tomorrow. It would save us two-thirds of a day's journey.'

The brahmarishi nodded. 'This is the reason why I halted our company, young Rama. Few travellers venture this far south, yet those who do so invariably face this very dilemma. To take the road through the hills or follow the long way around. As you have grasped already, the marg we intend to follow circumnavigates the entire range, taking us over five yojanas out of our way and adding a further two yojanas as well. At our current pace of one yojana per hour, that would be seven hours more than the direct route.'

The sage paused. 'But there is a reason why sensible travellers always take the long way. It is safer.' He indicated the narrow upward-winding path again. 'That wooded way is indeed quicker and easier. But there is a price to pay for taking it. As the Vajra captain reminded us this morning, those hills are rife with bandits and outlaws, as well as wild predatory beasts of several species. Hundreds, perhaps thousands of innocent travellers have lost their lives or their virtue, and surely all their valuables, upon those hills. If we were to take that route, we endanger the entire company.'

Rama inclined his head respectfully. 'Guru-dev, whatever your choice, we shall follow gladly. But may I say that in the event of our being waylaid by the bandits you speak of, my brother and I would not hesitate to protect every last life and limb in our entourage.'

Lakshman said, 'Rama speaks truly, maha-dev. If assaulted, we would ensure that not a single hair on a single brahmin's head should be harmed.'

Vishwamitra's eyes twinkled. 'Not that they have much hair to protect!'

Rama and Lakshman grinned involuntarily, surprised at the sage's sudden flash of humour.

Vishwamitra shook his head slowly. 'But jesting apart, rajkumars, I would rather that we avoid violence where possible. Our mission to cleanse the Southwoods was an unavoidable one, made even more imperative and urgent by the growing brazenness of the Lord of Lanka. But fighting bandits in the hills is not necessary to our cause. And as our studies teach us, even a kshatriya must do all he can to avoid violence, resorting to it only when all other means fail. In the present circumstance, violence is easily avoided. We shall take the main path and go around the hills.'

Rama wanted to ask the brahmarishi why, if his mind was already made up, he had stopped and discussed the whole question in the first place. But it didn't behove a shishya to question a guru on his motives. Besides, the brahmarishi's wisdom was unquestionable. Kshatriyas who wilfully sought out fights were looked down upon. Even so, he was surprised to feel a twinge of regret that they wouldn't be taking the more dangerous option. *It's almost as if I want a fight.* He dismissed the thought at once, feeling guilty for having even conceived it.

'Jaise aagya, Guru-dev,' he said, joining his palms together.

Vishwamitra raised his staff to order the company to resume their journey.

Just as he strode forward, the first scream erupted.

It was distinctly human. A man crying out hoarsely in extreme terror and agony. It was cut short abruptly.

Droves of birds of every colour and breed, disturbed by the blood-curdling cry, rose into the air, darkening the afternoon sky as they wheeled about. Bandaras chattered in the trees. Dry leaves and brush rustled as other smaller beasts of prey reacted to the sound of another being in mortal pain. Mirroring exclamations travelled through the brahmin procession.

Rama and Lakshman exchanged a glance. Ahead of them, the Vajra bigfoot had raised their trunks and were rolling them about excitedly, twitching their tails as well, but too well disciplined to issue a sound. A lookout seated facing backwards on the last bigfoot glanced up at the hills then back at the procession to see if he was expected to give the word to call a halt.

The brahmarishi strode on as if nothing had happened.

A second scream erupted, this one much louder and more startling than the first. It was more a clash of howls than a scream, really, as if two beings, human and inhuman, were fighting to the death. The throaty animal howl was cut off with brutal abruptness. Immediately after, the human voice issued a sharp, high-pitched cry.

The ensuing silence was more chilling than the screams.

18

Rama and Lakshman had drawn and strung their bows the instant the second scream began. Without slowing their pace, they scanned the hills intently. It was impossible to see anything through the dense, close-growing northern trees. Behind them, nervous murmurs broke out in the brahmin procession as the ashramites debated the source and cause of the blood-curdling screams. The Vajra bigfoot leading them had begun lowing uneasily, shaking their trunks from side to side and flapping their ears.

They're battle elephants, they know violence, Rama thought. Just as he now did.

'Guru-dev,' he said, 'it appears that someone is in trouble up in the hills.'

The seer-mage was so still and silent at first that Rama thought he might be absorbed in another trance state. Then Vishwamitra's fist opened and slid down the length of his wildwood staff, gripping it lower. He raised the staff, calling a halt yet again.

The procession lurched to a standstill.

Yet another outburst of screams and howls shattered the still, hot afternoon, causing a great commotion in the procession. Some brahmins were reciting mantras to ward off Asuras. But Rama didn't think those screams had been caused by Asuras. Those were some kind of animal. And humans of course. Locked in mortal conflict. A queer sensation rippled through the muscles of his back and arms. A brief memory of the battle in the Bhayanak-van flashed in his mind's eye. He tightened his grip on his bow, the string creaking as he drew it to its limit.

The sound of hoofbeats drummed steadily from the rear of the procession, growing louder and closer. Vajra Captain Bejoo was coming up again, and this time he didn't need to ask the reason why they had stopped. Ahead, the Vajra bigfoot squad also came to a lumbering, thumping stop.

The brahmarishi had remained curiously silent after calling the halt. Rama addressed him again.

'Guru-dev, my brother and I ask permission to go up into the hills to investigate the situation. If bandits or wild animals are preying on innocent wayfarers, it is our dharma to go to their aid.'

The seer-mage looked at Rama thoughtfully. 'True, rajkumar. But what if those are not innocent wayfarers but bandits themselves who are fighting the wild beasts of the hills? Whom would you save then? The savage beasts or the murdering mortals?'

Rama blinked. The question was completely unexpected. Did that mean that the brahmarishi knew what was happening up there? Of course he does, Rama admonished himself. If he could sniff out Lanka spies in a city as populous as Ayodhya, he can easily sense what's happening on the hill up there. He struggled to find an appropriate answer.

'If that were the case, Guru-dev, I should attempt to put a stop to the violence and send both groups their separate ways.'

The brahmarishi looked at Rama intently. His voice was

unusually soft, almost as if he was speaking to himself. 'Truly blessed, Rani Kausalya.'

A fresh burst of noise exploded into the nervous stillness. This one was a veritable orchestra of murderous shouts, yells of pain and rage, and a series of clashing sounds that were unmistakably weapons at work, including the familiar metallic ringing of steel striking steel. The sounds carried for miles around, disturbing the birds and fauna of the entire region and alarming the brahmin procession further. The youngest acolyte was lisping his 'Omharithwaaa!' frantically over and over again. This time nobody was laughing.

The brahmarishi cocked his head thoughtfully. 'It appears that your choice of opponents may have increased to three now, rajkumar.'

Rama waited but the brahmarishi didn't explain further.

Instead the sage added: 'Go with my blessings.'

Rama and Lakshman shot off at a pace that made the grassy ground blur beneath their feet. They thrashed through the undergrowth, reaching the narrow hill path in an instant. They plunged into the shadowy dimness together and vanished from the sight of the procession.

Bejoo had started once again towards the front of the procession on hearing the first scream. He was almost there when the second scream erupted. The blood-chilling sound alarmed a skittish calf just ahead and the distracted young brahmacharya minding it lost his grasp on the tethering rope. The calf turned, unnerved by the violent screams, and bolted left across a downy meadow, heading for the thicket. Two of its fellows followed eagerly, their dangling nose-rings tethered by the same rope. The brahmacharya called out in alarm and leapt down from the cart to chase after them. He landed directly in front of Bejoo's cantering horse and froze foolishly.

Bejoo pulled up sharply to avoid running him over. He held up his hand to indicate to his men following behind to halt as well, then gestured impatiently to the wide-eyed acolyte to get out of the way. A fresh round of screams from the hills confused and scared the boy further. He stayed firmly in Bejoo's way.

'Your calves are getting away, boy!' Bejoo said.

The boy whooped, slapping the side of his shaved head, setting his pigtail wagging, and ran after his animals. Several other young acolytes ran to help him.

By the time the path was clear for Bejoo to ride on, the rajkumars were already sprinting up the side of the hill. He cursed under his breath to avoid offending the brahmins and spurred his horse to a full gallop. As he rode past the seer-mage, he could have sworn Vishwamitra was smiling grimly up at him.

He veered off the path and up an overgrown hummock at the foot of the first hill. The two Vajra riders who were posted with the bigfoot regiment for purposes of co-ordination appeared ahead of him, still on the path.

He yelled at them to follow him and they swung their horses around with practised ease. From the thundering of hoofbeats behind him, he knew that at least half of the forty-odd horseback Vajra kshatriyas were already riding up to take up a defensive position around the procession. Those were standing instructions.

Bejoo cursed again, aloud this time, not caring if any holy men could hear him. He had anticipated a possible ambush on their way to Mithila. But his scenarios had not envisioned the rajkumars leaving the procession to go seeking out trouble, dammit! Now he was forced to make the difficult choice of leaving either the brahmins or the rajkumars unprotected.

He made his decision and yelled an order to one of the two horseback scouts who were on his flanks now. The man saluted and turned back towards the brahmin procession. He would ride to the acting lieutenant of the horse squad and convey Bejoo's order to bring the Vajra chariots up from the rear to form a picket formation around the brahmins, thus freeing the majority of the horse to ride after Bejoo as back-up. They would be a minute behind him now, but their presence might be invaluable. Judging by the number and variety of those screams, the fight up in the hills involved a sizeable number of participants.

He rode fiercely up the hillside, thrashing through wild brush and overgrown limbs, vines and creepers. He had to leap over fallen logs, and duck and swerve to avoid being knocked off by tangled vine-webs and mossy branches. The remaining scout followed him with difficulty. Bejoo ignored the scratches and minor slashes he received, pushing his mount as hard as he dared up the overgrown hilly path. The princes had run so swiftly, he knew they must be empowered by brahman shakti. If he didn't make a superhuman effort, he would reach them too late to help much. He didn't want another repeat of the Bhayanak-van battle, where he had arrived on the scene almost at the close of the fighting.

Up ahead, he heard another yell, this one less a scream than a cry of rage. Angry shouts followed. And above the drumming of his own heart and the pounding of the hoofs he caught a faint metallic sound that could only be weapons clashing. Someone was fighting up on the hill; several someones from the sound of it. He cursed again.

Why did the rajkumars have to get involved? What did they think they were doing anyway – acting as the Kosala nation's voluntary roving police force? This wasn't even Kosala territory. Whatever was going on up there, it wasn't their fight. If the rajkumars were so chivalrous and eager to protect the innocent, they could simply have asked Bejoo to send a quad or two to investigate. Did they stop to think? To consult Bejoo, a much-decorated veteran and a high-ranking kshatriya trusted by their father himself, a former teacher to them? No! They had simply discussed the matter with their new guru and gone running off into the wilderness to be heroes again.

Bejoo cursed once more and rode harder. An instant later, he broke out of the tortuous path and found more open ground. The going became a little easier as he rode on upwards through what seemed to be an ashwood grove. He was almost at the top now.

Bejoo knew this region. It was notorious for its high incidence of highway robberies and ambushes. After the Last Asura War, several kshatriyas of the armies of the united Arya nations, exhausted by their ordeal, had forsworn their oaths and taken to the hills. Usually they would be considered deserters, but the aftermath of the war had left everyone disturbed and confused and it had been decided to simply let them go their way and live their lives as generation-exiles, meaning that even their progeny could never claim citizenry of any Arya nation ever again.

The authorities had assumed the deserters wouldn't last long in this wild land anyway. That had been twenty-something years ago, back when the Bhayanak-van, whose still-smouldering ashes were situated only a few miles to the south-west, was still rife with Asuras, and this whole region had been desolate and uncharted. These hills had been so insignificant, they hadn't even been named.

As ashrams sprouted up across the southern boundaries of the nations and this route had slowly come into use, stray incidents of banditry had been reported with increasing regularity from the unnamed hills. But it hadn't been worth the manpower or effort to clean the place up. Besides, the hills were a no-man's-land, belonging neither to Videha nor to Banglar. And they were certainly no concern of Kosala.

So what am I doing, riding up a hillside after two princes of Ayodhya on a sunny spring afternoon? Exercising my Vajra? Something like that, Bejoo guessed.

He spurred his horse up a last bank, her hoofs scrabbling briefly. To her credit, she never made a sound of protest, just kept her head down and worked her way up with the bit held tight between her teeth. He breached the rise and gained relatively flatter ground running east by north-east. Sounds of weapons and angry cries were clearly audible now, coming from up ahead, and Bejoo led his horse that way.

He rode through shadow and clear light, tree shade and open patches, across a hard-packed coppery soil strewn with old leaf-fall. To his left, winking through gaps in branches, in a winding valley almost a thousand feet below, the placid waters of the River Shona gleamed silvery blue in the afternoon sunlight.

The sounds from up ahead grew increasingly strange and incomprehensible. As he caught echoes of unmistakable animal grunts and cries, Bejoo flashed back to a memory of the battle in the Bhayanak-van, when he and his men had finally caught up with Rama, Lakshman and the brahmarishi, battling hybrid Asuras in the deep Southwoods. That incredible sight would haunt his dreams for ever.

The memory reminded him of Bheriya for some reason, bringing an unexpected twinge of regret to his heart. Bheriya was gone, really gone. The man he had considered his surrogate son was dead. He brushed the thought aside fiercely. This was no time to think of dead surrogate sons. He had a duty to perform and two princes to protect, dammit!

Then he burst through into a clearing and his horse reared in alarm as they came across a sight almost as bizarre as the one they had encountered back at the Bhayanak-van. He reined her in with difficulty.

'In the name of Shani!' Bejoo exclaimed in sheer amazement. What had the rajkumars got him into this time?

Rama felt the surge of power in his veins as he breasted the top of the slope. He felt as if he had merely climbed a ten-yard-high hummock rather than a three-hundred-yard hill. Lakshman was right by his side.

'Which way, brother?' Lakshman asked, scanning the thickly wooded hilltop.

Rama replied by putting a hand to his right ear, miming listening. Lakshman nodded, listened, then pointed right. They sprinted that way.

Bright diamonds winked up at them from the valley to the left as they ran: the River Shona. Rama could see why travellers were tempted to cut across the hills. It was such a short way over. Besides, the hills – or at least this one thus far – seemed quite placid and tranquil. But he knew that was deceptive. Already, his awakening brahman-attuned senses were growing aware of a peculiar sensation. It was like a creeping, crawling itch on the back of his neck, like a thousand very tiny pinpricks being inflicted all at once, too tiny to do harm individually, but infuriating in sum. He sensed watchers in the woods, eyes gleaming darkly from treetops, behind trunks, even from loose soil and leaf-fall mounds on the ground. The population wasn't as sparse as first appearances suggested; they just didn't wish to show themselves to these two-legged intruders.

His feet pumping rhythmically beneath him, Rama dodged rabbit-holes, snake-holes, ant-hills, tree trunks, and a surprisingly large number of enormous beehives that hung low, almost at eye-level beneath the mishmash of banyan, oak, ash, pine and bitter elm trees, while his mind analysed the messages his other senses were receiving. What had the guru said? Remember the tiger. Restraint. A chisel, not a hammer. True enough: why use the hammer of brahman when his kshatriya skills might be enough to deal with the situation?

A part of him wanted to use that hammer, to give in to that electrifying surge of brahman shakti. To feel that numbing shock of divine effulgence passing through his cells, the indescribable ecstasy of drawing upon a power so vastly infinite, it could destroy universes and reshape existence itself. Not just that; he wanted to use the dev-astras again. To unleash forces so immense, they were named for their divine destructibility. Dev-astras: literally weapons of the gods.

He wanted to yield to the flow of brahman, to awaken the other Rama, the one who was a fighting machine, an unstoppable engine of destruction. And once unleashed, that Rama would not stop until every living foe in sight was dead. He forced himself to exercise self-restraint, to obey his guru's order.

The words of his first teacher, Guru Vashishta, rang in his ears like a mantra. First, assess. Then negotiate. Only when all else fails, resort reluctantly to violence. And even then, never strike the first blow.

The sounds from ahead grew louder. Rama had returned his arrow and bow to the rig on his back when Lakshman and he had begun running. Now, he drew his sword in a smooth motion, lopping off a tree trunk looming in his way. By the time the severed limb fell to the leaf-thick ground, he was twenty yards ahead. Lakshman followed him, perhaps just a stride after his brother. At Rama's current pace, that meant Lakshman was all of three yards behind.

Rama didn't know why his brother wasn't as empowered as he was by the shakti of the maha-mantras, but it was so. He accepted it just as he accepted the surge of energy that flooded his muscles, accentuating that indescribable feeling of . . . invincibility? Godlike power? Whatever it was, he was starting to like it now, and liked the way it made him feel, the way it made all other normal everyday considerations seem trivial and distant. Karma and dharma. His eagerness to return to Ayodhya. His concern for his mother's unexpectedly renewed relationship with his father. His father's fading health. His own approaching coronation. The real reason for this unscheduled detour to Mithila. All of it faded before the shakti of brahman like a trickle from a cupped hand drowned out by the roar of a waterfall. Right now, the only thing that mattered was sword and muscle. Blood and bone. Life and death.

Rama drew in a breath and leapt an enormous impossible leap. He arced up, up to almost five yards height, slashing easily at obstructing leaves and branches, scything his way through into the clearing ahead.

He exploded into the clearing like an apparition out of thin air, releasing an ululating cry that carried for miles around, and landed with an impact like a small tornado. A cloud of dust and leaves swirled around him.

'Ayodhya Anashya!' he cried. Ayodhya the Invincible!

Lakshman put every last bit of energy he had into keeping up with Rama, and found he couldn't. It wasn't so much that he couldn't run as fast, it was as if Rama was just physically so much more powerful that it was pointless even trying to keep up with him.

Lakshman guessed that he was running at a pace of at least ten yojanas an hour. Ninety miles an hour! That was amazing by any standards. But even so, he seemed to be struggling to catch up with Rama. His brother's legs were treadmilling as effortlessly as a sprinter doing a practice run on a training exercise, and even as he ran, Rama's head turned sharply this way, then that, scanning, observing, scouring the wooded slope like a tiger exploring its territory with preternaturally developed senses. Rama was changing again, he knew, into the killing machine he had become in the battle.

Somehow, that didn't make Lakshman feel very glad. For some reason, the sight of his brother transforming from a mild, soft-spoken, dutiful young kshatriya into a savage fighting machine beyond human comprehension disturbed him profoundly. But he could feel the brahman shakti throbbing in his own body and experienced a sense of overwhelming super-confidence. His doubts melted away as he entered a similar trance-like state.

As they approached the site of the disturbance, Lakshman watched Rama crouch low like a cheetah preparing to spring, then leap impossibly high into the air. He watched in admiration as Rama flew through the trees, sword slashing at obstructions, and disappeared from view.

Lakshman put all his effort into one final burst of speed, and exploded into the clearing ahead just in time to see his brother standing half crouched in the midst of a bizarre tableau, the air swirling angrily with the dust and disturbed leaves of his landing.

The reverberations of Rama's war cry rang through the air and Lakshman echoed him.

'Ayodhya Anashya!'

19

Prime Minister Sumantra scrutinised the young Vajra kshatriya standing before him. The soldier was clearly the worse for wear, his face revealing the rigours of his long, hard ride and his slashed uniform and blood-spattered limbs leaving no doubt that he had recently been at arms. He bore the three bands that marked his lieutenant rank, below the jagged lightning-slash symbol of the maharaja's Vajra regiment.

Sumantra didn't know Bheriya personally. His duties as prime minister of Kosala covered the entire gamut of administrative and governmental matters. Military affairs were only one part of his enormous responsibility, and while he was aware of every nuance of the overall picture, he could hardly be expected to know every soldier on sight. But Mantri Jabali, the minister for defence and military administration, recognised him and that was good enough for Pradhan Mantri Sumantra.

'Well met, Lieutenant Bheriya,' Mantri Jabali was saying now. 'Your appearance testifies to your need for rest, refreshment and, um, hygiene. But circumstances demand that you delay those graces and deliver your missive first.'

Vajra Lieutenant Bheriya inclined his head formally. 'Mantriji, I would have it no other way. My message is of far greater urgency than my personal needs. I am grateful to you and to Pradhan Mantri Sumantra for granting me this immediate audience.'

The prime minister nodded, acknowledging the man officially. 'Go ahead then, Lieutenant. Deliver your message. We are as eager to hear your words as you are to speak them.'

Bheriya looked up at Sumantra, who was standing at his formal post to the right hand of the sunwood throne of Ayodhya. The throne itself was empty, and the vast parliament hall nearly so. Sumantra, Jabali, Bheriya himself, Rajkumar Bharat, Rajkumar Shatrugan and an unusually large number of palace guards were the only persons present.

Bheriya bowed his head regretfully. 'Pradhan Mantriji, forgive my inability to fulfil your command. My message is for the ears of Maharaja Dasaratha alone. This was my captain's explicit command. To disobey it would be to dishonour my caste-oath.'

'Lieutenant,' Sumantra said with a trace of impatience, 'I understand that you would violate the oath of the kshatriya by not following your superior's orders. But Mantri Jabali is the minister in charge of military affairs, which makes him superior in authority to your Vajra captain. And I myself am prime minister of the kingdom of Kosala, entrusted by the maharaja as well as the people of this nation with the governance not just of the seat of Ayodhya, but of the entire Kosala nation. Your captain would not regard giving us your message to be a violation of his orders, let alone your caste-oath! Come now, time is wasting. Speak your message and I shall act on it immediately if so warranted. This is a direct command, good Bheriya. Speak!'

But the lieutenant shook his head regretfully. 'Pradhan Mantriji, once again, I beg your forgiveness. My master's orders brook no re-interpretation. Either I speak with the maharaja alone, or I do not speak at all.'

Sumantra was growing angry, a condition that wasn't common to his calm, measured disposition. Rajkumars Bharat and Shatrugan, who had escorted the lieutenant from the first gate to the palace for this audience, exchanged a glance. They had already told Sumantra about the man's refusal to speak to anyone but the king. But Sumantra's orders were equally clear: until prince-in-waiting Rama returned from the Southwoods, or Maharaja Dasaratha recovered enough to attend to his courtly duties, he was the one charged with governing the kingdom. Of course, he would not take any major action without consulting the maharaja himself, or at the least Guru Vashishta, to whom Dasaratha invariably turned for advice, but it was ridiculous to expect the maharaja to rise from his sickbed to attend to everyone who brought a vital message meant for his ears only.

'Kshatriya,' Sumantra said sharply, 'do you know how many couriers arrive with messages for the maharaja daily? Today alone four other riders have arrived since daybreak, bearing messages of the greatest urgency directly from the maharajas of four Arya nations and intended solely for Maharaja Dasaratha. All four messengers willingly entrusted their missives to me without delay or argument.'

Sumantra pulled out an ornately carved gold seal-ring from a pocket in his robe. 'I dictated the replies myself and sealed them with the maharaja's own seal-ring. As you can see, I am fully empowered to act and speak on his behalf. I command you for the last time, deliver your message to me, or face a trial for treason under martial law.'

He held up the hand bearing the seal-ring before the lieutenant could respond, and added, 'Think carefully before replying. Your honour as well as your life could well depend on what you choose to say.'

Mantri Jabali broke in hastily: 'I am sure the prime minister does not intend to impose this harsh penalty on you without cause, my good Bheriya. Pray, speak freely and trust us to bear your every word to the maharaja as if you spoke them directly into his very ears.'

The Vajra lieutenant glanced around the hall as if trying to collect his thoughts.

Sumantra added as an afterthought: 'One last point. I am willing to let you speak your message in private, to me alone if you prefer.' He gestured towards the rajkumars and the palace guards, including even Mantri Jabali. 'That is the last concession I make to you, soldier. Now speak.'

Bheriya looked up at the prime minister. 'Forgive me, Pradhan Mantriji. I cannot violate my orders.'

Mantri Jabali stifled a groan of dismay.

Sumantra nodded, seething inwardly. Stubborn kshatriya fool! 'Very well then. You leave me no choice. Guards, take this man to the city jail. He is to be charged with treasonous disobedience of the maharaja's law.'

A quad of guards marched forward and took charge of the Vajra lieutenant. Bheriya made no move to resist.

Mantri Jabali sighed. 'Most regretful. Pradhan Mantriji, I will go along with the arrested man to see to his arraignment.'

As Bheriya was led out of the hall, Rajkumar Bharat approached the prime minister.

'Sumantraji,' he said, a frown creasing his handsome features, 'that man has word of Rama and Lakshman and the outcome of their mission to the Southwoods. They may require our aid urgently, or . . .' He paused. 'Or worse.'

'I am aware of that, Rajkumar Bharat, and am as eager to learn of their condition. But you saw the man's stubbornness. He left me no choice under the law.'

The young prince chewed his lip anxiously. 'Yes. But perhaps if you speak to Guru Vashishta, he may find some way to release the man of his oath-obligation. The guru is wise in finding solutions to impossible problems.'

Pradhan Mantri Sumantra nodded. 'An excellent suggestion, young Bharat. That is exactly what I intend to do right away.'

A disturbance outside the hall attracted their attention. They turned to see Mantri Jabali returning with an uncharacteristic smile on his normally austere features. The guards and their prisoner followed in his wake.

'The devas are with us today,' Mantri Jabali said to Sumantra. 'The situation has been resolved.'

He turned and bowed his head to greet the person following close behind.

Maharaja Dasaratha, seated on a travelling chair carried by four palace guards, entered the parliament hall.

'Sumantra,' the maharaja said in a tone far softer than his usual booming baritone, but nevertheless as commanding, 'this messenger wishes to deliver an urgent missive to me personally. I will hear him without delay. See to it that we have complete privacy for a few moments.'

Pradhan Mantri Sumantra smiled. 'With pleasure, your majesty.'

Addressing the other occupants of the hall, the prime minister clapped his hands. 'You heard the maharaja. Everybody except Maharaja Dasaratha and the Vajra Lieutenant Bheriya is to leave at once.'

He descended the steps of the royal dais, passing the maharajah, who was carried up to the level of the throne and assisted in seating himself. In seconds, the hall was clear and Sumantra himself backed his way to the large, ornately carved wooden doors.

'Aagya, maharaja,' he said, taking leave formally. 'We shall be without these doors until you send for us.'

Sumantra emerged backwards from the hall and issued an order to the palace guards standing by to shut and bar the massive doors.

The stubborn kshatriya has his wish, he thought, relieved. He's alone with the maharaja and can do as his captain ordered.

The doors thundered shut. As the reverberating echoes faded away, Sumantra was reminded for some reason of the sound of the city war-gong. It was meant to summon citizens to the walls to prepare for battle, to announce the approach of an invading army. Ayodhya had never sounded that gong because the city had never been attacked or besieged. But if that relic were to be struck, Sumantra was certain it would make a sound not unlike the doors of the parliament hall had just made.

Bejoo controlled his horse with a nudge and a twitch of the reins. Her nostrils flared as she smelt the pungent scent of one of the large predators nearby, but she held steady as her master surveyed the scene in one quick sweep. Behind him, the solitary remaining scout reined in his mount as well.

'By the gods,' Bejoo muttered under his breath. What had the princes got themselves into this time?

The scene in the clearing was as exotic as any Ayodhyan artist could have imagined. Two different species were frozen in a tableau of brutal violence and hatred. On one hand were the humans, a motley assortment of men and women clad in garments roughly woven from bark and hemp-rope. They all looked much alike, as if they might be members of one vast family; this illusion owed more to their similarity in appearance than their features.

Their coarse henna-red hair was matted into knotted locks, their faces and bodies were uniformly filthy and unwashed, shiny with sweat, badly healed scars and more recent wounds. Their beggarly garments clung to ill-fed bodies taut with the aggressive, jumpy tension typical of lives lived in constant fear of violence.

A pathetic assortment of weapons were clutched in their fists – chipped swords, longknives, twisted daggers, sharpened rods, rusting tridents, a battered mace or two, and in the massively muscled arms of two enormous bearded brutes, solidly cast ironwood hammers each almost a yard long. They were about thirty-odd in number, and Bejoo had seen enough bandits to know a gang when he saw one.

The leader of the group seemed to be a man with a face uglier than any Bejoo had seen before: the flesh had been mauled brutally in some old encounter, gouged too deeply to allow regrowth. The man's teeth were clearly visible through three gaps in his left cheek; the cheek itself, if you could call it that, consisted of just three stringy strands of flesh hanging loosely. You can probably see his food being chewed when he eats, Bejoo thought, disgusted. He knew only one animal that could inflict such a wound: bear. But he had never seen a man clawed by a bear that badly who had survived to tell the tale.

As if in mute confirmation, the scarred leader of the gang wore an iron chain around his neck sporting at least a dozen bear claws, and predictably, his main garment was a faded chewed-up bearskin.

The other group in the fight were, not surprisingly, rksas. Bejoo, like all other Vajra kshatriyas, had a family totem which gave him his clan-name and was his protective mascot in life and battle. This totem was the black mountain bear, or Bejoo. Quite naturally, he had been brought up to regard rksas as a kind of guardian deity. Yet he was sensible enough not to let his reverence for the furry predators overcome his natural human wariness of their short-sighted, hard-hearing, bad-tempered natures. At this moment, however, his clan loyalty was calling out to him like conch-shell alarms, driving the blood through his veins and making him eager to join the fray.

There were four bears in the clearing. Ten if you counted corpses. The six bears that lay dead were horribly maimed and wounded, their black fur slashed with gaping flesh-bright wounds. Their snarling snouts testified to the struggle they had put up before yielding to superior numbers and metal weaponry. With every fallen bear, at least five bandits lay fallen too. Some were clasped in the crushing embrace that humans mistakenly called bear-hugs.

In fact, the so-called 'hug' was the bear's way of swivelling its torso from the hips, putting all its considerable upper-body bulk into a cuffing slash of its inches-long claws. The resulting force with which those lethal claws struck usually saw them embedding themselves deep within the victim's flesh, so a watcher would see the rksa appear to be hugging its prey closely. Each fallen bear had at least two humans apiece caught in its claws in this fashion. Even seeing the gruesome wounds on the bandits brought down by the dead bears didn't evoke any sympathy in Bejoo. It was clear who was the real predator here.

The four surviving bears were clustered together. Bejoo assessed the largest one to be a female in her early middle age. Behind her, partly concealed between her broad back and the trunk of a thick ancient oak, were three cubs of varying sizes. The cubs were very young, too young to be of any real use in a fight against so many armed enemies, but even so they peered out from behind their mother's flanks, snarling and growling fiercely at the humans who threatened her.

The female was bleeding from several small wounds, none significant enough to be fatal but cumulatively enough to cause great pain and hamper her movements. The bandits wore her down, slash by slash, jab by jab, Bejoo thought, his fury rising as he pictured the desperate last stand of the mother rksa after her adult companions were butchered. Those were the howls of rage we heard – they were sticking her like a dummy at a carnival pig-sticking contest.

Despite her wounds, the female stood on her rear legs, presenting the largest possible front, and bared her teeth silently at the ring of bandits who surrounded her. They held their weapons far ahead of their vulnerable bodies, clearly having learned from the example of their fallen companions that the mother bear still had enough fight left in her to take several more of them before she went down.

The man with the ruined face was closest to her, supervising the last part of what had been a difficult and brutal clash of the two species.

But the bandit leader's attention wasn't directed at the cornered bear and her cubs.

It was focused on the two humans who were threatening him and his band.

These last two were clearly not part of the bandit gang. They were both dressed in the all-black head-to-toe garb of kshatriyas-for-hire. Wandering mercenaries who travelled from kingdom to kingdom, hiring their swords out to rich merchants who needed bodyguards while ferrying their goods from marketplace to marketplace, entering mêlées and tourneys for the prize-money, occasionally even signing up with any army that was hiring and paying well.

Both had their heads covered with the same black roughcloth and their faces were veiled as well, only their bright eyes visible, shining fiercely. They were an odd couple, one a giant towering over everyone else in the clearing – everyone except the female bear, of course – and the other a slender, lithe kshatriya a third of his companion's size. They were armed with the familiar curved swords that Mithilan kshatriyas favoured, and their back-to-back stances revealed their own desperate struggle against the bandit gang. Four or five human corpses lay around them, confirming which side they were on.

Bejoo couldn't quite understand this set-up. He would have accepted the bandits attacking the family of rksas, perhaps slaughtering them for their valuable teeth, claws, fur, even their sexual organs for their mythical aphrodisiacal properties; or the gang attacking the pair of kshatriyas in the hope of stealing their purses – some of these wandering mercenaries did quite well for themselves, and this pair looked well-nourished and decently dressed. But he didn't understand how the mercenaries, rksas and the bandits all fitted together.

One thing *was* clear, though: the rksas and the kshatriyas were aligned on one side, the bandits on the other. Which made Bejoo's choice of loyalty crystal clear. If he and his men entered this fight, they would side with the kshatriyas, who were at least fellow-caste Aryas, and with the rksas, because they were the Vajra captain's totem. Besides, he hated bandits. They were nothing more than scum who preyed on unarmed travellers and slaughtered them for a few coins, keeping the women as sexual slaves and the children to be raised as additions to their gang. He would enjoy dispatching this lot to the realm of Yamaraj.

But the boys he was sworn to protect were right in the

midst of the tableau, between the bandits, the kshatriyas and the rksas.

As Bejoo watched, Rajkumar Rama began speaking.

Rama addressed everyone present in the clearing without regard for whether they were friend or foe, human or animal.

'In the name of Maharaja Dasaratha, king of Kosala, master of the sunwood throne of Ayodhya, I command you all to lay down your weapons at once and cease fighting.'

Sullen silence met his announcement.

Stunned by Rama's spectacular entrance, the bandits were still gaping at him, and at Lakshman, who was a few yards away to Rama's left. The two black-garbed kshatriyas exchanged a quick glance and seemed a little relieved at this dramatic change in their situation. But the bear and her frightened cubs continued to snarl and growl as fiercely as before.

Lakshman guessed that to the unfortunate bears, one human was much the same as the next. Even if they could have understood Rama's words, why should they trust him? He kept his focus as keenly on the rksas as on the bandits, figuring, as Bejoo had just done, that the kshatriya mercenaries were the only allies he could count on in this face-off. A cornered bear was ten times as dangerous as a bandit. There was no telling what that female might do, or at whom she might direct her wrath.

After a pause, someone laughed. The sound was grating, and unexpected. The man who spoke had an insolent tone, his accent a careless drawl that echoed the speech of the Garhwali Himalayas. A mountain man, Lakshman thought. If that was where the speaker was from originally, then he was a long way from his hilly homeland.

'Rajkumar Rama, we meet again! The devas must have entwined our horoscopes at birth. How else could we meet twice in less than one moon-cycle?'

Lakshman stared at the bandit who had spoken. It was the horribly scarred man, evidently the leader of this ragged band, judging from his appearance and the arrogant way he stood and spoke. For an instant, looking at the disfigured face, Lakshman thought the man's wounds had just been inflicted, in this very fight; after all, they were rksa-slashes, and the man and his band were fighting rksas. Then he realised that the scars – if you could call them that – were very old. He recalled Rama's encounter with the man named Bear-face, the leader of the gang of poachers hunting the deer near Ayodhya. This had to be the same man, although Lakshman couldn't figure out how the bandit leader could have got out of jail so soon.

'You do recognise me, rajkumar?' the man was saying to Rama. He gestured mockingly at his damaged features, making a coy hand-signal like a classical dancer. 'Or did you forget my pretty face so quickly?'

He clicked his tongue mockingly. 'Ah, I know why you're here. You didn't get to kiss my pretty mug the last time we met. So you decided to come a-hunting for me so you could fulfil your heart's desire!'

A burst of laughter exploded from the other bandits.

Some of the other men seemed to recognise Rama too, and one of the younger fellows was staring at the back of his head as if he was contemplating putting his dagger through it. Lakshman tightened his grip on his sword and waited to see what Rama did next.

Rama responded in the same measured tone he had used earlier. 'I repeat: throw down your weapons and live. Or fight on and die. The choice is yours.'

Bear-face hawked and spat on the corpse of a female

bear before him. Then he put a sandalled foot on the beast, unmindful of the still steaming mass of intestines oozing from the gashed belly.

'I seem to recall you giving me similar words on that prior occasion as well, young prince.'

He emphasised the last word as if it was the worst abuse any living being could speak. 'Right before you caught me unawares with that lucky stone-toss. Well, this time you won't be so lucky, and my numbers are better than on that occasion. What's more, you're in my territory now. No city guards to back you up, no city jail to throw me into.'

He made the infuriating clicking sound again. Lakshman saw the man's red tongue working inside his horribly exposed mouth and felt his stomach churn with disgust.

'Not that the city jail kept me long. Do you know the funniest thing?' Bear-face gestured to his band, all of whom were listening and watching attentively. 'The young rajkumar arrested me on the morning of Holi feast day, and I was released by the city warden on the same afternoon. Can you guess why?'

Nobody answered, not even the other men who seemed to recognise Rama. Obviously the bandit leader was accustomed to speaking without interruption. 'Believe it or not – or believe it a lot! – it was on account of this same rajkumar's coronation announcement! Those Ayodhyan wretches have a custom that when a rajkumar is to be crowned prince-heir, or even when he's just declared as such, they release all prisoners short of actual murderers! So the boys and I, though we didn't get to pick the purses we'd gone into town for, got off scot-free by the courtesy of this young king-in-waiting right here! Can you beat that? Arrested and then released, both by the grace of the same man on the same day. If that isn't karma, what is?'

'King-in-waiting,' one of the women bandits said

mockingly. 'Wonder what they feed them maharajas-to-be. The way he came leaping in here, I thought he was that vanar warrior, what do they call him?'

'Hanuman,' said another bandit, the oldest of the group.

'Shut up, you all,' Bear-face said casually. 'This here's no vanar warrior. Least of all a Hanuman. For all his fancy titles and big palace, he's just a boy. And boys can be killed twice as easy as men.'

Bear-face pointed his sword at Rama. 'You're poaching on my territory now, prince. Even jumping like a vanar won't help you get away this time. We'll show you how forest kshatriyas fight.'

Lakshman couldn't keep silent any longer. 'You insult the caste of kshatriya by daring to call yourself one. You're nothing but a common thief and highway brigand! Do as my brother asks and we may spare your life yet. Otherwise you will be shown no quarter, I promise you that!'

Bear-face turned his head slightly to squint at Lakshman. 'So this is another of Dasaratha's whelps, hey? You must be Lakshman then. I heard they sent you two with the seer to fight rakshasas in the Southwoods. What did you do there? Set fire to the forest and burn down all the wretched beasts?'

This provoked another burst of laughter. Several of the men who had looked nervous and unsure when Rama and Lakshman had first entered the clearing now seemed relaxed and supremely confident.

He's showing his men he isn't scared of us, while buying himself time to figure his way out of the situation. Lakshman found himself reluctantly admiring the bandit leader's shrewdness. But the man's words rankled. He was implying that Rama and he had simply burned down the Southwoods rather than confront the Asuras face to face. Lakshman couldn't let that insult pass.

'You don't know what you're talking about, bandit,' he replied. 'You'd probably wet your dhoti if you met a rakshasa right now. Why, look at this scene. It takes three dozen armed bandits to terrorise one female bear! And I'm sure you'd let your men kill her and only step forward to poke your sword at the poor cubs at the very end! Don't talk about things you know nothing of, vermin! Even a sudra gutter-cleaner can convert to kshatriya-caste more easily than a wretch like you!'

Bear-face's features darkened with sudden rage. 'Call me a sudra, will you? I'm a kshatriya, you hear? A kshatriya! I'd face an army of Asuras right now and skewer them alive! I'd face the Lord of Lanka and make him eat my steel! A kshatriya, damn you!'

His followers raised their left fists and echoed their leader's claim.

Rama's voice cut through it all. 'Then act like kshatriyas, bandit. Yield, or die. This is your last warning.'

Bear-face spat at Rama. The phlegmy effusion came nowhere near the prince of Ayodhya, but the vulgarity of the gesture itself shocked Lakshman.

The bandit leader yelled his response hoarsely. 'I didn't get to meet your mother last time, prince. You should introduce me to her now. I'll show her what a real kshatriya is like—'

That was as much as Lakshman could take. He was about to respond to the bandit's insult in the only language the man would understand when he saw Rama had reached the end of his patience as well.

Lakshman watched as Rama's eyes, clear and calm up to this point, suddenly blazed bright searing blue, casting a ghostly light that made the bandits nearest to him gape in astonishment. Motes of glittering gold swirled in those brahman-empowered eyes. His entire body vibrated with blood-madness.

Rama's voice rolled across the hills like the song of a creature neither wholly human nor animal.

'Your tongue is too sharp, bandit. You just cut yourself to death with it!'

And Rama swung his sword at the two bandits nearest to him, slicing their bodies in half with one lightning-quick slash. The slaughter had begun.

20

Dasaratha resisted the urge to groan aloud as he tried to make himself comfortable on the raj-gaddhi. He found it hard to believe that he had sat this throne for more than two-thirds of his sixty-year lifespan. Sat it, and governed the mightiest Arya nation from its high eminence. From this royal dais of Ayodhya, like the captain standing on the wheel deck of a great ship-of-war, he had steered this great nation through wars and famines, droughts and floods, earthquakes and avalanches. Governed and held united a crore of citizens, all of ten million strong, the largest Arya nation in population and prosperity, if not in geographical size.

And the largest in military strength. As a raj-kshatriya, a king-warrior by birth, Dasaratha had always learned that a strong army in times of peace was the most effective way to ensure the continuance of that peace. After the Kosala army was ravaged and depleted by the Last Asura War, Dasaratha had girded his loins, gritted his teeth, and, at a time when other monarchs might while away their days in feasting and carousing, rebuilt his nation's army to twice its former size and strength, restructuring, re-organising, re-arming, and in every way putting the bitter lessons of that last terrible conflict to good use. All right, so he had done his share of feasting and carousing as well – perhaps a bit more than his share, as his now-decrepit physique and a palace annexe filled with untitled concubines testified to – but he had never relented in the execution of his great Peace On A War Footing, as his campaign came to be called in time.

The result was an army so efficient, so powerful that no human nation would dare an act of aggression against it. In the old days of his ancestors, it was customary every ten years or so to hold an ashwamedha, the horse ritual. A white stallion was sent forth across the kingdom, to roam freely over the lands of smaller lords and nobles, rajas and ranis, self-ruling clans and insular districts. The king and his army followed close on its heels. Anyone who dared stop the horse, be he a solitary kshatriya stupidly seeking a good mount or a leader of a dozen clans, would have to contend with the army following in its wake.

In this manner, the ashwamedha would sweep the entire kingdom, ensuring that every last lord, raja and clan chief was still loyal and obedient to the maharaja. Dasaratha had performed the horse ritual too, a long time ago, but today, his democratic parliament was attended by representatives of every clan, tribe and district of the kingdom. There was no need to lead an army out to ensure the loyalty of all his people: they were glad to come to him and offer their vows as often as he summoned them.

Right now, it was all he could do to stay upright on the massive sunwood throne.

Even though he had been able to sit up since this dawn, he was already depleted and feeling through for the day. The early-morning incident with the drugged fruit punch had exhausted him further. He still didn't understand how Sumitra could have accidentally mixed vinaashe root into the punch. The Third Queen was soft-hearted, not soft-headed.

As he took a moment to settle himself on the throne and clear his throat to speak, he wondered for the umpteenth time if there had been an element of sabotage involved. Not on Sumitra's part of course, but on the part of some serving girl perhaps. Every employee of the palace was regularly screened and blindly loyal to the throne, but such things did happen in every house where power, wealth and glory lived beneath the same roof as mortal beings. It didn't bother him that Guru Vashishta and Rani Kausalya had dismissed his suspicions. They were more concerned about his recovery than about anything else. If they had known he was coming here to the parliament hall to meet this courier, they would have restrained him with their own hands.

Fortunately for him, when a court messenger had brought him the news, he had been alone for a brief spell – alone except for the confounded quad of guards that were now placed within his sick-chamber!

The guards had protested but he had over-ruled them by ordering them to carry him to the hall on the travelling seat. Only now had they been compelled to let him out of their sight, and only for the brief time it took this kshatriya to deliver his vital message.

He mustered as much dignity as his condition would allow and leaned forward.

'Go ahead, kshatriya. Speak your message.'

The Vajra lieutenant named Bheriya – Shatrugan had briefed his father on the way down – bowed and knelt at the foot of the royal dais. 'My lord honours me with this audience. Forgive me if I have caused any offence to Pradhan Mantri Sumantra, Mantri Jabali, or to anyone else in the commission of my duties. I was only following the explicit orders of my captain.'

'Yes, yes,' Dasaratha said impatiently. 'I understand

perfectly. You are forgiven for any lapses and hereby absolved of all charges levelled against you. I command you now, speak your message.'

The man rose to his feet once more. He lifted his head until he could stare up at his king. Dasaratha was briefly startled by the man's directness. It was not customary for a common kshatriya to meet the eyes of his sovereign when enthroned or otherwise.

He had already noted the kshatriya's dishevelled condition and minor injuries. He had seen far worse. Couriers often delivered their missives with their life-blood staining the floor and their bodies gaping with mortal wounds. This man seemed quite robust and able in comparison. He was young too, and not unattractive to look at. Dasaratha knew that if Bejoo had entrusted this warrior with the second-command of his prized regiment, then Bheriya must be a kshatriya to reckon with.

But all that was of no matter now. Right now, all Dasaratha cared about was the message the man carried. This was the reason why he had made this short but excruciatingly difficult journey in his present condition.

When the man didn't speak again for another long moment, Dasaratha frowned down at him.

'Kshatriya,' he said, 'I commanded you to speak. Deliver your message without further delay.'

What happened next took Dasaratha completely by surprise. Had he been in good health and alert, he would have sensed something amiss even before the hall doors thundered shut. But the Vajra lieutenant gave no sign of treachery until those massive doors were closed. And when the man began to change, he acted so swiftly that Dasaratha barely had time to register what was happening let alone react to it.

The man named Bheriya looked up at Dasaratha with

eyes as crimson as the wine of the angoor-grape. The grimace on his face was as white and as wide as the eternal grin on the face of a bleached skull.

'Aja-putra!' said the kshatriya in a voice so eerily familiar that it made Dasaratha's heart thud as though a hammer was striking his chest. 'We meet again. This time you will not escape the field as easily! I shall finish the job I began that day on the plains of Kaikeya!'

Dasaratha gripped the arms of the sunwood throne and watched in horrified amazement as the Vajra lieutenant began climbing the steps of the royal dais, coming directly at him with outstretched clawing hands reaching for his throat.

Bejoo watched as Rama leapt, rolled and ran through the clearing, hacking down bandits like a tiger let loose in a sheep pen. Most of the outlaws barely had time to raise their weapons before the rajkumar cut them down. The light of brahman shakti shone in the prince's eyes, and his sword reaped a terrible harvest.

Rajkumar Lakshman had joined the fray. He was slaying as fiercely as Rama, if not as fast. The two black-clad mercenaries were in the fight as well. Taking advantage of the distraction caused by Rama's attack, they were ridding themselves of the five bandits who had ringed them in.

And almost as if she understood that this was her best chance at freedom, the bear made her move, charging forward to swing mightily left, then right, impaling two screaming bandits on her claws. She howled in rage, biting deep into a third man's neck, his blood gushing into her open jaws and splashing across her shoulders, dyeing her black coat shiny red. Her cubs followed, staying close behind their mother while clawing in all directions. One lucky swipe tore through a female bandit's thigh, the same

woman who had compared Rama's leap to that of the
vanar Hanuman. She fell screaming to the ground, her leg
gouting blood.

Bear-face scanned the clearing, taking in the shocking
speed with which his band was being decimated. It was
barely a few seconds since the bandit leader had last
spoken. Already, half his followers lay butchered. And
Rama was wheeling through the air, cutting bloody
swathes and terrible arcs of destruction, hewing trees
and limbs alike, filling the air with splashes of blood,
bright jugular sprays that made dappled patterns across
trunks and leaves, slicing through flesh, punching through
bone, severing muscle and sinew, piercing, hacking, chop-
ping, jabbing, slashing, a one-man war machine.

Bejoo's sword was raised and he wheeled his horse
around, keeping a tight hold on her reins. No matter
how many battles she might have been through, the scent
of freshly spilled blood and the chaos of violent combat
always made her skittish. It was only her superb training
and character that made her stay in the thick of things. He
got in a few blows, bringing down one bandit who was
trying to impale one of the rksa cubs with a rusty spear.
But the fight was ending before it had begun, the bandits
shaken by the rajkumars' fighting power.

Bear-face looked furious, his mangled features con-
torted into a mask of screaming frustration, 'Kill them!
Kill them!' he screamed over and over again, shoving men
and women into Rama's and Lakshman's paths, but only
succeeding in adding more victims to the slaughter count.

Bejoo had felt the trembling of the earth beneath his seat
for several moments, but now he heard the familiar conch-
shell signal and the shouted exhortation from behind. His
Vajra riders had arrived. He swung his mount around,
waving his sword in a circle above his head. His acting

lieutenant, a young lad with the totem of the golden leopard named Sona Chita, understood the signal, and led the Vajra riders around the main action, fanning out to surround the clearing and fence in the enemies. Usually Bejoo would have ordered them directly into the thick of the fray; Vajras were trained for instant hit-and-run action, not protective or defensive manoeuvres. But it was obvious that the rajkumars needed no aid in finishing off the bandits, and Bejoo feared that in his current trance-like state Rama might even dispatch a few Vajra riders before realising that they were friend not foe. He waited as his men rode around the clearing. The outcome of the fight was now inevitable.

Seeing the arrival of reinforcements, Bear-face responded at once. The bandit leader knew when he was outnumbered beyond hope. Yelling to his surviving fellows to retreat, retreat, retreat, he ran as fast as his heels would take him, heading for the end of the clearing away from the approaching Vajra riders. The two enormous brutes who had flanked him escaped as well, their sheer bulk unmistakable as they followed their leader. Bejoo guessed they were the bandit chief's personal bodyguards.

Bejoo watched, chagrined, as the leader and a handful of his quicker-footed followers slipped into the woods while the Vajra reinforcements were still some twenty yards short. He considered sending them after the fleeing bandits but decided there would be time for that later. First, he had to focus on his primary responsibility.

In moments, the Vajra riders had completely closed the ring. The dust in the clearing began to settle, sunlight catching the motes and reflecting off blood-spattered metal and leaves. The rajkumars slowed and grew still at last, realising there were no more opponents left to fight.

As Bejoo watched with continued fascination, Rama's

eyes slowly lost their blue and gold light and returned to their natural black once more. The prince lowered his sword and scanned the clearing, examining the destruction he had wrought. Bejoo turned to look at what the rajku-mar was gazing at, trying to gain an insight into his mind. What was it like to experience such power? To have the divine shakti of brahman flowing through your body? To be possessed by the ability to face and defeat any foe? This was only the second time he had seen the rajkumar fight, but already he respected his prowess as highly as any of the greatest warriors he had seen in action.

The two black-clad mercenary kshatriyas also lowered their swords. They seemed stunned by the sheer extent and speed of the destruction. Looking around, the short, slender one appeared shocked by the number of bandits killed.

'How?' said the kshatriya, his voice husky with emo-tion. 'How did you do all that? So fast?'

Rama glanced around. The question was directed at him. 'My brother and I were inducted with the maha-mantras Bala and Atibala.' He added tersely, 'By Brah-marishi Vishwamitra, whom we are oath-sworn to serve.'

'Vishwamitra,' said the larger kshatriya, his voice low and strangely accented. 'The legendary one? Then the rumours are true. The Seven walk as One again. And the land will be bathed in fire until such time as either the Lord of Lanka or the Lord of Light remains. The Last Battle approaches.'

Lakshman and Rama exchanged glances. Rama replied: 'I do not know what you mean by that, friend. We are rajkumars of Ayodhya, heirs to the kingdom of Kosala. We were recruited by the sage to rid the Southwoods of Asuras, which we did. We don't know anything about Seven walking as One.'

'Who is the Lord of Light?' Lakshman asked curiously.

Bejoo decided it was time to step in.

'Rajkumars, we have not yet been introduced to these two strangers. You ought not to converse with them until I have questioned them and established their credentials. They could well be allies of the bandits who fell out with their leader.'

Almost as if to confirm his words, the larger of the two kshatriyas roared with fury and strode forward, brandishing his sword.

21

'Allies of bandits?' The larger kshatriya pointed his sword at Bejoo menacingly. 'Get off that horse and say that, kshatriya! I will show you whose allies we are!'

'Nakhu!' The shorter one barked the single word sharply, stepping forward. 'These are our friends. The captain meant no offence with his words.'

So the smaller one leads the pair. Bejoo was surprised. He gestured to the two Vajra riders who had galloped up behind the larger kshatriya, ready to defend their captain. They backed up their horses a yard or two, still eyeing the large warrior suspiciously.

The short kshatriya caught the arm of his companion and spoke into his ear.

The difference in their sizes was so immense, the shorter one's head only came up to the taller one's midriff. Bejoo estimated the shorter one to be at best five feet and seven inches of height, fairly below average for a grown kshatriya. The taller one was easily seven and three-quarters, or even more than eight feet tall. His head was almost at Bejoo's shoulder level, and Bejoo was mounted! Bejoo, himself substantially shorter than the six-foot average kshatriya height and overly sensitive about his lack of stature, found himself taking an instant dislike to the tall mercenary. From the glint in the veiled man's eyes, the disaffection was mutual.

The short one's whispered instructions seemed to pacify the taller kshatriya slightly. His eyes continued to glare angrily at Bejoo from above the veil but he lowered his sword, deferring to his shorter companion.

The short one nodded perfunctorily at Rama and Lakshman, then at Bejoo, speaking gruffly.

'My name is Janaki Kumar and this is my close companion Nakhu Dev. We are travelling kshatriyas currently between employers. We heard the sounds of the bears howling and tracked the sounds. When we saw the bandits slaughtering the innocent animals, we felt compelled to help. We were in the process of dealing with them when you arrived.'

Bejoo waited for a moment, then realised that was the end of the man's explanation. 'Is that all you wish to say, kshatriya? No thank you to the rajkumars for having saved your life?'

'Saved our lives?' said the tall one, eyes flashing again. 'What do we look like to you? Boys in need of daiimaas to protect us? Those bandit vermin were not fit to wet our swords. I could have handled all of them alone if I'd had to!'

Bejoo was needled by the man's tone and words. 'You were hopelessly outnumbered, man! Those bandits would have cut you down in another eye-blink if we had not arrived when we did. At least have the humility to admit when you're in over your head! There's no shame in admitting you're outmatched.'

The tall mercenary raised his sword again, shaking it threateningly at Bejoo. 'Outmatched is a word that you must be familiar with, Vajra! It's not a word in our speech. A single Jat kshatriya would have been sufficient to deal with that entire band of forest scum! Look to your own sword when admitting humility. I saw how you sat your horse and issued hand signals to your riders while the two rajkumars here did all the real work. You don't deserve to draw your coin this month! Your masters did all your work for you!'

Bejoo leapt off his horse and strode towards the mercenary. Dismounted, he was a good two feet below the man's eye level. He didn't care. He raised his sword in the two-handed grip he favoured, nodding his head at the same time to order his men to stay back.

'Put your sword where your fat mouth is. I won't have my courage questioned by cheap hire-by-the-day mercenaries like you! You want me off my horse? Here I am now. My men will not interfere. This is between you and me. Let's see if you can fight as well as you can boast now!'

'ENOUGH!'

The voice cut through the bristling tension, startling the scavenger birds that had begun to gather on the treetops above, scenting the sweet odour of dead flesh. A horse whinnied.

Rama strode forward, inserting himself directly between the towering kshatriya and the Vajra captain before either could make another move. He had sheathed his sword and was bare-handed. He held up his arms, facing the captain, leaving his back exposed and vulnerable to the tall kshatriya, whose sword was still drawn and raised.

'Captain Bejoo, in the name of my father Maharaja Dasaratha, your supreme commander and sovereign liege, I order you to sheathe your sword at once. I will not tolerate any more needless fighting. Instead of bartering words with your fellow warriors, you would do better to send your men after those escaping bandits. They can't have got far and your riders might yet catch up with them. I want that leader arrested and taken back to Ayodhya to stand trial. Do you hear and understand me?'

Bejoo backed away at once, lowering his weapon and sheathing it as he bowed to his prince.

'Yes, Rajkumar Rama.' He gestured to Sona Chita, his acting lieutenant. 'You heard the rajkumar! Send half your men after the escapees. The rest of you scour the woods immediately around us and make sure that the area is clear of danger. Move!'

The Vajra riders responded at once, galloping away to carry out their captain's orders.

Bejoo turned back to Rama. 'Forgive me, rajkumar. My sincere apologies for that unnecessary delay. I meant to give that order as soon as the fighting ended. It was this hulking dolt who distracted me with his egoistic boasts!'

Bejoo glared angrily over Rama's shoulder at the tall kshatriya. 'Truth be told, I would not be surprised if he was aligned with those forest vermin and was deliberately delaying us from chasing after them!'

The tall kshatriya raised his left fist, clenching it hard enough that the crunching knuckles sounded like an axeblade being driven into a tree trunk. 'Vajra! Heed your words! I respect the rajkumar's fighting prowess and lion-courage too much to raise my sword before him. But if the devas give me another chance, I shall slice you into small strips and feed you your own meat through every one of your nine orifices!'

Rama raised a hand, turning slowly to face the large kshatriya. 'Conserve your strength, giant-heart. Nobody questions your ability or valour. I saw fight. And had my brother and I not arrived here, I have no doubt that your sword alone would have been sufficient to send every last bandit to the arms of Yamaraj. Accept my admiration and my hand in friendship, and let us not fight any more, either in speech or in deed. Agreed?'

The kshatriya named Nakhu glared down at Rama's

outstretched hand. His eyes lost some of their gloss of anger and softened. He nodded slowly, and held out his own right hand, gripping Rama's tightly. Then he leaned forward and embraced Rama with fierce strength, clapping him on the back hard enough to raise an echo from the woods.

'Prince of Ayodhya, you fight like a legend reborn,' he said gruffly.

'And you like a legend waiting to be born,' Rama replied, clapping the kshatriya's back just as resoundingly.

The tension broken, all of them looked around the clearing, assessing the aftermath of the short but brutally violent conflict.

The shorter kshatriya, the one named Janaki Kumar, looked around at the fallen rksas. He shook his head sadly. 'What did they do to deserve this? Those butchers slew them neither for need nor greed.'

Lakshman came forward and stood by him. 'What do you mean? Surely they meant to fleece their skins and valuable parts? Why else would they kill bears?'

Janaki Kumar shrugged. 'I don't know. But when we came upon the lot of them, all surrounding that poor brave female and her brood, the leader, that horribly scarred man, he was ordering them to kill every last one.'

Rama joined them, looking down at the savagely gashed corpse of a large brown rksa. 'Our new friend is right, Lakshman. If they meant to skin these beasts, they would have been more cautious about how they killed them. Look at these wounds. This fleece would not fetch half the price with these slashes and rents. No, I think the one named Bear-face has some old enmity with them. Probably something to do with his own wounds.'

Janaki Kumar nodded sadly. 'I think Rajkumar Rama has the truth of it. This was meant to be a slaughter, not a capture. Those cubs alone would fetch good prices at any carnival or pit-fight. They would have been using nets and ropes, not weapons and violence.'

Rama turned to look at the shorter kshatriya. The man's eyes were a deep soft brown, betraying his intense sensitivity and intelligence. He reached out a hand of greeting.

'Well met, Janaki Kumar. It is good to come across a fellow kshatriya who abhors needless bloodletting as much as we do.'

Janaki Kumar took his hand, gripping it firmly. Rama clapped the man on the back as hard as he had done with Nakhu Dev. Janaki lurched forward, then recovered and returned the gesture less enthusiastically.

'I would not take you for a believer in peace, Rajkumar Rama,' he said sourly. 'Not after watching how you butchered those bandits.'

Rama shrugged. 'It was unavoidable. I made every attempt to talk them out of fighting. You saw how belligerent their leader was. He would not listen to reason—'

Bejoo interrupted. 'If you ask me, we should have cornered and killed every last one of them. Rid the earth of that scum.'

Nakhu Dev slapped the Vajra captain on the back, using more force than was necessary for the simple gesture. 'I second the Vajra kshatriya on that point. Even one bandit is one too many!'

Bejoo glared angrily at the Jat. He was about to say something when the sound of returning horses distracted his attention. The Vajra riders he had sent to scour the immediate area rode up, their leader saluting his captain.

'Bejoo,' he said, using the totem name as was customary for all Vajra kshatriyas, 'the area is clear of all danger. We had sight of the bear and her cubs, heading northwards. Do you wish us to chase them down?'

'No, you fool,' Bejoo snapped irritably. His back still smarted from the Jat's casual slap. 'Let the bears wander where they will, this is their land.'

A moment later, Son Chita came riding up as well, his face flushed and red with disappointment. 'A thousand times shama, Bejoo. We found tracks leading to a hole in the ground not far from here. I believe it leads into a tunnel that in turn connects with a grotto of caves within the hills. The bandits seem to have escaped into there. We would have to leave our horses to follow them and if it is one of those labyrinthine mazes, we could be a long while chasing them. What are your orders?'

Bejoo cursed and turned to Rama. 'Rajkumar, on you command, I can dispatch half my riders to pursue the bandits down the tunnels. The rest of us can continue our journey.'

Rama thought for a moment, a frown creasing his handsome face. 'No, Captain. They must know those tunnels and caves like the back of their hand. This is their territory. Your men would probably find them eventually, but if there are other bandits in those caves, we would only lose more good kshatriyas. Call off the search and let us all return to the procession. I must speak with Brahmarishi Vishwamitra about these events.'

Janaki Kumar exchanged an uneasy glance with his partner. Bejoo caught the glance and wondered what it meant. He still had his suspicions about these two. Rajkumar Rama had accepted their word and taken them at face value, but had Bejoo been in charge here, he would have liked to question them a while longer – at the tip of a sword preferably.

'Rajkumar Rama,' Janaki Kumar said, 'in that case we

shall take our leave and proceed on our way as well. The hour grows late and we have already been delayed much by this unhappy event.'

Rama nodded, looking distracted. He was still unhappy about not catching the bandit leader, Bejoo guessed.

'Very well, kshatriyas. Well met then. Safe journey.'

They returned his wishes and were about to go – with a distinct look of relief on the shorter one's face, Bejoo noted – when Rama thought of something else and turned back.

'Oh, by the way, friend,' he called out. 'Where exactly are you headed?'

Janaki Kumar called back, 'Nowhere near your fine city, prince of Ayodhya. Our road takes us the other way entirely. We go to Mithila.'

Rama looked at his brother Lakshman, then at Bejoo, then back again at the kshatriyas.

'That is our destination too,' he said to the black-clad warriors. 'And if you are headed there as well, then you must accompany us.'

Bejoo had to make an effort not to curse aloud – not at Rama's words but at the thought of enduring the arrogant tall kshatriya's company a moment longer. But he couldn't protest. His prince had already extended the invitation, and from the look on the face of the shorter kshatriya, it had been accepted.

22

Dasaratha was fighting for his life. The Vajra lieutenant's newly grown talons were gripping his throat in a vice, slowly choking the life out of him. Dasaratha struggled with all the meagre strength he had left. His legs kicked weakly out at his attacker, his arms flailing and beating the man's sides and chest. It was no use. The very suddenness of the assault had robbed him off the little strength he still had. The man was clearly possessed by some supernatural force. His eyes were glowing red as rubies. His head bulged at the sides, almost seeming to expand horizontally.

As Dasaratha gazed up through rapidly blurring vision, he realised with another shock that the man's head wasn't expanding, it was multiplying. Out of each of his ears something was emerging. As each lump of shapeless flesh emerged, it grew instantly larger, puffing up like an obscene balloon of flesh and cartilage and bone, to become a whole head as large as the man's original one. Now, Dasaratha saw with dazed horror, the man had three heads. Out of the ears of the two new heads, two more emerged. Now he had five heads, then seven, then nine.

And then, out of the one on the extreme left, one last head emerged, its mouth working soundlessly, like a newborn baby trying to scream its birth-pains. And to

Dasaratha's stunned surprise, the crushing hold on his throat was released and he fell back on the sunwood throne, gasping and choking and retching for breath, precious breath.

The man stepped back a yard, just enough to allow all ten of his heads a clear view of the Maharaja of Kosala.

'Aja-putra! We meet again!'

Dasaratha struggled to retain consciousness, fighting the waves of blackness and nausea that surged through his beleaguered senses. He could feel the parliament hall reeling and spinning madly, like the sky seen from one of the carousels he had ridden as a boy, astride a horse yoked to a central pole, a dozen boys and girls like himself riding round and round, clapping and laughing and singing. He could even see his father Aja standing by, watching carefully, ready to leap to the rescue if little Dasa should lose his balance. There were daiimaas and helpers all around the carousel, but it had taken Aja a lifetime to see a son born to his name, and little Dasa was more precious than a thousand thrones.

Dasa hadn't fallen. He had ridden that horse around the pole without once lurching or faltering. His father had taken him down proudly at the end of the contest – Dasa was still sitting long after the other children had cried and begged to be taken off – and had kissed his forehead lovingly.

'My son rides like a king,' his father had said aloud. And Dasa had smelled the familiar scent of betelnut and mint on Aja's breath. His father loved eating paan, and for the rest of his life Dasa would always associate that particular scent with his childhood.

There was no scent of betelnut and mint from the creature that stood before him. Only the stomach-churning reek of raw new-birthed flesh and the pungent musk of a wild beast of no discernible species, mingled with the unforgettable fetor of the battlefield – blood, urine, faeces, and the gases of organic decay. This was not his father. This was the beast that had haunted his dreams for the past twenty years, the creature that wanted nothing more than to erase him and his dynasty from existence, along with every other living being on earth.

'I see you are having some difficulty staying on your throne, Dasa! What is it your brahmins say? "Easier to sit an elephant in musth than to sit a gilded throne"? Something like that! Would you like some help staying upright? Or perhaps you'd simply like to move aside and let me take your place? I think I'd be able to bring more dignity to that seat than your pathetic choking and reeling!'

All the heads were speaking. Even through his agony, Dasaratha could tell that much. One spoke the first part of a sentence, another completed it. A third began the next statement, a fourth continued it, a fifth finished it . . . They all had distinctly different voices and accents. One or two even spoke in different languages, moving from Sanskrit highspeech to Awadhi commonspeak to Pali to Prakrit . . . it was a devil's legion of tongues. All the heads grinned and mocked him as he fought to stay conscious. Only the central head stared coldly, its eyes glinting with a deep inner light that seemed to observe all that was happening without actually involving itself. This central head no longer resembled the Vajra lieutenant Bheriya: he had been only a courier designed to carry this message to Ayodhya, Dasaratha now knew. And the message was Ravana himself. Ravana had always possessed great supernatural powers, but to transmit himself through another body across time and space was a feat Dasaratha had not known the demon lord was capable of. Clearly,

Ravana's powers had grown immeasurably since they had last confronted each other.

Gradually he managed to gain some semblance of balance. The brutal attack had shocked him more than hurt him physically. But in his ailing, weakened state, even that brief choking had been enough to exhaust his already drained resources. His throat was a rash of pain and wetness where the three-inch-long talons had gouged and pierced his flesh. His mind searched desperately for a means of calling for help while trying to decide what to do next. If this beast attacked him a second time, he would not survive. His only chance was to communicate his distress to Sumantra and the others standing outside.

But the doors were barred, at his own request, and the hall was large enough that even his loudest cry – should he somehow get a cry out through this crushed larynx – would go unheard. The massive doors were meant to keep in the cacophony of a thousand debating parliamentarians, not transmit the agonised distress cries of a dying maharaja.

Dying? Am I dying then? Is this how I am to go? Thrashing and retching on my own throne, staining the Suryavansha seat with my involuntary effluents? Despoiling this great chair which mighty Manu himself once sat on and whence he proclaimed the great laws of Arya civilisation? Never!

With one ferocious, heart-bursting effort he struggled to sit upright, gripping the arms of the throne to steady himself. Forcing himself to ignore the shooting pain in his chest, the pounding in the back of his head, the pain like a dozen splinters of glass in his throat, he spoke hoarsely to the ten-headed beast.

'Ravana. You're foolish enough to come to me. Good. You save me the effort of sending my army to fetch you then. You shall not leave this chamber alive.'

The ten heads stopped smirking and stared at him. Perhaps not all of them. At least two or three retained their fixed, mocking grins. But several others tried to glance at each other, rolling their eyes theatrically, and at least two that he could see – the ones at either end – grimaced and scowled menacingly at his threat. What threat? he thought as he fought to hold on to consciousness. What could I possibly do in my condition to hurt this being out of hell? Yet he felt better simply for having said that, for having put up some honourable show of dignified response.

The central head snarled at the one to its immediate right, then looked at Dasaratha and smiled with startling warmth. 'Very good! That's more like the Dasaratha I know. What is it your name means in the highspeech? He Who Rides His Chariot In Ten Directions At Once? Meaning that you were able to fight ten enemies at the same time? How quaint of your parents. I remember Aja. He was a good fighter, but much too vain about his looks. He never recovered from that double slash I inflicted on his cheeks. It completely ruined his handsome visage. His self-esteem couldn't stand the shock.'

The taloned hands shot out, imitating the way he had disfigured Dasaratha's father's face, slash-slash. Dasaratha resisted the impulse to wince even when those red-tipped claws came within millimetres of his eyes.

He spoke as coldly as he could, using his hoarseness to make himself sound harsh rather than weak and feeble as he really felt. 'If you have something to say to me, say it. I have no time to sit here and banter with you, Nagadeva.'

Seven out of the ten heads lit up with a variety of smiles.

'Nagadeva! It's been aeons since I was called by that name. Serpent-king. Of course you know that the real king of the nagas is Takshak, he who winds himself around the

blue throat of Shiva the Destroyer. But since I gained
control of the naga legions, it's quite accurate to call me
their king. Among many other titles, of course. And
speaking of nagas, they'll be visiting you soon. Along
with the pisaca legions, and the rakshasas, and uragas,
and vetaals and all my other creeping, crawling, lunging,
leaping and flying associates. Seething like a plague of
locusts across your kingdom, and every other Arya kingdom besides.'

The demon lord droned on sonorously, spelling out in
gory, gruesome detail the ravagement of the Arya nations
he had in mind. He spoke of warships already at sail,
landing soon at ports along the western coastline of the
subcontinental peninsula; teeming millions of Asura forces
starting to make their way towards Ayodhya and its
nearest neighbour, the north-western Arya nation of Kaikeya, from which Dasaratha's Second Queen hailed, the
site of the Last Asura War and the northernmost point the
Asura armies had reached before being pushed back by the
Arya armies led by Dasaratha himself.

He's telling the truth, thought Dasaratha. There was no
doubt that this was the reason the Asura king had come to
Ayodhya, to asassinate him, and before doing so, lecture
him on all the horrors he would visit on his race and his
kingdom, gloating over his final triumph. But as the
creature with ten heads continued his fiendish monologue,
Dasaratha's mind worked on another matter that had
unexpectedly come to his attention.

Even through his mist of pain and disorientation, the
maharaja had begun to see something very strange and
interesting. Each time the demon king spoke, the ten faces
took different sides in the utterance. As if some disagreed
violently, others concurred, and yet others were of a
wholly different but not disagreeable opinion. It was

not unlike some heated political debates Dasaratha had
administered; arguments over borders and river-sharing
where a dozen clan chiefs took as many different positions,
all appealing simultaneously to the maharaja to heed their
individual stand. The only difference was that the ten
heads in this case were not on ten different bodies but
on one.

And just as with the differing heads of state, so also with
these differing heads of Ravana, there was a pattern to the
apparent chaos. Each time the Lord of Lanka said something, there was always one head that remained silent.
While the words came from any or even all of the other
mouths, one mouth remained wordless, one pair of eyes
watched intently, one face stayed impassive and still,
sharply watchful. A glimmer of insight came to Dasaratha
then, even as he turned a deaf ear to Ravana's descriptions
of the Asura cities that would be built on the ashes of
Ayodhya and Kaikeya in the aftermath of the genocide.

That's the head that is in control at that moment. He can
use all the heads when thinking or acting, but when he
speaks, one head focuses completely on the task and you can
see which one it is just from its expression. The face in
question always had a look of rapt concentration, as if the
effort of speaking aloud took more effort than anything else.

And indeed, Dasaratha realised with that inspired insight that sometimes comes to minds pushed beyond the
limit of exhaustion and rational thought, might it not be
that a being with ten heads would find the simple act of
speech to be the most difficult of all physical actions?
Because while every other action required the head or
heads to control the rest of the body's limbs, speech
involved the heads themselves. What if speaking
was the action during which the demon lord was most
vulnerable?

He held his breath, unable to believe that he had been given such a major insight into the process of Ravana's inner workings. Not that he knew yet what to do with this information, but he was certain that it would be of some use, somehow, some day.

Rama, he thought for no particular reason, I must tell this to Rama when he comes home. It will be helpful to him at the crucial moment. The moment he thought this, he blinked, wondering why it had come to mind. Then it passed into the turmoil of warring thoughts and sensations battling for space in his consciousness.

Ravana fell silent suddenly, several of his heads peering suspiciously at the maharaja. Dasaratha realised he must have smiled involuntarily, unable to conceal the exultant pleasure of his unexpected inspiration. He knew that in another moment the demon lord would make his move and strike him down, washing the sunwood throne in his blood.

Still, the very fact that he had gained that brilliant insight into the inner workings of his arch-foe gave him renewed strength and hope. It provided the last ounce of extra courage he needed to put into action the plan he had formulated during the past few moments. He sent up a final prayer to his maker, fully aware that he would probably not survive this last foray. May the devas watch over my family and my people.

With a warrior's cry of rage, Dasaratha threw himself sideways, off the throne. He landed on the royal dais with an impact that felt as if he had broken a rib or three. He lay on the carpeted floor for an instant, then forced himself to rise to his feet again, staggering with all the grace of a drunken dancer to the object placed at the end of the dais.

The creature with ten heads bellowed as Dasaratha approached his goal.

'Foolish one! I was prepared to show you some mercy yet, for old times' sake. Now I will show you real pain! Pain such as you have never felt or dreamed of before.'

Dasaratha reached the ceremonial gong that stood beside the First Queen's throne. It was used to announce the formal start and end of a parliament session, indicating to the assembly that they should be seated or rise respectively. The long wooden ringer was hung on a rack above it. He didn't bother to try to fumble with the rope from which it was suspended. There wasn't time. He could feel the rushing wind and foul fetor of the demon lord at his back, flying at him with enough force to crush his organs and shatter his bones.

Dasaratha swung his clenched fist with all the energy he had left in his body and struck the gong with one resounding blow. The sound echoed through the chamber like a victory bell – or a death knell.

KAAND 2

THE TWO TOWERS

I

Sumantra was the first to hear the gong and react.

'Maharaja!' he cried. 'Open the doors! Open them now! Hurry!'

The palace guards rushed to do his bidding. Rajkumars Shatrugan and Bharat had been standing nearby, conversing with each other intently. The instant the gong sounded, they reacted as well, knowing something had happened in the hall.

Sumantra gestured agitatedly at them. 'Shatrugan, go fetch Guruji! Run!'

Shatrugan sprinted away. He was the faster runner of the two; Bharat's muscular bulk made him a formidable mace-fighter but slowed him somewhat. Bharat drew his sword and stood by Sumantra as four guards lifted the heavy teakwood bolt off the door and lurched sideways carrying it out of the way. Sumantra and Bharat threw their shoulders against the massive ten-yard-high doors, joining their strength to the ten other guards pushing against them. The doors opened as fast as the laws of gravity and motion allowed, seeming like an eternity. Even as he pushed, Sumantra yelled at a sergeant of the guards to fetch reinforcements and Captain Drishti Kumar, the commander of the maharaja's personal security.

As soon as the doors were ajar, Bharat and Sumantra

slipped inside. The prime minister had taken a lance from one of the guards and held it firmly in both hands like a two-handed sword, ready to lunge at the first sign of threat. They entered into pitch blackness: the torches in the hall had all been extinguished. Even the daylight spilling in through the open doorway barely illuminated a third of the long approach to the royal dais. Most of the hall's fifty-by-seventy-yard dimensions was utterly dark.

An eerie silence hung over the vast chamber. Their footfalls and the clanking of the guards' armour and weapons echoed and rang out through the empty space. Bharat and Sumantra reached the end of the gritty pool of light coming in from behind, and ventured into the sightless dark ahead, making their way towards the dais, not knowing what lay in wait for them.

'Maharaja Dasaratha?' Sumantra's voice was clear and filled with concern. 'Are you well?'

'Pitashree?' Bharat called, using the formal term of address required by propriety when addressing his father in public. 'Are you seated on the throne? Where are you?'

There was no answer to their queries. The deafening silence loomed before them like the thick, dense darkness through which they proceeded.

Sumantra gave a guard beside him an order to fetch torches. The man passed the message down the line, but Bharat guessed it might be several minutes before the light arrived. It was still bright afternoon outside and the torch-lighters would not be in use yet. They would have to be fetched, and that would take a moment or longer.

As he stepped slowly ahead into the wall-thick darkness, Bharat could feel the hairs standing on the back of his neck and hands, and a sensation like ants crawling up his thighs. Behind him, several guards spoke invocations softly, urgently. All Arya kshatriyas feared sorcery far more than they feared mortal injury. The unmistakable sense of magic was thick in the silent, dark assembly chamber.

Bharat felt his shin bang against an obstacle. He restrained the impulse to slash wildly with his sword, his mind reassuring his warrior instinct that it knew what the object was.

'The royal dais,' he said softly, more for his own benefit than for Sumantra's ears.

The prime minister replied nevertheless, whispering to be heard only by the prince: 'Bharat, you go to your left, I'll ascend from the right. We meet at the top in the centre of the dais, by the sunwood throne.'

Bharat whispered a curt 'Okay' in response. He moved left, knowing the prime minister would communicate the same message to the guards to ensure that they didn't tangle with each other in the darkness. Where were those torches? They ought to have arrived by now. He went up the high steps of the dais, lifting each booted foot carefully, trying to make as little sound as possible. The dais, like the rest of the chamber, was carpeted, but the structure itself was wood and would produce a muffled noise if he hit it with his heel. Surprisingly, even the guards behind him and on the other side of the dais made no sound as they ascended the seven foot-high steps to the topmost level.

As he lifted his foot to climb on to the seventh step, light returned to the hall. It blazed forth with such startling suddenness that Bharat was momentarily blinded. His sword hand instinctively flew up to shield his eyes, his kshatriya responses regarding the assault as being an attack like any physical strike.

If an assault, it was devastatingly effective: for a few precious seconds Bharat could see only stars exploding and bright colours flashing. If the enemy had chosen to strike him down at that very instant, he would have had no chance. As it was, he was loath to lash out with his sword for fear of accidentally hitting his father, whom he still expected to be somewhere about here. Somehow, the torches in the hall had all regained their light at once. It was impossible, he knew, but it had happened and he had no time to waste debating that trivial detail when all his attention was focused on seeing what the sudden infusion of light enabled him to witness.

The sight that met his eyes when they adjusted was the last thing on earth he expected to see.

Maharaja Dasaratha was seated on his throne, in that familiar pose in which Bharat had seen him countless times before. A forward-leaning posture, the maharaja's right elbow resting on the end of his right thigh, almost at his knee. His chin rested on his curled right fist, as he stared pensively into the distance. His crown was on his brow. Although still showing the wasted appearance caused by his cankerous disease, he sat with the dignity and majesty born of a lifetime of ruling and generations of Suryavansha kings.

'Pitashree?' Bharat approached the sunwood throne cautiously, lowering his sword but still unable to rid his mind of the certainty that something was still amiss here. From the far right of the large dais, the prime minister also approached, lance still in hand but point now lowered, his face reflecting the same confusion and suspicion that Bharat felt.

'Maharaj?' Sumantra said cautiously.

Dasaratha blinked twice, as if pulling his mind out of some vexing contemplation that had involved him for several moments. He looked up at Bharat and his face creased in a weary smile.

'Arya-putra,' he said, hoarsely but warmly. 'Approach me, my son.'

Bharat went to him, sheathing his sword. He felt curiously vulnerable doing so, but had no choice. He couldn't very well approach the enthroned king of Kosala with naked steel in hand, even if it was his own father – especially if it was his father! On the steps of the dais, caught by the abruptly returned illumination in various poses of stealthy climbing, the palace guards also blinked at one another and sheathed their weapons hastily. They retreated backwards down the steps as Bharat went to his father, bowing their heads and muttering formal apologies for their transgression.

Bharat stood before his father's throne and bent his knee. He felt Dasaratha's heavy hand rest on his head a moment. It felt unusually warm. The maharaja was running a fever. That was not unusual in itself; the maharaja was ill, after all.

'My son, rise now. I have important work for you. I wish you and your brother to take two divisions of the army apiece and ride separately to Kaikeya and to Gandahar at once. There you will warn your respective grandfathers of the imminent Asura invasion and stay to help them defend their cities. Only after you have repelled the invaders successfully will you return with whatever forces you can muster to help defend Ayodhya.'

Bharat looked up at his father after this astonishing speech. The maharaja's words left no room for confusion or question. But he still couldn't comprehend what he had just been told. More than that, it was the bizarre circumstances in which he had been given the command that disoriented him. One moment ago, he had been advancing through the pitch-black hall, anxious that his father had been attacked by some treacherous means, perhaps even by that very Vajra rider Bheriya – even though the man had been checked and found to be exactly what he claimed to be, a Vajra kshatriya come to deliver a message. And now here was his father issuing a command to Bharat to undertake the most momentous mission of his entire life. Two divisions apiece? With only four in total, that meant half the army would go with Bharat to Kaikeya, the other half with Shatrugan to Gandahar! The entire Kosala army, leaving its capital city unprotected.

Pradhan Mantri Sumantra came to his rescue. Bowing formally to his liege, the prime minister asked in his typical unassuming, sincere way, 'Maharaj, forgive my asking, but what makes you fear an Asura invasion of the capital cities of Kaikeya and Gandahar? We have no word of such enemy intrusions from these Arya nations.'

Maharaja Dasaratha raised his hand and gestured to the far right of the dais. All eyes, riveted on him these past few moments, turned to look at that part of the hall.

'He brought me the news, under instructions from the Brahmarishi Vishwamitra himself. The unfortunate man suffered mortal injuries and was not aware of it. After delivering his message his strength was drained and he dropped dead, accidentally striking that gong as he fell.'

The man named Bheriya lay at the foot of the ceremonial gong. Even from where he stood, Bharat could see the telltale trickles of blood from the man's ears, nostrils and mouth that could only mean deep internal injuries.

For that one instant, as every pair of eyes in the hall stared in amazement at the fallen courier at the corner of the dais, nobody noticed the maharaja's face change. For the briefest of moments, Dasaratha's features flickered like a shadow cast by a torch, seeming to ripple and alter into the visage of his greatest enemy, the Lord of Lanka. His eyes, naturally a clear greyish-blue, glowed and turned ruby-red for that same fraction of an instant, and his lips curled slowly to reveal his teeth in a shadow of a ghostly grin. Then, before anyone could spy this shocking change, his face composed itself once more, and he was Maharaja Dasaratha again.

2

Maharaja Dasaratha's weary eyes peered down at his sons and the captain of his guards.

Bharat and Shatrugan had expressions of relief on their faces. 'Pitashree,' Bharat said, 'thank the devas you're safe. When we heard the gong sound and rushed in to find the hall in pitch darkness, we feared the worst.'

Dasaratha nodded. 'I was alarmed too when all the torches went out at once. Captain Drishti Kumar, do you know what might have caused such an unusual phenomenon?'

The smartly uniformed young officer bowed his head to his sovereign. 'Forgive me, maharaj. I am equally at a loss to explain it.'

Bharat said thoughtfully, 'It must be sorcery. Our enemies were angered because the Vajra lieutenant succeeded in delivering his message and struck him down through the use of black powers. Then they darkened the hall, maybe with the intention of causing harm to you as well, Father.'

Dasaratha looked impressed. 'A commendable explanation. You may well be right, son. Who knows what powers the Lord of Lanka possesses?'

He rose to his feet unsteadily. Both Shatrugan and Bharat came forward to help him but he gestured them aside. He walked across the royal dais slowly, the effort showing on his illness-ravaged features.

Ignoring the corpse of the dead Vajra kshatriya, Dasaratha made his way to a large wall fresco that portrayed the fan-like shape of the subcontinent, with geographical features painstakingly depicted and the borders of the seven Arya nations clearly delineated. Pradhan Mantri Sumantra, anticipating his king's need, handed him a three-yard-long pointer which the maharaja used as he spoke.

'Once again, I'll explain my orders to make sure that both of you are clear on what you are to do. Bharat, you shall take two divisions of the army and ride post-haste to your grandfather's palace at Kaikeya. Shatrugan, you will take two divisions and proceed to your grandfather's palace at Gandahar. You will both remain there with your forces to defend those two great nations against the coming Asura invasion.

'As I have explained, the Asura armies will land on the western coast, travelling north-east up the Indus valley until they reach Gandahar and Kaikeya, followed by Bharata. If you stem the attack at those two northernmost kingdoms, they will never make it across the Sindhu Kush pass. We shall break their attack in the very first stage of the war. Once they have been repelled, they will attempt to make their way down to the great Kutch desert, then turn towards the north-east. They will avoid going fully north as that will put them between the Jat clans and the Five Rivers. Instead they will march further east until they reach Kosala and then Videha, where they will launch their second campaign.'

Shatrugan frowned. 'But Pitashree, if Bharat and I take our entire army with us, how will Ayodhya defend itself when that happens?'

Bharat spoke for his father. 'We shall have returned long before then. The Asura forces may be able to travel swiftly now because they cross the ocean in ships. But over land as harsh and hostile as the Kutch desert, it will take them several weeks to reach the borders of Kosala and Videha. We will be back home and ready to meet them long before they arrive.'

Shatrugan frowned. 'But what if they don't retreat down the Sindhu river valley? Or if they divide their forces into half and leave half to besiege Gandahar and Kaikeya while sending the other half to Kosala and Videha?'

'Well said, my son,' Dasaratha said. 'Guru Vashishta taught you well at his gurukul. As well as you, Bharat. Your grasp of military strategy makes me proud. It is indeed possible that Ravana may choose to divide his forces at that point. If he makes that mistake, then I shall send word to one of you, most likely Shatrugan, to return with his half of our army. Then all the seven nations shall unite our forces in a two-pronged attack,' Dasaratha jabbed with the pointer at the sinuously winding line of the Sindhu river and then at the western border of Kosala, 'and we shall drive them back into the briny ocean whence they came!'

He smiled as both the rajkumars broke out into spontaneous applause, joined by the palace guards who had been watching and listening to their king's explanation with rapt interest.

'It will take more than numbers to defeat us, I can promise you that,' he said, handing the pointer back to Sumantra. 'Whatever they may choose to do, we will prevail in the end.'

He gestured at the corpse of Bheriya lying beside him. 'Couriers such as this brave Vajra warrior will bring word of any new decisions I make to each of you. Now, I urge you to ride for Gandahar and for Kaikeya with all the speed that the devas and nature gifts you. Do not stay even to wish your mothers goodbye or to speak to anyone else. Captain Drishti Kumar and Pradhan Mantri Sumantra shall go with you to ensure that the army assembles at once. Since we are already on full alert, it will be a matter of only a few hours before they are ready to embark on the journey. Now, let us spend no more time on words when swords are what are needed. Go at once, my sons. Ayushmaanbhav!'

Bending to touch their father's feet to take his blessings in the traditional Arya way, Bharat and Shatrugan rose again with eyes glossy with emotion. They turned and strode out of the hall, followed closely by Drishti Kumar and Pradhan Mantri Sumantra, leaving only the maharaja's personal quad of bodyguards and a few other soldiers, who began removing the body of Bheriya.

Dasaratha descended the steps of the royal dais. He walked to his travelling seat. The four bodyguards were standing at its corners, waiting for him to be seated.

The maharaja glanced once again at the fallen Vajra lieutenant's body, now being carried out by the palace guards. His haggard mouth twitched with a faint ghostly smile as he watched the body being taken across the parliament hall to the yawning open doors.

A figure stood silhouetted in that open doorway, the outline leaving no doubt that it was Guru Vashishta.

As Dasaratha hesitated, his hand on the top of the travelling chair, the guru strode forward, advancing towards the maharaja.

Guru Vashishta gestured to the palace guards lined up alongside the royal dais.

'Leave us.'

The officer in charge of the quad glanced uneasily at

the maharaja. Dasaratha, standing by the travelling seat, his bodyguards ready to raise it once he sat, nodded once. The officer gestured to his men and they filed out quickly and efficiently. The maharaja looked at his bodyguards and dismissed them as well with a gesture. They left unhappily. Twice today they had been ordered to leave their master alone; both times, the maharaja had encountered trouble.

Without bothering to look back, Vashishta spoke briefly, a single line from a four-line verse.

The hall doors slowly swung shut of their own volition. The last of Dasaratha's bodyguards leapt out of the way just as the massive doors came together with a reverberating crash. As the echoes died away, the guru walked down the long approach to the royal dais.

'So, Dasaratha, you have dispatched the army to Gandahar and Kaikeya.'

Dasaratha inclined his head slightly, showing the spiritual adviser formal respect. 'Yes, Guru-dev.'

'And this information regarding the Asura invasion plan was brought to you by the Vajra kshatriya?'

'Indeed, Guru-dev.'

'A man named Bheriya, who served as second-in-command to Captain Bejoo, the trusted commander of your personal Vajra fighting force.'

'Yes, Guru-dev.'

'This Bheriya informed you in a private audience that Ravana's troops had set sail from Lanka and were heading towards the delta of the Sindhu river. Thence they would travel upriver as far as they could sail, then continue north on foot until they reached Gandahar.'

'Yes, Guru-dev.'

The guru had reached the travelling chair. He was a yard from the maharaja. The two men were face to face.

Despite his decrepit condition, Dasaratha was a large man, a big-boned, well-built warrior who had spent a lifetime engaged in martial pursuits. His muscles sagged sadly, his skin was liver-spotted and grey with age, his hair thinning, pouches under his eyes, deep furrows scarring his forehead and cheeks. But he still retained some vestige of his former glory; if not the full strength of the formidable raj-kshatriya personality that had made allies feel proud and enemies hesitate. He was still a maharaja, and he looked it.

He met the guru's eyes and held them for a moment. Then he looked down, as was appropriate in the presence of a seer-mage of such great stature. Vashishta had stood thus before each one of Dasaratha's ancestors, guiding the Suryavansha dynasty for over eight hundred years. And even those centuries of service were only a fraction of the seer's seven thousand years on this mortal plane. Dasaratha was king indeed; yet Vashishta was a maker of kings.

And a destroyer as well, should he choose to become one.

But it was not his awareness of the seer's superior power that caused Dasaratha to lower his gaze and incline his head. It was sanskriti: the Arya code of conduct that required that elders be shown respect and humility under all circumstances.

But what the maharaja did next was not called for by Arya sanskriti. He shut his eyes.

Guru Vashishta approached Dasaratha. As he came closer, the seer's eyes fastened on Dasaratha's face with the full intensity of his searching gaze. It was as if a blazing torch was being held to the maharaja's face.

The blue glow of brahman flashed in the guru's eyes, growing steadily brighter. It grew and grew until it was a beacon of searing intensity in the chamber. Had anyone been present at even the far ends of the vast empty hall, they would have been compelled to turn away or shield their eyes, so bright was the glow from the guru's pupils. Motes of gold and silver danced in the blue light, and a few strands of red winked in and out of the streaming waves emanating from the seer-mage's sun-bright pupils. The light swirled around Dasaratha, enveloping him in a cocoon of dazzling intensity. His white vastra caught the light and absorbed it, making his very skin seem to turn blue. Dasaratha gasped, his arms pulled away from his body by the uncontestable power of brahman.

The maharaja's eyes remained closed, but it was evident that the effort was taking a toll. Sweat poured freely down his face and neck, staining his vastra. The lines and furrows around his eyes deepened to knife cuts, his ashen colouring tinted deep blue by the supernatural light. He grunted, his head jerking this way, then that. A great struggle was taking place.

Dasaratha's feet left the ground. The blue cocoon of brahman light raised him up, and he rose towards the twenty-yard-high ceiling of the parliament hall. His arms were at right angles to his body, his legs apart, like a man bound akimbo by invisible ropes. His lips parted, showing once-strong white teeth now turning grey with age and decay. His nostrils flared, seeking to draw breath but inhaling only the pure aquamarine light. He floated upwards until he was midway between ceiling and floor. There he hung suspended in the cocoon of brahman.

Guru Vashishta began chanting a mantra. His voice was strong and clear but soft, loud enough to be heard by the maharaja suspended above, but not by anyone more than a few yards away. This mantra was not meant to be recited in the presence of mortals. It was a mantra reserved for devas. Yet Guru Vashishta had to resort to its use now; he had no other choice. There were no mantras that could free a mortal from the possession of an evil Asura aatma. Only this one, a mantra meant to give a mortal the power of a deva for the brief fraction of time needed to expel the demonaic spirit from his mortal form.

Vashishta continued chanting the mantra. He built to a climax, the musical Sanskrit rhythms rising in pitch and intensity until they were no longer mere words being spoken aloud, but threads knitting the eternal fabric of space and time itself, infusing the possessed maharaja with the light of brahman, forcing the shakti that held the universe together to enter into every pore, every cell, every atom of the maharaja's being. Suffusing them the way the blue light suffused every square inch of the assembly hall – even the far side of pillars and the depths of the darkest crevices. Leaving no place for the evil aatma to hide. Once the searing light of brahman became too much for it to bear, like a rat caught on a sinking ship the Asura aatma would either drown in the flood and be absorbed into the flow of brahman itself, or flee.

It resisted as long as it possibly could. Then it could withstand no more.

Ten yards above the floor of the hall, Dasaratha's mouth opened to release a shrill scream. A piercing banshee wail of dismay and disgust. The scream carried through the walls and doors, making the bodyguards and palace guards waiting outside look up nervously and shudder. Strange times had come to Ayodhya. Dark times.

Then the maharaja's eyes flew open.

They were blood-red. They resembled the eyes of the corpse of Bheriya when it had begun to transform into the imitation of its lord and master, sprouting the nine extra heads. But no heads sprouted from Dasaratha. Only the eyes glowed bright jewel-red for a moment, blazing with a fevered ruby light that tried to dispel and destroy the light of brahman. Tried but failed.

Then the eyes closed, and the maharaja slumped in mid-air, his body turning limp and lifeless.

The blue cocoon of brahman holding him up vanished, winking out as abruptly as a torch doused in a pond.

Dasaratha plummeted like a sack of grain.

The guru caught him easily.

On the tip of his right forefinger.

3

Once, the River Shona was a flourishing, powerful stream all of fifty yards wide. Now it was reduced to a mere ten yards of shallow but still cheerfully flowing clear water. To either side of this rivulet lay twenty yards of old riverbed, exposed to the sun and sloping upwards on either side until it joined the valley floor. The riverbed was mostly pebbles over gleaming yellow sand, literally the gold, or sona, that had given the river its name. Over time, the name had lapsed into the commonspeak pronunciation, which tended to turn the Sanksrit 's' sound into the easier-to-pronounce 'sh'. Hence, Sona became Shona, and so it stayed.

As the Siddh-ashrama procession emerged from the wooded hill road into the Shona valley, the evening sun picked out the mineral stones in the riverbed and turned them into a glittering display of jewellery fit for a queen. The first to step on to the bed were the Vajra bigfoot, their ponderous feet raising a crunching sound on the pebbles and shale that sounded like a thousand silbuttas grinding spices at once.

The crunching grew louder and more varied in intensity and rhythm as the brahmins and brahmacharyas followed, and by the time the Vajra horses and chariots joined in too, it sounded like a herd of elephants munching on sugarcane stalks.

Brahmarishi Vishwamitra went down to the edge of the water and stood gazing at the low evening sun, his staff held loosely in his right hand, ang-vastra flapping in the gentle breeze. It was cooler here than on the main marg they had been on before the incident in the hills, Rama realised, and the thickly wooded area alongside the river shielded them from the low sun's rays.

He and Lakshman stopped beside a large boulder that bore the signs of water erosion over centuries, perhaps even millennia. The boulder was still mossy in places, indicating that the river had been in spate last monsoon season. The two black-clad kshatriyas who had been walking just behind them stopped a little distance away, conferring quietly.

Lakshman indicated them without actually pointing or nodding his head. Rama and he were familiar enough with one another's looks and gestures to know what the other was referring to without needing to be led by the nose.

'What do you think their story is, brother?'

Rama shrugged. 'Why shouldn't they just be what they say they are?'

Lakshman shook his head. 'Something doesn't fit. The bigger one said he was a Jat. The other one clearly isn't a Jat. So what are they doing together? Jats don't mingle well, as you could see for yourself during that fight with Bejoo-chacha. They're fiercely loyal to other Jats but they regard all non-Jats as potential enemies until they've proven otherwise. A Jat wouldn't be travelling with a non-Jat and fighting back to back with him.'

'How do you know the shorter one isn't a Jat too?'

Lakshman sighed and looked down at his hands. They were still stained with blood from the encounter. Not his own blood though. 'Because if he is, then he's the shortest

Jat I've ever seen. The Jat clans are the tallest Aryas, remember?'

'Maybe he's young. He seemed young to me, maybe our age. Maybe he hasn't finished growing yet.'

Lakshman shook his head. 'I think there's a law that says even Jat newborn babes have to be at least six feet tall.'

Rama smiled. 'A law?'

'A maharaja's law,' Lakshman said solemnly.

Rama looked at his brother, trying to picture a newborn Jat babe, swaddled in black from head to toe, over six feet tall and lying on his back, bawling for milk. Lakshman seemed to be imagining the same picture: both brothers broke into helpless laughter, startling the brahmins bustling around the riverbed at first, then drawing smiles and grins as the ashramites understood that the paroxysm wasn't some rare variety of Ayodhyan affliction, simply two young boys sharing a good laugh. Even the gaunt, lined face of Vishwamitra, standing by the riverside, reflected a wisp of amusement at their hysterical attack.

When they had regained control of themselves, Rama punched Lakshman in the shoulder. 'Don't make jokes like that. These brahmins think of us as the heroes of Bhayanak-van. We have a reputation to live up to now.'

Lakshman punched him back. 'So? Heroes can't laugh once in a while? Next you'll say we can't go into the woods to relieve ourselves because they musn't suspect we're human! Or maybe you think we should wait until nobody's looking and then sneak away? And while we're at it, we should sleep with our eyes open and never drink or eat either so they think we're avatars!'

Rama put a hand on Lakshman's chest and pushed him. 'Who says avatars don't drink or eat or sleep or . . . act human? That's why they're called avatars, not devas, silly! They're just reincarnations of devas born in human guise.'

Lakshman pushed Rama back. 'So maybe the brahmins think we're devas. Immortal, invulnerable, superhuman.' He pretended to tap his chin thoughtfully. 'And I bet devas don't have to go into the woods to relieve themselves. Not more than once every thousand years or so!'

Rama wrinkled his nose and waved a hand at Lakshman. 'Go back to Ayodhya! I disown you. You can't be my brother.'

Lakshman pretended to gawp in amazement. 'I'm not your brother? That explains it all! No wonder you're always so serious and I'm always trying to make you relax and have a laugh or two. If you were maharaja, you would pass a law against jesting or laughing!'

Rama nodded. 'Like the law against Jat babies being less than six feet tall at birth.'

Lakshman looked at him.

Rama tried to keep a straight face.

A moment later, they were both laughing hysterically again.

'Rajkumars?'

Rama struggled to get his laughter under control and looked around. The original subject of his conversation with Lakshman stood before them. Nakhu Deva's dark eyes scowled suspiciously above his veil, while Janaki Kumar just looked curious, even a bit amused.

The shorter man's voice reflected his amusement. 'Are we interrupting something?'

Lakshman managed to stop laughing long enough to say, 'Just a little debate on the lawful size of babies.'

'Babies?' Janaki Kumar's eyes looked puzzled.

Rama nudged Lakshman in the ribs to make him stop laughing. 'You must excuse my brother. His head is addled by the sun.'

Janaki Kumar seemed to understand. His eyes twinkled. 'I see. I do hope he recovers quickly.'

Rama smiled. 'Was there something you desired, Janaki?'

'Janaki Kumar, please. I prefer to be called by my full name. Janaki is a very common name. It causes confusion.'

Rama wanted to add that Janaki Kumar was just as common. Instead he said, 'I apologise that you were unable to speak more fully to our guru. He was keen that we should reach the Shona so we could make camp well before sundown.'

He was referring to the aftermath of the fight in the hills. When they had returned to the procession and briefly outlined what had occurred, Vishwamitra had listened without comment, then had suggested that since the hills were clear of danger for the moment at least, they would take that road rather than the long way around and camp by the River Shona for the night. Rama had wanted to introduce the kshatriyas to the brahmarishi but Vishwamitra had immediately called the order to march forward again. Rama had told the kshatriyas he would formally introduce them when they were camped and the sage was more relaxed.

Janaki Kumar didn't seem to mind the delay. 'Please don't apologise, rajkumar. A sage of Brahmarishi Vishwamitra's stature has more important things on his mind than meeting every passing kshatriya on the road to Mithila. We just wanted to thank you and your brother once again for aiding us in that fight against the bandits and for inviting us to join your company.'

Rama noted that Lakshman had managed to get his hysterics under control at last. 'Truth be told, Janaki Kumar, it's a pleasure to have you with us. My brother and I are so eager for news of Mithila. Perhaps you'll sit with us awhile and talk with us about your fine capital city.'

Lakshman added with a painstakingly maintained straight face, 'And your fine rajkumaris Sita and Urmila.'

Rama kicked Lakshman in the shin. Lakshman cocked an eyebrow, then kicked Rama back.

Nakhu Dev looked at them suspiciously. 'What about Rajkumari Sita?'

Rama shook his head self-deprecatingly. 'Just a little jest between my brother and me.'

Nakhu Dev scowled at Lakshman. 'I don't like jests about my rajkumari.'

'Your rajkumari?' Lakshman raised his eyebrows and waggled them. 'I thought she was the whole kingdom's rajkumari. Unless Videha has begun allotting princesses to each citizen individually!'

Rama shot Lakshman a warning glance. 'My brother really doesn't know when to stop. He means no disrespect by his jests.'

'That's all right,' Janaki Kumar said in an odd tone of voice. Nakhu Dev continued to scowl angrily at both Rama and Lakshman. The giant looked as if he might challenge them to a fight at any second.

Rama looked about for some means to dislodge Lakshman from his childish mood and to change the track of the conversation. The Siddh-ashrama brahmins had begun to corral their livestock nearby, and the lowing and mooing of the cattle was growing louder and more distracting. He gestured at the riverbed.

'Shall we walk by the river a short way? We could talk more freely about Mithila and get to know one another better. I am keen to ask you many things about your beautiful city.'

Janaki Kumar's slender shoulders twitched in a small

shrug. 'As you please, Rajkumar Rama. But I must warn you, I am a simple wandering kshatriya with no great insight into the affairs of kings and kingdoms. I know nothing of Mithila politics apart from what is generally known.'

'And what is that?'

They walked downriver slowly, the gravelly sand crunching noisily underfoot. Rama and Janaki Kumar were abreast, with Lakshman and Nakhu Dev behind. A gentle breeze wafted from the west, bringing scents of wildflower and honey. The riverbed wound sharply around a bend, almost turning into its own course before unwinding to the right again. The curve took at least a hundred yards to straighten out and took them out of sight of the main campsite, although the noise from behind remained clearly audible.

Rama broached the conversation with the most innocuous question he could find. 'So, Janaki Kumar, which part of Videha do you and your companion hail from?'

Janaki Kumar glanced back at his tall companion before replying vaguely, 'Oh, you know the life of a travelling kshatriya, rajkumar. We belong to everywhere and no-where.'

Rama didn't comment on the answer. He wished they would remove their veils and headcloths. The masking added a layer of inscrutability. Although reading the shorter kshatriya's eyes wasn't that hard a chore: bright, alive, and very attractive to look at, they seemed to be clear indicators of the emotions and thoughts passing through the kshatriya's mind.

'Tell us about Mithila then. What business takes you there? A new assignment perhaps?'

Again that quick exchange of looks between the two, then Janaki Kumar replied, 'Yes. An assignment.'

'Whom will your swords serve there?'

Janaki Kumar slipped a finger between his ang-vastra's neckline and his skin. The cloth was damp with sweat-stains and the unmistakable salt-rings that revealed that the kshatriya hadn't changed garb in at least a day or two. He worked the finger around from side to side as if trying to loosen the tight upper garment.

'Nobody you would know, rajkumar. Just a client.'

'I know many people in Mithila, Janaki Kumar. By name if not personally. At least not for a few years – it's been a while since my brothers and I visited your fine capital.'

'Brothers,' Janaki Kumar said quickly. 'Yes, you have two more brothers, do you not? How are the rajkumars Bharat and Shatrugan?'

'They're well, thank you. At least they were well when I saw them last nine days past. We look forward to being reunited with them once more, as well as with the rest of our family. So, as I was saying, if you will tell me your new client, it's quite likely I might know him or her by name.'

'I sincerely doubt it, rajkumar,' Janaki Kumar said, deflecting the question once more.

They had reached a point where the side of the riverbed on which they were walking tilted as the river swung into the inward curve. They found themselves walking on the sloping sand-and-shale incline that grew more sharply graded by the yard. Janaki Kumar rose steadily to become a head higher than Rama, while Lakshman had the unusual opportunity of equalling the Jat kshatriya's formidable elevation. Rama sensed another of Lakshman's quips coming on and quickly continued before his brother said something else to offend the kshatriyas.

'Well, surely your new employer must be someone important if he or she has coin enough to hire two excellent kshatriyas such as yourselves. Is he a trader or merchant? A keeper of stores perhaps? A grain transporter? A brewer? A goldsmith?'

Janaki Kumar seemed to be growing hotter by the minute. His hands now played with his headcloth's band, as if it had suddenly grown too tight for comfort. He continued to sweat despite the pleasant breeze blowing downriver. His attention was riveted on negotiating the sloping curve of the bank and he didn't meet Rama's eyes, making it even more difficult to read his expression.

'Nobody of note, rajkumar.'

Lakshman spoke up. 'They work for the royal court of Mithila.'

Rama glanced back, as surprised as Janaki Kumar, whose eyes blinked rapidly as he looked back at Lakshman.

4

'W-w-what makes you say that, Rajkumar Lakshman?'
Janaki Kumar asked, faltering slightly.

Lakshman continued breezily, 'The way you fight. You
aren't just any ordinary travelling kshatriyas. You two are
army-schooled. As part of our training, my brothers and I
were made to study every notable fighting style in the Arya
nations as well as several major ones from foreign lands. I
know the Mithila martial style when I see it.' He paused
before adding with a smile, 'And I must say, I've not seen it
executed so well in my life.'

Nakhu Dev spoke unexpectedly. 'The rajkumar is generous. Both you and Rajkumar Rama fought magnifi-
cently as well. I saw you use several different styles.
Even some favoured by my clan.'

'You mean the Jat clan?' Rama said quickly, seeing his
opening at last.

This time Janaki Kumar's eyes flashed hotly at his companion. Rama actually saw the hulking kshatriya wince and
look down momentarily, as if bowing in apology.

Janaki Kumar answered for both of them. 'My friend is
of Jat origin, yes. But his sword in now in service to
Videha.'

'And Videha's king?' Lakshman added quickly.

Janaki Kumar stumbled. It was a steep slope and damp

from the last flood-rise, and the kshatriya was obviously distracted by the conversation. His foot gave way beneath him and he would have tumbled down the side of the bank. His legs flailed for purchase on the slippery pebbled slope. A shower of shale flew out from under his heels, pelting Lakshman's thighs. Rama reached out quickly and caught the kshatriya around the waist.

'Easy, friend.'

Janaki Kumar twisted around angrily. 'LET ME GO! RELEASE ME AT ONCE, OR I'LL HAVE YOUR HEAD OFF!'

Rama reacted, astonished. He released the man at once. Janaki Kumar, still not stable on his feet, fell promptly on his rear end and slid all the way down the slope. He landed with a splash in a puddle of thick brown river mud, where he sat, stunned.

Lakshman came up to Rama, touching his shoulder. 'What got into him?'

Nakhu Dev rushed past them both, hurrying down the slope to aid his friend. The man's sheer size worked against him. His right heel slipped on a mound of smooth river-polished pebbles and shot out at a right angle to his waist. He landed on his rump as well, began to slide, tried to halt himself with his hands, lost his balance and tumbled head over heels. Janaki Kumar was just trying to raise himself from the thick sucking mud when Nakhu Dev landed beside him with an enormous *whump*, splattering mud outwards in a radius of at least five yards. A few small drops reached Rama and Lakshman as well.

Nakhu Dev swore in guttural Jat dialect. 'By my mother's funeral pyre!'

They couldn't help it. Both princes burst into another paroxysm of helpless laughter.

*   *   *

Manthara raked her nails down her own cheeks. Her skin crackled like aged parchment, peeling and hanging loose in ragged strips. There was little flesh on her bony face, but what little was there gaped wound-red. Wetness trickled down her face, dripping slowly on to the chaukat before which she sat. The flame was doused but the metal rim of the chaukat was searing hot, and as her bowed head touched it she smelled the familiar stench of singed hair and burnt skin; it mingled with the aromas of the burnt remains of the brahmin boy that lay in the chaukat. Her latest victim, procured by Manthara herself on a late-night foray.

She tore her arms and shoulders, ripping whole shreds from her withered body. Her hunched back quivered with the ecstasy of the agony. She ripped, tore, clawed, gouged, until it was impossible to tell her own blood and gristle from that of the sacrificed child. The chaukat and the area around the yagna square was splattered with the evidence of her self-inflicted injuries.

Finally, after several minutes of this torture, the fire blazed up, black as coal and glowing at its heart with a hypnotically compelling image. It was the ten-headed visage of the Lord of Lanka, her master. Her god. Manthara exuded a squeal of ecstatic pleasure and paid obeisance to her deity.

'Swami, I am blessed to be graced by your divine presence.'

Dispense with the formalities. I have other matters to attend to – and other devotees. Is it done?

'Yes, my lord. I was able to create a diversion that prevented the guru from reaching the parliament hall in time this morning, thus giving the twice-lifer the time it needed to transfer its aatma to the unconscious body of the maharaja. I extinguished the torches in the hall and relit them only after the transfer was accomplished.'

Not the details, hunchbacked hag. Just the results! Was it done, I asked, not how it was done!

'It was done, master. Possessed by the aatma, the maharaja delivered the orders to send the army to Gandahar and Kaikeya, just as you desired. They left this morning.'

And that leaves Ayodhya defenceless now?

'As utterly as a common whore! Your forces can ride into the city with no fear of substantial opposition!'

Substantial? Does that mean that there might be some opposition after all?

'Nothing worthy of concern, great one. Just the PF garrison. Old doddering veterans and raw green recruits. You could hack through them single-handedly!' She added with a smirk, 'And I will be here to sabotage their pathetic efforts and hasten their collapse. Ayodhya is yours for the taking, my master!'

So it seems.

She hesitated; then, when she realised that nothing further was forthcoming, she said cautiously, 'Swami, may I ask when you propose to invade?'

The fire sprang out at her, catching her unawares. It put out both her eyes, poking fingers of flame into her eye-sockets. Her visual organs bubbled and boiled in her skull. She screamed with the pain.

Concern yourself with matters of your own level, hag. I don't discuss my strategy with my own wife Mandodhari; why should I reveal it to you!

'Forgive me, my lord!' she babbled. Trickles of eye-fluid ran into her open mouth, sizzling. 'I meant no offence! I merely thought perhaps I could serve you better if I knew—'

You can serve me by completing the mission I entrusted you with before this one.

'Swami? You mean the poisoning of Dasaratha? I did my best, my master. But the seer is always vigilant for attacks on the maharaja's person. Now more than ever.'

Then attack him from a direction the seer does not foresee and cannot prevent.

'How, my lord? I am feeble of mind, but if you instruct, I will follow dutifully.'

Use his own family against him. Put the last phase of our plan into action now. Use Kaikeyi to attack Dasaratha. If we can't poison his body, we shall poison his mind.

'Your wish is my command, swami! I have prepared her well for precisely this moment. I shall send her at once.'

Not at once, you fool. Wait awhile. I will let you know when the time is right. Meanwhile, continue to breed discontent between the other members of the royal family. You did well to separate Kausalya and Sumitra. They had grown sickeningly close to each other and to the maharaja. Focus your attention there and keep Kaikeyi ready for the final step.

'It shall be as you say, my master. I shall—'

The fire died out. Manthara could feel its absence, as well as the absence of the king of the Asuras. He had left her presence. She rose shakily to her feet, and made her way blindly to the door. It was only when she was leaving the secret chamber that she realised that her sight had been restored. Her self-inflicted wounds had been repaired as well. It took great pain and damage to summon up the lord of the Asuras, but once he was satisfied with the acolyte's devotion, he always healed the damage through his mastery of brahman. She shuddered to think what might happen if some day Ravana failed to be pleased by her efforts and left her in that state of agony. She put the thought out of her mind and focused on the task at hand.

She would need that wretched serving girl again. Where was the wench?

As the hunchbacked daiimaa scurried out of her apartment in the Second Queen's palace and down the long torchlit corridors, she failed to notice the pair of eyes observing her discreetly.

The eyes were almond-shaped, as delicate as a doe's, and as pure and gentle. But on this occasion, they were also filled with righteous conviction and distrust. Third Queen Sumitra stepped from the alcove where she had lain in wait for the past few hours. After a glance back to make sure that Manthara was well away, she entered the daiimaa's apartment and began to search.

The two kshatriyas had managed to clean themselves off in the river as best they could. They were both still sulky and silent, and Janaki Kumar kept shooting fiery glances at Rama and Lakshman as if they had been responsible for the mishap. It was all the princes could do to keep from laughing again.

When they were presentable again, Janaki Kumar rose swiftly and said, 'Rajkumar Rama, my companion and I have had a change of heart. We desire to go directly to Mithila rather than camp overnight with you and then journey tomorrow.' He added gruffly, 'Our business is urgent and we would rather not waste time sleeping when we could be halfway to Mithila by dawn.'

Lakshman raised his eyebrows. 'You mean to journey by night?'

He addressed his question to the taller kshatriya, Nakhu Dev, but it was Janaki Kumar who replied again, speaking for both of them. The slender kshatriya's tone was sharp enough to cut glass. 'Rajkumar, I'll have you know that the raj-marg to Mithila is the safest in the Arya nations. A virgin could walk naked clad in the finest jewels and arrive at the capital unmolested.'

Lakshman's mouth fell open. 'Do they usually do that? Travel naked clad in fine jewellery down the raj-marg? I had no idea Mithila virgins were that adventurous!'

Janaki Kumar glared up at Lakshman. His veil was still crusted with drying mud, causing it to droop in some places and cling in others. 'It was meant to be a figure of speech.'

'Ah, but I hear Mithila virgins have fine figures too! You really know how to provoke a man's imagination.' Lakshman looked up at the sky and whistled. 'I'll be dreaming all night of naked virgins prancing down the raj-marg!' He added mischievously: 'Clad in fine jewellery, of course. By the way, would that be silver or gold?'

Janaki Kumar turned haughtily to Rama. 'Is your brother prince always this offensive when referring to women, Rajkumar Rama? Or does he derive some insidious pleasure from insulting Mithila women in particular?'

Rama smiled apologetically. 'Lakshman was just making a jest, friend. You mustn't take offence at his innocent remarks. He's always been something of a mischief-maker.'

Lakshman raised his arms. 'That's me! Master of mischief and good times!' He grinned and winked at the two kshatriyas. 'Don't Mithila kshatriyas tell jokes about their women? Or would you prefer that I joke about Ayodhyan women instead? They look quite splendid too when walking naked down the raj-marg clad in fine—'

Rama broke in hastily. 'Lakshman, go see if Guruji is inclined to meet our new friends formally. Quickly, before it's time for us to perform our evening rituals.'

Lakshman shrugged good-naturedly and sauntered off upriver towards the brahmarishi.

Rama turned back to Janaki Kumar. Suddenly, Nakhu Dev emitted a choking sound. People twenty yards away turned to look at him curiously. The enormous kshatriya coughed apologetically into his fist.

'Forgive me, rajkumar. I just now pictured Rajkumar Lakshman's description of naked virgins prancing down the raj-marg, and . . .' The warrior paused, his face twitching beneath the veil. 'It is quite funny, you have to admit, Janaki.'

'Nakhu Dev,' his shorter companion retorted sourly, 'if you're going to start getting giddy-headed and join in that chauvinistic jesting, maybe you'd rather join the Vajra kshatriyas instead of journeying to Mithila with me. Nakhu?'

He put a peculiar emphasis on the last word, making Rama wonder if that was the taller kshatriya's real name or just an alias. And why did the shorter man insist on being called by his full name, Janaki Kumar, even by his travelling companion? They were surely an odd couple!

He was about to suggest to the kshatriyas that they at least join them for the evening ritual and some hot supper before setting off when Lakshman returned, followed closely by a Vajra rider.

It was Sona Chita, the acting lieutenant of the Vajra. He had ridden close to the river to avoid the slanting, slippery slope of the right bank. He reined in as he approached them, saluting smartly.

'Rajkumars,' he said, his horse's hoofs splashing as it pranced in the shallow water of the river. 'Brahmarishi Vishwamitra requests your presence back at the camp to perform the evening rituals. And Captain Bejoo requests you not to wander this far from our invigilance again.'

Lakshman snorted. 'Tell Bejoo-chacha we're not little boys with runny noses any more. We can take care of ourselves now, as you probably witnessed up on the hills a while ago.'

Sona Chita grinned. 'No argument on that account, Rajkumar Lakshman. But the captain takes his responsibility very seriously. These are unfriendly woods and there's no telling what might assail you.'

Rama gestured to Lakshman not to retort again, and said to the Vajra kshatriya, 'Thank you for the message. We are turning back towards camp.'

Sona Chita saluted smartly and turned his horse around, splashing water energetically. He raised the reins to give the horse its head then added belatedly:

'And the brahmarishi also said to make sure our new kshatriya friends join us. He insists that they share our humble hospitality tonight.'

As the Vajra lieutenant rode away noisily, Rama found himself feeling oddly pleased. The kshatriyas wouldn't be able to refuse the brahmarishi's invitation; to do so would be to insult him grossly. It would give him a chance to spend more time with Janaki Kumar. He didn't know why, but he found the slender kshatriya's company and conversation strangely pleasing. He was looking forward to talking to him about several topics of minor interest.

Just then he happened to glance at Janaki Kumar. He was surprised at what he saw. The expression in the kshatriya's eyes couldn't have been more sour if he had just bitten into an imli ka butta.

The two rajkumars and their black-clad companions made their way up the riverbed, bare feet crunching softly on the gravel. None of them noticed the eyes watching them from the shadowy depths. Four pairs of them, all softly glowing like fireflies in the lush darkness. As they went around the curve of the riverbed, four pairs of snouts, three small and one large, pushed their way through the bush they were standing behind.

One of the bear cubs made a low mewling sound, reaching up to pluck what looked like a clump of blueberries from the bush. It put the clump in its mouth, chewed, then growled and spat out the mouthful, only a few yards behind the sentry, who continued downriver slowly, swinging his pike. The mother bear slapped the cub on its snout, soliciting a babyish mewl.

The female turned her snout in the direction the two rajkumars had gone and sniffed several times, as if trying to memorise a certain scent.

Then she opened her jaws slightly and emitted a sound that sounded curiously like human speech, except gruffer.

'Rama,' the bear said tenderly, the affection and gratitude in her voice unmistakable. 'Rama.'

'Rama,' repeated her cubs obediently. 'Rama.' All except the smallest one, who was still snuffling over being cuffed by his mother. His sister nudged him.

'Vaba,' he said sulkily.

5

The company was too large to be accommodated at one fire. They had done the next best thing: building a dozen fires in a circular formation. The riverbed at this point was wide, almost thirty yards across, and the fires were perhaps five or six yards apart. The Siddh-ashrama brahmins had seated themselves in such a manner that everyone faced inwards but slightly to the north. The result was a roughly circular congregation of seated brahmins all converging towards a point at the top of the circle, not the centre. Brahmarishi Vishwamitra sat on a rock at this focal point, his staff lying behind him.

On the outer rim of the circle of brahmins sat the Vajra kshatriyas, forming a protective perimeter. Captain Bejoo stood almost apart from the whole group, his face still clouded with conflicting emotions, sharpening the blade of his shortsword with a pumice stone. He glanced up sourly as the rajkumars joined the congregation, nodding perfunctorily. He spat a mouthful of blood-red tobacco-stained paan juice every now and then to the side, evoking irritated stares from the nearest brahmins, who disapproved of tobacco consumption in any form.

Everybody seemed quite comfortably settled by the time Rama and Lakshman arrived and took their places. Rama scanned the assembled faces quickly but couldn't see

Janaki Kumar and Nakhu Dev right away. The two princes made their way through the ranks of brahmins, seated cross-legged with their hands on their knees. Several brahmins were standing by the fires, supervising the cooking. The smells coming from the enormous pots were delicious and Rama could see the younger acolytes waiting eagerly to be fed. Except for a little fruit and water on the journey, nobody had eaten since that morning.

They found a space reserved for them right up front, immediately before the boulder on which the sage was seated. The kshatriyas were there already. All four of them seated themselves cross-legged and waited for the brahmarishi to begin speaking. Rama found himself seated diagonally opposite Janaki Kumar, and for some reason found his attention drawn to the slender kshatriya's face. The mercenary had performed the evening ritual with them, and his piercing eyes caught the firelight in a way that was oddly hypnotic.

Janaki's eyes were surprisingly bright, brighter than anyone else's in the congregation that Rama could see. They had seemed dark and soft earlier in the sunlight, but now they had a way of catching the light and holding it within that was fascinating to see. Like the eyes of predators which caught light at night-time, except that his eyes were neither feline nor feral. They were very human and very striking, filled with a glowing intensity that collected every sight, every observation around, sparing nothing. Rama found himself compelled to glance often in the lad's direction until the sage began speaking. Janaki seemed not to notice at first, but at one point, when Rama glanced that way suddenly, he found the kshatriya watching him with the cool, studied gaze of a fisherman watching a dolphin race alongside his boat – neither as a potential catch nor as a threat, simply watching. Janaki raised his gaze to meet Rama's eyes, their views locked, and it seemed to Rama that a faint flicker of a smile passed over the youth's face. But it was hard to tell with the veil.

The brahmarishi began speaking, and Rama's attention turned to the sage.

Vishwamitra spoke quietly, yet his voice seemed to carry across the riverbed to even the farthest listener, who was Bejoo. The Vajra captain put down his sword and sharpening stone and listened to the seer.

'I know all of you are eager to partake of some nourishment. This has been a long day and the past days have been difficult ones too. In a few moments, we shall eat together. I know that some of us,' here the seer's eyes passed over the two princes of Ayodhya and the black-clad mercenaries and then flicked to where Bejoo sat, 'have weighty concerns on their mind. All doubts will be pacified, all questions answered. This shall be done after we nourish ourselves. But first an important sandesh to all of you. From this point onwards, our company will divide into two groups.'

A ripple of surprise met this announcement.

Vishwamitra went on, 'My good brahmins of Siddh-ashrama, you will travel to Mithila directly via the raj-marg. Maharishi Tulsidas will lead you well.'

He indicated the elderly rishi who had stood up when his name was spoken and now greeted the congregation with a namaskar. He resumed his seat as the guru continued.

'The rajkumars and I will take the Visala road to Mithila. I invite the our new kshatriya friends to accompany us as well.'

Rama glanced at Janaki Kumar. The lad looked startled by the seer's announcement, as if unsure of how to respond.

Fortunately for the young warrior, Captain Bejoo spoke at that moment. 'Swami, may I enquire as to why the company must split up?'

Vishwamitra replied, 'Owing to certain developments too complex to explain here and now, the rajkumars and I must visit Visala before travelling on to Mithila. I do not wish to delay the rest of the company. The good ashramites of Siddh-ashrama have waited eagerly all year to attend this philosophical festival. Taking this detour would cause them to miss the first day and also the inaugural yagna. Hence the rajkumars and I shall travel separately from this point onwards.'

The sage added as an after thought: 'However, you and your Vajra kshatriyas may freely choose which group you wish to travel with. After all, you are not under my spiritual guidance and may do as you please.'

Without waiting for an answer, the sage went on, 'We shall all meet in Mithila then. I urge all you good brahmins to make directly for the congregation halls specially provided in the fields adjacent to the royal complex. There you will be well cared for and all your needs met. Those of you who have attended this annual conference will know full well that Maharaja Janak's love for men of faith and philosophical debate is matched only by his generous and warm hospitality. I am sure we shall all come away from this trip a little wiser and more insightful about matters that are central to our way of life and thought.'

Vishwamitra raised his head. The sky was a deep dusky blue, and few birds were flying now. The sounds of night insects were growing steadily louder as twilight fell as rapidly as a black scarf descending.

'It is past sunset now. Let us all perform our agnihotra and then take some nourishment prepared by our brahmins. The kshatriyas shall be fed at the two cookfires further upriver. This segregation is unavoidable as they consume flesh and our brahmins do not. After breaking my fast with my good ashramites, I will join the kshatriyas for a while in order to discuss tomorrow's journey. I urge all of you to take an early night's rest and be refreshed before the long journey tomorrow. Swaha.'

'Swaha!' responded the congregation in one resounding chorus. Everybody began moving eagerly towards the cookfires. There was only one thing brahmins loved more than prayer and penance, and that was good food.

It took Guru Vashishta the better part of the day to complete the ritual spiritual cleansing and make sure that Dasaratha was totally free of all evil influences. Both the healer and the afflicted remained through those many hours locked in a bond of brahman. The evening shadows were lengthening across the assembly hall floor when Vashishta ceased chanting the smriti mantras – the most secret Vedic knowledge of all – and was finally satisfied that this new crisis was also past.

Still holding the maharaja on the tip of his finger, the guru lowered Dasaratha gently to the floor. This part of the hall was furnished with large, comfortably stuffed mattresses that Aryas liked to stretch out on while conducting business or pleasure. He placed the unconscious king on one such seat. Dasaratha returned to gravity, his bulk indenting the overstuffed mattress. The guru watched him closely for several moments, then finally felt satisfied that the maharaja was breathing normally and out of danger.

He rose to his feet and strode towards the doors of the hall with an energy that belied his considerable age. A single phrase from his lips parted the towering doors. The palace guards moved aside to let the seer pass.

He gestured to their leader.

'The maharaja is exhausted and needs rest. Have him taken to his sick-chamber.'

The guards rushed to do his bidding.

Vashishta turned to face the sizeable group that awaited him anxiously. First Queen Kausalya was there, but the other two titled queens were conspicuous by their absence. Pradhan Mantri Sumantra, Captain Drishti Kumar and his father Senapati Dheeraj Kumar were present as well, along with Mantri Jabali, Mantri Ashok and the other members of the ministerial cabinet, and several other nobles and officials of the court. The anxiety on all their faces was as plain as a spoken question.

'Council of Ayodhya, pray, enter within the assembly hall. We have important matters to discuss.'

They followed him in without question. Their wan, anxious faces and small number were a stark contrast to the busy, bustling, clamour that normally filled the vast chamber. Vashishta stood at the foot of the royal dais and turned to face the council of ministers and the First Queen of Kosala.

A volley of questions erupted, everybody speaking at once, eager to know the meaning behind the sage's cryptic comments. Only the maharani awaited her chance to speak.

Vashishta raised a hand, showing them his palm.

'Silence. The maharaja is well. He is tired now and will sleep long and deeply. But when he awakens he will be refreshed and well.'

A hoarse cheer rose from the assembly. Two or three assistants ran down towards the exit to convey the news to the criers, who would pass it on to the citizenry. The others remained, still looking anxiously at the guru. He resisted the urge to sigh. The exorcism had taken a great deal out of him. But their questions would have to be answered.

First Queen Kausalya spoke first, asking anxiously, 'Guru-dev? Was there an attack on the maharaja?'

Vashishta sighed. 'It vexes me to say aye, maharani. This morning the attempt on his life was physical and brought him to the very brink of mortality. But the later attack was spiritual.'

'Spiritual, maha-dev?'

Vashishta nodded. 'Yes, maharani. The courier who arrived this morning was no normal kshatriya. He was one of Ravana's own minions.'

Consternation and dismay met this announcement. Pradhan Mantri Sumantra's face creased into a mask of anger.

The guru held up his hand. 'But do not fear. The danger is past. Twice today the Lord of Lanka has attempted to take our liege's life. Twice he has been foiled. The devas watch over Maharaja Dasaratha. The man named Bheriya was in truth a twice-lifer. He was ambushed and killed last night on the road to Ayodhya. The king of the Asuras infused the empty vessel of his body with the aatma of another long-dead man. This wretched being was sent here by the Lord of Lanka to deliver a false message.'

The faces of the ministers and the maharani were chalk-white with shock.

The sage turned to the First Queen and said gently, 'Maharani, the king has need of your healing touch. I request you, attend him in his sick-chamber and let me know the minute he awakens.'

Kausalya nodded and withdrew without any argument. The First Queen had sat the sunwood throne long enough to know that even a maharani could not deal with every problem at once. This was a matter for the guru and the royal council. She also understood from the subtle change of tone in the guru's voice that he wished her to stay close to the maharaja. An enemy who could make two attempts on the king of Ayodhya's life was capable of making another. She exited the hall with the same quiet grace and dignity with which she always conducted herself.

After she was gone, the guru had the doors closed again. For the third time that day, they were barred shut.

6

Bejoo wished the brahmin caste had never been created.

The Vajra captain sat on his bundled saddle and horse armour, scowling darkly enough to keep everyone else at bay. He wanted to be left alone. Around him, his kshatriyas had already finished their meal and were sipping some fermented grape juice in place of their nightly soma. He would have paid a hundred rupees for some soma or even some cheap local wine, but there was none to be had for love or money in this godly part of the country.

A plantain leaf with chunks of roasted meat, charcoaled vegetables on a stick and segments of fruit lay in the captain's hands. As he ate, he watched the brahmin camp downriver. The Siddh-ashramites had already finished their supper and were now singing, clanging their bell-clappers together in noisy rhythm to the beat of their devotional chanting. He wondered how they got their energy, carrying on that way after covering a dozen yojanas on foot and supping on vegetarian fare. What was it they said? 'Prayer is meat and soma to the true devotee?' Maybe there was something to it after all.

As for himself, his bones ached as if he had walked those hundred-plus miles beside them instead of having ridden them out on his mount. He suspected that it was the stress of riding without any definite purpose that had worn him down more than the distance covered. O Shani-deva, he thought wearily, I'm getting too old for this traipsing around with brahmins, going nowhere and doing nothing useful. If not for the little stir-up on the hill, he would barely have been able to put food in his mouth; a true kshatriya earned his meat. Even there, it was the raj-kumars who had done most of the fighting.

A few yards to his left, the two rajkumars and their new kshatriya friends sat eating and talking to one another. Bejoo noticed Rajkumar Rama laughing whole-heartedly at something Janaki Kumar had just said. Clearly, the prince enjoyed the slender mercenary's company – they had spent their meal-hour talking and laughing more than eating. The wind was blowing across the river and Bejoo had heard several of the lad's words as well. The kshatriya clearly had a nimble mind and a witty tongue. Rajkumar Lakshman didn't seem as taken by the kshatriya – the junior prince had found himself on the receiving end of that sharp tongue more than once, to Bejoo's delight. It wouldn't hurt Lakshman to realise that there were wits sharper than his own.

Around the kshatriya campsite, Bejoo could hear the sounds of his men laying down pallets for the night. Despite the fact that it was early spring, the weather had turned surprisingly warm. After sunset a little bite had come into the wind, but it was barely a nip compared to the freezing chill of the northern nations. Bejoo and his Vajra had camped out without tents in temperatures close to freezing in the mountains of Gandahar. This was like a summer bask in comparison.

He was still having some difficulty dealing with this whole trip to Mithila. And now the sage wanted to take them sightseeing! At least, that was what it sounded like to Bejoo's ears. Why would they want to leave the main company and take a detour to Visala? To see the Ganga, that was why. The holy river of the Arya nations, its waters regarded as sacred and magical, the Ganga flowed past Visala, right through the Gautama groves. Bejoo was prepared to bet his horse that the sage wanted to bathe in the holy water and offer prayers. The Ganga was the holiest of rivers and the place where it flowed through the Gautama groves was of special significance to seers. No doubt the sage would want to take his ceremonial dip in the waters there before proceeding to Mithila. Maybe even spend another day or two showing the rajkumars the botanical wonders of the Videha plains. Why, at this rate, they would be lucky to return to Ayodhya in time for Deepavali!

At times like this it seemed to Bejoo that these stubborn, aloof and superior-aired pundits had been put on earth only to vex and frustrate kshatriyas. And the brahmarishi in particular was probably a fully ordained maestro of the art of kshatriya vexation!

The subject of his ire appeared just then, a tall, strong figure making his way upriver over the pebbled bank, his staff crunching as loud as a bigfoot hoof each time it struck the ground. Bejoo didn't fail to notice the faint blue sparks that rose from each contact of the staff. That was the other thing that made him uneasy about brahmins: they leaked brahman power like a firefly leaked light. It made his hackles rise. Bejoo trusted things that could be seen, touched, tasted, felt, smelled – and hacked, stabbed and lopped off, not to put too fine a point on it.

The very sight of the brahman sparks made his stomach queasy. How did one fight powers like that? He put his leaf of food aside, unfinished, and stood up. Protocol, always protocol. Until the brahmins decided to listen to the voice of the devas instead of Arya rules, at which point protocol, with everything else mortal, went out of the window and down into the stinky moat. Bejoo slapped his hands on his flanks, carelessly wiping them clean, and went to receive the brahmarishi.

When he saw the sage making his way towards the rajkumars, however, he stopped and waited. He was within hearing distance of the group and watched as all four young men rose at once at the sight of the seer-mage. They had finished their meal and their leaf-plates had been disposed of moments earlier.

The rajkumars bowed and performed reverent namaskars to their guru.

'Pranaam, Guru-dev,' Rajkumar Rama said. Lakshman echoed his brother.

The sage's voice was as serene as the idyllic valley in which they stood. 'Pranaam, rajkumars. Have you eaten and rested well?'

'Yes, Guru-dev.'

'Good,' the sage replied. 'For we shall be leaving in moments.'

Rama looked surprised. 'Leaving, Guru-dev?'

'We shall travel by night to hasten our arrival at Mithila.'

'Then we shall not be stopping at Visala en route?'

'We shall indeed. Without visiting Visala our journey to Mithila would be fruitless.'

Rama and Lakshman exchanged a puzzled look. Bejoo noticed Janaki Kumar glancing at his companion as well, his eloquent eyes speaking silent words to the larger kshatriya.

'Jaise aagya, Guru-dev,' Rama replied.

'Very good, rajkumars. Now prepare yourselves for departure. We shall leave shortly.'

Bejoo stepped forward. This was all news to him.

'Maha-dev,' he said, forcing a tone of polite reverence into his voice. 'It would not be safe to travel by night. My Vajra—'

'Your Vajra will slow us down, Captain Bejoo,' Vishwamitra said calmly but firmly. 'They must travel to Mithila by the raj-marg with the Siddh-ashrama procession. However, if you so wish, you may accompany us. But you must hurry and give your men last instructions. My company will not wait for stragglers.'

Stragglers? Who did the mage think he was talking to? Bejoo swallowed his indignation and said in as level a voice as he could manage, 'But Guru-dev, I am oathsworn to protect the rajkumars. Without my Vajra—'

The seer cut him short. 'Bejoo, in the nine days you have been with the rajkumars and myself, have you ever felt that they lacked protection in any way?'

Bejoo tried hard to come up with a suitable retort but found himself unable to think of a single word. The rajkumars were more than able to protect themselves. Bejoo's duty had become purely ceremonial.

'No, maharaja,' he said at last.

The moment he said it, he wanted to bite his tongue off. He had addressed the sage as 'maharaja', implying that he now accepted Vishwamitra as his supreme liege. But it was too late to take back the error. If the seer noticed, he gave no sign.

'Then let us end this tired line of argument,' Vishwamitra said. 'Decide now. Will you accompany us on our mission or will you ride with your Vajra? Remember also, we walk in the light of brahman. We are not permitted the luxury of chariots or mounts. If you come with us, you must come on foot. What is your decision?'

'I shall come with you,' Bejoo said. 'Maha-dev.'

The sage's penetrating gaze stayed on Bejoo for a long

moment. 'Good,' Vishwamitra said. 'I am glad to hear it, Captain Bejoo. You are a fine kshatriya and we shall need every sword and bow before we reach Mithila.'

Bejoo didn't know whether to blush or to blink at the unexpected compliment. And was he mistaken or had the sage addressed him with a mite more respect than he had earlier? 'Captain Bejoo' instead of the perfunctory 'kshatriya'?

Then the full implications of the seer's last words sank in. What did the sage mean by saying they would need every sword and bow? It sounded ominous. Was he planning to get into a scuffle with bandits on the road again? And what had he meant by their 'mission' to Visala? Bejoo had heard nothing of any mission before now.

But Vishwamitra had already turned away to face the four young men again.

'Now, Rajkumar Rama, I think it is time for you to introduce me to our new fellow-travellers. Our road to Mithila is long and fraught with many perils. It would be best if we all get to know one another as closely as possible.'

The sage's diamond-bright eyes glinted in the flickering firelight as he looked at the two kshatriyas. 'It would not do to travel together without knowing one another's identities, would it?'

Bejoo saw that the sage directed his words pointedly at the slender kshatriya. The young man dropped his eyes at once, but Bejoo thought he did so out of respect, not fear.

Bejoo observed not for the first time that the shorter kshatriya was unusually small-proportioned and thin. Bejoo himself was very short for a kshatriya, or for an Arya, and as a young boy he had been thin and weak as well, until he had come under the tutelage of a senior

warrior who had chalked out a diet and training programme that had slapped on the slabs of muscle bulk that
he now possessed. That man had been Senapati Dheeraj
Kumar, and under the veteran general's tutelage Bejoo had
blossomed into a champion wrestler, kabbadi player and
mace thrower, winning several dozen tournaments before
he was given command of the Vajra. He made a mental
note to take the slender kshatriya aside later and give him
some pointed tips on how to turn that delicate frame into a
muscular body.

Rama presented the two black-clad kshatriyas formally
to the brahmarishi. 'Guru-dev, this is kshatriya Janaki
Kumar and kshatriya Nakhu Dev. They are travelling
warriors for hire. They were on their way to Mithila when
they heard the sounds of the bear family being attacked on
the hill and went to their rescue. We fought the bandits
together.'

To the mercenaries Rama said: 'Kshatriyas, pay your
respects to the brahmarishi Vishwamitra. His legendary
stature is too great for me to have to repeat here. My
brother Lakshman and I are both oathsworn to the great
sage. He is our guru.'

'Pranaam, Guru-dev,' both kshatriyas said, almost at
once. They had already greeted the sage as he approached,
but did so again without hesitation, paying their respects
formally this time.

Bejoo noted curiously that both lads avoided meeting
the seer's eyes directly. He assumed it to be the effect of the
brahmarishi's formidable reputation and imposing personality. He was about to find out how wrong that
assumption was.

7

'False message, Guru-dev?' Sumantra's voice sounded like a choked cry for help from the bottom of a deep well.

'Indeed, prime minister. The news of the Asura army's impending invasion.'

Everybody began speaking at once. Mantri Ashok spoke loudest. 'Guru-dev, do you mean to say that there will be no invasion?'

'Alas, mantriji. If only things could be that simple. Nay, there will surely be an invasion. Even as we speak, Ravana's forces are making their way across the subcontinent like a venomous serpent slithering towards its prey. This part of the message was true enough. It was the point of first attack that was falsely given.'

The seer-mage paused. He had everyone's undivided attention. 'The Asura forces will indeed attack Gandahar and Kaikeya. Their ships will carry them up the Sindhu river to those two north-western Arya kingdoms just as you have been informed.'

The guru paused, glancing around to make sure he had the undivided attention of the entire council of ministers. 'But those ships will carry only a small fragment of the Asura forces, not the entire army as you have been led to believe. Because the attacks on Gandahar and Kaikeya are merely diversionary tactics intended to draw the Arya armies to those distant nations, and away from the real target of the Lord of Lanka.'

Sumantra sat forward in his seat, looking alarmed. 'The real target, Guru-dev? You mean, apart from Gandahar and Kaikeya, there will be an attack on another Arya city or kingdom?'

'Exactly, prime minister. While a fraction of the Asura armada is making its way up the Sindhu river, the majority of that vast fleet has already landed on the shores of Salset and Kerall, and are even now working their way northwards.'

Northwards! Every face in the hall turned to the map on the wall. Their eyes focused on the western coastal regions of Salset and Kerall and travelled upwards . . . to the kingdom of Kosala, with the city of Ayodhya marked in bold, right in the centre of that trajectory.

'Ayodhya?' Mantri Jabali cried out in frustration and rage. 'But our army has been sent to the north and the north-west already, split into two halves travelling in two separate directions! They are both already a full day's march away. It will take a night and another day to send a messenger after them to call them back!'

'Maha-dev,' the prime minister said agitatedly. 'Pardon my questioning your actions thus, but why did you not inform us of this vital news earlier, when there was still time to stop our army from marching?'

Guru Vashishta was standing nearest to Sumantra. He laid a large, gentle hand on the prime minister's shoulder.

'Because, good Sumantra, I myself only learned of it a few moments ago. It took me that much time to rid the maharaja's evil-infected soul and brain of the havoc the possession had caused. After delivering its message, the evil aatma left the re-animated corpse of the messenger and passed into our maharaja's body. It was no easy task to exorcise it from his being. My first concern was saving Dasaratha; only then could I attempt to discover the true motive behind the possession.'

A deathly pall of silence fell over the group.

'We are lost then,' Mantri Jabali said at last. 'If the Asura hordes attack before our army returns, we stand no chance. Even mighty Ayodhya cannot withstand an Asura invasion without sufficient soldiers to man its defences. Our siege infrastructure itself requires twenty-five thousand soldiers working at all times to operate efficiently. Even if we put all the PFs to work round the clock, it will be insufficient.'

'Calm yourself, Mantri Jabali,' the guru said calmly. 'The Asuras will not attack Ayodhya.'

'They will not?' Sumantra said, looking as confused as the minister of war and the rest of the council. 'But mahadev, you just said—'

'Trust me, good Sumantra, all you wise and brave ministers of Kosala. The Lord of Lanka's first goal is not our seven-walled city. He knows that Ayodhya the Unconquerable is too formidable a target against which to pit his forces directly. He will come here, but only after he has cleared a space around us and isolated our proud land from the other Arya nations. In order to do that, he intends to first focus his attack on our sister kingdom of Videha. It is the capital of that peaceful country that he first intends to overrun.'

The sage directed their attention back to the wall map.

'His main target in the first crucial offensive will be the city of brahmins, Mithila.'

Vishwamitra looked at the shorter kshatriya intently.

'Janaki,' he said, his hand stroking his flowing beard thoughtfully. 'An interesting name. It literally means "of

Janak". And Janak of course is Maharaja Janak, king of
Videha and master of the moonwood throne of Mithila.
What is your relation to his majesty, lord of Mithila?'

The slender kshatriya kept his head bowed, clearly awed
by the brahmarishi. 'Guru-dev, despite the meaning of my
given title, I am not of the blood of royals. Although
Maharaja Janak is my liege, as he is the liege of every
citizen of Videha.'

Bejoo thought he saw a faint wisp of a smile play across
the sage's weathered, beard-enshrouded face. What had the
brahmin found so amusing about the kshatriya's reply? It
had sounded straightforward enough to Bejoo. The lad was
probably just some knockaround bastard, conceived of a
prostitute or dancer, had learned the sword from some army
irregulars and when he was old enough to walk straight had
decided to go into business for himself and make a few
rupees. It was a tediously common history.

'A very interesting reply,' Vishwamitra said. 'Observe,
rajkumars, how intelligently your new friend plays with
the vocabulary and grammar of our great national language. "My given title" is what was said, not "my given
name". And indeed, Janaki can be a title as well as a name,
its meaning being "of Janak" as I have already mentioned.
Then your friend says, "I am not of the blood of royals".
And that is another shrewd choice of phrase. For Maharaja Janak's heir, titled "Janaki", was indeed adopted by
the lord of Mithila, rather than birthed by his queen. And
of course, every citizen of the Videha nation, highborn or
low, regards Janak as his liege. So your new friend cleverly
answered my direct question with an elegantly worded
and quite suitable response that nonetheless succeeded in
revealing nothing of the speaker's true identity.'

Bejoo stood up straighter, frowning. What was this new
twist?

Rama and Lakshman was looking at the sage with perfectly matched expressions of befuddlement.

'Guru-dev,' Lakshman said in a puzzled tone, 'are you saying that Janaki Kumar lied to you just now? That he is in fact related to Maharaja Janak?'

'Not just related, Rajkumar Lakshman,' the brahmarishi replied. 'I say your new friend is none other than Janak's own adopted child. The heir to the moonwood throne and future ruler of Videha in the same way that your brother Rama is prince-heir of Kosala.'

Bejoo blinked. What was the sage talking about? That delicate-looking fellow there? Royalty? Heir to the throne of Videha? Impossible! The fellow was a good fighter, that was true, but . . . but . . .

Bejoo was unable to restrain himself any longer. He had drifted slowly closer as the dialogue between the sage and the kshatriyas had grown more intriguing. Now he said, 'Forgive me, maha-dev. I apologise for interrupting. But the maharaja of Videha has no sons. There is no prince-heir to the throne of Videha!'

The sage smiled, his ancient grey eyes twinkling in the warm reflected light of the campfires.

'I did not say that Janaki here was a prince. I merely said that this person was the heir to Videha's throne and Janak's own adopted child.'

Lakshman said, 'But, Guru-dev, Bejoo-chacha is right. Maharaja Janak has no sons, so how can Janaki Kumar be his adopted child?'

Vishwamitra turned his eyes again to the slender kshatriya. 'Janaki Kumari, not Janaki Kumar. A title that is cleverly used in place of a name, concealing the user's true identity, just as the black veil and garb of the travelling kshatriya is cleverly used to disguise the wearer's true form and appearance.'

Bejoo looked at the slender kshatriya, still not fully understanding what the sage meant. Then it registered with the sharp clicking of a final bolt falling into place.

'IMPOSTER!' Bejoo roared, drawing his sword and stepping forward. 'VAJRA! TO ME!'

The riverbed exploded into a flurry of activity as half a hundred Vajra kshatriyas left off whatever chore they were engaged in to run to their leader's side. Some of them tossed aside chunks of roast meat to lunge for their weapons. In an instant, Bejoo's yell still echoing through the upper slopes of the hill behind them, every Vajra kshatriya was within ten yards of the brahmarishi and the four young men, their swords, lances and bows out and ready for action. Their boots crunched noisily on the riverbed as they shifted slowly closer, directing their weapons at the two black-clad figures.

The taller kshatriya had already drawn his sword and turned to face the Vajra kshatriyas. Nakhu Dev made a gesture of warning to the nearest of Bejoo's men, cautioning them against coming any closer.

Downriver, the brahmins of Siddh-ashrama ceased their devotional chanting and fell silent, peering towards the kshatriya camp as they tried to make out what this new crisis entailed.

Bejoo took a step forward. 'Rajkumars! Step back, away from those two. My men and I will deal with the Asuras.'

'Asuras? When did I say these were Asuras, Captain Bejoo?'

The tone of amusement in the bramarishi's voice confused Bejoo further.

He glanced at the sage. 'Guru-dev, did you not just pronounce this man an imposter in disguise?'

'Not at all,' Vishwamitra replied calmly. 'I merely said that Janaki Kumar is in fact Janaki Kumari.'

Bejoo stared at the sage. 'So doesn't that mean—' He broke off abruptly. 'Kumari? But that would be a girl's title.'

'Indeed, which is precisely why our young kshatriya friend here removed the last vowel, to masculinise it.'

Bejoo turned his attention to the slender mercenary. 'Kumari?' he repeated, feeling foolish. 'But that would make him a her!' He gaped at the kshatriya-for-hire. 'A woman? In disguise?'

'Two women in fact, Captain Bejoo. Her companion is in fact named Nakhudi Devi, which was cleverly altered into Nakhu Dev to sound more masculine.'

Bejoo stared at the two black-clad figures. Rama and Lakshman had turned to look at them as well, giving the Vajra captain a clear line of sight. He quickly re-appraised the shorter and more slender of the two. Yes, that one could certainly be a woman. That would explain his . . . um, her delicate shape and lack of musculature. But the bigger one? That hulking giant with shoulders like a bigfoot's knee? Could that towering mass really be a woman?

'Don't fret, Captain Bejoo,' the sage went on. 'Anyone would have been deceived. Those black garbs are quite effective. Their voices made them appear young men. And Nakhudi Devi's enviable size and strength defied the usual expectation. If it's any consolation to your injured ego, you should know that Nakhudi Devi is in fact the chief of the princess's royal bodyguards and her closest trusted companion. Naturally, I have not laid eyes on either of them before as I have only recently emerged from my long bhor tapasya, but it is not the first time that I have met a princess travelling incognito in her own kingdom. Who else would she choose to accompany her on her adventure except her most trusted bodyguard? Besides, I doubt that Nakhudi Devi, like any sworn personal retainer, would allow herself to live if she ever let her mistress out of her sight. Even if the rajkumari wished to travel alone, the very idea of her dearly loved bodyguard committing aatma-hatya for having failed in her duties would give her pause. By accompanying her, the princess avoids an unnecessary tragedy while Nakhudi Devi continues to fulfil her sworn duty to protect the rajkumari.'

'Rajkumari?' Bejoo barely recognised his own voice, it was so hoarse with surprise.

The seer-mage gestured sorcerously. As if whipped off by an invisible and powerful wind, the veils on the faces of the two kshatriyas were peeled away. They fell on the pebbled floor of the riverbed. Amazed eyes stared at the delicate if grimy features of the two women, one flushed with embarrassment and impotent fury, the other still suspicious and aggressive.

Vishwamitra spoke aloud, adding a touch of theatri-cality to his voice: 'I give you the princess-heir of Videha and the future ruler of the moonwood throne of Mithila, Rajkumari Sita Janaki!'

8

'Mithila?' Mantri Ashok seemed unable to believe the guru's words. 'But they are followers of ahimsa. Their army is not even a standing force. Ayodhya city alone has twice the kshatriyas of the entire kingdom of Videha!'

'Besides,' Sumantra added, 'with their annual philosophical festival in progress, their attention will be diverted to spiritual matters. Their gates will be opened to all visitors, their defences lowered. They are least prepared to face an outright assault by . . .' The prime minister's voice trailed off as he realised the implications of his own words. 'They will be as easy prey as fledgling swans in a pond filled with gharial!'

'Indeed,' the sage agreed sadly. 'This is the very reason the Lord of Lanka proposes to attack Mithila first. Once he has control of Mithila, his path is clear to Ayodhya. Banglar is too distant to send forces in time, and Gandahar and Kaikeya will be occupied with their own sieges. The lord of Asuras will finally be able to lay siege to the one Arya city that has never been besieged before. And to do this, he must first storm Mithila. From what I gleaned from the wretched mind of the Asura spirit that possessed our liege, I learned that the Asura armies are already making their way northwards. They will reach Mithila in two days or less.'

'But that's even worse,' Mantri Ashok cried out. 'Mithila is three days' march from here. Even if we call our army back and instruct them to go to Mithila, it will take all of five nights and four days to reach Maharaja Janak's city. We will be too late to help them!'

'Even so,' the sage said grimly, 'this is our only recourse. Couriers must be sent out at once, asking rajkumars Bharat and Shatrugan to turn their divisions around. Better we reach our fellow Aryas in Mithila in four days than never. Pradhan Mantri Sumantra, I propose you ride personally to warn Rajkumar Bharat, while you Mantri Jabali go after Rajkumar Shatrugan. You must leave within the hour. From the information I gathered, the Asura attack on Mithila will begin tomorrow at nightfall. As you know, contrary to the Arya code of war, Asuras fight at night as well as by day. By sundown tomorrow, Mithila will face the most hideous army of Asuras ever assembled.'

Mantri Kasyapa spoke, his normally austere façade giving way to open anxiety. 'But what will be the use, Guru-dev? We will be too late. Including the time taken to contact our forces and turn them around, it will take four days of hard marching to reach Mithila, even if we wear out our animals and soldiers getting there. Surely Mithila cannot hold out that long?'

He looked around at the other ministers for confirmation.

Mantri Jabali nodded grimly. 'Mithila will not stand one night against such an assault, let alone four! With the philosophical festival to add to the burden on their already meagre security forces, I'd wager they'll fall within an hour or two. It will be a slaughter worse than the First Asura War. Those unfortunate Videhans will be as innocent and unsuspecting as our founding fathers were when they faced the horror and fury of the first Asura invasion.'

The minister raised his piercing eyes to the guru and to the prime minister. 'Forgive me, Guru-dev, pradhan mantriji. I would make a suggestion which may not sound very Arya in its aspect, but I would make this offer for the good of all our citizens whom we are sworn to protect.'

'Speak, Jabali,' Sumantra said. Vashishta nodded his encouragement.

Jabali took a deep breath, released it as a sigh and said, 'As minister of defence it is my duty to propose a military strategy that ensures the continued safety of our own kingdom and capital city. If Ayodhya falls, all Arya falls. This is not just a homily handed down from generations, but a basic military fact. We are the only Arya nation positioned geographically in a manner that enables us to aid any or all of our neighbour nations. As we have seen from past encounters with the Asura vermin, our only hope lies in unity. If the Lord of Lanka were to capture Ayodhya,' he bowed his head for a fraction of a second, 'and note that I still say "if" . . . if that foul day ever fell upon us, then Ravana would have the most advantageous base from which to launch assaults on all the Arya lands. The guru has already informed us that smaller but significant Asura forces will attack the other Arya nations. With Ayodhya as his centre, the lord of Asuras can catch all our brother Aryas in pincer-actions, besieging them until their resources run out. Within months, perhaps as long as a year at best, all of the subcontinent will be in his fist.'

The mantri made a fist of his own right hand and clenched it tight. The knuckles and joints cracked loudly in the silent assembly hall. Jabali looked at the faces of each person present in turn.

'This is the only reason why I propose what I am about to say. I submit to this council that we recall our army to

Ayodhya and redeploy them in preparation for a siege. If Mithila is to be attacked tomorrow night, then the Asura armies will be at our gates in three, perhaps four days. This gives us enough time to stock our granaries, bring as many citizens as possible within the city walls and strengthen our defences. Thus, we may yet withstand the might of the Asura hordes and repel the Lord of Lanka.'

The silence that met this proposal was broken by Mantri Kasyapa, his voice almost a sob. 'You mean that we should leave Mithila to face the Asura armies alone? That we should abandon our brothers and sisters? How can you suggest such a thing, Jabali? I know you are hard of heart, you must be to become minister of war, but this is beyond hardness. This borders on betrayal!'

Mantri Ashok said, 'I agree with Kasyapa, Jabali. I see the logic of what you propose, but how can we save Ayodhya and let Mithila fall? How can we not go to the aid of our fellow Aryas?'

Pradhan Mantri Sumantra raised his hand. 'Let us not grow too emotional. I too feel outraged at the thought of leaving the Videhans unaided. Yet Mantri Jabali speaks wise words. If we go to the Mithilans' aid and are too late, our army will be caught between the two kingdoms, on the open road, exposed and vulnerable. Under such conditions, we will be no match for the superior numbers and strength of the enemy. We all recall the titanic struggle Maharaja Dasaratha had to endure on the fields of Kaikeya. What Mantri Jabali has proposed seems harsh and cold, it's true. Yet the alternative may be harsher still.'

Mantri Kasyapa rose to his feet angrily. 'If we are to choose between helping Mithila and saving our own skins, I will vote for Mithila no matter what the outcome. Better that we die fighting on the open road than cluster here behind our seven walls while the Videhan nation is raped and razed by Ravana's monstrous hordes. We have all seen how hideously the Asura species treat their enemy. This is no Arya civil conflict we speak of, where rules of war are maintained and the code of the kshatriyas is upheld even in the thick of battle. The survival of an entire kingdom is at stake!'

Guru Vashishta spoke calmly. 'There is a third alternative. Neither abandon Mithila, nor abandon Ayodhya.'

Everybody turned curious eyes to the sage.

Vashishta said, 'Mithila must hold out until our army reaches them. They must put up a fight fierce enough to keep the Asura armies from reaching the Sarayu river. If they hold the enemy there for four more days, our forces can reach them and press them back. Meanwhile, we also send word to Banglar in the east and Marwar in the west to join our army at Mithila. They ought to reach Mithila at best a day after our forces, just in time to press home the attack.'

The council exchanged glances, their expressions varying from surprise to wonder.

Sumantra spoke for all of them when he said slowly, 'A brilliant plan, maha-dev. Truly magnificent. The open plains of the Videha nation would then be our ally rather than our foe. We could attack the Asura force on three fronts, and drive them back southwards. What do you say, Mantri Jabali, might not this be a viable strategy?'

The pinched face of Jabali cleared slightly. 'Oh yes. It would work. The Asuras are not good on flatland, we've seen that before. And they get confused and disoriented when attacked from more than one direction – it forces each species to transgress into the other's area and causes huge internal conflict and outright fighting. They could even end up fighting one another as much as our armies. It could certainly work.' The minister's face clouded again.

'But I have a pertinent question for Guru Vashishta. Guru-dev, how can we expect Mithila to hold out for those four crucial days? Everything would depend on that. If they fell even a day too soon, all would be lost. For the plan to work successfully, it is imperative that Mithila must make a stand like no other stand in Arya history. It would be like pitting a herd of elephants against an ant-hill.'

The guru nodded.

'Well spoken, mantriji. But I believe these ants of Mithila might just be able to keep the elephants at bay long enough to save the ant-hill from destruction.'

Jabali looked confused. His expression was mirrored on the faces of the other council ministers. Only Sumantra watched the guru's face earnestly. He had spent enough time with the sage to know when he was speaking of matters that were beyond mortal ken.

Guru Vashishta looked around at the anxious and curious ministers. 'Ants can sting,' he said. 'And when enough ants work together, their sting can be enough to bring down even an elephant. I think Mithila might just be able to produce one giant surprise.'

9

For one long, stunned moment, the entire company was silent. The sounds of the river valley seemed to grow louder to fill the sudden vacuum: leaves whispering in the wind, the gurgling of the rivulet, horses nickering softly, bigfoot pawing the shale and noisily eating the grass and fruits collected by their mahouts. The scents of wildwood and honey, roses and thyme, neem and chandanwood filled the air. The pungent but not unpleasant animal odours of horse and elephant mingled with the strong perfume of nightqueen blossom, reminding Sita of the compound behind the princess gardens where she had learned to ride as a little girl. Its wall separated that end of the princess's palace from the stables, and the bougainvillea creeper overhanging that wall was interwoven with the branches of a nightqueen blossom tree, its strong scent mingling with the aroma of horses.

But this she noticed only in an abstract, subconscious way, just as her ears took in the natural, animal and human sounds around her without her mind fully registering the meaning of those sounds. Right now, the only sound Sita could hear was the deafening thudding of her own heart. The only scent in her nostrils was the scent of her own fear. When the veil was removed by the brahmarishi's sorcery, she felt bare, vulnerable. She wanted to pick it up and cover herself at once. To scream out loud and run away from these gawking, gaping people. To sink into the earth and be embraced by the all-encompassing arms of Prithvi Maa, the form in which the Mother Goddess Sri presided over the world, and Sita's own patron deity.

She was exposed. Unmasked. Humiliated. It was bad enough to have her identity revealed, it was unbearable to have it done thus, so publicly. She could feel every pair of eyes as keenly as if they were two-tined pitchforks goring her flesh. Most of all, she could see Rama, standing closest to her, staring at her with an expression that was all the more shocking because it wasn't displaying shock or horror or disbelief, like the other faces around her. Rama was smiling. As if his jest-prone brother Lakshman had just voiced another of his silly, grossly unfunny jokes.

'It isn't funny,' she snapped at him. 'This isn't a joke for your pleasure.'

Rama's smile remained unchanged. His dark pupils gleamed, twin campfires reflected in them. Wind ruffled his dark locks gently. He continued to smile at Sita.

She turned her attention to the gawking crowd of brahmins who had drifted upriver to watch the unfolding drama. They were staring at her in stunned amazement.

'And the rest of you, if you want entertainment, go find the nearest tavern or dance hall! This isn't a free show provided for your amusement!'

Several of the more senior rishis exclaimed, offended by her tone as well as her words. To tell a brahmin to go to a wine hall or dance performance was akin to asking him to deny his faith. Perhaps there were a few dissolute brahmins somewhere in the world who did indulge such fleshly pleasures clandestinely, but these were Siddh-ashrama hermits not city pundits! As she had expected, the sharpness of her words did the trick. In moments, most of the brahmins had moved away, returning to their evening chores. Only a few brahmacharya acolytes continued to steal guilty glances at the two women.

Sita flashed her angry eyes at the Vajra captain next. Bejoo was literally gaping at her, his lips parted as he stared at the two women. More specifically, he was staring at the taller of the pair. He seemed to be physically unable to take his eyes off Nakhudi.

'And if *you* don't order your men to move away and sheathe their weapons, you'll see a bloodier fight than that little encounter with the bandits!'

Bejoo blinked. He rasped shortly: 'Vajra. Stand down.'

The Vajra soldiers retreated, still staring curiously at the women in black. Nakhudi made one final menacing gesture with her curved sword before sheathing it expertly in its waist harness without even a downward glance. Sita saw Bejoo's eyes flick down, following the sword's descent, then return at once to the bodyguard's face. He looked like a man who had just offered a flower gift to a deity then raised his eyes to gaze upon the deity's visage.

'And you can put your eyes back in your head, Captain. She won't grow any taller if you keep staring.'

Bejoo looked suddenly embarrassed. He sheathed his own sword and glanced briefly at Sita. 'Why does the princess-heir of this great nation travel in disguise and without adequate protection?'

'The first question answers the second,' Sita said curtly.

Bejoo stared at her dumbly.

Rama spoke, addressing the captain while keeping his amused eyes on Sita. 'The rajkumari means that since she is travelling in disguise, it would be pointless to bring along her entire royal entourage. She might as well hang a sign around her neck announcing who she is.'

Understanding dawned on Bejoo's face. He kept his eyes on a point midway between Rama and Sita. He seemed to be deliberately avoiding looking at the taller woman again.

Rama went on, 'As for why she's travelling in disguise, I have a fair idea what her motive might be, but perhaps the rajkumari would like to tell us in her own words?'

'The rajkumari would rather jump in the River Shona and drown,' Sita said.

Lakshman made a show of looking at the shallow stream flowing beside them. 'Better find another river. Frogs couldn't drown in this one.'

Nakhudi glared down at Lakshman. 'When you address my mistress, you must speak politely and preface your words with her title, rajkumari.'

Lakshman waggled his eyebrows at the bodyguard. 'In case you've forgotten, Rama and I are rajkumars. So if we do as you say, we'd all be adding a lot of extra syllables to our sentences. What do you say we drop the formalities and just use our first names and save all of us a lot of breath and energy?'

He ended with a broad wink.

Nakhudi strode forward, her face darkening.

'Enough!' Sita moved to join her companion, turning to face the others. Now Vishwamitra, Rama, Lakshman and Bejoo were on one side, facing into the light of the camp-fires, their faces clearly illuminated, while Nakhudi and she had their backs to the fires, their faces shrouded by flickering shadows.

'What my motives were in travelling incognito are none of your concern, rajkumars,' Sita said. 'But out of respect for the venerated brahmarishi, I shall share this information with you.'

'Your graciousness makes me want to supplicate myself in undying gratitude,' Lakshman said.

Rama nudged his brother. 'Enough,' he said softly. Lakshman subsided reluctantly.

Sita studiously ignored Lakshman. Instead she directed her attention to the sage. Inclining her head, she joined her hands in a namaskar. Her tone lost its sharp edge and grew humble and respectful. 'Guru-dev, it was foolish of me to expect to deceive your infinite wisdom and insight. But such was not my intention. I had no expectation of meeting such a venerated seer-mage on the road to—'

She broke off abruptly. 'On the road,' she finished simply.

'On the road to Dandaka.' The seer's tone was final. He was telling, not asking.

Sita stared up at Vishwamitra dumbly for a moment before answering, unable to conceal the shock she felt at the seer's words.

She found her voice at last. 'Indeed, maha-dev. That is where my companion and I were headed.'

Vishwamitra nodded grimly. 'You heard the tales then. Of Asuras massing in the Dandaka-van and Bhayanak-van, and other areas south of the sacred rivers. And you requested your father to send scouts to investigate the rumours. But Maharaja Janak's preoccupation with spiritual matters precluded him from seeing the depth of your anxiety. And so, when he failed to be moved by your entreaties, you decided to take matters into your own hands.'

Sita nodded, awed by the seer's intimate knowledge. 'It was just as you said, Guru-dev. My father is a good man, but his days are spent increasingly in philosophical discussions and the performing of yagnas. More and more, he has come to believe that ahimsa is the only road to salvation. He has almost completely disbanded the armed forces. The entire kingdom of Videha now has barely one full division to guard its borders and police its capital city. Every time we receive news of some new Asura movement or attack – such as the recent invasion attempt on Ayodhya – he dismisses it as idle gossip with no basis in fact.'

She shook her head in frustration, remembering how hard she had tried to convince her father on that last morning, and how he had smiled indulgently and nonchalantly at her and tried to change the topic to her marriage plans.

The sage nodded. Sita felt as if he understood every thought, every emotion she was experiencing now and had ever experienced. His eyes were filled with such bottomless empathy. When he spoke his voice were tinged with a hint of sadness. 'And so you decided to bring him proof that this was not idle gossip. You took your trusted bodyguard into your confidence and convinced her of the merit of your plan.'

Nakhudi spoke, her gruff voice softened by her respect for the seer. 'My people have known of the Lord of Lanka's plans for many moons now, sire. But city kshatriyas regard our clans as warmongers and refuse to listen. They forget that back when war was a way of life, it was the rakshak clans and our clans that watched and warned all the Arya nations. Too many years of peace have made the people soft and thick-bellied. We have forgotten the lessons of our mothers and gurus.'

The large warrior chanted aloud: 'Always watch, always prepare. Carry a sword with you to prayer. Never forget, never forgive. No rest as long as our enemies live.'

She ended by making a gesture of grief at a lost one's memory. 'My father, mother, four sisters and two brothers all died in the Last Asura War. I was too young to fight, or I would have gone to Vaikunta with them.'

She clenched her fist on the pommel of her sword. The sound of the leather was audible to Bejoo, five yards away.

The seer nodded. 'Strong words, Jat. Angry words. As one who has walked the earth from the time of the First Asura War to the present day, I understand your anger and feel for your pain. But Maharaja Janak too saw many loved ones lost in the same war; his own bow and sword were drenched with Asura blood in that last terrible conflict. I know this even though I was engaged in bhor tapasya, for events of such magnitude cannot escape even a seer absorbed in transcendental devotion.'

Nakhudi and Sita frowned at the sage, trying to understand his meaning. He went on gently, 'Both of you misjudge Maharaja Janak's desire for peace and non-violence as a failing. Yet it is the very opposite of a fault, it is a great virtue. The desire for peace and ahimsa is the true sign of the enlightened Arya. It takes great courage to embrace the way of the word over the way of the sword. Maharaja Janak's acceptance of the principles of ahimsa and peace are just as brave as the taking up of arms.'

The two women were silent. Vishwamitra smiled. 'You disagree. After all, you reason, I am a brahmin, and a brahmin would of course favour peaceful non-violence over armed aggression any day.' He shook his head. 'I will not preach to you. These things you must understand through direct experience.'

He glanced up at the dark night sky. 'But the hour grows late and we have a mission to fulfil tonight. Go on, Rajkumari Sita. Continue your tale. After your father rejected your advice yet again, you and your companion donned the black garb of travelling kshatriyas and left the palace and the capital city unrecognised. You travelled southwards, heading for Dandaka-van, the unexplored forests beyond the vale of Chitrakut hermitage. For this was the part of Videha that was mentioned in most of the rumours. You wished to see if there were Asuras there, perhaps even slay a few yourself. Then you could return home and convince your father to allow you to lead an armed contingent back to the Dandaka-van to deal with the menace.'

Sita nodded, her eyes still reflecting her awe at the seer's insight. 'Yes, Guru-dev. It was as you said. But we never reached the Dandaka-van. We were crossing the hills when Nakhudi smelled bandits nearby.'

Nakhudi nodded. 'Even a noseless man could smell them a yojana away.'

Nobody argued the point. Sita went on.

'We crept close to the bandits. They were waiting for something, we saw. We assumed they were laying an ambush for some unsuspecting merchant carting spices or silkworms up from the southern territories where such natural wealth is profuse. We did not know then that they were lying in wait for rksas. We overheard the leader of the clan, the scarred one they called Bear-face, speaking to another bandit. He was speaking of the coming Asura invasion, of how the Lord of Lanka's hordes were already making their way across the great ocean.

'He said that once the Asura armies came north, they would swarm across the land like a plague, laying waste to all in their path. But he and his gang would be spared, for they served the dark lord in their own small way. By slaying the vanars, rksas and kachuas which are the only enemies of Ravana among the animal species. That was why it was important for them to kill as many rksas as possible before the Asuras came. Then they would be able to travel as allies with the hordes and join in the sacking and plundering of Ayodhya.

'He spoke of a jail warder there whom he would torture to death in his own dungeon, and of things he and his gang would do to the female members of the royal family.'

Sita glanced to the right, her eyes meeting Rama's briefly. Then she looked down, clenching her fist in exactly the same way that Nakhudi had done. 'It was horrible hearing such things. Nakhudi and I wanted to rush them and cut them down right there and then. But there were too many of them. Then the rksas came by and the bandits attacked and began . . . began slaughtering them. And we could take no more. We jumped into the fray. And moments later, you appeared.'

She shrugged. 'The rest you know already. Once again, I am grateful to you for assisting us in our attempt to save the rksas from those vile miscreants. But now that you know who I truly am, you will probably understand why I must leave you as well. It is imperative that Nakhudi and I return to the capital as soon as possible. We must return to Mithila and inform my father of these things I have heard and seen. He must be persuaded to arm the city and prepare for its defence.'

She focused her attention on Rama, her voice reflecting her urgency.

'More importantly, Rama, Lakshman and you, with the permission of Guru-dev of course, must return to Ayodhya at once. There was no doubt in the bandit leader's mind that Ayodhya is the primary target of the Asura invasion.'

Sita turned back to the brahmarishi, folding her hands, and went on earnestly.

'Guru-dev, I humbly request you to permit us to leave your company and proceed directly to Mithila. I shall inform my father of your imminent arrival and we shall receive you in Mithila with all due respect and hospitality. But you must allow my companion and I leave to go to the capital with all speed. We cannot afford to take the long diversion to Visala.'

Vishwamitra moved his hand a few inches down the length of his staff, the wildwood rasping against his palm.

'Rajkumari Sita, your father has raised you well and wisely. You are a young woman of great resourcefulness, intelligence and maturity, and I assume, once you have washed the grime of the road off your face and garbed yourself in more alluring garments, great beauty as well. However, you are mistaken in your assumption. The news you seek to carry home to your father is not only inaccurate and grossly misleading, it is in fact planted in your ear by those very forces that you seek to warn Maharaja Janak against.'

Sita stared at the sage in dismay. 'Guru-dev?'

Nakhudi swore. Then immediately apologised to the seer. Vishwamitra ignored both the curse and the apology.

He said instead, 'My good princess, your intentions and efforts were admirable. But you only heard a small part of the full information and deduced the rest from it. It is true that the ultimate goal of the Asura invasion is to take Ayodhya. But it is not their first goal!'

Sita stared up at the sage. 'But maha-dev, if not Ayodhya, then where? What other target could the Lord of Lanka have in mind?'

Vishwamitra's face darkened as he raised his staff and brought it down once resoundingly on the gravelly riverbed. It made a crunching sound like glass breaking underfoot. Sita glanced down and saw that the small smooth stones of the riverbed had shattered into fragments and splinters beneath the force of the apparently small blow.

'The main Asura army will attack neither Banglar nor Kosala, nor even Gandahar or Kaikeya. While there will be sorties carried out on all the Arya nations, the main thrust of Ravana's forces will be directed at only one capital city. The Asura army will pass through these very lands, across this riverbed on which we now stand.'

The sage lifted his staff and pointed in a north-eastern direction. The blazing intensity of the campfires turned the seven-foot staff into a twenty-yard-long shadow racing across the riverbed to the far bank and the edge of the woods. There it vanished into dense darkness.

The seer's voice was so quiet, it was almost lost beneath the crackling of the logs in the fires and the renewed chanting of the brahmins in their camp downriver. Yet every one of them heard his words clearly, and felt the chill they brought to their hearts.

'The attack will be directed at Mithila.'

10

Jatayu was overcome by a great desire to spread its wings and emit the loudest, most ear-shattering screech it was capable of producing. It was slowly going mad with impatience and frustration. How much longer was it expected to wait like a common lackey or steward-at-table?

Was it not Jatayu, king of vultures, proud descendant of the mighty Garuda himself, creator of all birdkind? Had it not led its black-winged hordes in numerous battles, often providing the decisive advantage that swung the seesaw of victory? Had it not slain over a thousand brave kshatriyas with its own talons and beak? Had it not dispatched uncounted thousands of other mortals, brahmins, women, children, and other castemen who dared to oppose its master, the dark Lord of Lanka?

Even in the cosmic assault on Swarga-lok, the celestial realm of the devas, had it not led the sky attack, swooping down through a barrage of brahman bolts that decimated more than half its fellows in a few eye-blinks? Had it not personally avenged its felled companions by setting ablaze the towers of the heavenly city, distracting the king of devas Lord Indra long enough for Ravana's ground troops to gain a vital ingress in the city's battlements?

Did it not father a thousand thousand fledglings each

year, every one devoted from birth to the bloody cause of the king of Asuras? And now, on this momentous day, did it not come bearing vital news for Ravana's many ears? News that the Lord of Lanka himself had commissioned it to seek out? Then why was it kept waiting here in this hall of horrors like a common foot-soldier on dog duty? Not just a few moments but several days had it waited for an audience with its lord and master, precious days in which its valuable news was losing its potency as surely as water leaking from a punctured water-skin.

It started to unfold its leathery wings, sorely tempted to vent its fury in the natural way of its species. It was not the way of the Jatayus and garudas to be treated thus. To be kept waiting in hallways for audiences. To be ignored and neglected. Creatures of wing, masters of the open sky, a Jatayu was free to roam the world, unfettered and un-bound by the puny limitations of mortal limbs. Why should a Jatayu wait when it could simply leap out of a window and soar away?

But there were no windows in the Hall. And the winding corridors down which it had been led by the pair of grunting kumbha-rakshasas – imbeciles! dolts! – had been too la-byrinthine. It would never find its way up again to the Roost, the large terrace where the Jatayu forces massed. The Fortress of Lanka was one of the few places that managed to physically intimidate Jatayu. It had no desire to lose its way in these endlessly winding dark, slime-encrusted corridors and hallways. There were nagas and uragas here, hundreds of thousands of them. And nagas and uragas loved to eat birdfood. Large as he was, ferocious and fierce and re-nowned as he was, even Jatayu was ultimately mortal. Landlocked, within an enclosed stone-walled structure like this one, confronted by an army of nagas and uragas, even it would succumb eventually.

It shuddered, its powerful shoulder and wing muscles rippling to produce a sound like a thousand pigeons fluttering. No, it decided, its burst of temper subsiding as suddenly as it had simmered. Better to stay here and wait a while longer. No need to go wandering in those unholy places. At least here in the Hall there were others of its kind. And whatever a being's individual size or strength, there was always more safety in numbers.

Still, it peered unhappily down the dark, pillared length of chamber. It had been kept waiting much too long. And it was hungry. If the Lord of Lanka didn't take audience with Jatayu soon, it would do something, anything. There came a point when even the king of man-vultures lost patience.

A sound echoed in the depths of the Hall.

Jatayu opened its rheumy yellow eyes, abruptly alert, and scoured the chamber.

That was easier said than done. The Hall of the Fortress of Lanka was no mere assembly chamber. It was vast.

Even if Jatayu were to spread its enormous wings right now, the vulture-king's twenty-yard wingspan would barely stretch across a quarter of the width of the chamber. And if it flapped its powerful wings and flew upwards, it would not achieve any opposition for well over a hundred yards above its scraggy bald head. In fact, several dozen of its own kin were flying high above even now, small, dark silhouettes as small as bats in the uppermost reaches of the vaulted ceiling. Maybe even hundreds. It was too shadowy in the Hall to see much beyond a few yards clearly.

And, like all else in Lanka, there was something about the architecture that defied close scrutiny or accurate assessment. Jatayu had heard the muttered rumour that the interiors of the Fortress of Lanka changed each night, its stones reshaping themselves to the Lord of Lanka's wishes, even its chambers, corridors, hallways, alcoves, pillars and beams shifting and reknitting themselves into new patterns like a vast architectural kaleidoscope shaken by a monstrous child. Nobody, not even the oldest residents of Lanka – and there were few enough of those – knew for certain just how or when it happened. But there was no question that it did change. Jatayu itself found the Fortress a little different each time it returned. It was unsettling to say the least.

It had even heard tell that Asuras who dared to brood or plot against their lord simply vanished in the depths of night, their entire chambers replaced by spiralling stairwells that led nowhere, or enormous bulkhead walls, as if the beasts had never existed at all. Such individuals were never spoken of again, by tacit unanimity. It made for a cautious and remarkably loyal populace: who would dare speak against the lord of a fortress whose very stones obeyed his every command – perhaps even to the point of eavesdropping on his minions?

And of all the chambers in the Fortress, the Hall was the most intimidating.

Even now, as Jatayu scanned the vast chamber for the source of the strangely unsettling sound, the Hall seemed to defy its attempt to plumb its depths. It stretched out before the vulture-king in an apparently unending succession of pillared arches that extended as far as its keen eyes could discern. A thousand yards? Two thousand? There was no telling for sure, with the far end shrouded in semi-darkness, illuminated only by an occasional flickering torch.

The sound came again, this time from right beside Jatayu. The vulture-king started, its wings starting to flap instinctively, its yard-long talons scrabbling noisily for purchase on the slippery floor that seemed to have not a single level flagstone. Its anxiety resulted in more noise than the creature that had materialised beside it.

Jatayu screeched in alarm, rearing up to defend itself against the Arya mortal who had appeared out of thin air. The man was clad in the rich garb of a royal house. Gold bracelets adorned his muscular forearms and clasped his taut biceps. Necklaces of solid gold inlaid with precious stones encased his neck. The sound that had attracted Jatayu's attention had come from the man's weighty jewellery. His handsome head was adorned by a crown that glittered with fine diamonds, each worth a maharaja's ransom. His fair skin, muscular form, striking good looks and poised stance marked him out for nobility, certainly a prince from a great house, perhaps even a maharaja.

Jatayu raised its talons, prepared to strike out at the enemy. Its leathery wings had unfurled to almost half their length, looming above the puny two-yard-tall human, dwarfing him. One slash of those black talons and the man's head would lie severed from its body on the floor of the Hall.

Before Jatayu could strike, the man raised a hand, gold bracelets jangling again, and smiled beatifically.

'You might not want to raise arms against your lord, Jatayu.'

The voice was that of Ravana, Lord of Lanka.

Jatayu stared, its yellow eyes glaring as fiercely as large bright lamps in the murky dimness of the Hall. Its talons, barely a yard above the human's head, froze. There was no mistaking that voice: the gravelly, grinding sound of the king of Asuras speaking was horrible to hear the first time, and once heard, it was never forgotten.

The man smiled sweetly, his handsome face as cheerful

as an Arya prince at a royal feast. 'Does my appearance surprise you?'

Jatayu lowered its talons slowly, trying to contain the sudden urge to shriek and fly screaming up to the rafters. It sheathed its talons, withdrawing them to a third of their formidable length, and its wings shuddered shut with a sound like a canvas tent collapsing. It slumped lower, reducing its height until its eyes were below the level of the human who spoke with Ravana's voice.

'My lord, I did not recognise you in that garb.'

The man raised one perfectly shaped eyebrow. 'Garb? This is more than a garb surely? It's a human body. A quite real and functional one, I assure you. Not the work of maya.'

Jatayu blinked. It could understand maya, the subtle sorcerous art of illusion that Asuras had developed over the millennia to aid them in their unending war against the devas and the mortals. It had been maya that had changed Kala-Nemi's appearance to match that of the seer-mage Vishwamitra when the uncle of Ravana had carried out his intrusion into Ayodhya. But maya was just what the name suggested: illusion. He had never heard of a rakshasa being able to assume a living human body.

The man laughed. 'You're befuddled, my feathered friend. Unable to grasp the concept. It's simple enough really. Remind me to tell you about it sometime. Right now, though, we have work to do. I have a mission for you, bird-master.'

Jatayu tried to bow its head. It was difficult, with its body already scrunched down this low. 'Lanka-naresh,' it said in as respectful a voice as it could muster, 'I have yet to report to you on the result of my last mission. I have returned from Ayodhya with news of great import.'

The man waved dismissively. 'I already know what

transpired on your mission, Jatayu. Let's move on, shall we? Time is short and I have many other urgent matters to attend to.' The handsome face creased in another winning smile. 'Many more matters than I have heads, you might say!'

Jatayu didn't know how to laugh. That emotional expression was not a part of its physiological make-up. It screeched as softly as it could manage, trying to emulate the peculiar sound mortals made when indulging in this inane expression of pleasure.

The mortal who spoke with Ravana's voice grimaced, raising a gold-bedecked hand to shield his delicate human ears from the high-pitched sound. 'Ah, you need to consider taking voice modulation lessons from the gandharvas! But now, let's get to the point, shall we?'

'But master, I have flown a long way to bring you this news.'

'And you will fly a long way to carry out the next mission. Pay heed now. I have places to go and cities to ravage, bald-headed one.'

'But master, my news—'

The change was astonishing. One moment the Arya human's demeanour was all smiles and cheerful patience; the next it was a raging mask of fury.

'SILENCE! YOU DARE TO QUESTION THE LORD OF LANKA? WHO DO YOU THINK YOU ARE, YOU WRETCHED CARRION-EATER?'

If Jatayu's high-pitched attempt at laughter had been offensive to the human's ears, then the glass-grinding, mirror-shattering timbre of the mortal's voice was equally painful to the man-vulture's ears. It reared back several steps, sheathed talons skittering helplessly on the slippery floor, cringing at the low, booming tones of the Asura king's voice, as well as at Ravana's anger.

11

The echoes of the Lord of Lanka's shouted words reverberated down the enormous chamber, travelling until they seemed to reach the ends of the island fortress. The chittering, clicking, grunting, hissing, flapping and other bestial sounds of Asuras scattered throughout the Hall ceased momentarily as every creature in Lanka shivered in anticipation of the demon king's temper.

With a visible effort, the human composed his face into an unconvincing simile of a smile. 'Let's have no more of that, shall we? I have a very important function to attend and I don't wish to arrive in a bad mood. After all,' he added, visibly trying to regain the cheerful demeanour he had presented before his outburst, 'it wouldn't do for a prince to arrive at a swayamvara in a bad temper!'

Jatayu cringed and grovelled as best as its anatomy permitted. The stones of the Hall's floor stank of old ichor and other vital fluids from a dozen different Asura species. 'Forgive my impudence, Lanka-naresh. I meant you no disrespect.'

The man waved the apology away self-deprecatingly. 'Don't bother. You were just eager to do your job, that's all. Just remember, Jatayu, that I oversee not merely some military campaign over here. I am orchestrating the invasion of all of the earth! Sometimes an individual shred of news, important as it may seem to the soldier who has spent so much effort in procuring it, becomes insignificant when the larger picture changes. Since I dispatched you to Ayodhya to report on Kala-Nemi and Supanakha's intrusion, much has changed. The very fact that the intrusion itself failed made your mission redundant. I've long since moved on to other, more important considerations. As for your news itself, well, I have excellent sources in Ayodhya that provide me with all I need to know. There's nothing you can tell me that I have not heard and acted on several days ago.'

That's because you made me wait several days for an audience. And if my news was so unimportant, why didn't you just tell me so earlier instead of keeping me waiting like a lackey in this horrible cold and damp hall for all this time? These thoughts flashed across Jatayu's mind silently, but it saw a flicker of irritation cross the demon-lord's human features and forced itself to say aloud quickly, 'Forgive me, great lord. I await your next command.'

Ravana looked at the giant man-vulture for a moment. Despite the ludicruous difference in size, it was the relatively puny-seeming mortal who exuded danger and power. Jatayu kept its beak dipped and its eyes cast downwards. It was more difficult to keep its thoughts blank and devoid of the frustration and resentment it felt, but it made an effort.

Finally, the king of Asuras spoke again, quietly this time. 'Take your flock to Mithila. They must be in position to attack in three days' time. Do not commence the attack until I personally give you the order. Until then, make sure none of your flock is seen by any mortal. Naturally, they should not be spotted while travelling there either.'

Jatayu shifted uncomfortably from one clawed foot to

the other. 'My lord, I shall do as you say. But it will prove difficult to avoid being seen in the course of the journey. It is a long way to Mithila and there are many ashrams and rakshak outposts that will spot us and send warning of our approach.'

Ravana sighed. 'Did you think I would forget that? The outposts are taken care of. There will be no warnings given. As for ashrams and gurukuls, fly high, stay above the clouds. And on the day of the attack, there will be ample cloud cover. I shall see to that.'

That means I leave today. What about rest and food? What does he take me for? One of his dispensable rakshasa minions? Jatayu struggled to compose itself before replying.

'Very well, my lord. In that case, I suggest that I remain at a high vantage until such time as you call upon us to attack.'

'That would be appropriate,' Ravana agreed, looking suddenly distracted. 'One more thing. When you attack, I wish your flock to direct itself to certain key targets.'

'Key targets, my lord?'

'Yes,' Ravana went on. 'You will focus your attack primarily on brahmins.'

'Brahmins?' Jatayu blinked in surprise.

'You heard me the first time,' Ravana snapped. 'The kshatriyas will be on the walls, defending the city. But the brahmins will mostly be within the city enclave, protected for the most part from our ground assault by all those stupid walls the Aryas love to build. Eventually, we'll ram through and get them all. But I wish to remove as many of the cursed deva-worshippers as possible early in the battle. And walls will be no protection for them against an assault from the skies.'

Ravana gestured with a raised finger before continuing.

'So when I give the word, I want you and every last one of your flock to swoop down like hawks on cobras, killing as many brahmins, seers, rishis, maharishis, sadhus, pundits and their ilk as you can manage in one mass attack. It should be as quick and unexpected as a horde of eagles falling on a nest of newborn serpents. Within moments, every last brahmin in Mithila should lie dead, savagely shredded by your beautiful talons and razor beaks!'

His eyes gleamed, filled with the epic vision of slaughter. 'The Aryas will never know what hit them. Without their seers and priests, they will still be able to fight physically. But spiritually, mentally, they will be crippled beyond repair.'

He laughed, gesturing. 'Because every brahmin in the kingdom of Videha, as well as the highest-ranked brahmin representatives from the other seven Arya kingdoms, will be present there, like a field full of fatted calves awaiting slaughter!'

Jatayu resisted the urge to screech in response. 'Master, it is an ingenious plan. After we are done with the destruction of the brahmins of Mithila, what would you have us do next?'

Ravana blinked rapidly, as if he had forgotten for a moment that he was addressing someone. He focused his blue-grey mortal eyes on the vulture-king.

'After Mithila?' He chuckled sardonically. 'After Mithila, then Ayodhya. And after that, nothing will stand in our way. But first accomplish this much and show me, bird-king! Don't underestimate mortals, like so many Asuras have done before. They are weak of flesh and short of life but their other qualities more than compensate for those shortcomings.'

Ravana's eyes glimmered darkly. 'If you do this for me successfully, if you can show me the ravaged, worm-eaten corpse of every last brahmin in Mithila city, then I will give you an opportunity for advancement such as you have never dreamed of before.'

The disguised demon-king chuckled again, seductively. 'What am I saying? Of course you would have dreamed of it. But I can put it within your grasp at last. Do you know what I speak of, vulture-lord? I mean to make you the new king of your kind!'

Jatayu frowned. What new insult was this? It was already king of its kind.

Ravana smiled, his mortal face cheerful and handsome again. 'Not just king of the vultures and foragers, Jatayu. I mean king of all birds. I will place you above even the lord of birdkind himself, the Maharaja of Pakshis!'

Jatayu peered disbelievingly. Could the Lord of Lanka mean what it thought he did?

Ravana nodded. 'That's right, Jatayu. Do this for me and your path to ascension will be clear of all hurdles. And by the end of my campaign, when the Arya nations lie smashed and bleeding across the land, I will crown you king of Pakshis. You will replace Garuda himself and rule over every last winged being in the three worlds for all eternity!'

Jatayu had nothing to offer in response to that astonishing beak-bending statement. Not even the tiniest of screeches. It was struck speechless and immobile.

It was still searching for words to express its inexpressible response to that amazing promise when the Lord of Lanka raised his hand. 'Enough talk. I will leave you now, my feathered senapati. When we meet next, we shall both have mortal blood on our hands.'

Ravana flashed a brilliant smile. 'And on our beaks as well! But now, you will excuse me. I have a marriage to attend and little time to waste.'

'A marriage?' Jatayu heard itself say stupidly. It was still dazed at the prospect of being king of all birdkind.

'Yes. Well, first a swayamvar, of course. But they are generally followed by a marriage, as even you, my un-mortal friend, probably know.'

Jatayu couldn't understand what attending a marriage had to do with waging a war. So it asked before it could stop itself: 'Whose marriage, sire?'

Ravana flashed another brilliant smile. This time, it was so dazzling, the vulture-king was actually blinded for a moment. Then Jatayu realised that the brilliance came from the Asura lord's use of brahman magic, not the whiteness of his teeth. Ravana was transporting himself instantaneously to another location, using the flow of brahman.

An instant before the Lord of Lanka winked out of sight, he spoke one last word, answering Jatayu's question.

'Mine,' Ravana said.

Rama had a hundred questions, a hundred things he wished to say to Vishwamitra. About the unmasking of the rajkumari Sita, about the things she had overheard the bandit leader saying in the hills, about the Asura invasion that was coming. But moments after announcing that Mithila, not Ayodhya, was to be the first target of the invaders, the seer had abruptly ended the dialogue and told them all to prepare to leave. Bejoo was already giving Sona Chita last-minute instructions about the Vajra, and Lakshman and Rama had begun strapping on their rigs, which they had taken off for the evening ritual and meal.

Nearby, Sita and Nakhudi, their faces bare now that they had no reason to mask themselves, were using the brief respite to have a few words privately. Rama found himself unable to keep his eyes off the rajkumari. He was still trying to adjust to the realisation that Janaki Kumar was a woman. Lakshman, on the other hand, seemed mostly embarrassed by the unmasking and studiously avoided both women. Even when Rama tried to catch his brother's eye, Lakshman grinned sheepishly and looked away.

Brahmarishi Vishwamitra walked down to the riverside, his robes flapping in the sudden chill wind from the north that was growing steadily in intensity and coldness. Just a little while earlier, the weather had seemed calm, almost balmy. Now, as if churned up by the drama on the riverbank, it seemed to be confused and agitated. The wind blowing in from the north had a wet, icy edge to it that could mean either hail or rain, or maybe even both.

Rama found himself thinking that if he found the wind so cold, surely Sita must find it even more uncomfortable. She had no maha-mantras to shield her from the vagaries of nature. He mentally chided himself for thinking such thoughts. What did he think he could do? Offer her the maha-mantras the way you might offer a lady a cloak?

Lakshman nudged him. When Rama glanced at him, he found his brother watching him with a strange expression. For once, he seemed to have no smart witticism to offer. He looked pointedly at Sita and then back at Rama in a manner that was a comment in itself. Rama raised an eyebrow in warning. Lakshman nodded and gestured at the riverbank, at the brahmarishi.

Rama and his brother watched as the sage stopped by the edge of the water, standing as he had earlier that evening when they had reached the Shona, and raised his head to gaze in a north-easterly direction. The sage's arms were raised as well, the wildwood staff clutched in his right hand casting an enormously long shadow that stretched across the meagre river and pointed into the dark depths of the woods bordering the north bank.

Bejoo wasn't entirely certain, but he thought he could hear – feel? – the brahmarishi mouthing mantras in that internalised manner of transcendental meditators. Was the sage praying for their safe journey? It was true that travel by night was unadvisable, as Bejoo himself had pointed out, especially in this part of the country where bandit gangs and wild predators were rife. But somehow he didn't think the brahmarishi would be this anxious about mere dacoits and a few baghs or rksas. There was something else in the air, something imminent.

Bejoo could smell the threat of violence already. What was the sage leading them into this time? Not just a holy dip in the Ganga, that was for sure. What was at Visala anyway? And what was their mission there? Most of all, what did it have to do with the impending Asura invasion?

That was what Bejoo cared most about: the invasion. The instant he'd heard the seer speak of it with such conviction, his first instinct had been to leap on to his horse and ride back to Ayodhya. That was where his place was if war was breaking out again. Not traipsing around the countryside playing daiimaa to a bunch of bald brahmins and two rajkumars who could take care of themselves.

The wind changed just then, carrying the unmistakable drone of sub-auditory incantation, and Bejoo observed with a start that golden and blue motes were issuing from the brahmarishi's mouth, floating towards Bejoo and the rajkumars and their companions like fire-sparks on the wind. From all around, Bejoo heard the uneasy mutters of his Vajra kshatriyas as they watched the seer-mage work his brahman sorcery. Even the Vajra horses and bigfoot grew unusually silent and still. The night seemed to gather in around them, the cookfires flickering and gasping in the wailing wind that had begun to blow, stirring up ashes and leaves.

If Bejoo had had any doubts before, he had none now. Clearly, the brahmarishi was speaking an incantation to ensure their safe and successful journey. What vital mission could they be embarking on now that even a brahmarishi of Vishwamitra's stature felt compelled to ask the blessings of the devas before setting out?

He wasn't entirely sure he wanted to know. He was beginning to think that with the brahmarishi Vishwamitra and the rajkumars Rama and Lakshman, it might simply be best to follow them on their adventures rather than be forewarned about what to expect. That way he could focus on being a warrior, not a worry-wart. There were things in this world that a simple Vajra kshatriya was better off not knowing in advance.

Sita felt the chill in the air and resisted the urge to shiver. She felt Rama's eyes on her. She didn't want him thinking she was . . . what? Weak? Cold? Why not? He must be cold too in this weather. Then she remembered, he was protected by the maha-mantras. By concentrating, he could dispel physical discomfort, even sleep, hunger and exhaustion if he desired.

But that wasn't the reason she felt reluctant to display weakness before him. It's because he's a man. And they're all so quick to assume they're stronger, faster, smarter. Except that she didn't really think Rama was like that. He was . . . different somehow. Not just because he was a prince of the greatest Arya nation. Or the recent champion of Bhayanak-van. If anything, he seemed almost embarrassed about that heroic achievement.

It had taken her – in her guise as Janaki Kumar – almost half an hour of indirect and direct probing and clever questioning to get him to reveal some of his true feelings about the battle in the Southwoods. And even then, she kept feeling he was holding something back. Sita had known many champions before; as a princess she had a line of national heroes seeking her hand in marriage at any given time. She was all too familiar with that particular breed of macho, overbearing, full-of-themselves kshatriya heroes. The champions she had known never held back any details of their conquests or triumphs. Yes, there was something different about Rama. She just wasn't quite sure what it was.

She was drawn out of her thoughts by Nahkudi's gentle nudge. A gentle nudge from the hulking Jat was like a punch in the shoulder from most ordinary men.

Sita looked in the direction Nakhudi was pointing just in time to see the scene unfolding by the riverside. As the brahmarishi's chanting grew louder, something was starting to happen. The sky immediately above the seer-mage had grown darker and angrier, not just night-black but a deep scarlet-edged, purple-hearted black, like a storm approaching. Except that the storm was restricted to a single cloud that grew steadily, boiling and seething more frenetically with every line the mage uttered.

Sita could see blue-tinged lightning flashes exploding within the belly of the supernaturally created cloud. As she watched, it came steadily closer, descending over the section of the Shona riverbed where the kshatriya camp was situated, bringing with it a darkness deeper than night. As she watched, the seer roared his final words and the cloud roared back at him like a herd of wild elephant, opening a dark maw with which it swallowed up the brahmarishi. Vishwamitra was enveloped completely by the seething cloud that now obscured the riverbed for several dozen yards in a northward direction.

Beside her, Sita heard Nakhudi cry out and start to move towards the spot where the brahmarishi had last been visible. Rama and Lakshman and the Vajra captain had seen what had happened and were running down the bank. Sita began running as well.

Within the cloud, Vishwamitra chanted a calming mantra. The seething and boiling reduced gradually, the

thundering died down, until he was surrounded by a
relatively benign fog. It remained thicker than any ordinary natural fog, its texture that of volcanic effusion rather
than condensation mist, but unlike the offal of a volcanic
emission, this cloud did not suffocate or choke. If anything, it was warm and comforting, a blanket against the
abruptly chill early spring night.

Tiny lightning bolts flashed at the periphery of the
brahmarishi's vision. Using his hands and a few carefully
chosen verses he had composed spontaneously for this
specific purpose, he began to reshape the cloud. Controlled by his incantations, it rolled slowly across the
river and into the woods in a roughly straight line, like
the dust-plume of a speeding chariot disappearing down
a raj-marg. The sage's hands blurred as they gestured
and sketched mudras in the air, carving a passageway
through the heart of the midnight-blue fog. After a
pause, he pointed the head of his staff and recited
another incantation: the centre of the long line of fog
opened up, creating a hollow corridor large enough for a
man as tall as the seer-mage – or the Jat bodyguard – to
move through easily. The seer-mage studied the corridor
of brahman fog, then sketched another mudra with his
right hand. The corridor expanded laterally by a half-
yard.

Satisfied, the seer pushed a palm outwards, as if commanding the passageway to go. At once, the brahman
corridor expanded in that direction, unrolling into the
distance for as far as the eye could see.

Behind him, he heard the voices of the rajkumars
approaching. Rama was the first to reach him.

'Guru-dev?'

Vishwamitra turned to Rama. 'It is imperative we reach
Visala before dawn, and Mithila before noon, Rama. Yet,

owing to my penitential vows, I may not ride a mount or seat a carriage. Visala is forty-five yojanas from here, and Mithila another thirty yojanas thence. The combined distance is close to seven hundred miles. Only brahman shakti can help our company reach there in such a short time.'

Rama glanced at the unfurling corridor of dark blue fog still working its way into the distance. 'My brother and I can run that distance, maha-dev. But the rajkumari Sita—'

'And her associate and the Vajra captain,' Vishwamitra continued for him, 'would be unable to match your speed. Hence I have created this corridor. Within this brahman-infused space, all of you will possess the ability to run as fast as you desire. I will lead the way, Rama. Then will come the rajkumari and her bodyguard. Followed by your brother and yourself. The Vajra captain shall bring up the rear. Inform them accordingly.'

'Yes, Guru-dev.' Rama turned to carry out the seer's order. The others were waiting a few yards away, watching anxiously. Rama hesitated, then turned back.

'Speak, Rama.' The sage's voice was quiet.

Rama said, 'Guru-dev, did you know from the very first moment that Janaki Kumar was a woman? I mean, that the kshatriya was actually Rajkumari Sita travelling incognito?'

The sage looked at him. Vishwamitra's eyes were still flecked with the gold and blue motes of brahman shakti.

'Are you asking me why I did not expose her the moment you returned to the procession, rajkumar?'

'Yes, Guru-dev.'

The sage permitted himself a small smile. 'Because all things serve the purpose of brahman, Rama. And because, if I had revealed her true identity at that time, then you would have lost the opportunity to make a new friend.

And I repeat the word "friend". Does that answer your question?'

Rama thought for a moment. Then his expression changed. 'Yes, Guru-dev.'

He turned back to the others.

The night had turned deathly cold by the time they set out. They entered the corridor of fog and made their way across the river. They were able to walk on the water or, rather, on the flimsy translucent smoke. Through the fog they could see the world outside as through a misty window. Colours were dimmed, illumination faded – the lights of the cookfires seemed like glow-worms nesting, and shapes were obscured. It was a strange state of being, neither of the world of waking nor of the world of dreams. Real, yet unreal. Rama was reminded of being underwater. It was a curiously intimate sensation.

The fog itself felt oddly firm beneath their feet but it was the firmness of well-packed damp sand or clay. No pebbles dug into their soles, no dips caught their toes, no rough patches slowed their feet, no smooth places made them slippery. It was like running on an endless undulating platform made of a substance that was like sand, but a perfect, non-gritty sand. That was the only way Rama could manage to describe it to himself.

Already he could feel the shakti of the maha-mantras coursing through his veins, empowering him, sending his feet treadmilling ever faster through the dark foliage at a speed no normal mortal could achieve.

They crossed the River Shona, plunging directly into the dense woods on the north bank, travelling sharply north-east. The lack of a moon made the thick jungle easier to navigate rather than harder. The sage led them, and his staff emitted a blueish glow that was surprisingly effective in illuminating the path ahead, while obscuring everything to either side. Where a moon would have cast a silver net over their entire surroundings, the sage's brahman light lit up only the area ahead that they needed to see as they ran.

He's blinkering us, the way we blinker horses, Rama thought as he picked up speed to match the sage's accelerating pace. He also knew that the seer was somehow using his brahman shakti to expand the corridor ahead as they advanced, just as he was collapsing the corridor behind them as they covered the ground.

As he ran, Rama could smell the Vajra captain sweating liberally behind him. Bejoo was bringing up the rear, and as their speed increased to a level impossible to achieve by normal means, Rama could sense his fear and nervousness. The Vajra captain, like most older kshatriyas, had a palpable fear of brahman sorcery, whether benign or otherwise.

Not just older kshatriyas.

Even now, Rama knew, Lakshman still harboured some vestige of resistance. That fact alone made him that much slower and less strong than Rama, who knew he had passed the point of acceptance and was now ready to explore new levels of the shakti. He felt as if he had discovered the secret that underlay all of creation: and in many ways, he had. Brahman was the power that the universe was made up of. He hoped Lakshman would learn to embrace and accept it in time.

As they ran, his brahman-accentuated senses smelled the odours of the woods: the rich variety of Videha flora and fauna. The jungle was rife with predators of all shapes and species; several balked nervously at their passing, cringing or snarling menacingly as the seer's band sprinted impossibly fast through the pitch-dark jungle. The prey animals only stared dumbly, uncomprehending. Somewhere to his right, Rama sensed a bagheera tensing, preparing to spring. By the time it landed, they were already fifty yards ahead. The bagheera pawed the forest floor frantically, unable to understand how it had missed.

Glancing up, Rama could see stars visible faintly through gaps in the foliage. There was the constellation of Makar the Crab, an ominous sign. From the speed at which the foliage cut the starlight, he estimated that the sage was leading them at a pace of roughly four yojanas an hour. Thirty-six miles. Still too slow.

Ahead of him, he sensed Rajkumari Sita and her bodyguard Nakhudi struggling to keep up the pace. Even though they knew that the sage was using his own shakti to speed them up, Nakhudi had refused to accept that such a thing was possible. Blinkered by the sage's corridored illumination, the hulking bodyguard had probably convinced herself that they were sprinting fast, not superhumanly swiftly. It was difficult to tell speed without clearly visible signposts. Rama wondered how Nakhudi was able to explain the lack of obstacles in their path. But he wasn't really concerned about what Nakhudi was thinking and feeling. He wished, though, he could read what was passing through Rajkumari Sita's mind at this moment.

Rajkumari Sita. It would take some getting used to, calling her Sita now. But he could hardly call her Janaki Kumar any more. He remembered the fall by the river, when he had tried to catch her and stop her slipping into the mud-pool, and she had screamed and batted him away. He had felt the softness of her upper body briefly, but she had pushed him away so hard, he hadn't had a chance to truly suspect anything amiss.

Only now that he knew it was a woman he had caught, not a man, did he understand that unexpected softness and the vehemence with which she had resisted his touch. Everything, her sweating overly, her nervousness at certain questions, her blustering arrogance at others, made sense now. It even added to her personality as he had come to perceive it: the witty, sharp-tongued roving sword-for-hire Janaki Kumar was not entirely fictional. It was just that he was a she with an extraordinary lack of the coy artifice that most noble-born Arya women usually affected.

Rama had met several princesses before – his social status dictated that he would eventually have to marry one – but he had never met a woman quite like Sita. More importantly, he had never met a man quite like her either. That last insight, he realised, went to the heart of the matter. There was something so unusual and attractive about her, it almost seemed irrelevant whether she was a woman or a man. Either way, Rama knew he liked her, him, Janaki Kumar, Janaki Kumari. Sita.

He smiled to himself in the darkness as they ran. The sage was picking up the pace, he sensed. Five yojanas an hour, six . . . seven . . . Now he could no longer tell their relative speed from the starlight and foliage overhead. It took all his concentration to keep pumping his legs and swivelling his arms for balance.

Yet he knew that no matter what he did, the sage had control of them now; they were all being carried by the flow of brahman. Their windmilling limbs were merely allowed to keep moving to provide a rational physical explanation for their progress. If the brahmarishi desired, he could probably whisk them across half the nation in the blink of an eye.

Then why didn't he? Rama wondered idly as the night blended into one endless blur of darkness and wind. Why did seer-mages of Vishwamitra and Guru Vashishta's stature need to bother with physical niceties at all? Why not simply accomplish everything through a wave of a hand and by reciting a mantra or three? It was something to ask the sage when he got a chance.

Right now, he decided to stop thinking and simply run.

13

Sumitra scanned the room in frustration. Manthara's private chambers were so utterly immaculate. The Third Queen had never seen any woman's chamber this clean – except maybe a palace concubine's room, and then only when she expected a visit from her lord. The thought of the withered spinster hunchback entertaining men was ludicrous but it brought no smile to Sumitra's delicate features. She was running out of time. Already she had spent several minutes searching the daiimaa's rooms, without any luck. She had no idea where the woman had gone or when she would be back, but it couldn't be very long. The hour was late already.

Sumitra was beginning to think this had been a foolish idea. Her suspicion of the daiimaa had begun when she had decided to undertake her own investigation of the morning's incident in the maharaja's sick-chamber. After the heart-breaking encounter with Kausalya, Sumitra had realised that if she was to clear her name of this slur, she would have to work alone.

Shatrugan was gone, sent to his grandfather with two divisions to prepare for the imminent invasion; there was still no news of Lakshman's return; and there was nobody else in the palace she could trust to carry out this delicate task.

Besides, who better to do it than herself? She would only grow more miserable sitting in her chambers alone, and while a trusted serving girl would be unable to explore the queens' palaces, Sumitra herself could roam freely without being stopped or questioned. Angry as she was with Kausalya for having believed that she could do such a thing as poison Dasaratha – even by accident – she also had to admit that the First Queen had been gracious enough not to spread her assumption about the palace. Sumitra still retained all her privileges and honour.

Still, it rankled that Kausalya of all people would even entertain such a notion against her. Sumitra would die before she let such a thing happen. But she didn't hold it against Kausalya personally; these were trying times and everybody was under a lot of pressure. She was certain that if she could only find some shred of evidence to support her story, Kausalya would change her assumptions in a trice. That was what had motivated Sumitra the most: the knowledge that Kausalya still loved her, despite the misunderstanding. And that she herself wanted desperately to make Kausalya see that she had misjudged her.

Prosaic, sensible, logical, that was Kausalya. It was what made her so dependable and so perfect. The complete opposite of Second Queen Kaikeyi, who was always a blathering mass of extreme emotions. Kausalya never touched intoxicants; Kaikeyi drank like a fish, although she denied it hotly. Kausalya never ate living flesh, neither meat nor fowl nor fish, and she even avoided any preparation cooked in animal fat; Kaikeyi relished her meat, demolishing skewers and platters at the same rate as any kshatriya male. Kausalya could be passionate, Sumitra knew, but her passion was banked, controlled and always kept strictly within the circumference of propriety; Kaikeyi was wild, wanton, out of control. No wonder then that men found Kaikeyi irresistible and women envied her, while women admired Kausalya and men respected her!

Sumitra sighed. Now she was being unduly harsh. Yes, her comparison of the two senior queens was accurate but it left out one essential factor: heart. For all her prim propriety and rigid adherence to protocol and sanskriti, Kausalya's heart was always in the right place. Kaikeyi, on the other hand, reminded Sumitra of the darkest avatars of the devi that she and Kausalya worshipped. Not the Earth-Mother's Durga avatar, or even her Lakshmi or Saraswati avatars. Those were benign, maternal, affectionate. Kaikeyi resembled the more bloody brooding forms of the ur-goddess. Parvati. Uma. Kali. Or even . . .

The idea came to Sumitra with the suddenness of a flame sparking.

Avatars. Goddesses. Deities.

Pooja room.

What had she smelled the minute Manthara emerged from her chambers and hustled down the corridor like a serpent out of its subterranean lair?

Smoke. Fires. Burnt . . . something. That unmistakable scorched odor of a yagna. Or a cookfire.

Why a cookfire? Sumitra wondered for an instant if she really was suffering from some kind of delirium. How could she have smelled a cookfire in the daiimaa's chambers?

Then it struck her.

Balidaan.

A sacrificial rite.

That was exactly what that odour had been. The distinct, unmistakable smell of a balidaan yagna, like the ones conducted at certain festivals. Less popular now, and generally falling out of fashion as the Arya nations attempted to encourage more rational and scientific behaviour, advocating the necessity of moving on from the superstitions of their ancestors. But indisputably the smell of roasting flesh.

Sumitra searched now with renewed hope, seeking with her nose, not her eyes.

She found it in moments. A faint ashy odour coming from the daiimaa's pooja room. At first, she doubted her nasal sense, thinking that it was probably just some combination of agar, myrrh, camphor, phosphor, the familiar perennially lingering smell of all unaired pooja rooms. But then, as she went further into the room, towards the deity altar, she caught it again. This time it was so pungent and putrid there could be no mistake. This was no blend of wax and camphor or any such thing. It was the smell of burned flesh.

After a few more moments of searching, her nose told her the odour was coming not from the pooja room itself, but from somewhere behind it.

She found the narrow space between the back of the altar and the rear wall a few minutes later. Knocking on the rear wall, she was soon convinced it was hollow. She had expected to find something, but not such concrete evidence. There could be no good reason to have a secret chamber in such a place.

She debated calling for help, thinking through her options carefully.

Her suspicion had been right: someone had been using black sorcery in the palace, just as Guru Vashishta himself had suspected. But unlike the guru, Sumitra had not hesitated to point a mental finger at even the highest-ranking members of the royal family. After all, she reasoned, if she could be accused of having carelessly almost poisoned the maharaja, surely someone could have deliberately attempted to do so. Someone like Kaikeyi. Even when she had learned that Kaikeyi had genuinely been cloistered in her chambers these past nine days, she hadn't been discouraged. That was the whole point of sorcery, that it used maya to deceive and alter perceptions.

Kausalya had found a theory that fitted the facts, however unlikely, and had moved on. But the facts she had considered failed to take into account Sumitra's eye-witness account of what had transpired in the sick-chamber. Now, Sumitra had a theory that fitted the facts that she knew.

Suppose for a moment, she had mused, that Kaikeyi hadn't been in the maharaja's sick-chamber this morning, then perhaps someone else had been there, someone whose appearance had been altered to make her seem to be Kaikeyi. On that assumption, she had questioned all the guards independently, this time asking not if they had seen the Second Queen enter the sick-chamber, but if they had seen anyone else, however innocuous.

The answer had come quickly enough. All the guards had seen a serving girl go in at almost exactly the same time that the incident with Kaikeyi-the-snake had occurred. They hadn't mentioned this earlier to Kausalya because the First Queen had been asking specifically about Second Queen Kaikeyi and nobody else. The guards even recalled noticing that the serving girl had seemed a little flushed and out of breath when she emerged from the maharaja's sick-chamber. But it wasn't the first time they had seen serving girls look that way after a visit to the maharaja and had assumed she was simply reacting to an unusually strong compliment or perhaps an inadvertent brush of the king's arm in passing.

From that revelation, it hadn't taken much further investigation to trace the serving girl back to her point of origin: Manthara-daiimaa's chambers. And Manthara-daiimaa served Kaikeyi. Which made her part of the dark devi camp. Which made her a prime suspect.

Sumitra was not one of those who foolishly harboured irrational prejudices against people who were physically or otherwise challenged. She knew that outward appearance didn't always reflect the inner being. But Manthara was a famous exception to the assumption that beauty was within and not skin-deep.

This wasn't just Sumitra's point of view. There had always been something about Manthara that set her apart, not only from the bustling and lovable daiimaas like Sakuntala-daiimaa or Susama-daiimaa, but from women in general. There was an air about Manthara that made even women want to stay far away from her. An air of deep self-pity that bordered on masochistic tendencies combined with an exaggerated sense of ego and false pride. It made for an unattractive combination. The fact that the wet-nurse was hunchbacked and club-footed would not have deterred her from finding friends and even loyal companions in the royal palace; but her dreaded foul temper, acid tongue and penchant for inflicting brutal corporal punishment on those below her station had given her a notoriety uglier than any physical deformity. She was that saddest of all the devi's girl-children, a woman as ugly on the outside as within.

Now, as Sumitra sought a way to enter the secret chamber behind the daiimaa's pooja room, she wondered what Manthara's game was. Was she using sorcery to try and keep Kaikeyi in the maharaja's favour? Or was it more than that? After all, this morning's near-poisoning had been close to an assassination attempt. Anyone who could have accomplished such a powerful sorcery had surely been practising the dark arts for a long time. And to what purpose? Most troubling of all, was Kaikeyi aware of Manthara's evil activities? How could she not be aware?

Sumitra was so absorbed in her thoughts and search that she failed to notice the figure that had entered the pooja room and now stood behind her, watching with eyes that blazed with fury. Though she had been alert for any signs of the daiimaa's return, she hadn't reckoned with the woman's ability to cloak her own presence through the same sorcery that occupied Sumitra's thoughts.

The first hint she had of Manthara's presence was when the daiimaa spoke a short, harsh incantation.

Before Sumitra could even turn around, the entrance she was seeking so eagerly flew open abruptly. Caught unawares, she fell directly into the secret chamber. At once the stench assaulted and disoriented her. She scrambled to her feet, turning back the way she had fallen in.

But the wall had closed behind her magically. It was seamless and solid once more. More solid on the inside that it had been on the outside, for Manthara's spells had been designed to keep sounds from going out of the yagna chamber, not the other way around. Sumitra was trapped within the very secret chamber she had been trying to find.

14

Among the more incredible sights of that long night run was the view of the Ganga. It was toward the end of the first half of their journey and Rama sensed that they were nearing Visala. Until now, they had been travelling through heavily wooded plains and rolling hills. They emerged into open plains for a few yojanas, mostly brush-land except for a handful of farms.

A field full of cows lowed in sleepy surprise as they shot past. Rama wondered what they saw, or thought they saw. By now, the brahmarishi's party was racing through the brahman corridor at a speed easily seven yojanas an hour. At that rate, all the cows would have seen was a dark-blue cloud of some foggy substance rolling across the field, with some human-like forms within it. The reverse was also true. A pair of dark shuddering figures looming in their path turned out to be two elephants in musth, indulging in the oldest dance of all. The brahman corridor curved upward, over the furiously mating bigfoot, and then down again. The elephants never even noticed their passing, or if they did, it was probably absorbed in the tantric energies of their dance of bliss. They sped over the rutting beasts, then down again, and were gone in a flash.

They came over one final rise, the familiar hump of a millennia-old alluvial deposit that Rama knew at once was the ridge of a river valley. He was right. A moment later, the corridor curved sharply upward, then steeply down the far side of the ridge. They shot down almost vertically, then the corridor straightened out into a more gradual incline, and that was when Rama and his companions were given a clear view of the valley of the Ganga.

Even at night, shrouded in the darkness of an almost completely moonless night – the moon had risen and set an hour earlier, too weak and weary to offer much help – the beauty of the vale was breathtaking. Or perhaps it was just the knowledge that this was no ordinary river vale but the blessed and sacred Ganga herself that added a final sheen of lustre. Whatever the reason, that instant was the first time that Rama wished he could actually stop right there, on that downward-sloping incline, and wait for sunrise. But like so many other incredible sights and experiences since he had left Ayodhya, this sacred vision was not meant for him to enjoy at leisure. And so they had sped on, descending further into the valley, until they were on the famous flat plains of the sacred river's banks, the brahman corridor undulating below and before them then straightening out to shoot ahead until it reached the very edge of the silver ribbon that lay a yojana or so ahead.

The corridor ended at the bank of the Ganga. Previously, when it had encountered obstacles like the rutting elephants or a stream, or even a deep ditch or pit, it had simply carried them across or over. But this time, Rama saw, it was actually stopping. He could see the end of the corridor dissipating as he watched, the fog unravelling and melting away into the darkness.

Rama sensed himself slowing. The brahmarishi was altering their speed to give them sufficient time to halt before they reached the end of the corridor.

He felt a vague sense of disappointment; in its own way,

the running had been enjoyable. In that state of physical challenge, he could simply give himself over to the extreme exertion, blanking his thoughts and emotions for the duration of the exercise. With a return to normality came the return of mundane thoughts, feelings, anxieties. How was Ayodhya preparing for the invasion? Were they sending a force to support Mithila? Did they even know there was an invasion imminent? How was his father's health? How had his mother received the news of his success – and of his delay in returning home?

As he came to a halt, body dripping with sweat, his whole life seemed to come rushing at him like a bandit lying in wait to ambush him. No wonder then that each time he gave himself over to the flow of brahman, he felt more reluctant to return to his own self, to the real world of everyday cares. In that magical plane, everything seemed possible, no problem unsurmountable, every dream achievable. Here, it was the complete opposite. Well, not complete, but close.

The night rushed back in like a wave descending, washing over him. Smells, night sounds, the coldness of the air, the familiar but briefly unfamiliar sensation of standing on solid ground once more.

From what he could tell, they had landed on a knoll near the south bank of the Ganga. He could hear what sounded like rapids up ahead over the rise. Like the rest of this part of the Gangetic plain, the knoll was heavily shrouded in a profuse variety of semi-tropical as well as northern flora. Papaya and banyan stood beside date palm and coconut. Hibiscus reared their intensely coloured heads beside marigold and lionface. Rama could smell the rich soil, could almost feel the fertile power of this land. Only the Sindhu river to the distant north-west across the Hindu Kush range was as fertile as the land irrigated by the

Ganga's flow. Some day, he imagined, great Arya cities would rise here too and flourish. Cities as magnificent as Ayodhya and Mithila, Gandahar and Kaikeya. As long as the Ganga flowed, mortal life would surely go on.

Then he recalled the shadow that fell across their lives in this historic crisis and his proud thoughts turned grim. There was still the Asura invasion to survive.

Ahead of him, Nakhudi and Sita turned around, examining their surroundings. Sita's eyes sought him out. He nodded briefly at her. She turned away abruptly, ignoring the gesture.

Lakshman came up beside him. He spoke softly in Rama's right ear, 'Looks like someone's still sore as a mule at being outed, brother. Watch out for her back-kick!'

Rama dug his elbow into Lakshman's ribs. Lakshman anticipated and dodged the elbow. He collided with Bejoo, who was coming up to join them.

'Easy there, rajkumar. Takes a moment or two finding your land feet again after that magic flight, doesn't it? Now I know how geese must feel when they touch ground again after flying across the earth.'

Rama gestured to them both to be quiet. 'Guru-dev calls.'

The sage was beckoning to them. They went to him. The ground was covered with deep roots and trailing vines and creepers. They made their way up the side of the knoll to where the seer stood with his staff extended to arm's length, facing them. The head of the staff glowed softly blue, casting enough light to see by.

'Walk with me,' the brahmarishi said. He led them to the top of the knoll, parting the bushes that blocked their way. The sound of the river grew louder as they went further. They emerged from the shrubbery on to a small shoulder of land that jutted out sharply.

They were looking down at the Ganga, dark and resplendent as a rope of black velvet in the darkness of the moonless night. The sage stood at the edge of the knoll and pointed down with his staff. The head glowed intensely brighter, illuminating the calm clear waters flowing below.

'Behold the Ganga,' he said, 'the destination of every devout Arya. Blessed are those who seek it. Graced are those who find it. Tonight, it is our goal as well.'

He pointed with his staff to a pathway leading down from the knoll to the riverbank.

'Come,' he said, leading the way. As they went down the path, the seer continued:

'We shall cross from the bank below. But first, I have words to say to all of you. These words will save your lives tonight and perhaps even ensure the survival of Mithila tomorrow.'

Vishwamitra led them down the path to the bank below. The bank was clear for several yards, like many spots Rama had seen along the Sarayu that were marked for ferry crossings. Sure enough, a boat was moored to a rod embedded on the bank. It bobbed gently in the river, a sturdy, well-constructed little vessel that seemed just right to carry the six of them.

They sat by the bank of the Ganga. The river flowed gently beside them, its passage soft and musical. This was not the fierce roaring of the Sarayu, glacial and ferocious as a kshatriya army descending from the mountains. The Ganga was a brahmin body, flowing serenely across the subcontinent from west to east.

Vishwamitra hardly needed to raise his voice to be heard by his band. 'In a few moments we shall cross these blessed waters. Our destination lies on the north bank, a few yards downstream.'

Bejoo frowned. 'Forgive me, maha-dev. I am not overly familiar with this area and it is difficult to tell where exactly we are at night without landmarks visible. But I would think that Visala is at least half a yojana's walk from here downriver.'

The Vajra captain indicated the sky above. 'At least that is what I would deduce from the position of the Makar constellation in the seventh house.'

'Well mapped, Captain. But we have a task to complete before we enter the gates of Visala. In fact, this task is the reason we came here. Back by the banks of the Shona, I deliberately emphasised Visala to avoid letting our enemies know our real destination.'

'Our enemies, maha-dev?' Lakshman looked surprised. 'But there was nobody to hear us by the Shona. Only our own kshatriyas and brahmins.'

Vishwamitra's voice was unruffled and serene. 'So it often seems, rajkumar. Yet in these hours of crisis, you can be certain that our foes have eyes and ears everywhere, observing us as closely as a cobra watches the jaws of the mongoose.'

Everybody looked around uncertainly. Nakhudi's hand went to her sword pommel, her deep-set eyes darting from side to side as if expecting an ambush at any moment. Bejoo, still the rearmost, turned a complete circle before returning to his original stance, his hand also gripping his sword's hilt.

'Keep your swords sheathed, brave kshatriyas,' the seer went on calmly. 'You will have need of them before the night is past, but not yet. Now I must take a few moments to explain our task ahead. For though our mission tonight will seem simple enough, it is fraught with any number of hidden dangers that even I cannot describe clearly.'

The sage's voice grew sombre. 'The task we undertake is of a delicate and dangerous nature. As the one who leads you, I must warn you what lies at stake. It is likely that some of us may not live to see the sun rise this morning. And yet, if we fail to achieve this task, the proud city of Mithila will not survive to see the same sun set this same evening. This I know for a certainty.'

The brahmarishi gestured with his staff, pointing towards the east. 'As Captain Bejoo rightly informed us, Visala is but a few short miles further east of here. On the outskirts of the city is the hermitage of the sage Gautama. I need hardly explain his history to you well-educated Aryas.'

'The sage Gautama of yore?' Sita asked, sounding astonished and reverential. 'He of the Seven Seers?'

'The very same,' Vishwamitra replied. 'Along with Vashishta, Bharadwaja, Jamadagni, Kasyapa, Atri and myself, Gautama makes up the fellowship of seven that mighty Brahma himself ordained for the protection and overseeing of mortalkind's spiritual progress.'

'But maha-dev,' Sita said, 'Maharishi Gautama no longer resides there. It is true that his ashram is situated on the outskirts of Visala. And many fortunate Arya sons and daughters are schooled at the gurukul there by the able rishis of Gautama's order. But the great sage himself has been absent from that place for more years than anyone can count.'

'I can count,' the sage said. 'And by my estimate, close to two thousand and three hundred years have elapsed since Gautama took the vows of samadhi.'

Rama spoke. 'Guru-dev, by your own admission, the maharishi took samadhi. Is that not the same as leaving the mortal plane?'

'Nearly so, Rama. Yet not quite. Samadhi is the ultimate

penance. A total surrendering of one's physical body in order to immerse oneself completely in the flow of brahman. When a mortal undertakes it, it is equivalent to fasting unto death. But the Seven Seers may sustain themselves on brahman itself, eschewing mortal necessities such as food and air indefinitely. Gautama remains alive within the ashram that he built himself several thousand years ago. Yet his vital signs have been slowed to such an extent that it is as if he lives no more. He has become akin to an effigy of his own self.'

Sita said, 'Maha-dev, there is an effigy of Maharishi Gautama within the ashram, beside the tulsi plant in the temple. It is made of earth and painted with chunna. Due to its extreme age, it is overgrown with vines and creepers. Birds nest in its crevices and cracks. Yet if you look at it closely, you can see that it is amazingly lifelike in resemblance to the portraits of the sage in my father's palace at Mithila.'

Vishwamitra looked at Sita. 'Have you seen the statue yourself, rajkumari?'

'Oh yes,' she said. 'I have touched its feet and prostrated myself before it, as all the shishyas do each morning before starting their lessons for the day. It is a part of the daily ritual at Gautama-ashrama.'

Vishwamitra allowed himself a small smile. 'Then you have met the maharishi already. That statue is Gautama himself, frozen by the sheer force of will into a state of suspended animation for the past two millennia and almost three hundred years!'

Sita stared at the brahmarishi. Her mouth opened and shut without saying anything.

Vishwamitra nodded understandingly. 'Say no more, rajkumari. The night is short and I have an important sandesh to give you yet. As I have just explained, the sage

Gautama took samadhi. Every Arya child knows this. But do you also know why?'

He answered his own question. 'Of course you do. The great sage was blessed with a wife named Ahilya. An avatar of Ratri, the goddess of night, who herself was one of the countless avatars of Sri, the Mother-Goddess, creator of the universe. Ahilya was the most beautiful woman ever to walk the earth. Her visage was said to be so splendid to behold that if she walked by the ocean at sunset, the sun god Surya would delay his descent, making the day last as long as she continued to walk, just so that he could gaze on her beauty. On one occasion, it was said, Gautama and Ahilya decided to sleep out of doors at night. The sun never set all that long night. After that, Ahilya decided she would sleep indoors to prevent causing nuisance to the other inhabitants of Prithvi.

'Talk of Ahilya's beauty spread through the three worlds until one day it reached the ears of Lord Indra, raja of Swarga-lok, the realm of the devas. Apart from his prowess as a warrior, Indra was notorious for his love of feminine beauty and renowned for his mastery of the art of love. He descended to earth to gaze upon Ahilya's beauty. He doubted that she could possibly be as beautiful as her admirers claimed, but Indra was a man who would stop a battle in order to dally with a mistress! So he visited the sage Gautama's ashram near here, on the banks of the blessed Ganga.'

Bejoo spoke apologetically. 'Forgive me, maha-dev, but a moment ago you spoke of the maharishi's ashram on the outskirts of Visala. How then could it also be situated here, five miles upriver?'

The brahmarishi's voice was forbidding. 'That is part of the story, Captain. If you would only listen instead of interrupting like a kai-kai bird, you would learn the answer to that and several other questions as well.'

Rama glanced at Bejoo. The Vajra captain looked chastised but not put out. Evidently he had begun to feel some respect for the brahmarishi after all. Then again, Rama mused, perhaps it had something to do with the brahmarishi softening his attitude to the Vajra captain as well. The fact that Vishwamitra addressed Bejoo as 'Captain' instead of 'kshatriya' even when scolding him just now was telling. Rama smiled to himself and turned his attention back to the brahmarishi's tale.

'As I was saying, Indra came to the maharishi's ashram to see Ahilya. But he did not wish to be recognised by either Ahilya or her venerated husband. So, as he often did on such escapades, Indra took the guise of sage Gautama himself. He also chose the moment of sunrise, when the sage was certain to be down by the river performing his morning ritual.

'Ahilya had just completed her morning ablutions and was enjoying a few moments' respite before preparing breakfast for her husband. Her hair was wet, freshly washed in the river, and her ang-vastra was still drenched and clung to her ivory-pale body. She sat in the first rays of sunlight in a grove, drying her hair and body. In a moment she would rise and go within the ashram to dress and finish preparing the maharishi's morning repast. But for now, she was content to sit there on a cot, stretching her limbs carelessly.

'As she sat there, she was unaware that she was being watched by a pair of eyes that belonged to one of the most lascivious men in the three worlds. For Indra had stopped in his tracks the instant he laid eyes on Ahilya. And he was watching her with rapt attention.

'Soon, Ahilya rose and went within the ashram. Indra's

eyes wept, for he had not blinked or looked away since seeing her. The deva was tumescent with uncontrollable desire. He could not resist the allure of Ahilya's beauty. He decided there and then that he must have her. As it had done on many occasions before, Indra's priapic lust overcame his sense of duty, and he stalked into the ashram to bed the wife of another man.

'He found Ahilya in her private room, in the very act of disrobing completely. The sight was too much for the deva to bear. He took hold of the sage's wife and began to shower her with passionate kisses, all the while reciting praises of her beauty. Ahilya was taken aback at first. But to her innocent eyes, the man making love to her was her own husband. It was strange, she felt, that he had finished his morning ritual so quickly and that he was displaying such extraordinary passion at this early hour. For Gautama, though a bull among men, was a man of strict spiritual discipline and had perfect mastery of his appetites. Yet she was swept away by the sheer vehemence of Indra's love making and succumbed.

'But there came a moment in the heat of their passion when Indra's control over his garb slipped momentarily. Just for a fraction of an instant, he was visible to Ahilya as himself, Lord Indra, raja of the devas. The moment passed in a flash, and then he appeared to be sage Gautama once more. An instant later, he reached the climax of his passion and spent himself.

'In that moment, Ahilya faced a terrible dilemma. Though she had seen through Indra's disguise, the revelation had come too late for her to prevent her seduction. Had she seen the truth earlier, she might have stopped him or called to her husband for help. But at such a climactic moment, she could do nothing except throw him off. And knowing then that he was Indra himself, she was too shocked to act. The instant had passed and she had been used. The deed was done and nothing could change that fact.'

15

Manthara wanted to kill the woman and be done with it. Wanted to go into the secret chamber, seal it with yet another cloaking mantra to ensure that even the most agonised of screams didn't emerge as so much as a whisper of a whisper, and then kill Sumitra-maa.

She still thought of the Third Queen as Sumitra-maa because her first role in this house had been that of wet-nurse, and all the wet-nurses referred to the queens as maa. But right now, it wasn't Sumitra's motherly stature that was filling her with rage, it was the impudence of the Third Queen. She had entered Manthara's private rooms! She had violated her inner sanctum! And why? There could be no good reason for such an intrusion. Obviously the Third Queen suspected something after this morning's encounter in the maharaja's sick-chamber.

Manthara had always thought of the frail, delicate, bird-like little queen as a koel. So pretty to look at, such delicate colouring and plumage. So sweet to hear. And so easy to crush. Just one bunched fist and the Third Queen would be a heap of crumpled bones and mangled flesh. Of all the people in the palace, Manthara had feared Kausalya, Guru Vashishta, Sumantra even. But never Sumitra-maa. And yet life had a way of surprising you sometimes.

She had left her chambers in such a hurry, forgetting

even to lock her doors. After all, nobody ever came there except Kaikeyi. And the Second Queen was in no condition to go wandering around right now; she was still lying in her bed in the same drug-addled state in which Manthara had kept her these past nine days. Soon, when the time was right for her to fulfil her lord's final command, she would revive Kaikeyi and send her on one last mission. The last thrust of the dagger into the bleeding heart of Ayodhya's royal house.

But first she had to deal with this new nuisance.

How had Sumitra-maa found the secret chamber? Had someone said something? Manthara cursed herself for not getting rid of that serving girl after the morning's work was done. The girl knew too much. Not about the presence of the secret chamber, but she knew that Manthara had been paying the tantrik in the Old Quarter to kidnap brahmin infants for her to offer as sacrifices. That was enough to destroy Manthara. Yet she had let the girl live. Why? Because she had been useful. And because the day of the lord's coming was nigh. Any day now, Manthara's true liege would ride through Ayodhya's burning streets before an army of Asuras and none of this would matter any more.

But until that day came, Manthara had to abide by the rules of this world, this society. Which meant that she would have to deal with the Third Queen somehow. And quickly. She doubted the queen would be missed until morning, and even then a likely explanation could be cooked up to justify her absence. A spontaneous urge to travel to Gandahar perhaps, to follow her son Shatrugan to the seat of her family. She might have left unexpectedly in the middle of the night, taking only a serving girl or two and very few possessions – after all, she was going to her father's house.

Yes, that might do. Manthara thought she could use a maya spell to convince Susama-daiimaa of Sumitra's unexpected night journey. And once Shatrugan and Lakshman's wet-nurse was convinced, she in turn would pass on the news with unshakeable conviction to the rest of the palace. Nobody would suspect anything amiss or think to check with Gandahar; and even if someone did, or if a courier came from Gandahar and denied that Sumitra had ever arrived there, it would be too late. The invasion would have occurred by then, and nothing would matter any more.

But it still left one vexing question. How was Manthara to deal with the Third Queen? She was still angry enough at the violation of her privacy to want to burst into the secret room and tear the woman to shreds. She licked her lips at the prospect. It was no challenge to sacrifice little boys; they were too terrified and much too small to struggle. But she had a feeling Sumitra would put up a good fight. Despite her apparently delicate physical appearance, the Third Queen seemed to harbour a deep inner strength that would make her a worthy opponent.

Manthara's lips curled in a smile. Yes, it would be interesting to kill the Third Queen and offer her up as a sacrifice to Ravana. She had no doubt she would be able to murder Sumitra-maa. After all, even if they were evenly matched physically – which she doubted – Manthara still possessed the powers given her by the Lord of Lanka. She would win easily, but it would be fun to let Sumitra think otherwise for a while. It would heighten the pleasure of the sport.

And then, when she was done toying with the Third Queen, she would unleash her shakti and show the foolish woman her real face. Did she think she was dealing with merely a retired wet-nurse? A hunchbacked cripple?

Stupid woman! She would see what Manthara was truly capable of. Manthara would show her how she dealt with those who tried to thwart her ambitions . . . and she would take her time showing her.

The only question then left to answer was what to do about that stupid serving girl. Manthara had no doubt that the girl had outlived her usefulness and would now bring only needless risk. She must be dealt with at once. Very well. First she would go out and search the taverns and dance halls, find the wench, and kill her in some dark alley if possible, or bring her here and throw her into the hidden chamber as well, to be killed along with the Third Queen. Either way, Manthara would get rid of these two nuisances tonight, and tomorrow, when the word from Ravana came, she would embark on the final stage of their great master plan. And soon it would all be over.

She raised her cowl, preparing to leave her chambers and go out once more, to search for the serving girl. Just then a voice came from the outer room. Manthara went out, frowning at this new intrusion. Her withered, arthritis-stricken hand twisted into a claw, ready to cast a maya spell at the visitor. Her heart thudded once, hard, at the thought that it might be Kausalya-maa, come in search of Sumitra. Then she remembered: Kausalya-maa hadn't left the maharaja's side since the guru had exorcised him. And before that, she hadn't had any contact with Sumitra-maa all day. Sumitra had been acting entirely on her own, for the express purpose of proving her innocence to Kausalya. That was the beauty of it.

Still, Manthara whispered the first syllables of a powerful mantra before she emerged into the outer room. If the visitor was an unwanted one, she would be that much closer to blasting the unfortunate intruder out of his or her shoes.

The girl in the outer room swung around, startled at Manthara's quiet appearance. 'Mistress! I was about to leave. I thought you weren't here.'

Manthara's eyes narrowed suspiciously. 'What brings you here at this hour, foolish thing?' She couldn't accept the fact that she had just been saved a long night's searching through the more disreputable part of the city. Surely the serving girl's appearance wasn't just a lucky coincidence?

The girl came forward excitedly, swaying slightly. She was quite drunk, Manthara saw – and smelled. 'It's about the coins you gave me, mistress. One of them's a counterfeit! It has the maharaja's seal and all on it, but it's not pure gold as it should be, it's only part gold, and part brass, and mostly silver.'

The girl held out a gold rupee embossed with the profile of a much younger and handsomer Dasaratha.

Manthara recognised the coin well; it was one of a large batch she had had forged herself, providing the stolen king's seal as well as the gold and silver portions. It was part of the earlier, more mundane phases of the Lord of Lanka's master plan for undermining the strength and supremacy of Ayodhya and the House Suryavansha. Manthara commonly paid her accomplices in counterfeit coin: the scoundrels were doing dishonest work anyway, they were in no position to protest to the city magistrates!

Manthara knew then that the serving girl was here alone, that her coming was destined. She took it as an omen that her success was assured tonight. She smiled invitingly at the girl, beckoning to her.

'Follow me then. I'll take that back and pay you in the coin you deserve. In here.'

She led the serving girl into the pooja room and to the rear of the altar. The girl was too drunk to suspect anything, and by the time she realised where she was, it was too late.

'Mistress?' she said, peering drunkenly into the dimness behind the altar. 'What—'

Manthara shoved her as hard as she could. The serving girl gasped once and fell through the portal, into the secret room. The portal closed with the speed of an eye blinking. Manthara barely had time to see the Third Queen's face before it winked shut.

She cackled to herself, wringing her hands in anxious relief. Now she had two birds on the same stick. And roast fowl was her favourite meal!

'The sage Gautama returned at that very moment and found his wife in bed with the imposter. Lord Indra's garb fell away like a dried leaf in autumn, exposing his true self. He sprang up from the sage's bed and prostrated himself before Gautama. He lamented his loss of self-control and asked the sage to forgive him.

'But Gautama could not forgive. This was no simple ravishment by some vile Asura. Nor even a gandharva consorting with a wanton apsara. This was his wife. He had been cuckolded. And the cuckolder was none other than a deva, a being who possessed the power of life and death over mortals. If Indra could perpetrate such an atrocity and be allowed to go unpunished, what weight would the laws of dharma have? Nay, as one of those chosen to school mortals in the laws of dharma, Gautama the seer could not permit Indra to escape unpunished, any more than Gautama the man could forgive the deva for this vile transgression.

'So Gautama inflicted on Indra the most terrible punishment he was empowered to give. With a single spoken incantation, he gelded the deva, rendering him impotent and incapable of repeating the act of fornication for the rest of his eternal existence. Thus he stripped the deva of his ability not only to procreate but to perpetuate his own line until the end of time.

'In addition, so that the entire world might always be reminded of Indra's shameful crime, Gautama issued a second incantation. This one punished Indra for the crime of seeing and coveting another man's wife. He willed that since Indra had eyes for so many women, he ought to be covered with a thousand eyes. And thus Indra was doubly penalised and marked for ever.'

Vishwamitra paused. 'How Indra attempted to overcome the maharishi's curse and whether he succeeded or not is another tale and one that I will not tell tonight. But hear now what befell Ahilya.

'Perceiving that his wife had been deceived and seduced by the deva, Gautama's anger cooled marginally and he was inclined to forgive her for this inadvertent transgression. But because he was still inflamed by the sight of his wife lying naked beside the deva, he asked her one question.

'Had she known that she was being bedded by Indra or had she truly been deceived by his guise?

'Now, Ahilya was a virtuous and honourable woman. So despite fearing her husband's ire, she replied honestly. Her truthful answer was, Yes, she had known that it was Indra who lay with her and not Gautama, but—

'Alas, poor Ahilya was unable to complete her explanation. To her husband's enraged mind, the word "yes" itself was a condemnation. Her admission rang in his ears like the bells of the great temple at Mithila. She had knowingly fornicated with another man? In her own marital bed? Unspeakable! The maharishi's rage was of such proportions that Lord Indra, minus his testicles and covered from head to toe with a thousand staring eyes, fled the ashram without daring to ask the sage's forgiveness once again.

'Ahilya's curse, spoken by Gautama with lightning swiftness, took effect before she could utter another word of explanation. Had she been given the opportunity to tell her side of the story, certainly the maharishi would have seen that she was blameless and innocent of any guilt. But her own honesty had condemned her.

'Gautama decreed his wife's fate with a single gesture and incantation. Since she had transgressed by yielding to physical desire and pleasure, she would be deprived of any physical sensation or pleasure for the rest of her days. And since, as the wife of one of the Seven Seers, she would live a considerable lifespan, the curse would be in effect indefinite. In order to enforce it, the sage sent her along with the entire hermitage, to the bottom of a pool nearby. This was no ordinary pool though. It was the Pit of Vasuki.

'The Pit of Vasuki was the hole that was dug in the ground when the devas called up the serpent lord that dwells in the bowels of the earth. They required Vasuki to wind around the mountain Himavat, and churn the great ocean of Sagara in order to produce the amrit, the nectar of immortality. That is the tale of the Amrit-Manthan, and that too is a tale that you shall hear another time.

'All you need know now is that when the Amrit-Manthan was done and the amrit was collected, along with many other miraculous by-products of the churning, a deep hole remained in the ground. That is the Pit of Vasuki. Many fantastic events occurred after the churning, one of which was the bringing of the Ganga from the realm of Swarga-lok down to earth. When the Ganga fell to earth, flowing from the bound tresses of Lord Shiva himself, the three-eyed deva took great care to let it fall gently so as not to harm any living creature. For, despite his notoriety as the Great and Terrible Destroyer, Shiva in truth has great love and respect for all creatures mortal and otherwise. This is why he is also named Pashupati, or lord of animals.

'But at the instant that he was pouring the Ganga on to the earth, his elephant-headed son Ganesha and his younger brother Kartikeya were playfully wrestling nearby. In the course of their play, Ganesha's trunk flicked up and brushed against his father's hand. So Shiva's control slipped by the tiniest fraction. He corrected himself at once and told his wife Parvati Devi to take the boys outside to play their boyish games, but in that moment a single drop of the Ganga splashed out of its chosen course. That drop fell into the Pit of Vasuki, and being a drop of divine Ganga water, it filled the vast pit from top to bottom.

'At the bottom of the Pit of Vasuki, Ahilya lies still, trapped for all eternity. For her husband took samadhi soon after this tragic incident. Since Gautama, as one of the Seven Seers, possesses the power to prolong his life indefinitely through the pursuit of bhor tapasya, and since by taking samadhi he is frozen in the ultimate penitential form, he can continue thus for ever. And as long as he lives, Ahilya will live as well. If you can call such an existence living. Imprisoned at the bottom of the Pit of Vasuki, chained by the sage's curse, she endures still, feeling no pleasurable emotions, only pain, sorrow, regret and guilt. Physically her condition is even worse. Her body is as stone, it can feel no sensation at all. She is condemned to a life of the mind and the spirit.'

Silence greeted the seer as he lowered his staff, indicating the end of the story. All the five travellers, eager and brimming with questions and comments at the start of the narration, were silent now.

Vishwamitra looked at each one in turn, lingering on Sita a moment longer than the others, then his piercing eyes sought out Rama.

'Your silence is eloquent, good kshatriyas. I see you have taken this tale to heart. Yet you must prepare yourself. For one last chapter remains in the tale of Gautama and Ahilya. And that chapter will be written by us this very night.'

He pointed at the far bank of the river. 'There, in the heart of that vinaashe-wood thicket, lies the Pit of Vasuki. That is our first destination on this arduous mission. We shall cross the river now and enter the thicket. When we find the pit, Rajkumar Rama shall enter it and descend to the bottom of its waters. There he will revive Ahilya and return with her to the surface. Then we shall all proceed to Gautama-ashrama, to reunite the sage with his wife and plead her case to him. After that, we may proceed to Mithila. But we must act with haste and boldness, for already the night grows old and the sun god has almost completed his circuit of the far side of Prithvi. In a few hours, it will be dawn. That is how long we have to complete this task. Now, let us board the boat and cross the sacred river.'

Rama stopped the brahmarishi. 'Guru-dev, may I ask a single question?'

'Swiftly then, Rama. Time is scarce. We have much to accomplish this night and the coming day. The fate of at least one Arya nation, a great holy city, and perhaps the future of all mortalkind rests on our success or failure. Ask your question, but once it is answered, we shall speak no more until we are at the Pit of Vasuki.'

'Yes, Guru-dev,' Rama said. 'My question is, how can I, a mere mortal, overturn the curse issued by a seer of Maharishi Gautama's eminence? I am willing and eager to fulfil your every command diligently and with all the knowledge and wisdom in my possession, but this question troubles me. How can I overturn a curse when I know nothing of such things? I am a kshatriya after all. Perhaps you, with your infinite knowledge of brahman, might—'

'Say no more, Rama,' Vishwamitra broke in. 'Your question is pertinent, so I shall attempt to answer it as briefly as possible. After the curse was pronounced and put into effect, the devas themselves sent a delegation to the sage Gautama. This was shortly before he took samadhi. They pleaded with him on behalf of Lord Indra as well as on Ahilya's behalf. Indra's fate does not concern us, but when the devas, by dint of their divine knowledge of mortal affairs, revealed to Gautama the full explanation that his wife herself had been unable to give him, he was filled with remorse at the harshness of the penalty he had imposed upon her. He regretted his curse but could not take it back completely. For that would undermine the value of his words. What would people think if a sage penalised a deva so harshly but allowed his own wife to go unpunished? So he spoke a codicil to the curse, an amendment that allowed for a means of Ahilya's liberation.'

'Of course!' Sita said excitedly. She added apologetically: 'With your permission, Guru-dev. If I may continue? Every visitor to Gautama-ashrama is told about this part. The maharishi Gautama proclaimed then that if and when a young boy pure of body, mind and spirit should be willing to risk his life to free Ahilya without any ulterior motive, she would be freed of the curse!'

Everybody turned to look at Rama. He felt his face burn with embarrassment.

'Pure of mind and spirit I follow,' Nakhudi's gruff nasal voice said. 'But what exactly does it mean, pure of body?'

It was Lakshman who spoke, saving Rama the

embarrassment of replying himself. 'It means a man who has not loved a woman yet. In other words, a virgin.'

'Indeed,' Vishwamitra said drily. 'A virgin. Now your question is answered, Rama, and our task still remains to be done. Do you have any more questions?'

Rama shook his head silently.

The sage gestured impatiently. 'Come then, waste no more time. Board the boat and let us cross the river.'

16

The crossing took very little time. The ferry was a pull-across. Bejoo and Nakhudi took hold of the rope and began dragging them over. The Ganga was barely fifty yards wide at this place, one of the narrowest points in the river's mighty course. They disembarked on the north bank moments later. Sita had run her hands in the river as they were pulled across vigorously by her bodyguard and the Vajra captain. Nakhudi noticed her damp garments as they left the ferry and frowned disapprovingly. Sita responded by flicking water in her face. Nakhudi raised her hand to wipe it off, then remembered it was Ganga water and let it dry. It was considered inauspicious to wipe off water from the sacred river, and Jat kshatriyas were perhaps the most superstitious of all the kshatriya clans.

The night was still moonless and pitch-black but their eyes had adapted by this time. Or so Sita thought at first. When she looked around and began recognising species of flowers and even night insects scurrying underfoot, she knew that her vision couldn't possibly be this good. She turned her head back and found she could see clear across the river to the south bank, right to the place on the knoll where the brahman corridor had deposited them. Even Nakhudi's owl-like night vision wasn't that sharp.

When she turned back, Rama was beside her, watching her curiously.

'Night vision?' he asked.

She nodded.

He gestured with a nod at the brahmarishi.

Ah, that explained it. The seer had used his powers to enhance their vision. What else had he done to them? She wondered if maybe he had infused the three of them with some mysterious shakti as well, the way he had infused Rama and Lakshman.

She found Rama still watching her. As if reading her thoughts, he shook his head. 'No,' he said softly. 'Just the night vision. And a cloaking spell to prevent us from being seen too easily.'

'Seen by what?' she asked.

The sage spoke quietly then, calling them forward. Rama and Sita had lagged behind by a few yards. They ran to the edge of the vinaashe thicket where the others waited on their haunches, crouched over behind a clump of bushes. Nakhudi shot her an admonishing glance at the exact same time that Lakshman gave Rama a raised-eyebrows look. Sita resisted the urge to laugh out loud.

'We shall go into the woods separately,' the sage said quietly. 'That way, it will be difficult to tell which of us intends to enter the Pit of Vasuki. If we are attacked, which is more than likely, we shall try our best to lead the attackers back this way, towards the bank of the Ganga, away from the pit. Our opponents will assume that we are retreating out of the thicket and will not pursue us. Their only goal is to keep us away from the pit. Rama will use the ensuing confusion to proceed.'

The sage turned his attention to Rama. 'Now, rajkumar, listen carefully. Before you enter the pit, you must throw these stones into the water.'

He handed Rama a small cloth bag bound at the top by a string. The bag clinked softly as Rama stuffed it into his ang-vastra.

'They are infused with brahman and will illuminate your way at the bottom of the pit. Remember, the pit is very deep, perhaps a hundred yards or more. Yet you will be able to hold your breath at its lowermost depth and sustain yourself for as long as you desire without taking fresh breath. You have only to will it! The maha-mantras will do the rest. But when you enter the pit, you must leave all your weapons behind.'

Rama looked startled. 'My weapons?'

'Yes, this is imperative. From that point on, the flow of brahman itself will protect you and guide you to the fulfilment of your task. Remember, if it is not ordained that you are the right person to save Ahilya, then you will fail no matter what you do. Therefore your only hope lies in trusting the shakti of brahman itself. Do you understand?'

'Yes, Guru-dev.'

Sita wondered how Rama could just take a command from the seer and accept it so easily. She would have debated the point about the weapons until she was satisfied or until she had convinced the seer to let her keep them. How could a kshatriya hope to defend himself in such a place without weapons? The devas alone knew what lay in that pit, waiting to snare unwary—

'Do you wish to say something, rajkumari?' The seer's voice was deadly quiet.

Sita looked at Vishwamitra. He knows what I'm thinking. She felt as embarrassed as a shishya caught peeping at her companion's slate at gurukul. 'No, Guru-dev,' she said meekly.

'Very well,' Vishwamitra said. 'Then let us proceed.'

Bejoo spoke hesitantly. 'Maha-dev, what are these opponents who are likely to attack us within the vinaashe-wood?'

'That's exactly the question I was about to ask,' Na-khudi whispered agitatedly. 'How can we fight without knowing what we fight?'

Vishwamitra replied without looking back.

'Vetaals.'

Nakhudi exclaimed and clutched Sita's shoulder tightly enough to hurt. Beside her, Bejoo swore softly. The Vajra captain had stopped dead in his tracks as if pole-axed by the seer's last word.

Apparently unaware of the agitation he had caused, the brahmarishi was already at the edge of the thicket. He gestured to the others to go different ways and entered a gap between two twisted trunks. He was swallowed by the darkness and was gone.

The rest of them had no choice but to follow his lead. Rama and Lakshman went next, moving to the left and right of the gap through which the brahmarishi had entered the thicket. In an instant, they too had vanished into the vinaashe grove.

Sita stepped forward, accompanied by Nakhudi, who was swearing freely under her breath now that the seer was out of earshot. The Vajra captain followed them, muttering incoherently. Sita only heard his last words.

'Vetaals,' Bejoo said grimly. 'And the seer said some of us may not emerge alive from this thicket? I say none of us will.'

Sita and Nakhudi entered the thicket.

Sumitra stared at the serving girl. She recognised the woman from around the palace. She was a part of the Second Queen's staff.

She searched for the girl's name. She was usually good at remembering the names of servants and even their families. It was one of the reasons she was nicknamed Queen of Angels, for her charitable work and her empathy for even the lowest of castes.

'Sulekha?' she said. 'It is you, isn't it?'

The woman stopped beating her fists against the stone wall through which she had appeared a few moments ago. She turned a tear-streaked face to Sumitra. She seemed to have difficulty focusing and keeping her balance. She tottered to the right, on the verge of falling. Sumitra shot out a hand and caught her in the nick of time. She helped the girl seat herself on the floor.

'What's wrong? Are you not well, girl?'

The serving girl's head dropped, her hair falling over her face. She looked up at Sumitra through gaps in her hair.

'The Third Queen,' she said in a tone of shocked amazement. 'Queen of Angels.'

Sumitra touched the girl's forehead. She didn't seem to have a fever. 'What happened? Does she beat you?'

'Beat me?' The girl looked puzzled for a moment. Then she seemed to recall whom they were speaking about. 'Oh, she! Manthara? She beats me sometimes. Yes. She beats everybody.' She leaned forward, whispering conspiratorially. 'There's worse things than beating though, my queen. Worse!'

Sumitra realised with a start that the girl wasn't ill as she had first thought. She was drunk! Her breath was as heavy with soma-wine as any Sumitra had ever smelled.

'Sulekha,' she said gently. 'You've been drinking.'

The girl's hand flew to her mouth. She nodded slowly, several times, as if unable to stop. She looked as guilty as a maid caught stealing her mistress's jewellery. Sumitra put a hand on her shoulder, calming her.

'Never mind that now. Tell me, what is this place? What does Manthara-daiimaa do here?'

The girl peered at Sumitra blankly for a moment. Her head lolled to one side as if in danger of dragging her body in that direction, then she registered the question posed to her and straightened up with some difficulty. She looked at the ceiling, then the walls, then scanned the room. It was so plain and bare, there was nothing really to see. None of the decorative fluting or carving or plasterwork that the rest of the palace was ornamented with. Just a large rectangular room. Except for one thing. In the centre of the room.

The serving girl's eyes found the chaukat. Sumitra had already deduced that the stench coming from the fire-square was the same odour that had helped her locate the secret chamber in the first place. She had assumed the stench to be small goats, maybe even calves. She had heard there were people who still made such sacrifices to the dark pagan gods, devi alone knew why.

Sulekha froze as she saw the chaukat. It took her soma-addled brain a moment to accept the reality of what the chaukat implied and therefore where she was right now. She rose shakily to her feet, staring at the secret room with horrified eyes, wide and showing more white than pupils. She turned around, like a girl lost in the throes of some childhood game.

'The witch's lair,' she said in a tone drained of all inflection. 'We're in the witch's lair, the witch's lair, the witch's lair . . .'

Sumitra rose and caught the girl by the shoulders.

'Sit down, Sulekha, you'll make yourself dizzy that way.'

The girl looked at the chaukat then back at the queen, then back at the wall through which she'd come. Her eyes flew one way then another like a person watching an archery contest in progress. Sumitra saw that only now was she truly seeing and accepting the reality of her situation.

'Maharani!'

Sulekha's voice rose shrilly. She grew suddenly violent, her arms flailing in panic. 'Maharani Sumitra! You mustn't be here! You must leave this place at once! You don't know what she does in here. We must leave at once, before she comes back. Go!'

She pushed Sumitra hard, caught in the grip of her panic attack. 'Go, my rani! Go now or she'll kill us both and sacrifice us to her black god!' She sobbed suddenly. 'The way she sacrifices the little boys to show her obeisance to He Who Makes The Universe Scream.'

Sumitra felt a dagger of ice pierce her heart. She looked at the chaukat. The small charred bones in the fire-square suddenly had a new meaning altogether. A horrible, unspeakable meaning. A shudder of revulsion shook her. She let go of the serving girl, her head reeling.

Suddenly she felt this had been a bad idea. Coming here on her own, searching for a sign of Manthara's complicity, seeking out the secret room. It had all been a very bad idea.

And now she was caught. In the witch's lair.

17

Lakshman moved through the vinaashe grove as silently and carefully as he could manage. The shakti of the maha-mantras throbbed in his veins, enhancing his senses and keeping him preternaturally aware, yet he felt a tinge of doubt prick his heart. There were too many things about this particular mission that disturbed him. Not least was the sage's sending Rama alone to perform the most vital task.

Ever since he had been old enough to walk and talk, Lakshman had been devoted to his older brother. The bond was stronger than the biological one between Laksh-man and his twin, Shatrugan. Never had he felt the faintest envy for Rama over anything, from the sharing of a favourite sweet to driving his brother's chariot while Rama shot the arrow that won the chariot-archery con-test.

But tonight he felt something stir within his heart. A question. It was a very simple one, hardly worth speaking aloud. Yet it existed. Why only Rama? That was what troubled Lakshman. Not envy that his brother had been selected over him, but anxiety over their separation. He didn't know what horrors might lie in the Pit of Vasuki. But he was certain Rama would be obstructed by some-thing formidable, perhaps even worse than the hybrids in the Bhayanak-van, worse even than Tataka herself. Mortal danger was implied in the very nature of the mission. And the sage's grim warning had left no doubt that while they were protected by the power of brahman, they were not invulnerable.

And Rama was being compelled to face the danger alone. Without Lakshman.

Lakshman could understand leaving the others behind, they had joined the company incidentally. But Rama and he were oathsworn to obey the sage's commands and fight the creatures that threatened their people. The sage ought not to have separated him from Rama for this task. His sword belonged beside his brother, defending Rama's back, watching over him. Lakshman never doubted that Rama's superior skill and the shakti of the maha-mantras made him almost deva-like in battle – he had seen evidence of that superiority first-hand in the Bhayanak-van. But he was uneasy at not being by his brother's side in this moment of extreme danger. His place was with Rama, not running back to the river at the first sign of trouble as the sage had ordered them to do.

Lakshman made up his mind. He couldn't openly disobey Vishwamitra's command by following Rama into the pit, much as that command frustrated him, but he could do the next best thing.

He moved in the direction he had seen Rama go, deeper into the heart of the thicket. His eyes glowed softly blueish in the moonless night, seeking out his brother. So absorbed was he in this task, so preoccupied with his thoughts, that despite his preternatural awareness, he failed to notice the shadows gathering around and above him. Even the maha-mantras could not help a person who ignored their shakti. Lakshman was concentrating all his brahman-given power on finding Rama rather than on protecting himself.

As Lakshman moved forward slowly, the shadows moved too, stalking him.

Bejoo cursed steadily as he moved through the thicket. He cursed almost everything he could think of at that moment. But he did so silently.

There was only one thing he disliked more than taking orders from a brahmin, and that was vetaals. He loathed the creatures more than even rakshasas. Rakshasas were powerful, bestial demons that came charging at you, roaring like fiends, and used brute force to try to destroy you.

In that sense, they weren't unlike mortals – well, they were quite different, but he was thinking only of their style of attack. As far as that went, vetaals were completely different from mortals. They didn't attack directly, they stalked you. And they didn't attack you when you were armed and ready, they came upon you when you were sleeping, resting, eating, praying, performing your ablutions, at any time except when you were armed and ready to fight. It violated every Arya code of warfare. But it was more than that. After all, all the Asura races disregarded the Arya rules of war; why should they bother with civilised human rules when they were inhuman? But at least the other Asuras sought mainly to kill mortals either outright, as rakshasas did, or slowly and painfully, as pisacas did.

But vetaals never killed. Not truly. Instead, they fed on you, and kept you alive enough so they could feed on you some more. And then, perhaps when they'd had enough, or when it pleased them, they turned you into one of them. Like twice-lifers, the walking dead, who could infect you with a single bite. Except that even twice-lifers did so in a brainless, instinctive way, driven by some compulsion beyond human understanding.

Vetaals, on the other hand, were very aware, very alive, very much driven by the same motivations and impulses as humans. They weren't dead, as some ignorant people foolishly believed, or undead, as other even more foolish people assumed. They were simply humans who had been infected by other vetaals and had turned over to the vetaal way of life, either gradually, over days, weeks or even years and decades, or all at once.

And once turned, they could never regain their humanity. For by then they had committed the most unspeakable human sin of all – they had fed on fellow humans. And having fed, had developed a taste for it that could never be ignored or forgotten. Like a merchant driven by the canny lure of gold, they were driven by the lust for human blood – and in some cases, human flesh, and certain choice organs. Their pleasure was derived from enslaving others and feeding off them, in much the same way that humans themselves corralled and fed on cattle or fowl. With one major difference – the vetaals never killed their human cattle.

Because with their very first bite, they infected you with the gift of immortality.

Bejoo cursed silently again and moved through the densely clustered thicket. He came around a large tree and found the way ahead slightly easier than before. The trees grew less close here than on the outskirts of the thicket, the brambly leaves less irksome.

He guessed he was reaching some kind of clearing, perhaps the central one of which the brahmarishi had spoken. If so, that would mean he should be turning back soon. But where were the vetaals? Why hadn't they attacked him yet? He had been alert for any sign that he was being stalked and was reasonably certain that none were on his trail. But they must have been aware of his presence by now. Vetaals could smell humans from yojanas away. Where were they then?

A moment later, he emerged into a clearing and had his answer. It was not the clearing he had expected to find – there was no pit or pool anywhere in sight. Just a round corral made of a low vinaashe-wood fence barely a yard high. The cattle cloistered within could easily have stepped over the fence and escaped. But it was obvious that they had no desire to do so. They merely sat or stood around the roughly circular enclosure, staring as mutely as sheep or pigs.

They were human cattle. Bejoo had found the vetaals' food store. What was more, he realised, as the two-dozen-odd men and women within the corral grew aware of his presence and began to shuffle towards the fence, they had all been turned, every last one of them. It was obvious from their red-irised eyes, glowing wetly in the pitch-darkness. And the greedy way they looked at him as they became aware that he was that rarest of rare things, a human as yet untouched by their vetaal masters.

They smiled at him, by way of attempting a grotesque greeting. To his horror, some even attempted namaskars. He understood at once why the vetaals hadn't tracked him into the thicket. He had headed straight to the one spot where they would have taken him anyway.

The vetaal cattle began creeping towards him, smelling his fresh, untainted blood and uninfected body. Several of them began to grin, their teeth flashing in the darkness.

They began climbing over the low fence, reaching out longingly. Touching him, tugging at his clothes, even trying to clasp the point of his sword. Their movements grew agitated, their smiles broader.

They wanted him.

Sita knew at once that she was being stalked. She felt the familiar prickling on the nape of her neck and the itchy sensation at her wrists that meant she was under threat. She glanced at Nakhudi. The Jat kshatriya had obeyed the brahmarishi's instructions by finding her own course through the thicket, but she had followed her own immutable life-oath by staying within sight of her ward.

Nakhudi's large head bobbed once, briefly. Signalling that she was aware of their stalkers too. Sita felt better at the Jat's presence. She would have willingly ventured into the thicket alone if the sage had commanded, but having Nakhudi in sight made her feel complete. She had been intrigued to see how similarly Rama and his brother were bonded.

She had always wished that her sisters would take an interest in swordplay and warfare the way she did, but they had stayed with their girlish pursuits while her interests had taken her in these less effeminate directions. As her daiimaa had once put it, she was obsessed with martial pursuits, while her sisters were obsessed with marital pursuits! Thank devi she had Nakhudi at least. She re-affirmed Sita's conviction that a girl didn't have to wear oiled tresses and red saris in order to assert her femininity, and that wielding a sword and riding a horse bareback wasn't the exclusive pursuit of men.

Sita made a fist, bent it forward, then raised one finger and twirled it around. Nakhudi raised her open palm sideways to show she had understood. They were to pretend to move forward, then circle back very quickly and try to force their stalkers into a confrontation.

Sita followed her own strategy, moving forward at the same careful pace until she found a thick clump of brambly poisonwood bushes ahead. She slipped behind the bushes then crouched down low for a moment before darting sharply round them to the left. She sprinted between tree trunks and wildflower clumps, circling around several yards, sword raised and ready for action.

She stopped abruptly.

They were waiting for her. Arrayed in a crescent, their deep ruby eyes gleaming in the darkness. As she froze, they closed the gap behind her, surrounding her completely. They had seen and understood her signal and waited for her to circle around and return to them. She had forgotten: they weren't like other Asuras. They understood human speech and communication. They thought like humans.

They moved in, teeth flashing whitely, talons held ready by their sides. She smelled the familiar acrid odour of fresh human blood from their open mouths. They had fed just moments ago. She had a fraction of an instant to wonder who might have been the hapless victim. Where was Nakhudi? Caught in a similar trap of her own probably.

The circle closed completely and she was alone with her own private group of suitors. What they sought from her was much more intimate than marital bliss. They sought her immortal aatma.

Lakshman burst out of the thicket and into the clearing moments behind his brother. The dull glassy gleam ahead told him that Rama had found the Pit of Vasuki. The clearing was not large, perhaps twenty yards in circumference, but the mind boggled at the thought of a snake that thick being pulled out of the ground. The pit – rather, the pool – occupied almost all the clearing, with only a thin lip of about two yards between the woods and the water. Rama was standing a yard from the pool, almost close enough to leap in and continue to the next phase of his mission.

But he had run into trouble.

The clearing swarmed with light-skinned, dark-eyed beings that had lost the right to call themselves human a long time ago. Their eyes and teeth were the only things that were clearly visible, flashing blood-red and ivory-white respectively. They were between Rama and the pool.

Lakshman had the impression that they knew that Rama desired to enter the water and were determined to prevent him. Although Rama was swinging his sword ruthlessly, slaughtering them left and right, more of them kept coming to take the places of their downed comrades, swarming from the woods, rushing out in endless numbers.

Lakshman roared his battle cry and leapt beside Rama, wielding his own sword.

'Rama, go! I'll deal with these vermin!' he shouted.

Rama needed no more urging. Together they cut a swathe down to the edge of the water. Lakshman swung around, shielding Rama from the vetaals. As they rushed him, screaming silently, eyes glistening with tears of blood, Lakshman fought them bitterly. Without turning, he heard the sound of Rama's sword falling to the ground beside him, then his rig and bow and arrows.

An instant later, he heard a gentle splash. Rama had dived into the pool. The vetaals produced a strange throaty sound, a rasping, grating noise like a creature's death rattle, and even greater numbers swarmed out of the thicket to bear down on Lakshman with murderous zeal.

'Ayodhya Anashya!' Lakshman roared, and fought on with renewed fury.

He didn't stop to wonder if he could possibly hold out until Rama returned. He had to hold out. That was all there was to it.

18

Rama fell slowly. The water pushed his arms away from him, and he didn't resist. His elbows rose to the level of his chest and stayed there, bent inwards. At first, he was aware only of the water encasing his body, embracing it, caressing it. It was cool and soft and felt like a thousand tickling feathers. As he descended lower, it seemed to grow warmer but there were moments when a swathe of colder water would pass by suddenly and once he was swept sideways by the force of one such swathe.

There were bubbles in the cold swathe, as if something that breathed air had pushed its way through at great speed and with great force. But each time he tried to turn his head slowly to see what it might be, there was only the murky dimness of the pool. He continued to fall slowly, seeming to grow heavier with each yard he descended, as if the water above was now greater in mass and weight than the water below. He had learned about water pressure in his gurukul days, but the store of Arya knowledge on the subject of sub-marine science was limited by the national fear of deep water.

He saw little of his surroundings as he descended. For the first several moments there wasn't sufficient light to see anything; even his hands before his chest seemed insubstantial, ghostly. He had to touch his chest repeatedly to remind himself that he was still solid. When the descent was smooth, it felt as if he was floating in the same place, immobile. This must be what an insect trapped in ancient amber must feel like. Suspended. Frozen eternally.

But after a while, sight began to return to him. He began to see colours first. Swirls of dark hues at the edge of the spectrum, the deep ochres of spiritual enlightenment. Then the softer, warmer tints of the tertiary colours. And eventually, as he felt his descent slowing, natural colours. They danced and flowed, one way then another, never still, always changing form, shape, size, direction. He tried to puzzle out what they might be. Weeds? Fish? Coral?

When he reached out to touch one of the streams of colour, it seemed to avoid his hand deftly, dancing out of his reach then returning to swirl close by, as if taunting him to try to catch it again. He shook his head, smiling, and kept his arms before his chest. This was no time to play.

He knew he was reaching the bottom when the gloaming illumination of the brahman-infused stones lit up the area around him in a wide circle of blue light. Each stone seemed to physically bleed light, the blue effusion rising upward like a string of bubbles. These rising bubbles had given him the dim light with which he had been able to see at the lower end of the descent. Here at the bottom of the pool, they glowed as brightly as small glassy lamps, their cerulean emission suffusing the water and staining it a glaucous blue-green.

His feet found bottom with a gentle impact that he barely felt. He felt weightless, as if he could begin to float up at any moment, or be buffeted aside by the slightest current. But there were no currents in a pool. The water was still here, and startlingly clear. He had expected mossy murkiness at the bottom, obscure darkness even. Instead, he could see for several dozen yards in every direction. He could see an assortment of natural objects on the floor of the pool. Boulders and rocks mainly, of all shapes and sizes. Gleaming yellow-gold fish darted through hollows in the rocks. The floor itself was surprisingly regular and firm rather than soft and muddy as he might have expected. After peering down closely he discerned that the reason for this was simple: it was a man-made surface, slightly weathered by millennia beneath water but otherwise as unbroken and regular as stone. That struck him as odd. After all, if this were the sage Gautama's hermitage, how would it have a stone floor? He probed with the toe of his sandal and found that it wasn't stone at all, just a bitumen coating over a thatch-mud surface, like the floors of most ordinary Arya homes. The stillness of the pool had prevented it from decaying much.

He marvelled at the thought that perhaps two thousand years ago, human hands had laid and carefully smoothed this floor, applying layer upon layer until it formed a surface almost as strong as woodplank to walk on. Then had used the shakti of Surya, direct sunlight, to bake the surface hard. And eventually, the same hands had raised walls made of the same material and a roof of thatched straw over it all. Which raised the question: what had happened to the roof and walls of the ashram? After all, if this was the floor of the original hermitage, then the rest of the structure ought to be—

He looked up then and had the first real shock since his descent.

The swirling colours he had descended through, the ones that had seemed to dance playfully just out of his reach, were still there. They filled the pool in every direction, forming a dense wall that had evidently opened briefly to allow his passage then closed ranks once more.

The colours were indeed breathtaking and beautiful, mesmerising in their pattern of sway and swirl, turn and twist. It was the most amazing display in nature he had ever seen. As gaily decorative as a Holi festival or a troupe of Marwari folk dancers.

But they were neither rang colours nor gaily hued mirrorworked fabric.

They were snakes.

Rama reached for his sword, remembering too late that he had no sword. No bow and arrows. No weapon at all. He could only stand and look up at the incredible profusion that teemed just yards above his head.

Water serpents. Thousands upon thousands of them, all of different hues and tints. The swirling dance was a result of their ceaseless writhing. They formed a thick carpet, the bottom of which was perhaps ten yards above the floor of the pool. He had been unable to see them properly while descending because the light was too dim. But standing here on the floor of the pool, the brahman stones gave off enough light to illuminate them clearly.

The thickness of the whole group was impossible to discern from where he stood, but based on the time it had taken him to descend through the colours, he deduced that they formed a mass perhaps fifteen yards from top to bottom. Each serpent was at least three yards long, while several were ten times that length.

Their thicknesses varied with their lengths, some as thick as his fist, others the size of his head, and a few enormous ones as wide as his chest. Their mouths opened and closed, releasing bubbles constantly, which meant that they breathed air and must rise to the surface periodically to take in fresh air before descending again. He wondered how long they could breathe at one go, and if they were venomous.

He had always heard that the bites of water serpents were deadlier than those of their landlocked brethren. The thought of his bare skin passing within lunging distance of those fanged mouths made him want to scream. He stayed still and watched the serpents dance; unable to believe he had descended safely through their midst. Yet he had, somehow. That must mean they were benign. Or that he wasn't their natural prey. Either way, he was here, unharmed, and they seemed unconcerned or unaware of his presence. Their dance continued, the colours swirling into obscure patterns and combinations of hues, a mesmerising interweaving and mingling that demanded to be watched. He had the impression that if he didn't exert his will and look away, he could stand here and watch them for ever. He forced his eyes down. He had a task to perform.

He knelt down and picked up two of the brahman-infused stones, gripping one in each fist. They felt warm and soft to the touch, like something living rather than dead stone. The instant his hands touched them, they glowed brighter, turning almost blueish-white in the intensity of their effusion.

He blinked and held them up, away from his eyes. They cast a wide swathe of light several yards in every direction, lighting his way more effectively than a pair of torches would have illuminated the forest above at night.

He began walking slowly, unaccustomed to the strange experience of meeting resistance at every step. It was oddly pleasing yet frustrating. If he moved one side, one limb, too forcefully, his entire body twisted and he found himself corkscrewing around, feet leaving the floor of the pool. He forced himself to walk slowly, with gradual sweeping movements rather than short quick ones as he would have used above ground. After a few yards, he began to move more efficiently, and soon he was able to make fairly good progress. He glanced up once and saw that the mass of serpents still hung above him, at the same height.

He had a sudden insight: the fauna of the pool consisted of creatures living at varying depths. The serpents occupied the lowermost level short of the floor. At that depth, they probably filled the entire circumference of the pool. He had a sense that every few dozen yards the fauna changed in species and variety. He recalled the powerful waves that had buffeted him soon after the start of his descent. What had those been caused by? Something large and powerful certainly. And if his theory was right, then what dwelled at the very bottom of the pool?

The brahman stones clutched in his fists, he walked on. After a few yards, the landscape of the floor changed. It had been damaged here, and a fine spiderweb of minute cracks were splayed across the hand-smoothed surface. He knelt down, still holding the stones. It took him only a moment to see that the cracks had been caused by the impact of some enormous object. He looked around. The area was clear of boulders and rocks. Only a few under-water plants struggled to sustain themselves in the cracks. There were no fish or crabs to be seen here either. Not a living thing moved. He rose slowly to his feet, puzzling over this mystery.

The first warning he had that something was amiss was from the water serpents.

A flicker of movement caught his eye. He held the stones to his side and stared up.

The serpents were fleeing.

They were moving in agitated circles completely unlike the slow, sensual swirls he had seen earlier. Moving upwards. Frantically spiralling away from him, from the bottom of the pool. For yards in every direction, the same thing was happening, spreading in ripples, as if the message was being passed on, beginning at the centre where he stood, and travelling outwards.

He felt a tremor beneath his feet. It grew into a series of vibrations, blending into one continuous pounding rhythm. The small plants poking out of the cracks in the floor swayed and shuddered with the impact.

Above ground, he would have said at once that a bigfoot was approaching. From the intensity, spacing and measure of the successive impacts, he could have estimated the size of the beast, its distance and the speed with which it was coming. A kshatriya's life depended on his ability to make such judgements. He could even have distinguished a rhino herd from a hippo herd simply from the difference in the way they moved – rhinos thudding flat-footed clumsily, hippos high-stepping almost gracefully.

But here at the bottom of a hundred-yard-deep pool of water, all he knew was that something was coming. Fast. And it was either one massively enormous beast or many smaller ones. But not too small, judging from the impact.

He looked around for something to use as a weapon, anything that might provide a defence against that numbing moment of first contact. If he could only stand long enough to tell what manner of foe he was facing, he could figure out how to fight it – or how to flee if it came to that! After all, even brahman shakti wouldn't turn his fingers into blades or his arms into maces. To fight, a warrior needed a weapon.

There was nothing of use in sight.

He was still searching when the first of the creatures appeared, thundering across the bottom of the pool as it came into the circle of brahman light cast by the stones in his fists. It never paused or hesitated, never stopped to examine him or judge his strength warily. It just came on, barrelling at him like a herd of raging wild boar.

Close on its heels, swarming like a small army, came its fellows. He counted at least a dozen of them, maybe many more. But their numbers didn't really matter.

Just one of them was large and dangerous enough to deal with him on its own.

Rama tightened his grip on the stones and stood his ground, bracing himself for the impact of the leading beast's onward rush. As it approached, he found himself raising his head to look up at its gaping maw and gelid eyes. It was at least three yards high at the head. And its head was the lowest part of its body.

19

Sumitra slapped the serving girl. The girl stopped screaming and tearing at herself and stared blankly at the Third
Queen.

'Get a hold of yourself,' Sumitra said firmly. 'Screaming
won't help. We have to find a way out of here. I have to
warn the royal family.'

The girl continued to stare dumbly. After a moment, she
began crying. The tears flowed down her face like rain, but
her mouth moved, talking incessantly, as if she wasn't
aware that she was crying. She confessed everything to
Sumitra. About the eavesdropping at different doors. Spying on various members of the royal household, including
Maharani Kaikeyi at times. Sumitra blushed when she
heard about Kaikeyi's midnight escapades with strange
men in nameless taverns. The girl went on relentlessly.
About how she had accompanied Manthara on her trips
to the houses of tantriks, sorcerers and other unsavoury,
even criminal types. About the daiimaa paying to have
brahmin boys kidnapped for her gruesome yagnas – again,
Sumitra shuddered and avoided looking back at the chaukat. About how the daiimaa bullied, tortured and beat her
own mistress, and took especial pleasure in inflicting even
greater pain on the maidservants, guards, cooks, stable boys
and other menial staff who served under her.

About how, from time to time, a serving girl or cleaning boy who had displeased Manthara more than usual would abruptly vanish, and about how the rest of the staff would rationalise aloud that the poor wretch had been unable to take more of the hunchback's abuse and had simply run away, but of course, they all knew what had truly happened: Manthara had gone too far and ended up with a corpse instead of a badly beaten employee.

The litany of horror went on and on, until Sumitra found herself wondering if she was trapped not in a secret chamber but in someone else's nightmare. How could so many atrocities have been perpetrated under the very roof beneath which she slept? How could nobody have suspected? The answer was painfully obvious: nobody had thought to read the signs. Each of them had their own section of the enormous palace complex – their own palaces to all intents and purposes – and it was easier to live your own life without prying incessantly into the affairs of your neighbouring queens. Besides, it didn't pay to look at Kaikeyi too closely.

As the half-hysterical, half-drunk girl droned on in an epic fit of remorse and guilt, Sumitra found herself understanding one thing that had misled them all. They had always assumed that Kaikeyi was the royal troublemaker. And so she was. But it was Manthara who was the truly rotten apple. A very fetid, corrupted, worm-riddled apple. And because they were so busy casting blame on Kaikeyi, they had never thought of looking at Manthara. That had been a grave mistake. One which might cost Sumitra her life now.

She tried to ignore Sulekha's babbling, tried to think her way through this situation. She couldn't escape, that much was clear. She couldn't communicate with anyone outside. So what was she to do? Simply wait here until the daiimaa returned from wherever she had gone and let the hunch-back do with her as she willed? Was she to share the same fate as those tragic boys?

There was only one thing she could think of in the end. That was to wait for Manthara to enter the secret room and attack her the minute she came in. The element of surprise might win her a moment or two. And in that moment, she might be able to slip out. Her heart sank as she recalled how suddenly the wall had opened and closed each time, like a tissue-thin cloth being ripped apart, then sealed shut as if the rip had never been made.

It seemed impossible. And the daiimaa knew black magic. How could Sumitra fight sorcery?

But she had to do something.

Her hair had come loose in the fall into the room. Now she tied it up tightly, keeping her face and eyes clear. Then she stood up and forced herself to look around the chamber for something she might use as a weapon of sorts. Anything.

Her eyes came to rest on an object lying beside the chaukat. And at the exact same instant, for some inexplic-able reason, the faces of her twin sons flashed into her mind. Lakshman and Shatrugan. She must survive and escape from here for their sake. Exposing this conspiracy at the heart of Ayodhya could save the entire kingdom, perhaps even tilt the balance in the war. But patriotism and citizenship apart, she had to do it for the sake of her sons.

She picked up the loose folds of her sari and knotted them tightly to keep her legs free.

Then she walked over to the chaukat and picked up the blackened, blood-encrusted trident that Manthara had left behind. She hefted it, forcing herself to ignore the reek of human remains that came from it, thinking of it only as what it now represented to her. A weapon.

She spoke a silent prayer, and picked a spot in front of the wall, sitting on her haunches and waiting for the daiimaa to return. The trident lay clutched in both hands, its trio of sharply tipped tines pointing at the wall, ready to strike.

After a moment, Sulekha stopped her babbling and calmed down, staring at Sumitra then at the trident. She seemed to be wonderstruck by the implication of the object in the Third Queen's hands. Finally, her mouth worked and she spoke three words with surprising confidence.

'Jai Mata Di,' the girl said. It was an invocation to the devi in her avatar as avenger of the wronged and the innocent. In that particular avatar, the devi was usually portrayed with a trident in her hands. To the girl's addled senses, Sumitra probably resembled the devi's avatar. It was a startling thought and one that almost made Sumitra blush and put down the trident. What in the world was she doing anyway? Using a weapon stained with the blood of sacrificed children to attack a hunchback wet-nurse who might or might not be a spy for the Lord of Lanka?

To hear it described that way, it sounded ridiculous. She, Sumitra, was going to attack a witch who was empowered by the most powerful Asura in the three worlds? Her hand trembled and she began to lower the trident.

Then she remembered her sons again. For Lakshman and Shatrugan's sake.

Sulekha's invocation stirred an idea within her brain. Something better than just a trident. Something that could make that crucial difference between a successful surprise attack and just an attempt at an attack.

She turned to the chaukat and forced herself to look at it properly for the first time. Yes, everything she needed was right there. With the grace of the devi, her idea would work just long enough for her to gain the upper hand over Manthara.

'Jai Mata Di,' she said, striding over to the chaukat and bending down before it.

Sita had downed six of the vetaals and was struggling to fend off the remaining four or five when they stopped dead in their tracks. She slashed one's arm off at the elbow, her sword slicing through it as neatly as if cutting a sugarcane stalk. The amputated limb gaped blackly, oozing a thick syrupy goo. She observed with revulsion that in place of flesh the creature had a kind of mushy purplish-black substance that had the approximate texture of flesh when covered with skin but was altogether different when viewed in cross-section.

She fought down her rising gorge and plunged the tip of the sword into the vetaal's chest. It released a throaty rattling sound and fell to the ground, corkscrewing to land face-down. She turned, ready to deal with the others, and was shocked to see them skulking away.

For one surprised instant, she thought she had scared them off. Then she saw more silhouetted shapes ambling through the woods around her. Several came from behind her and went past without giving her a sideways glance. She was horrified to see how many there were. Dozens, maybe even hundreds. If they had all attacked her at once, she wouldn't have stood a chance. As it was, she had been hard pressed to defend herself, keenly aware that the greatest danger she faced was not being brought down and killed but simply being bitten. One nick of those razor-sharp teeth and she would be no longer able to resist.

She followed them, curious to see where they went. They were shambling silently through the woods, carelessly walking through poisonwood bushes that ripped their skin and tore at their eyes. Pain was pleasure to a vetaal. Wounds healed in moments. Such was the nature of their existence.

She emerged into the clearing just as Bejoo appeared, a few feet away. The Vajra captain seemed startled to see her. As if he had forgotten that there were others here besides him. For an instant he looked as if he was about to rush her, then recognition dawned on his face and he lowered his sword slowly, nodding a cursory greeting. She returned the nod just as sharply.

She had no idea what individual horror the captain had faced in the vinaashe thicket but she thought she understood how he must feel at this moment. While fighting those creatures in the dark, she had felt utterly alone. Part of that had been the lack of Nakhudi. But another part had been the odd silence in which the vetaals fought. It was like fighting ghosts. Except that her sword could cut these ghosts down at least. Thank devi for small mercies.

The clearing was the one the brahmarishi had spoken of, she saw that at once. There was the pit. And there was Lakshman, his back to the pool, sword raised, as if he had been fighting to keep the vetaals away from the water. She saw the discarded weapons at the edge of the pool and understood. Lakshman had been keeping the vetaals at bay while Rama dived in. So they had reached that far at least.

She looked around, seeking out the last two members of their band. Nakhudi and the seer.

Nakhudi appeared after a moment, her face grimacing in distrust as she emerged cautiously into the clearing. Sita flashed her a smile and a toss of her chin which asked silently, where the devil were you? Nakhudi shrugged sullenly in response, looking abashed. Her sword and her vastra were splattered with the purple-black ichor that the vetaals had for blood.

'Shishyas!'

Sita turned at the sound of the brahmarishi's voice. The word he used to address them jointly, students, was usual for a seer. All those who followed a guru were shishyas.

The brahmarishi was cross-legged, floating above the pool of water. A bubble of brilliant blue light encased him, pulsing alternately sky-blue and cloud-white with lightning flashes of gold. When he spoke again, she realised that he was addressing them through telepathy, not by the use of his vocal organs. Those organs were busy chanting mantras. She could hear the recitation continuing uninterrupted even as the seer's words burned their way directly into her brain.

'I have drawn the vetaals away from each of you by the use of this mantra. As long as I continue this recitation, they will be unable to resist its attraction and will stand immobilised as they are now. But once I cease the recitation, as I must do soon, they will renew their attack on you with greater ferocity. As you have all seen fit to disobey my direct orders and have come further into danger rather than returning to the safety of the river, I offer you one last chance of salvation.

'Drive the vetaals into the pool. Every last one of them. Do it swiftly, do it now. Move!'

Sita needed no further urging. She sprang into action, sprinting to the edge of the pool. The vetaals had all clustered here, gazing up reverentially at the brahmarishi in his bubble of brahman. She didn't stop to count them but her eyes told her there were close to a hundred of them. Those were greater odds than they could survive. And yet all of them had preferred to die fighting than retreat dishonourably. She didn't know if that made them foolish or noble.

Right now, it didn't matter either way.

She raised her sword and issued the battle cry of her kingdom and the House Chandravanha.

'Satyamev Jaitey!'

Truth Always Triumphs!

Beside her, Nakhudi echoed the cry and together they attacked the vetaals. It was a strange, cumbersome slaughter, for most of the creatures hardly seemed aware of their presence – even when their swords hewed their limbs and cut them down like animals at a slaughterhouse. Some snarled, showing their gleaming teeth, and backed away. Working together, Sita, Nakhudi, Bejoo and Lakshman formed a line of flailing swords, steadily pushing the crowd of dazed vetaals towards the pool.

The vetaal closest to the pool stumbled and fell into the water. Sita watched as the creature raised its hands and thrashed about in obvious agony. It was if it had been immersed in a vat of boiling water. Or acid, she thought grimly, as smoke began to issue from the vetaal's flailing limbs.

Gradually, the creature's struggle diminished and it began to sink, literally melting into the water. In seconds, nothing remained except a bubbling mass of ichor that was quickly absorbed. Several more began to fall in, tripping over one another, and they all met the same fate.

'It's the Ganga water,' Sita whispered in wonderment, speaking to herself as much as to the others. 'Their corrupted flesh is being absorbed by the sacred water, freeing their trapped souls!'

What had felt like butchery a moment ago suddenly became a ritual of salvation. The four of them renewed their efforts, driving the remaining vetaals into the pool of sacred water. Above them, the brahmarishi continued reciting the mantras, the light from his bubble illuminating the strange yet miraculous scene below.

Manthara expected to be met with weeping appeals and hysterical cries when she entered the secret chamber at last. She had taken the time required to dismiss the rest of her staff for the night and lock her rooms. It wouldn't do to have another foolish servant come wandering in now.

When she was certain she would not be disturbed, she recited the mantra that opened the portal and stepped through the wall.

The sight that met her was so unexpected, she froze for a moment, unable to accept the evidence of her eyes.

The devi herself stood before her, terrible in her black-skinned beauty. Her lips smeared with fresh blood, her eyes large and white in her dark face, her mouth gaping open, tongue lolling loosely. Her four hands were raised to either side. Her feet were splayed in the tandav posture, celebrating her victory over evil through the dance of death. And in her upper right hand was the traditional trident, its razor-sharp tines glistening with fresh blood.

Manthara gasped, her hands flying to her breast. Her heart stopped still for an instant. All her years of evil-doing, of inflicting torture and abuse and pain on the innocent, the young and the harmless, came roaring at her with the ferocity of a black bull charging. She forgot that she possessed immense power, enough to defend herself against a devi if need be. Perhaps not to win but enough to thwart a first blow or two and attempt to flee. She forgot everything except her sins and her awful acts, and believed wholeheartedly that the devi herself had descended to earth to punish her for her crimes against humanity.

She saw what she feared most, not the reality, which was far simpler: Third Queen Sumitra with her face and arms smeared with ash from the chaukat, posing in the familiar stance, the serving girl Sulekha crouching behind her like a dancer at a court performance, holding out her hands to create the illusion of a single woman with four arms.

That moment of disorientation was all the time Sumitra needed.

In that instant, as Manthara stepped in through the widening portal and gasped in shocked amazement, Sumitra reared forward and plunged the trident into the daiimaa's breast.

Manthara shrieked and fell back, the weapon embedded an inch deep in her chest.

Beside her, the portal gaped, the mantra that commanded it to shut still unuttered.

KAAND 3

THE FORGE OF GOD

Mithila. City of saints and singers. Home to a million Videhans of all castes and creeds. Host to as many visitors on this annual festival. Wood fires blazed at the gates of the city and at every street corner, performing a dual function – keeping the city free of malaria-bearing mosquitoes as well as scenting the air. Mithilan women stood downwind of the fires, talking and laughing happily, letting the scented smoke blow through their freshly washed tresses. The fragrance would linger for days.

Unmarried girls walked carelessly through the market stalls, admiring, selecting, bargaining; in liberal Mithilan fashion, they went blouseless, their bare breasts visible beneath their flimsy translucent chunnris and odhinis.

Mithilan men, inured to the fashion, smiled and greeted men and women alike, unmindful of any sexual divide. Women merchants dominated the city's trade, entire orders of women sadhunis clad in white attended the seminars and discourses taking place at various heavily attended venues.

Male brahmins visiting the city for the first time walked with their hands raised high in the air. Freshly bathed and purified in Ganges waters en route, they were intent on avoiding accidentally touching their own nether organs as well as the bodies of other worshippers. Children tossed

down handfuls of flower petals from the terraces and roof-
windows of houses in the narrow winding streets, showering the visitors and citizens and shouting greetings. The
streets, clean-swept each morning by the city's meticulous
administrators, were strewn with the petals, which would
be allowed to lie until dawn the next morning.

Conch shells, trumpets and drums sounded from
around the city, the high ululating voices of town criers
calling the programme for the day's events at the festival.
Musicians, both secular and pious, filled the dance halls,
music houses and even the streets with their songs. Bards
held forth with ballads and endless epic compositions of
their own devising at the city taverns, where soma and
wine and ale flowed as lavishly as Ganges water at the
ritual baths for the pilgrims. There were two types of
spiritually inclined: brahmins who walked naked and
goosepimpled from the cold through the streets after their
purifying baths, hurrying to attend special morning ceremonies; and soldiers and citizens tottering out of taverns.
As the Videhan adage went, spirits were always high in the
liberated city of Mithila!

An air of festivity and holiday abounded. Several citizens still carried rang powder left over from the Holi
festival and tossed handfuls into the air, producing clouds
of red ochre, saffron, mauve, and parrot green. An entire
rainbow spectrum of garments clad the Mithilans, con-
trasting brilliantly with the whites of the pilgrims. Soldiers
and sadhus conversed at the large square junctions
marked clearly with signs directing visitors to their desti-
nations.

On the city's fairgrounds a vast carnival was in progress. Gypsies, jugglers, acrobats, snake charmers, bear
wrestlers, hawk-hunters . . . a hundred different varieties
of entertainment jostled for attention and rupees. They

had arrived for the Holi fair and had never left; their money bags sagged with coins. Chariot races, archery contests, sprint races, wrestling bouts, every manner of sport was going on.

Gambling halls raked in the money, occasionally paying out happily as well – cards, betting on sports, guessing games, even strip gambling, everything was fair game. But the most popular betting game of all was chaupat, the game of war strategy played on a board with carved pieces representing the four divisions of an Arya army, cavalry, elephant, chariot and foot-kshatriya, with the maharaja, maharani and mantri presiding over all. The dice rolled endlessly, pieces took or were taken and coins changed hands endlessly, fortunes passing over the chaupat board and returning the same hour or day.

The four castes mingled and socialised in happy harmony. Mixed marriages were common; women kept multiple husbands if it pleased them – or multiple lovers; men kept more than one wife if they so desired. What one did in one's bedroom was a private affair; marriage was a sanctified public ritual but one governed by the choices of its participants, not the state. Men went with men, women with women if it so pleased them; and some went both ways and enjoyed it.

The city police intervened only to break up fights, prevent brawls and drunken disagreements, arrest pickpockets and burglars, or encourage order over chaos, not to control and rule. City magistrates urged complainants to settle their differences independently and come to higher authorities only as a last resort. Property disputes were the most common cause of litigation.

An hour before noon the town criers interrupted their seminar programme announcements to present a different engagement. The swayamvara of the rajkumari Sita

Janaki, princess of Mithila. Today was the day the princess was to view suitors and, if it so pleased her, choose one as her husband.

It was not the first swayamvara conducted for the rajkumari. She was notorious for turning down suitors by the hundreds. But a rumour had spread through the city and the kingdom that today would be different.

It was whispered that this was the day when the rajkumari would actually choose a mate, finally ending years of speculation and broken hearts.

Like most rumours, this one had its basis in fact.

The assembly hall of Mithila's palace was large enough to accommodate a hundred designated courtiers and nine times as many observers. It was filled to capacity today. The crowd thronging Devarata Avenue easily numbered over twenty thousand and was growing larger by the minute. A portly brahmin trader seated on an ass with three servants on foot following gaped at the throng and compared it to the far smaller crowd outside the Hrasvaroma Hall nearby. A first-time visitor to the city, the rich brahmin had come to attend a lecture at the Hrasvaroma Hall. The potentially titillating subject of the discourse was the inter-relationship between kama and bhakti: sex and devotion. Live demonstrations were to accompany the lecture.

The brahmin licked his lips and tried to decide whether to attend the lecture as planned or to visit the assembly hall. He decided to ask one of the palace guards milling with the crowd, lightly directing people to leave room for traffic to pass on the avenue.

'Kshatriya,' the brahmin said, 'what manner of programme takes place here today?'

The guard looked the stranger up and down, sizing him

up quickly as one of those brahmins who regarded the pursuit of spiritual and material enrichment to be closely related. 'It's the maharaja's assembly hall, friend. No programmes here. Only official court business.'

The brahmin frowned, sweat trickling down his heavy jowls. The sun was almost directly overhead and it was hot for a spring day.

'Is there a war council on or something then?' He gestured at the crowd milling about excitedly. There was an air of nervous expectation in the air. 'What official business attracts a bigger audience than a kama demonstration?'

The guard looked at him with a raised eyebrow. So the brahmin included sensual enrichment in his list of pursuits as well. Well, it took all kinds. 'A swayamvara,' he explained shortly. 'The rajkumari Sita's.' He added curtly, 'Today's her fourth, I think.'

'Her fourth birthday?' the brahmin asked, wiping his bald pate with his ang-vastra and gesturing to a servant to bring him the waterskin.

The guard grimaced. 'I don't know where you come from, friend, but here in Videha we don't marry off our children before they come of age. I meant it's her fourth swayamvara. She's a finicky one, the rajkumari. But they say she's going to catch one today.'

He glanced at the brahmin's swelling belly and gleaming jewellery. 'Maybe you'd like to try your luck as well, hey? Every man of marriageable age is free to present himself without prejudice. That's the law. Besides, they say if Rajkumari Sita finally makes a choice today, her sisters will consent to marry as well. You look like a man who could use a wife. Or four!'

The guard moved away, chuckling to himself.

The brahmin was used to disparaging comments from

kshatriyas about his bulk and his wealth. Unoffended, he sat thinking for a moment, drank a gulp of pomegranate juice, then motioned to his servant to give him a piece of betelnut. He put it in his right cheek, grinding it lightly to release the flavour as he pondered his choices.

He turned his donkey's head towards the assembly hall. 'Who needs another boring lecture,' he told his servants. 'Let's go see if we can get ourselves a Mithilan princess as a wife!'

2

Maharaja Janak handed the water jug back to his prime minister and folded his hands respectfully before the brahmarishi Vishwamitra.

'Maha-dev,' he said, 'you honour the House Chandra-vansha and all of Videha with your presence. I am truly fortunate to have this opportunity to offer you the hospitality of my humble dwelling. Pray, do me the honour of gracing my palace.'

Vishwamitra entered the vaulting façade of Chandra-vansha Mahal, the seat of Maharaja Janak and the centre of power of the Videha nation. It had been three hundred years since he had last come here. On that occasion, the palace was a mass of half-caved-in ruins, the result of an Asura assault. Looking at it now, it was hard to tell it was the same place.

Two decades of peace and prosperity had restored the palace to its former glory. Enormous sculpted likenesses of the great ancestors of Janak watched benevolently as the brahmarishi and the two rajkumars followed the maharaja up the sweeping marble stairway that led to the administrative annexe of the palace. A sense of majesty and magnificence swept one's senses, yet it was a spiritual rather than a rich majesty. The colour white dominated the architectural design rather than the traditional gold and silver bejewelled patterns of Ayodhya; Chandravan-sha Mahal, like all of Mithila, celebrated the majesty of the aatma, not regal splendour and wealth.

As they ascended the vaulting stairs, Vishwamitra recognised almost every one of the larger-than-life sculptures, and those he had not met personally, he could name by their position in the order of ascendance. Nimi, founder of the dynasty, his son Mithi, who built this capital city, Janak the First, Udavasu, Nandivardhana, Suketu, Devarata, Brhadratha . . . all the way up the stairway through twenty-one generations, the last of which was Janak himself and his younger brother Kusadhvaja. From the garlands and joss sticks adorning each statue, it was evident that Janak respected and honoured his ancestors in true Arya tradition.

But none of this distracted Vishwamitra's sharp eyes from noting the absence of armed guards in the palace. Except for the pair of lightly armed sentries at the main gate and an occasional guard walking his rounds, there was almost no palace security visible. It was a sharp contrast to Ayodhya's heavily guarded royal residences.

They entered the throne room, a smaller chamber than the enormous assembly hall of Ayodhya. Unlike Dasaratha, who presided over his own court and made all major decisions himself, consulting his prime minister and council only when required, Maharaja Janak left the daily administrative part of governance entirely to his ministers. The maharaja spent far more time in prayer, meditation and philosophical and spiritual discussions than on statecraft.

Vishwamitra knew all this despite his long retreat from the physical world during his two-hundred-and-forty-year bhor tapasya; he knew it in the same way that he knew that Janak had renounced the eating of flesh and the taking of intoxicants in any form twenty years ago. The flow of brahman revealed everything to those who had the power to see.

After a further round of formalities and ritual greetings, Maharaja Janak turned his attention to the rajkumars standing beside Vishwamitra.

Rama and Lakshman were still in the same ang-vastras and dhotis they had worn when they left Siddh-ashrama the previous morning. Although only a day, a night and another morning had passed since then, so much had happened that they looked less like princes of Ayodhya and more like travellers who had been on the road for weeks. Their clothes were soiled by dust and mud and various dubious stains that the sage knew was the blood of vetaals spilled during the fight last night. Their vastras were torn in several places, ripped by the clinging barbs of the vinaashe-wood bushes and leaves. Their hair was unkempt and matted with dust and dirt, their skin grimy. And this was despite their having bathed in the sacred Ganga at dawn today.

Yet none of this seemed to trouble Maharaja Janak. He was accustomed to meeting with sadhus and rishis who regarded any concern for personal hygiene as being a sacrilegious waste of precious time needed for devotion and meditation, the twin goals of every brahmin.

The maharaja smiled warmly at the princes as they greeted him with polite namasakars.

'You are fortunate to be travelling in such illustrious company, young shishyas. Your proud bearing and gracious manner impresses me. Guru-dev, are they the sons of some noble sage? Or perhaps the scions of some great brahmin house? Clearly, they have spent their young lives devoted to religious pursuits and holy activities only. They have an enviable brahmin air of serenity and peace about them.'

Vishwamitra replied without preamble.

'They are kshatriyas. Valiant warriors both. Their serenity comes from following the path of dharma scrupulously.'

Maharaja Janak blinked, taken aback. He looked disappointed but smiled on regardless, acknowledging the namaskars performed by the two princes. 'Well met, young Arya-putras.'

'Well met, Janak-chacha,' Rama said, echoed by Lakshman.

In Mithila, the royal dais was on the same level as the rest of the chamber, reflecting Janak's famous writ that a king was no different from his subjects. Only the moon-wood throne, massive and magnificent, suggested the maharaja's great warrior ancestry and hinted at the heritage of the Chandravansha dynasty. Dwarfed by its looming carved bulk, the lithe, slim and smiling Janak looked more like a young prince than the descendant of a great line of warrior-kings.

Rama approached the throne and bent low to touch the feet of the maharaja. Lakshman did likewise. Janak gave them his ashirwaad without showing any sign of recognition. Even Rama's affectionate use of the term 'chacha' hadn't rung a bell. It was customary in Arya society to politely address any older man as 'uncle' and woman as 'auntie'. Janak would have to be given more than a subtle hint to recognise the two rajkumars, Vishwamitra saw.

The sage said, 'The grime of the road conceals their true identities from you, Mithila-naresh Janak. When last you saw these two lads they were probably little more than half as high and certainly no more than half as old as they are now. Eight years at Guru Vashishta's gurukul, the inevitable progress of time, the appearance of maturity on their faces and bodies, and their adventures these past ten days have lent them an air of the unfamiliar to your eyes. Yet they are your own distant relatives by marriage, the rajkumars Rama Chandra and Lakshmana, sons of Dasaratha, Maharaja of Ayodhya, ruler of Kosala.'

Janak sprang up from his throne. 'Rama and Lakshman? Impossible!'

He came forward, taking Rama by the shoulders, then Lakshman, looking at each one with stunned amazement. 'Yes! Of course. I see the resemblance now. You, Rama, have inherited Maharani Kausalya's striking beauty and complexion as well as your father's magnificent physique. While you, Lakshman, have inherited your father's features and gentle Maharani Sumitra's grace and charm! What magnificent young men you have become!'

He embraced them both, unmindful of their grimy clothes and unwashed bodies. 'When last I saw you both, you were mere boys! You were still innocent enough to run around and play childish games with my daughters, I recall! Look at you now. It makes my heart proud to see you grown so well. And under the tutelage of such a great brahmarishi no less. Truly, this is a doubly happy day. I knew the omens were unmistakable: this day shall go down in history, mark my words. I have studied the configuration of the constellations and cast my predictions at daybreak, as I do every day after my pre-dawn meditation. Great things shall happen in Mithila before the sun sets on this happy day.'

Rama and Lakshman exchanged a glance. Rama spoke for them both. 'Janak-chacha, we are happy to see you as well. But—'

'But, raje,' Vishwamitra said, 'as you yourself have read in the stars, today is destined to be an eventful day in your kingdom's history. Much as you would like to sit and pass the time talking with the rajkumars about how the intervening years have treated them, we have important matters to discuss and much to do.'

'Yes, yes, of course,' Janak said. 'In the excitement of hearing of your arrival, Guru-dev, I neglected to mention that I have a swayamvara to preside over as well. It would do my house great honour if you would join me there. The rajkumars as well, of course.'

Janak laughed as he looked disbelievingly at the two princes. 'Rama and Lakshman. With the brahmarishi Vishwamitra. On a feast day no less. Who would have believed it?'

'A swayamvara?' Vishwamitra kept his voice devoid of inflection. It was good to be able to know all by dint of the powers of brahman, but it was not always appropriate to let others know that you knew. 'Who is it who will choose a husband today? Is it one of your daughters?'

Janak's smile reduced in intensity. 'Yes, Guru-dev. My daughter Sita.'

'Then this is a fortunate coincidence indeed. It will give me great joy to see you give away your daughter Sita today, raje. You can count on my attending both the swayamvara and the marriage.'

Janak laughed nervously. 'You honour me, maha-dev. But I must inform you of all the facts of the matter. If left up to me alone, I would have given my daughter away years ago. But as you must know already, we of the Chandravansha and Suryavansha dynasties do not wed children. We believe an Arya has the right to choose his or her own life-partner. Hence the practice of a swayamvara, which enables any suitor, regardless of stature, wealth, appearance, caste or creed, to come forward and seek the hand of my daughter. Whom she chooses, or even whether or not she chooses at all, is entirely up to her. I can only watch and offer suggestions when called upon.'

'An excellent and commendable attitude, raje. In my experience, most swayamvaras result in marriage. After all, when a mature young woman has every imaginable choice before her, it's usual that she will make her pick wisely and well. You must expect that Rajkumari Sita will find a groom worthy of her taste and inclination this very day.'

Janak's face lost its smile entirely. 'One would normally expect that from a swayamvara. But, maha-dev, my eldest daughter is as particular about her choices as I am particular about my prayer rituals. On several previous occasions, at occasions much like this one, she has rejected more suitors than I could count using a bead-table!

'Even today, I hesitate to raise my hopes yet again. But I am heartened by the fact that the stars are most auspicious for a marital match. That is why I have set the swayamvara for the hour of noon. If the devas – and my daughter – so decree, then I shall give her away in a marriage ceremony this very afternoon. Nothing would give me greater pleasure. Guru-dev, you must say a mantra to ensure this fruitful union. I am aware of the power you wield. It would give my ageing heart great relief to see my Sita settle down with a suitable husband this very day, blessed by your auspicious ashirwaad. It would ensure her long and blissful cohabitation.'

Vishwamitra nodded before replying. 'I should gladly speak the most powerful mantra I have knowledge of, good Janak. But even I cannot change the mind of a woman who knows what she wants. Sita is right to wait for the groom of her choice and to refuse to lower her standards and expectations.'

Janak's face showed his disappointment.

Vishwamitra went on, 'However, take heart from this, raje. I too see propitious stars aligning themselves. And like yourself, I predict that before the sun sets on this auspicious day, not just your daughter Sita but all four of your daughters shall have husbands of their choosing. And shall live long and happily married lives.'

Janak cried out happily, falling to his knees before the sage. 'Maha-dev, may your words be heard by the devas themselves! If it is so then I shall undertake a pilgrimage to every holy site in the world to offer thanks to every deity. I shall give my worldly possessions to the needy and less fortunate. I shall grant the brahmins of Mithila any guru-dakshina their hearts desire.'

Vishwamitra held up a hand. 'All this and more you may do. But first, the rajkumars and I have important matters to discuss with you. Matters that exceed the vexing concern of a loving father for his daughters' future welfare. We must discuss these matters at once that you may prepare yourself and your beautiful city for the approaching crisis.'

Janak frowned. 'Crisis, maha-dev? What crisis do you foretell? Pray, do not speak inauspicious words on this most excellent of days. I have forsworn all material joys and pleasures for over twenty years. The only ambition I retain for this lifetime is to see my daughters married and settled happily in good houses. Tell me not that some ugly shadow shall darken this hope. I beg of you, do not deprive this father of the only pleasurable dream he has left.

'When my wife passed away, I took not another woman as wife or even as mistress, not for a single night. When my brother passed away, I raised his daughters under my own roof, counting my daughters as four, not two. I have performed every yagna, every sacrifice, every ritual, every obeisance to the devas, asking only two things: peace on earth to all men; and the happiness of my daughters. They are the jewels in my crown. Just now when you spoke those beautiful words, predicting marriage and happy lives for all of them, I felt the greatest pleasure of my life.

'I pray to you, maha-dev, do not cast any shadow over this happy day. Whatever threat approaches me or my people, I shall confront it gladly and with open arms. But let this swayamvara be completed successfully and my daughters be well placed in their lives. This boon I beg of you.'

Maharaja Janak prostrated himself on the ground before Vishwamitra, clutching and kissing the seer's feet, tears pouring from his eyes.

Vishwamitra was silent for a long moment. When he spoke at last his voice betrayed neither anger nor impatience. Instead, he said affectionately, 'Rise up, good Janak. You have lived a pious and honourable life. This boon you ask is within my power. I shall grant it to you in recognition of your great devoutness and adherence to the twofold path of dharma and karma. We shall talk of other matters afterwards. Come now, walk with me. Lead the way to the hall where this auspicious swayamvara is being held. Let us go and see for ourselves as your daughter Sita selects her mate for life.'

3

Sita entered the packed and silent assembly hall with her head covered and eyes lowered as befitted an Arya princess at her swayamvara. Given the freedom to survey, interview, test and finally judge her suitors at this ritual event, it was nonetheless considered unseemly for a woman to simply strut about and look boldly at the men on display. She would have time to gaze at them at the right moment. Right now, it was she who was presenting herself before them. And tradition required that she present herself as a princess and a potential bride. Even though, right now, she thought of herself as neither.

Sita's mind was still preoccupied with the events of the previous day and night. At several moments during that short span of time, she had actually doubted if she would be back home in time for this swayamvara. Not that it would have mattered much to her, but her father would have been bitterly anguished.

He would also have discovered her absence. Her sisters had covered up for her from the night before last, when she had slipped away incognito, making excuses and pleading a variety of different feminine and princessly reasons for her non-appearances at meals and other family occasions. It hadn't been difficult for them to convince her father that she was fraught with anxiety over the swayamvara; it had made him think that if she was this anxious, perhaps she was finally going to choose a husband! On all the three previous swayamvaras, she had been so non-chalant and disinterested, he had known even before the event began that he would not be finding a son-in-law on that particular day. Any emotional response on her part would have given him hope.

But he would have been heartbroken if she had failed to show up at the event itself. He would assume that she had deliberately missed it to avoid finding a husband. And there was more than a little truth in that assumption. One of the reasons she had left Mithila incognito had been because she wanted space and time to think. The mission to Dandaka-van had been an excuse. Now that she knew how grave the Asura menace really was, her little escapade seemed foolish and ineffectual. But at the time it had seemed to her that this was her one last chance to enjoy the freedom of being just herself, a person and not a princess.

Now that freedom was in danger of being stolen from her for ever. She walked slowly, with cautious steps – she had always been uncomfortable in these complicated garments and heavy ornaments – as she traversed the rows upon rows of seated men, presenting herself for the ritual viewing.

For the first time in the past year, she actually peeped out occasionally from beneath the pallo hanging over her forehead, glancing curiously at the faces she passed.

A few were middle-aged and sagging, one or two aged and decrepit, there was even a fat red-faced brahmin grinning idiotically at her as he chewed noisily on a paan, but the vast majority were young, handsome, robust-looking men, bursting with youthful confidence and the glow of good health. Very few were nervous or less than good-looking. She guessed that these must be sons of rich fathers, pushed forward by their parents, eager to make a match with the biggest house in all Videha.

Sita knew the realities of her situation. She wasn't a coy nymphet toying with the power given to her by this age-old Arya ritual. A swayamvara wasn't an opportunity to see the handsomest and wealthiest men jump through burning hoops to provide a day's entertainment. It was a serious affair. An opportunity for a woman to carefully select the very best mate available. She considered herself lucky in one way: at least she didn't have a father who believed that it was a parent's right to make every important choice for his child; or worse, a chauvinist who refused a daughter her right to choose while letting his sons marry as they pleased. There were parts of the Arya nations where such practices were traditional and swayamvaras were unheard of. Mithila was not one of those places and she was grateful for it.

But that didn't mean that she had to be pressured into marrying if she wasn't ready. Or into marrying at all.

She reached the far end of the hall and was guided across the width of the aisle to the other side by her sakshis – her bridesmaids, if she chose to marry today. Starting with the first suitor seated on that side, nearest the door, she began working her way up the hall.

As she walked, and occasionally glanced at the men seated on the comfortable thrones designed to make every suitor feel like a prince, she thought back to the moment at the Pit of Vasuki.

After they had driven the vetaals into the water and watched them all melt away, they had nothing to do but wait for Rama's return. Even the seer had descended to solid ground again and sat with them by the edge of the pool.

As the minutes passed, then turned into hours, Lakshman had grown anxious and agitated, becoming convinced that

Rama had encountered some obstacle or opponent that he could not overcome. He wanted to dive into the pool and go to his brother's aid. Each time, Brahmarishi Vishwamitra restrained him with a firm command.

Finally, when Sita herself had begun to think they should all leap into the pool and go to Rama's rescue, Rama had returned. And with him had been a woman of the most astonishing beauty Sita had ever seen. She was like an effigy made out of fine bonewood, or porcelain. In contrast to Sita's own dusky complexion and sharp features, the legendary Ahilya was the epitome of classical Arya beauty.

White as a summer rose, she was delicately boned and featured, full breasts and wide hips divided by a waist a wasp would have envied, with a smile that could have melted the snows on Mount Kailasa and eyes so mesmerising, even Sita found herself unable to look away. When she and Rama had stepped ashore, Rama had wanted to tell them about his experience finding and then freeing Ahilya, but the brahmarishi had insisted that they proceed to the next stop on their route.

So they had gone to Gautama-ashrama on the outskirts of Visala. And there, standing before the statue-like maharishi frozen in his meditative state for two thousand years, the sage had chanted mantras that cleared away the vines and creepers and detritus of the centuries, then issued an incantation that had caused a blinding flash of lightning, and when they were able to see again, the sage Gautama—

'Rajkumari, you have already finished that side! It's now time to take your seat.'

Sita returned to the here and now with a start. Lost in her recollections, she had traversed the entire left side of the hall as well, and had been about to walk down the right side for the second time. How embarrassing! Luckily for her, Sundari, her first sakshi and childhood friend, had stopped her in time.

She let her sakshis guide her, giggling softly at her near-mistake, and took her seat on the raised dais at the head of the hall. Her father was already seated in the seat to her left. Beside him, preferring to stand, was the brahmarishi Vishwamitra.

But there was still no sign of Rama and Lakshman. Where were they? Surely they would at least do her the courtesy of attending the swayamvara. It wasn't as if she was expecting them to participate in it! Just to attend and give her some moral support. Was that too much to ask?

Nakhudi and Bejoo were standing at opposite ends of the dais, watching the assembled suitors with grim, forbidding eyes. The Vajra captain had volunteered to share Nakhudi's duty for the event, just before Sita and her bodyguard had parted from the rest of the company at the gates of Mithila this morning. Sita had hoped Rama would say something about her swayamvara, or at least promise to call on her in her apartments. After all, she knew the rajkumars and the seer were here to meet her father and discuss the imminent Asura invasion.

She had been so consumed by thoughts of that approaching storm and their adventures these past two days that it had been very hard for her to say goodbye to them and return to her role as princess. This was the kind of thing she had always dreaded about marriage. Although Arya law and social custom dictated that men and women had equal status, it was a well-known fact that unless checked, men invariably tended to treat their women, be they wives, daughters or sisters, as wards to be protected and watched over at all times. Sita found it humiliating to have men think she was in need of their protection when she could probably knock them flat on their rear ends in a fighting contest.

But she wanted Rama and Lakshman here as friends, not brothers-in-waiting. Or as cousins – which was tenuous since they were only vaguely and distantly related through marriage and couldn't technically be considered to be family.

The past two days had been by far the most exciting and exhilarating of her life. And a large part of that was due to Rama. She had been unsure of him at their first meeting, especially when he had come flying into the clearing in the hills like some kind of vanar-king. Hanuman indeed!

But when they parted this morning at the city gates, she felt as if she had just met and lost the best friend she had ever known. Could that be possible after just a day and a night and a morning? Certainly. She had been attached to Nakhudi from the first instant the hulking Jat had been introduced to her.

And those hours with Rama when he still thought she was a man, that had been an extraordinary experience. She had gone incognito before, and had met and spent time with many kshatriyas and other castes. But Rama had been different by far. One test she always applied was how men spoke of women when they were in the company of other men – or so they thought. Every last one of them ended up making at least one or two chauvinistic remarks that made her want to throw something at their faces – on one occeasion, she had done just that, flinging a leaf-full of fried beans and potatoes, still steaming from the cookfire, straight in the face of one obnoxious oaf! And some were so outright misogynistic that it was all she could do to keep from having at them with her sword.

But Rama really was different.

Not only did he seem to genuinely not see any difference between men and women, he also didn't regard women as sexual objects. Even Lakshman, in a good-natured, adolescent way, made ribald jokes and observations so natural and normal that Nakhudi herself sniggered at a few. Rama smiled distractedly at them, as if acknowledging that they were clever and had humorous appeal, but he never truly seemed to relish such banter. As if, to him, there were more important matters to talk about.

It wasn't even that he was totally humourless. She herself had tested that by making him laugh out loud several times. It was that he had such a healthy, open, unprejudiced mind that the concept of attaching himself to one group – the male of the species – and regarding the world from that limited perspective simply didn't occur to him. He was a free thinker in the truest sense of the word.

And that, she had realised with a lightning burst of insight at one point last night, was why he took orders from the brahmarishi so well. Where other men would need to prove their masculinity, or at least their princely stature, Rama was content to simply do the job at hand and let people perceive him as they would. Totally unselfconcious, even after he knew she was a woman.

Sita had never met anyone like him.

And right now, she wanted him here very badly. More than she wanted anything else in her life.

But it was her swayamvara. And she had to go through with it. With or without Rama.

As her father finished making the customary announcements about the formal process of the ritual, she rose with a fixed, glassy smile on her face, trying not to show how she really felt – lost and alone and friendless – and stood before the assembled men, preparing to announce the test for this swayamvara.

4

Rama watched as Sita rose and took a step forward on the dais. The princess seemed very unsure and hesitant, as if she were distracted by other matters. It lent her an air of snobbery that he knew she didn't possess. Even though he had known the rajkumari less than two days, he was sure she was not spoilt or snobbish. He had met his share of royal snobs and Sita was about as far at the opposite end of the scale as could be imagined. But he wondered what was on her mind that was causing her such trepidation. She had even walked past him without so much as a second glance! It was as if she hadn't seen him at all, even though her eyes had been open and she had passed within a few yards, led by those giggling and blushing sakshi maids.

Lakshman and he were seated on the left side of the hall, in the seats nearest to the podium. He would have been content to sit with the public audience on the matting at the far end of the hall. At least that way they could simply watch the whole show and relax. This way, he felt as if he were one of the dozens of suitors arrayed like so many new army recruits waiting to be given their marching orders! He had never taken part in a swayamvara before, and never intended to in his life. At the moment, marriage was the remotest thing on his mind.

His immediate concern was the Asura invasion. Why had the brahmarishi not told Maharaja Janak about it? True, Janak-chacha's eloquent appeal had been heart-wringing. But Sita's marriage would hardly matter if Mithila didn't prepare itself to face the oncoming hordes. Rama shuddered mentally at the memory of his recurring nightmare. The brahmarishi himself had turned the night-mare into a living vision before all of Ayodhya on the feast of Holi, ten days ago. If that was the horror that Mithila now faced, then the devas help them all. From what he had seen, Mithila was not even one tenth as prepared as Ayodhya was. Even though both cities had been built with similar seven-wall, seven-gate defensive circuits, Mithila had allowed her security procedures to lapse years ago. Now, all gates stood open at all hours, people came and went as they pleased, and brahmins outnumbered kshatriyas a hundred to one because of the current annual festival. When the attack came, as Rama knew it would, Mithila would be torn to shreds like a sheet of wet parchment. The Videhans stood no chance of putting up a defence, let alone resisting such a formidable invading force.

Perhaps that was why the brahmarishi had agreed to discuss the matter later. Maybe Vishwamitra knew that Maharaja Janak could do little in these last few remaining hours to stem the Lord of Lanka's progress, and had decided to grant the king his last wish out of sheer sympathy. Yet even that didn't make sense. If Mithila was such a lost cause, then why had Vishwamitra both-ered to take them on that mission last night? Why had they travelled using the power of brahman to the Pit of Vasuki and risked their lives to free Ahilya?

He recalled the moment of utter helplessness at the bottom of that deep pit. The instant when the giant kachuas had appeared, storming along the bottom of the pool. When their mottled bald green heads had reared at him, exposing maws large enough to swallow him whole – after those half-yard-long teeth crunched him into chowder – he had thought that was it. Even the shakti of the maha-mantras would be unable to save him from these lumbering amphibian beasts. They had seemed as imposing and fearsome as the Ancient Ones themselves, the giant turtles that were once believed to have borne the universe on their backs.

But instead of attacking him, the kachuas had simply examined him. Sniffed at him. Nudged him. And when he gripped the brahman stones harder in his fist, certain that they would lunge and rip out his belly at any moment, they had tilted their heads and looked at him with renewed interest, as he might look at a dancing ant or a rabbit that had suddenly burst into lyrical song.

The kachuas had taken him to a deep grotto, a cave within the side of the pit. Because it curved upwards, it was dry at the end, with air brought in through unseen fluted passages. He could breathe and speak in that place.

There he had found a woman as immobile and unblinking as a statue. Ahilya. Frozen by her husband's ancient curse, incapable of feeling anything physically, locked in an endless inner existence of pain and guilt and remorse at her transgression with the lord of lightning and thunder. Rama had only a few moments to wonder what to do next when his foot had accidentally kicked up some loose soil from the ground of the underwater cavern. The soil touched the statue, and to his everlasting amazement, Ahilya had begun to move and speak.

She had thanked him for freeing her from the curse and had asked him his name and identity. He had told him about the brahmarishi Vishwamitra. At the mention of the seer-mage's name, Ahilya's beautiful green eyes had lit up. She said that she had always known it would take another sage as great and powerful as Gautama himself to undo the curse. But she had not counted on a boy, and a mortal at that, to come to her aid.

Ahilya and Rama had left the cave and risen to the surface of the pool, neither the kachuas nor the snakes, nor even the enormous dolphin-like creatures at the upper levels of the pool, giving them any trouble whatsoever. They had found Vishwamitra and the others waiting for them, and after a few words with Ahilya, the brahmarishi had told them that they must now go to Gautama-ashrama. There, he had performed his brahman sorcery once more, awakening Maharishi Gautama from his long, deep tapasya and reuniting husband and wife.

Afterwards, Gautama had thanked Rama profusely for daring to be the one who braved the depths of the Pit of Vasuki and freed his wife. He had become a victim of his own anger, he admitted, warning Rama that young as he was, he ought to learn from his example and never speak an angry word without first considering its effect carefully. The maharishi had then had words privately with brahmarishi Vishwamitra and Rama had seen the maharishi speak an arcane mantra and hand over a small object of some kind to Vishwamitra, who had accepted it with the same reverential gratitude that most shishyas displayed before their guru. In a way, Rama realised, Vishwamitra was like a shishya to Gautama. Despite his five thousand years on the earth, he was junior in stature to Gautama, who had been ordained all of eight thousand years ago.

After that, they had performed their morning ritual, bathed in the Ganga, and proceeded to Mithila. That was the whole purpose of their mission, Rama recalled. To obtain something from Gautama that would help strengthen Mithila's defence against the Asura invaders. That was why he had rescued Ahilya, why they had fought vetaals in the vinaashe wood, why they had rushed to Visala through the brahman corridor, why they had left the rest of the Siddh-ashrama procession in the thick of night.

And yet, what were they doing now that they were finally here in Mithila? Not discussing last-minute defence strategies, urging Maharaja Janak to deploy his troops, nor sending word to Ayodhya or the other Arya nations to ask for urgent aid; not doing anything constructive that might help ease the heavily stacked odds against the Videha kingdom in the coming war.

Instead, they were attending a swayamvara and watching Rajkumari Sita choose herself a suitable husband. And, if the rajkumari obliged by finding one of these fine young Arya-putras acceptable as a mate for life, why then they would continue to watch as Sita's sisters did likewise! And once those good ladies were done with their browsing and shopping, all four couples would then be united in matrimonial alliance with full Vedic rites, which would take at least another hour or three.

And before it all, the test itself had to be performed, to eliminate the unworthy suitors. At this rate, the whole charade could go on until sunset! By which time the Lord of Lanka would have arrived at the gates of Mithila and led his army in to ravage and plunder as they pleased.

The whole situation just didn't make sense at all. While Rama had faith in the brahmarishi Vishwamitra's infinite wisdom and knew that the sage had a good reason for everything he said or did, he couldn't fathom what attending this silly swayamvara had to do with anything. If Sita had to return to being a dutiful princess and pick a husband out of this line-up then let her do it. Why did

Lakshman and he have to endure the whole spectacle? Worse, why were they sitting here like eager suitors on display along with these hundred and ten other fools?

Rama watched in seething indignation as Sita finally found her voice and addressed the hall. The princess had decided her test for the swayamvara and was informing the assembly. A roar of consternation met her announcement, snapping Rama out of his thoughts.

He frowned and looked around. Men were standing up and shouting. Several seemed to be complaining that if the rajkumari didn't want to be married, why did she waste their time by calling this swayamvara? Rama scanned the length of the hall. Almost every suitor was on his feet, supporting the general complaint. Apart from Lakshman and himself, only one elegant-looking young man remained seated. He occupied the first seat on the right side of the hall, directly opposite to Rama.

He smiled as Rama's eyes lingered on his face, and Rama blinked and looked away. Did he know the man? He didn't think so. The face was completely unfamiliar. Yet there was something about the way the man had looked at him, as if he knew Rama. Well, maybe he did. Rama supposed that many citizens of Ayodhya must know him, and he could hardly know them all on sight. He avoided looking in the man's direction again.

Maharaja Janak stood up and called for silence. As the hue and cry died down, he said firmly, 'The rajkumari has spoken. The test is declared. Those of you who do not wish to participate may leave at any time. Those of you who have the courage to proceed, please be seated in dignified silence.'

The maharaja clapped his hands and called to his prime minister, standing beside the dais, 'Have the Bow of Siva brought to the assembly hall at once.'

A fresh murmur of protest rippled through the hall as the prime minister left the hall to do the maharaja's bidding.

Rama leaned across the arm of his chair and said softly to Lakshman, 'What exactly is the test that Sita announced?'

Lakshman looked at him. 'You're joking, aren't you? Where were you when she spoke just a moment ago? Gone fishing in the Pit of Vasuki for sages' wives?'

Rama shot him an irritated glance. 'Just answer the question.'

Lakshman shrugged. 'Our new friend said that she has only one test for us. Anyone who can lift the Bow of Siva single-handed, string an arrow and fire it will have her hand in marriage.'

Rama waved an admonishing hand. 'You mean them.'

'What?'

'She set that test for *them*.' Rama gestured at the disgruntled suitors down the length of the hall. 'Not us. We're just spectators here.'

Lakshman leaned over and looked at him closely. 'Are you feeling well, brother? Did you hear what I just said?'

'Yes, she wants them to fire an arrow from Siva's bow. The man that does it will be her husband. What's the tie-breaker? What if more than one man passes the test?'

Lakshman pinched Rama's arm hard. Rama winced but didn't make a sound.

'That dive into the pool must have melted your wits,' Lakshman said, 'the way it melted those vetaals. I don't think you know what you're saying right now.'

Rama looked at him, frowning. 'What are you talking about, Lakshman?'

Lakshman shook his head sadly. 'I don't know what's wrong with you but you're obviously not thinking straight. This is the Bow of Siva we're talking about. Remember it? It's the enormous one that stands in the armoury of the royal museum at the back of the throne room in Janak-chacha's palace. We used to peek in at it when we were children. We peeked in because we were forbidden to go into the armoury. Not that it stopped you and Sita from hiding in there during our hide-and-seek game. You two—'

Rama snapped at him, keeping his voice low, 'What's the point, Luck? Get to it.'

'Well, if you remembered the bow, you'd also remember that it's made of solid iron yet never rusts. That it's a million years old. Or ten million. I forget which. And that it's called the Bow of Siva because it once belonged to Lord Siva himself. Only he of all the devas can lift it. There's no question of any mortal ever being able to do it. Let alone one of these eager young Arya-putras!'

Rama shrugged. 'So? A swayamvara test is supposed to be difficult.'

'Difficult?' Lakshman chuckled softly. 'Difficult is what you are, my brother. Difficult is what climbing Mount Himavat in winter might be. Difficult is what flying to the stars and back home in time for breakfast would be called. Sita's test isn't difficult. It's impossible.'

Rama still didn't see what Lakshman's point was. He was trying not to look at Sita on the dais. Apparently, she had finally noticed him and was now trying to catch his attention. He studiously avoided her. 'So?'

'So don't you see the point? She's specified an impossible task because she doesn't want anyone to succeed. She isn't interested in getting married, Rama. Not today, and if you ask my opinion, not any day. Nobody in the three worlds can lift the Bow of Siva. Let alone anyone in this room!'

5

It took five hundred men the better part of an hour to drag the bow on a wheeled platform into the assembly hall. The crowd of citizens gathered on the avenue outside had swelled to over a hundred thousand as word of the rajkumari's test spread through the city. They watched in awed silence as the entire palace guard strained and sweated to drag the wheeled platform across the fifty yards separating the armoury museum from the assembly hall.

Finally, the platform was in the hall. And the Bow of Siva stood in the centre of the chamber, its lustreless arc gleaming dully in the afternoon sunlight. It was close to two hours past noon and the assembled suitors were already sweating profusely in their heavy rich garments and jewellery. None of them had left the hall, not because they thought they could lift the bow but because nobody wanted to be remembered as the first to leave. So until one of them had the courage to stand up, admit defeat and walk out, they would all remain. They were the sons and brothers of the greatest houses in the kingdom, heroes of countless contests and champions of various sports. To walk out without even attempting the test, however impossible, would be humiliating. And to these proud sons of Arya, failure was acceptable; humiliation was not.

A strapping young kshatriya took first try. A court crier

called out the suitor's name as he stepped up to the platform and walked around it, examining the bow from every angle. It was huge, no doubt about that, at least twice the length and width of any normal bow. Its double-ribbed design was in the fashion of ancient bows from the early days of the Arya nations. Apart from that, it didn't look extraordinary. There was no polish, no shine, no gleaming jewels imbedded in it. Just a seven-foot-long curved shape cast from solid iron.

The courageous – or foolishly deluded – suitor stepped up to the bow, arching his back in anticipation of its weight, and bent down. Laying his right hand on the centre of the bow, he heaved with all his strength.

Nothing happened.

Sweat began to pop out on his forehead, then on his neck and back. His muscles strained and stood out as sharply as bamboos beneath an upraised tent. He gripped his right forearm with his left hand, bracing it while keeping only one hand on the bow as the rajkumari's rule demanded.

After an eternity of straining, he let go and fell back on the ground, panting heavily.

The watching assembly released a huge sigh. Word of the failed attempt rippled through the public spectators to the crowd on the avenue outside. The suitor rose slowly to his feet, head bowed, and looked around at his rivals, eyes shining wetly with frustration.

'It's impossible, my brothers,' he cried out. 'I can life three hundred kilos with one hand, yet that bow didn't move a fraction of an inch. I tell you, no mortal can move it!'

He left the hall amid a pandemonium of cries, catcalls and renewed complaints.

The rest went much the same way.

After the first dozen or so failures, the others barely made an effort. Several left the assembly hall then, unable to stand the humiliation any longer. At the outset, the crowd had started placing bets with city bookmakers on the odds of individual suitors. The bets had dwindled to almost nil by the tenth attempt. Now, the bookmakers themselves had stopped accepting further wagers, on the grounds that it wasn't fair to take people's money for impossible odds.

Maharaja Janak rose to his feet and addressed the assembly. There were still about two dozen suitors left, perhaps hoping that some miracle would save them from having to lose face by walking out as failures. They were from the twenty biggest houses in Videha, fiercely loyal to the maharaja. Most of them had grown up watching Sita and her sisters blossom, and had dreamed of winning one of them as a wife some day. They sat silently, sullenly, waiting for something to happen.

'Good Mithilans,' the maharaja said brightly. His manner seemed undimmed by the crushing failure of the suitors or by the obvious impossibility of the task. 'Take heart from this news. The brahmarishi Vishwamitra, whom I introduced to you at the start of this function, spoke to me before we began. The good sage, with his infinite knowledge of all things past, present and future, predicted that today's swayamvara will have a successful conclusion. He predicted that not only will my daughter Sita choose a suitable husband, but her sisters will find husbands as well before the fall of sunset this evening.'

Amazed murmurs met the maharaja's announcement. Janak looked around at the few seats that remained occupied, greeting each suitor with a smile. 'I believe implicitly in the seer's prediction. The man who is destined to wed my daughter is in this very hall today. Let him step forward and try his hand at the bow, and I am certain he will succeed. The might of dharma itself will give him the strength he requires to lift it. Come forward then, and show yourself.'

In the silence that followed, the remaining suitors looked around at one another. Each was thinking the same thing: Is it true? And if it is, then who is the chosen one? Is it me?

Before anyone else could say another word, a solitary suitor rose to his feet. It was the man seated in the first throne on the right hand of the rajkumari Sita. He strode forward, his handsome face creasing with a confident smile.

'I am the man chosen to be your son-in-law, raje. I am the one destined to lift the bow. Give me your blessing now and let me fulfil my destiny.'

Janak's smile could hardly be brighter or more intense. 'Well said, Arya-putra! It would be my pleasure to bless you. May Siva himself give you strength.'

The man accepted the maharaja's ashirwaad. He walked to the platform and approached the bow. Without so much as an intake of breath, he reached down and clutched it with his left hand.

Flexing his arm, he lifted the bow above his head in a single smooth motion.

Sita watched in amazement as the handsome suitor lifted Siva's bow single-handedly. The strain was evident; she could see the young man's jaw clench with the effort. But he had done it! He had completed the first part of the task she had set.

A stunned silence fell across the assembly hall. It spread like a fire to the crowd outside, hushing them. Over a hundred and fifty thousand people now watched and waited with bated breath as the young man in the assembly hall attempted the next part of the test.

Taking up the end of the leather cord wound around the head of the bow, the suitor unwound it slowly, using his right hand. All the while, he kept the bow suspended overhead with his left hand. Sweat poured down his face and arms, but his grip never yielded for an instant. His concentration was absolute, his focus impressive. Sita watched with growing disbelief as the man finished unwinding the cord and pulled it across to the other end of the bow.

The man strung the bow tight and wound the end of the cord around the pointed horn at the tip of the curve. He tested the stretched cord with a flick of his right forefinger. It twanged audibly, the reverberations echoing through the vast hall.

Eyes widened, hands flew to open mouths.

Sita couldn't believe what she was seeing.

The man picked up one of the arrows provided, a perfect longbow arrow with a peacock feather trim at the end. It was dwarfed by the size of the bow, reduced to looking like an ordinary shortbow arrow, but it fitted, just. He set it on the bow, fixed its end to the cord and pulled tight.

Then he turned the bow slowly around, seeking a suitable target, and loosed the arrow.

Brahmarishi Vishwamitra didn't blink an eye as the arrow struck a crossbeam a yard over his head and embedded itself a foot deep, shuddering.

The roar of exultation from the spectators was deafening. The people went wild with ecstasy. They had just watched the impossible being done. It was a feat that would be talked about to the end of their days. They would tell their grandchildren about this amazing day.

Nay. Their grandchildren would tell *their* grandchildren about it! Word spread through Mithila like a fire out of control. The town criers galloped to the farthest corners of the city carrying the news.

In the assembly hall, Maharaja Janak stared at the arrow embedded in the beam above the brahmarishi. The maharaja turned to the suitor, who was still holding the bow in one hand. The smile on his face was still as smug and confident as before; he seemed to have grown accustomed to the strain of the bow, but the crinkles around his eyes and the straining muscles of his arm suggested that it still took all his strength to keep it aloft.

His eyes sought out and fixed on the rajkumari Sita. Janak glanced at his daughter. Her face was as white as chalk.

'Young man,' the maharaja said, 'you have accomplished what nobody thought possible. Not even my strongest kshatriyas were able to lift the Bow of Siva. Yet you did so single-handedly, strung it, and fired an arrow from it as easily as other men might fire from any ordinary longbow.'

The maharaja gestured uncertainly at the beam. 'I assume you did not mean the brahmarishi any disrespect by aiming the arrow in his direction. No doubt your aim is excellent and you knew you would not endanger the esteemed sage in the slightest degree. Still, a brief apology would be in order. If you could merely offer your regret to the sage and take his forgiveness, we can proceed with the rest of the ceremony.'

The young man reached down to the quiver provided for the test and pulled out another arrow. He strung this one as well, and aimed the bow once more at Vishwamitra.

'I would rather put an arrow through the seer's heart than apologise to him,' he said.

Janak stared at the man as if he had just spoken in a foreign tongue. 'Arya-putra,' the maharaja said sharply, 'I will not condone an insult to a brahmin in my kingdom. Apologise to the seer at once!'

The young man insolently released the cord and dropped the arrow on the floor. Then, with a loud crash, he let the bow fall on to the platform. The platform shattered and sank to the floor, its two-inch-thick wooden planks splintered by the impact.

'I have passed your daughter's test,' the suitor said, his tone arrogant and demanding. 'Now I demand her hand in marriage. Fulfil your promise, Janak of Mithila! Give me Sita!'

Janak frowned down at the suitor. 'Arya-putra, it is true that you have passed the test, and displayed amazing talent. Yet that is no excuse for speaking thus. First you insult my honoured visitor, now you speak to me arrogantly. Mind your tone, young . . .' The maharaja glanced at the crier deputed with calling out the names of suitors. 'What is this man's name?'

'Maharaj,' the crier said nervously, 'he refused to give his name at the start of the swayamvara.'

'My name is Jay,' the man said, striding up to the edge of the dais. He leapt up on to it with a single bound.

Maharaja Janak stepped back, surprised at the suitor's boldness. Both Nakhudi and Bejoo, as well as the other guards posted by the dais, started for the man, their weapons drawn. The maharaja shook his head, gesturing to them to stay back. Nakhudi retreated reluctantly, staring balefully at the arrogant young man.

The maharaja pointed sternly at the suitor.

'Young Jay, I do not know from which part of our

kingdom your family hails, but if you are to be my son-in-law, I suggest you learn how to conduct yourself in the presence of—'

'I am not from your kingdom,' the man said. There was menace in his tone now, and a challenge in his eyes. He swung around, addressing the entire assembly. 'I am not a Videhan and I would be ashamed if I were one!'

Janak's face coloured at that. 'That is enough insolence. How dare you insult our proud nation?'

Jay turned back to the maharaja. 'I am not an Arya either,' he said. 'Do you understand now? I am not one of you!'

Janak stared at the suitor with irritated incomprehension. 'What do you mean? If you are not Arya, then who are you? Where are you from?'

The suitor shrugged carelessly. 'Originally I am of Vaikunta. But presently I call Lanka my home.'

'Lanka?' The maharaja looked around, as if to confirm whether he had heard correctly. 'You make a poor jest, young Jay. There are no mortals in Lanka. Only Asuras.'

The man was silent. Only his smile spoke.

Janak's voice faltered. 'What manner of story is this? Where are you from really, boy? What is your family crest? Who are your parents?'

Brahmarishi Vishwamitra stepped forward, his staff thumping the wooden dais. 'He speaks the truth, Mithila-naresh. His birth-name is indeed Jay, although it is millennia since he used that name. He was originally of Vaikunta, celestial home of Lord Vishnu Deva, and his present residence is Lanka. But you are right as well, raje. There are no mortals in Lanka, only Asuras. Behold then, the lord of Asuras himself!'

And the sage threw his staff at the young suitor as hard as he could. The man named Jay had no choice but to catch it to avoid being struck. The instant the staff touched his hand, a blinding flash of brilliant blue exploded, dazzling everybody.

When Sita was able to see clearly again, she looked at the spot where the handsome young suitor had stood.

Jay was gone.

In his place was Ravana.

6

Rama sprang to his feet, his hand reaching for his bow. Lakshman was beside him in the same instant. Bejoo and Nakhudi were by Sita in a trice, swords drawn. The hulking Jat grabbed her mistress in one powerful arm, lifting Sita as easily as she might a child, and retreated to the rear of the dais, her sword keeping any aggressors at bay.

But Ravana already had Maharaja Janak by the throat. The Lord of Lanka's ten heads quivered, ranted and screamed with fury in as many different languages as they had tongues. Their eyes blazed with ten different expressions of rage, exultation, lust and triumph. The rakshasa stood over seventeen feet high, the maharaja clutched in one yellow-taloned hand. Janak's feet were a whole yard off the ground, the veins on his neck standing out like cords. If the Asura lord squeezed just once, the king of Videha would die on the spot.

The guards saw this and kept their distance, staring fearfully at the demon lord's many heads, unable to tell which one to look at or how to proceed.

The spectators at the far end of the hall had screamed and begun exiting the chamber in panic when the rakshasa king appeared. One or two of the suitors had left as well, running for their lives – a portly brahmin was one of them, an elderly merchant another. The rest stood and watched with impotent rage as this new drama unfolded on the stage. They were kshatriyas all and would have come to the maharaja's rescue, but by swayamvara rules none were armed, and they were too far away to be of any help in the drama taking place on the raised dais.

Only Vishwamitra seemed calm and unruffled. The sage strode forward and picked up his staff from where it had fallen. The move brought the sage within the target area of Rama's bow. Rama saw that the place where the rakshasa king had grasped the staff bore the imprint of his six long, inhumanly shaped fingers. The handprint stood out in sheer pitch-black against the ivory whiteness of the wild-wood staff. A glance at the rakshasa's left hand revealed a matching scar. Where the demon lord's hand had clutched the staff, a mark of its length and texture lay imprinted on the skin, stark white against Ravana's night-black complexion. Wisps of smoke still trailed from the burn. For a burn was what it was, a brahman burn. The Asura had been scorched by righteous shakti.

'What did you hope to accomplish by coming here?' Vishwamitra said quietly. 'Did you believe you would be able to come into our midst and escape unscathed, demon? Did you forget the fate that befell your mother's brother Kala-Nemi, whom you sent to infiltrate Ayodhya? He reached only as far as the palace gate before Vashishta and I despatched him to another nether destination!'

One of Ravana's heads roared in fury. Another cried out a single word in an alien tongue.

'I have already come farther than my uncle, brahmin! I have the life of the king of Videha in my hands.'

Another head chuckled. 'In one of my hands, I should say.' He turned around slowly to face the brahmarishi, the maharaja spinning through the air with him like a rag doll suspended from a string. 'Should I show you how much more capable I am than my uncle now? By dispatching Janak to a nether destination as well?'

'NO!' Sita's voice rang through the hall. 'I beg you, please, don't harm my father. He is a man of peace. He would not hurt a living soul.'

Ravana turned a head to look at her. 'Just the princess I wanted to speak with. You do recall the terms of your test, don't you, girl? I fulfilled your conditions and passed with flying colours. Now come with me as my bride and I will spare your father's life.'

Sita stared at her father's face with anguish. Janak's already pale complexion had turned as white as limestone. The maharaja was starting to lose consciousness, the bloodflow to his brain suspended by the immense pressure on his neck, Rama saw. If he was not lowered to the ground, he might die in minutes.

'But you're an Asura!' she screamed. 'You had no right to come to my swayamvara. You don't belong here. Why don't you go back to your island-fortress and leave us alone!'

'My lady,' Nakhudi growled, restraining Sita, who would otherwise have run to her father's aid and physically assaulted the rakshasa king.

'Come now,' Ravana said. 'I had every right to be here. Even the sage recalls days when Asuras and mortals attended swayamvaras together. And as often as not, it would be a mortal who rode away with the prize even though he had failed the test. I recall those days full well. Do you not remember them, sage?'

'I have nothing to say to you, rakshasa. Except to command you to release the maharaja at once, or face the consequences.'

Ravana's heads snarled balefully. 'Threats! Always

threats! Can't you be honest for once, brahmin mortal! I played by your rules. I passed the swayamvara test fair and square. I won the rajkumari's hand in marriage. Give her to me, and I will leave you!'

'You lie,' Vishwamitra said. 'Your army is only yojanas away from Mithila. You came here to steal away the rajkumari and undermine the people's confidence by showing off your superhuman strength. You wish to take Sita Janaki away not as a wife but as a prize commemorating your victory over the Videha nation.'

'And the sacking of Mithila, don't forget that, sage,' Ravana said quietly. 'It's what any mortal invader would do. How do you think Janak got the Bow of Siva in the first place? As a boon from the three-eyed deva himself? Never! Videha was invaded by a usurper, Sudhanva of Samkasya, who laid siege to its capital. Janak murdered Sudhanva and stole the bow from him. He doesn't deserve to keep it. When I leave, I will take it with me as well. Spoils of war!'

'That's not true!' Sita cried as she saw Janak's eyes flutter and close. 'My father challenged Sudhanva to single combat, to spare his people the horrors of another needless war. He won fairly and the bow was given freely by Sudhanva's widow.'

Ravana laughed. 'If you care so much for your father, Sita Janaki, then make your decision quickly. Already I feel his life ebbing. Or tell me, should I clench my fist and end it for him mercifully?'

Sita fell to her knees. 'Please. I will do as you wish. You passed the test, it is true. You are my champion. I will wed you and go with you where you please. But spare my father's life. In the name of the devi, mother of all creation, I beg of you. Spare him!'

Ravana grinned with pleasure, raising his heads to the

ceiling and roaring his exultation. 'FINALLY! A MOR-
TAL WHO HONOURS HER WORD!'

He flicked his wrist as if he was brushing away a drop of
water. Maharaja Janak flew across the dais and landed
sideways on a trio of palace guards and Captain Bejoo.
Bejoo had the presence of mind to grab hold of the
maharaja's arms and cradle his head against his own chest
as he fell back on to the floor.

Lakshman and Rama loosed arrows at the exact same
instant. Each aimed at a different head of the rakshasa
king. But when the arrows reached their targets, the
demon lord was gone from that place. He had leapt into
the air, landing with a deafening impact beside Sita. This
put Vishwamitra between him and the rajkumars, who
were now forced to stay their arrows, reluctant to shoot
and risk hitting their guru, or Sita and Nakhudi should
Ravana move again.

Before anyone could react, Ravana reached out to grab
Sita's hair. Instead, he found Nakhudi's sword at his chest.

'Touch her and I'll cut you to ribbons, monster!' the Jat
said.

Ravana's eyes smouldered with rage. 'Rajkumari? Is
this how you honour your word?'

Sita's hand shot out, knocking Nakhudi's sword aside.
'Back off, Nakhu. He kept his word. He let Father go.
Now I have to keep my part of the bargain. I have to go
with him.'

Nakhudi stared at her mistress, her friend. 'Are you
insane? He's a monster! You owe him nothing! Let me at
him. I'll kill him with my bare hands.'

'NO!' Sita yelled. 'We are Aryas. We keep our word. I
made a pact. Pass the test and I marry the man. He passed
the test! Move aside, Nakhu.'

'He's not a man!' the Jat screamed back. But she moved

aside sullenly. Her eyes never left Ravana, scouring across the demon lord's ten heads. Ten pairs of eyes watched her suspiciously.

Sita turned to Bejoo. 'Captain, my father . . . ?'

Bejoo nodded shakily. 'Alive. Unconscious but alive.'

Sita turned to Ravana. 'Then I am yours.'

'WAIT!'

Vishwamitra strode forward.

Ravana snarled and stepped back.

'Sage, again you try to cheat me of my just reward. You heard the rajkumari. She comes with me of her own free will.'

'Nay, Asura. She comes with you because she believes you won the contest. But the contest is not yet over.'

Ravana growled malevolently. 'What new sorcery is this, mage? You saw it with your own eyes. I was the last to try my skill at the bow. Nobody else could even move it!'

Vishwamitra shook his head. 'Her condition was that who ever picks up the bow single-handedly, strings it, and fires an arrow shall be her groom. But she meant that the arrow should be fired at the target, not at that beam.'

The brahmarishi pointed at the target provided for the contest, at the far end of the hall, high up by the rafters, where a miss would not risk harming anyone. Then he pointed with his staff at the crossbeam where Ravana had shot his single arrow. It was nowhere near the target.

'The point is moot, sage,' Ravana said. 'Nobody else could lift the bow, let alone string and shoot it. Therefore I win. The princess is mine. Let me have her and leave before I change my mind and decide to kill all of you.'

'The contest is not won yet, demon,' Vishwamitra said calmly. 'Two contestants remain. Only if they are unable to pass the test will you win by default.'

Ravana's heads scanned the assembly hall. 'Which two contestants? All these other young fools declared in my favour the minute I picked up the bow! Ask them yourself! Why do you seek to cheat me of my fairly won prize?'

Vishwamitra shook his head. 'I speak of these two contestants, Ravana.'

He pointed his staff at Rama and Lakshman.

7

Lakshman stepped forward and looked at the bow. It lay mutely on the smashed planks of the wheeled platform, oblivious to the human conflict raging around it. Its cord was still strung.

Lakshman took a deep breath and reached a decision. He stepped back, shaking his head.

Rama stepped forward. 'Lakshman?'

Lakshman looked at his brother, then at the brahmarishi. He knew what he was doing was right. Even if he won the contest, he had no desire to wed Sita. If there was anyone here who was suited for the rajkumari, it was Rama. Lakshman had seen how Rama and she looked at each other. How the air between them seemed to sparkle with magic.

There was no point in playing if the prize wasn't yours to covet. He could probably complete the test with the help of brahman shakti, but what would be the point? If he stepped out now, Rama would try his hand, and he would win. Lakshman never doubted that for a moment.

He looked at Rama, his mind made up. 'I withdraw. Your turn, brother.'

Ravana laughed. 'There goes one of your champions, sage! Your other one will fare no better, I warrant!'

Vishwamitra said nothing. All eyes were on Rama as he stepped past his brother. He looked at Lakshman, search-

ing his face to make sure he was all right. Lakshman
nodded reassuringly and squeezed Rama's hand.

Rama stepped up to the broken platform. He looked
down at the Bow of Siva for a moment, discarded as
carelessly as an unwanted toy. His heart burned with
anger at such foul treatment of a treasured relic.

He bent down and picked up the bow with one hand. It
came easily. On the dais, someone released a long-held
breath. It sounded like Nakhudi.

Rama looked at the cord of the bow. The terms of the
contest were clear. He reached up and carefully began to
unwind it. It took several moments. Finally, it was done.
He loosed the cord, held it in his free hand to show all
those present that it was untied, then began to wind it
again.

When it was done, he picked up an arrow and strung it.

He took aim at the target.

He loosed the arrow.

It flew straight to the heart of the painted wooden
target, striking the centre, and quivered there. The silence
in the assembly hall was deafening.

Then a roar of triumph rose from the throats of all
assembled in the sabha hall filling the air for miles around.

'Satyamev Jaitey!' Lakshman yelled punching a fist into
the air. *Truth always triumphs!*

Ravana roared and sprang down from the platform.
'GIVE ME THE BOW. GIVE IT TO ME, BOY! YOU
THINK I CAN'T HIT THAT TARGET? I CAN HIT IT
BLINDFOLDED IF I WISH.'

He strode across the hall, his powerfully muscled body
thrice as tall as Rama and twice as wide. Vishwamitra's
voice stopped him in his tracks.

'The rajkumari called for one shot. Nothing was mentioned of a retrial. You had your chance, demon. Rama is

the victor. Accept your defeat now and show how honourable you are!'

Ravana roared. His remaining arms, hidden until now within their sheaths of flesh, emerged and spread wide, each pair strong enough to tear a grown man in two.

'The princes of Ayodhya were only watching, sage. You know that as well as I. You connived to let them take part to cheat me once again. I allowed that. Now you will not deny me the same licence! I will shoot that bow again and place my arrow in the tail of this young whelp's. Then I shall wed and bed the rajkumari!'

Rama raised the Bow of Siva over his head. His eyes were glowing with blue fury now. 'Ravana!'

The Lord of Lanka turned to look at him.

'You want this bow?'

Ravana watched him suspiciously. 'Give it to me, boy. Or die. It's the same to me.'

Rama took the bow in both hands and bent it. Ravana watched him curiously. 'What would you do now, boy? That is the Bow of Siva. The Three-Eyed One himself anointed it with everlasting endurance. It cannot be broken. What do you think you will do?'

'WATCH, DEMON!' Rama shouted, his eyes spitting gold and blue fire. 'WATCH AND LEARN! THIS IS THE POWER OF THE LIGHT!'

And with one massive scissoring of his arms, Rama snapped the Bow of Siva in two.

The sound that came from the cracking of the bow was monstrous. It rolled through the assembly hall, through the palace, and through the city entire. It swept the streets like a wind with lightning in its breath. Like a rolling tidal wave of thunder, the sound rumbled through Mithila, carrying to the distant fields outside the city, to the Siddh-ashrama procession arriving just now at the crossroads leading to the capital. It was like a crack of the mightiest thunder ever heard, like the snapping of the backbone of the world itself.

Birds fell from the skies, killed outright by the sound. Small creatures ran gibbering to their holes for safety. Large predators mewled in fear and cowered in dark thickets. Glass shattered throughout the city, cracks appeared in walls and floors, and in the highest point in Mithila, the Sage's Brow, an enormous bell that had not been rung for twenty-two years sounded a single pealing toll, then was silent again.

Sita couldn't believe her eyes. Rama had outmatched Ravana. And now he had broken Siva's bow. Broken it! But that was impossible.

She heard Vishwamitra speak a single phrase: 'Om Namay Shiva.' All around her, everyone repeated the invocation, praying to the three-eyed god to forgive the destruction of his weapon.

'Om Namay Shiva,' Sita said.

Her father stirred in her lap. She had gone to him while Rama and Lakshman went to try their hand at the bow. She looked at his wan, bloodless face. His eyes fluttered, then opened slowly. He peered up at her with difficulty, groaning.

'Sita,' he said, relieved. 'That monster . . .?'

'It's over, Father. Rama bested him in the contest.'

Janak sat up with difficulty, peering across the assembly hall.

Sita followed his gaze.

Ravana was staring at the two broken halves of the bow in disbelief. He looked at Rama, whose eyes had returned to their normal deer-brown colour.

'So,' Ravana said softly, 'the boy has learned some new tricks.'

'These were old when the world was young, demon,' Rama replied.

Ravana laughed. 'You try to teach me, boy? Me? *I* was old when the world was young! I!'

'No, demon. You weren't even born at the time. You're no deva, no god. Only an anti-god. That's easy enough. Far more difficult to be a god. Or even aspire to that divine status.'

Ravana looked startled. Then he recovered, his faces breaking out in a variety of enraged expressions. 'Enough banter! Do you think by breaking the bow you have ended this? Nothing has ended! The sage said it truly. Already my army masses on the north bank of the Ganga. In hours they will be here, tearing down the gates of Mithila, laying waste to this city. And after we finish raping the city, I will do the same to Rajkumari Sita! Enjoy your ill-won wife while you can. I will be back before nightfall to take her from you. And this time, your puny brahman tricks will not save you. I will make your nightmares come true tonight. You do remember your nightmares, don't you, boy? Sita remembers too! Don't you, princess?'

'Rama! Cut him down now. Use your shakti and bring him down! Together we can take him! Now, Rama! Now!' Lakshman sprang forward, his sword ready. 'Come on, brother. Don't let him leave alive. He's alone and unarmed now. We can kill him together. If he leaves, he'll return with a million of his kind and we won't even get close enough to strike at him.'

Ravana turned to Lakshman. The demon lord's eyes glinted and gleamed with dark anger. His mouths snarled silently, fangs bared, dripping saliva as thick and viscous as insect ichor.

'You mortals. Always dishonourable, yet you pretend that you are the only honourable ones. You would fight me now? Come! Fight me! I will take your odds and to hell with your honour and your so-called eternal souls!'

Rama stepped forward, drawing his sword. The blue light of brahman flashed in his eyes again. Nakhudi whooped with exultation and leapt down from the dais, ready to join in. Bejoo jumped down beside her. The seer-mage Vishwamitra strode forward, his staff held high, preparing to chant.

'No,' Maharaja Janak cried. His voice was cracked and hoarse, but his authority was indisputable. This was his roof, his city. He was liege here.

Everybody froze. They looked at him.

Sita helped her father to his feet. He said hoarsely, 'You cannot attack this creature under my roof. It violates the law of dharma. A guest is as a god by our Arya traditions. To cause harm to this guest, monster though he may be, would dishonour the Chandravansha dynasty and the Arya people.'

'But he harmed you, Father,' Sita said urgently. 'And if they allow him to leave, he will return with an army! Lakshman spoke truly. We must kill him now and end it. It's our only chance.'

'No.' Janak shook his head, adamant. 'He knows our ways. That is why he came here alone and unarmed. He knows that Arya law dictates that no guest can ever be attacked beneath his host's roof. If we kill him, we will put the lie to every Arya tradition. People will stop believing in our nobility and say we are not worthy of the title Arya. What face will we show to the world then?'

Turning to the tableau of warriors and sage in the assembly hall, Janak raised his voice with difficulty, continuing, 'I command all of you, my own people and visitors from Ayodhya alike. This guest must be allowed to leave unharmed. If he chooses to return with hostile intentions, then he will be answered in like fashion. But for now he has come to attend a ceremonial function and as such he must be permitted to leave safely. Go now, demon king, go and never darken my door again!'

Ravana raised his head and laughed. 'A fine way to speak to a man you were willing to make your son-in-law a little while ago! But I think it's for the best. You and I would have had a hard time getting along under the same roof, wouldn't we? I don't think you would have liked hearing a rakshasa bed your beautiful daughter every night! It might have tested your Arya honour more than you could bear!'

'Begone, demon!' Janak shouted fiercely, his damaged voice cracking with strain. 'Begone before I rescind my words and turn you over to your enemies.'

Ravana chuckled and began sheathing his arms again, pair by pair. His muscled torso glistened darkly as he strode to the doorway. Citizens watching wonderstruck fled away like rabbits before a wolf. Some spat at the demon's feet before they ran. 'I shall go, Janak. But I will be back this very eve. And then we shall see who owns this roof. Or even if you have a roof left, for that matter!'

The rakshasa lord sketched a series of symbol in the air as he walked. A misty sheen formed before him, like an oval doorway, and he stepped through it. Briefly at the edges, over his shoulder, Sita glimpsed a green field of grass and a great body of water flowing beyond.

The Ganga's north bank. And there, just at the periphery of the portal, the unmistakable dark mass of an alien army.

The portal closed behind the demon lord and the air sparkled briefly before resuming its normal appearance. The laughter of Ravana echoed through the hall.

8

Kausalya ran down the winding corridor, forcing the leader of her personal guard to run as well. The woman, a short but strapping Banglar named Sengupta, tried to answer a question the First Queen had asked a moment ago. 'She seems all right, my queen. But she looks like she's been at a funeral pyre.'

'A what?' Kausalya didn't slow her pace, but her face registered her surprise. 'I thought you said you found her in the south corridor of the palace.'

'That we did. But she was wandering around in a daze. And her vastra, her face, her arms . . . well, she looks like she's been rolling in ashes.' Sengupta wrinkled her dark snubby nose. 'And the stench of her, my queen . . . How can I describe it?'

Rolling in ashes? What in the world had Sumitra been up to? Where had she been?

Kausalya had got word of Sumitra's disappearance this morning, when the Third Queen's maids had taken her some breakfast and had found Sumitra's bedroom door ajar and the maharani nowhere in sight. Kausalya had been alarmed at the news. She hadn't stopped feeling guilty and miserable since placing Sumitra under palace arrest the previous day. But she'd had no choice in the matter. She'd done it as much to protect dear Sumitra as to prevent further mishap. Too much was happening to take any risks.

She had hoped to be able to discuss the matter with Guru Vashishta and see if he still felt that Sumitra had accidentally dropped the vinaashe poison in the maharaja's punch yesterday, or if it had been more supernatural mischief perpetrated by some agent of the Lord of Lanka. After all, if their enemy could reanimate a dead man and send him within strangling distance of Maharaja Dasaratha himself, might he not possess the ability to somehow poison the maharaja as well?

Kausalya reached the place where the corridors bifurcated, heading south and west. She took the former and ran past a clutch of serving girls, maids and daiimaas all trying to catch a glimpse of the latest mishap to befall the House Suryavansha. O Sri, Kausalya prayed silently as she approached the jewelled arch that marked a titled queen's palace annexe, let Sumitra be okay. Let her not be culpable of any further mischief, deliberate or otherwise.

She entered the Third Queen's private apartment, slowing to give herself a moment to catch her breath, and breezed past a clutch of Sumitra's private guards and servants. The alert ang-rakshaks, the birth-caste of personal bodyguards sworn to live and die protecting the Third Queen, glanced sharply at the First Queen as she entered. It was yet another sign of how much Ayodhya had changed in just a few days. The recent spate of intrusions, attempts, supernatural occurrences and grim news had left the capital city shaken.

The result was that even she, the Maharani of Kosala, was now scrutinised as sharply as anyone else. Distrust and suspicion was visible on every palace guard's face, and even the servants and daiimaas glanced nervously at her as she strode past. She reached the closed doors of Sumitra's chamber and was about to knock on them herself rather than wait to be announced and shown in formally, when the doors flew open and an apparition straight out of a tribal folk play appeared before her.

'Kausalya!' The apparition oddly resembled Sumitra in its low-pitched voice, tall stature and excessively slender build. 'I found the witch's lair!'

'Sumitra?' Kausalya stared at the ash-covered face and arms. 'What happened to you? Where have you been?' She sniffed the air around the Third Queen. 'What have you been doing?'

Sumitra looked around the foyer full of women. They had fallen silent and were watching the two queens with open and avid curiosity.

Kausalya saw an uncharacteristic look of caution steal over Sumitra's ash-smeared features as she took in the huddle of servants.

Sumitra turned and took Kausalya's elbow. 'We have to talk privately,' she said softly. 'There are surely others in the conspiracy. Come.'

What conspiracy? Kausalya wondered as she allowed herself to be led into the bedchamber. It looked much as it had appeared when Kausalya had left Sumitra here under house arrest the previous afternoon. She watched, puzzled, as Sumitra shut, barred and bolted the door. The precautions themselves had been recently installed in the past few days. Previously, it had been unheard of for any royal family member to need to bar or bolt a door. But since Holi, a great deal had changed.

Sumitra turned to face Kausalya, a grin breaking the powdery grey mask coating her face. 'You won't believe what I discovered! The enemy has spies within the palace. They are the ones who poisoned the punch yesterday. And they've been working secretly for years, sabotaging a hundred different things. Guru Vashishta could never find them because they were in the heart of the royal family itself, in a place where he never looked. But I know it all now. I know who the ringleader of the conspiracy is and I've got her trapped in her own secret chamber! We've got to get the guru to confront her and disable her shakti. She's too powerful for us to face on our own.'

Kausalya held up her hands. 'Hush, Sumitra. Slow down and tell me everything from the beginning. What conspiracy are you talking about? Who's this ringleader?'

'It's Manthara-daiimaa! She's an acolyte of Ravana, can you believe it? She's been loyal to him since before she came to the palace. And she's recruited a few palace staff over the years, using her ill-gotten shakti to control and manipulate them. Kausalya, it's horrible, the way she carried on all this time, right under our noses. She beat and tortured people, did you know that? She tried to attack our sons even. Remember the time the royal wheel-house broke a wheel and almost fell into the ravine at Chindig? That was Manthara's foul sorcery. The boys were barely five years old at the time and would have been killed. She tried to murder our sons, Kausalya. That's how heartless she is. She sacrifices little brahmin boys to appease her lord. In a secret yagna room within her own private chambers, right here in the palace!'

Kausalya's head was spinning. For a moment, she wondered if Sumitra was suffering from the same delusional state that had afflicted her the previous day. From hallucinations of Kaikeyi as a giant serpent to visions of Manthara performing black magic wasn't a big leap. But there was something in Sumitra's voice and eyes that was very convincing.

'Slow down, Sumitra,' she said again. 'Sit down here and explain it to me properly.'

Sumitra did as she was told, although she was too excited to sit calmly. Her hands kept clenching and unclenching, as if she held some invisible object in her fists. Kausalya put her hands over Sumitra's, stilling them.

'Calm down, Sumitra. Take deep breaths and slow your heartbeat. You have to calm yourself first.'

Sumitra did as Kausalya suggested. After a moment of breathing deeply in the pranayam yoga method, the Third Queen's demeanour became less agitated and excited. Her hands stopped twitching. Kausalya released them and looked at Sumitra's face closely. She rubbed at Sumitra's right cheek with her forefinger and examined the tip of her finger.

It was unmistakably ash. Not just firewood ash, but the particular grainy particled grey-black ash produced by sandalwood and moonwood with copious amounts of ghee and various ritual condiments. Yagna ash.

'First of all,' Kausalya said, 'before you say anything else, explain this to me. Why in the three worlds are you coated with yagna ash?'

Sumitra took another deep breath, then explained everything. Kausalya listened raptly. Ten days ago, if Sumitra had told her this tale, she would have sent for the royal vaids and had her fellow maharani examined closely for signs of a head injury or mental illness. But too much had happened these past ten days, and in the last day and night, for her to dismiss even such a fantastic tale out of hand.

So she asked calmly, 'And then what happened? After you leapt back through this . . . hole, or whatever?'

'I came straight here to my chambers and sent for you,' Sumitra said. 'On the way I told my personal guards to take post outside Manthara's door and if she emerged then to hold her there and send word to me.'

Kausalya frowned. 'And that was how long ago?'

'A few minutes. You came very quickly. All my women,' Sumitra gestured at the closed door, 'bombarded me with questions. I told them nothing. Some of them may be working for Manthara for all we know.'

'I thought you said the serving girl was the only one who did these . . . things.'

'That's what she said. But who knows? Maybe others were secretly in league with the witch without Sulekha's knowing. Manthara didn't exactly confide in her, Kausalya. Whatever the girl knew, she picked up by seeing things, hearing things. Besides,' Sumitra smiled sheepishly, 'she was very intoxicated, very scared, and not very intelligent to begin with.'

Which was what Kausalya found oddest about the tale. Everything else was within the bounds of possibility, however remote it seemed – even the horrifying notion of brahmin boys being sacrificed under the very roof she slept beneath – but the serving girl was a loose thread that didn't fit the overall pattern.

If Manthara was the scheming sorcerous witch-spy of the king of Asuras, as Sumitra said, then why would she be foolish enough to have a witness to her every crime? One obvious reason suggested itself: Manthara was bodily incapacitated. She could hardly do some of the more physically demanding things that she would have to if Sumitra's tale was true.

And even if she could, and had done so herself, with or without the aid of black sorcery, it would have raised suspicions at once. The incident in the maharaja's sick-chamber the previous day was one example. Had it been Manthara who had gone into the room, the guards would have been very curious and would have told Kausalya later. But because it was an ordinary serving girl, one of hundreds, nay thousands, in the enormous royal complex, it had raised no suspicions at all. Still, could Manthara afford to risk her ambitious world-spanning schemes by trusting the loose tongue of a slip of a girl? Loyalty could be bought and sold like any other commodity perhaps, even in the dharmic and honourable nation of Kosala, but no sum of gold could guarantee silence.

Finally, she decided, Sumitra's entire story rested on just one thing: this girl Sulekha. If she could back up even a tenth of what Sumitra had just told her, or describe a single misdeed that Manthara had committed, Kausalya would bear down on the daiimaa with all the force she could muster. And with the maharaja ill and the princes away, all the force of Ayodhya was at her sole command. Even if the army was not at hand, the PF battalion and palace guard were sufficient to take care of one depraved daiimaa, surely. And if Sumitra had indeed injured her as mortally as she said she had, then even Manthara's sorcery would logically be diminished, perhaps incapacitated.

Sumitra was watching her intently, an anxious look on her face. Her eyes flickered as she tried to read Kausalya's thoughts. Kausalya could see that the first flush of excitement had passed and now Sumitra was weighing the pros and cons of her situation. Kausalya didn't need to explain to the Third Queen that by reeling off such an outrageous story, she had put herself at risk of being thought totally insane.

Which ironically was the most credible aspect of the whole thing. Why would Sumitra make up such an extravagant fantasy when it could be proved or disproved within a few minutes? Especially when she had been discredited yesterday and fallen under suspicion? No, she didn't think Sumitra was making this whole thing up, but she might be labouring under another elaborate hallucination again. After all, if the Lord of Lanka could send the re-animated corpse of a Vajra kshatriya into the very heart of Ayodhya, surely he could delude a sensitive, susceptible, emotionally overwrought maharani?

'Kausalya,' Sumitra said shakily, 'you do believe me, don't you? It all happened just the way I said it did. I'm not making any of this up. Why would I? What would be the point, when just yesterday you and Guruji refused to believe me?'

Kausalya nodded. 'That's true. Why would you make up such a tale?'

Sumitra's face brightened cautiously. 'Then you believe me?'

Sri, guide me. Kausalya took Sumitra's hands in her own again and nodded slowly. 'I think I do.'

Sumitra's smile was as brilliant as a harvest moon. 'Devi be praised!'

She rose to her feet, pulling Kausalya up. 'Come quickly then. Let's go to Guru Vashishta and take him to the witch's lair. He'll be able to confront her and cleanse that awful place. The sooner it's done, the better. Come, Kausalya, we must hurry before she does something.'

'Sumitra, Sumitra, wait a moment. I'll have to get Drishti Kumar to get a contingent of palace guards to come with us. It will take a few minutes. Meanwhile, maybe you should cleanse yourself.'

'There isn't time! We must go now. We don't need guards. Guru Vashishta is sufficient. Let's go call him, Kausalya!'

Kausalya pulled herself away from Sumitra. 'Guruji isn't here, Sumitra. He's gone to Mithila. You probably haven't heard, but the Asuras are invading the Arya nations. Guruji expects the main force to come through Mithila, so he's gone there to help them make a stand.'

Sumitra stared at Kausalya. 'He's gone? But how will we face the witch without him? Rishi Vamadeva and Punditji are strong, but if Manthara is as powerful as I think she is, then they may not be able to confront her. We need a seer-mage of brahmarishi stature. Guru Vashishta or Vishwamitra. Have Rama and Lakshman returned with the sage yet?'

'No, Sumitra. And Bharat and Shatrugan aren't here either. So much has happened since last evening, you've been out of touch. The army was sent away on false information; it was divided and sent to Gandahar and Kaikeya yesterday. Bharat and Shatrugan went as well. Pradhan Mantri Sumantra is occupied with organising the PFs for a full city defence in case the Asuras make it this far. There's only you and me to take care of this problem now. That's why we have to fetch Captain Drishti Kumar.'

Sumitra's face reflected her anxiety and confusion. But to her credit, she didn't react with hysterics or melodrama. Instead she said, 'All right. Then let's get him and go to Manthara's rooms. We have to act quickly.'

That response, so sure and sensible and logical, impressed Kausalya more than anything else. Now she was certain that whatever the truth might be, Sumitra wasn't perpetrating a deception. She was either the victim of another elaborate illusion, or she was telling the truth. Even though she wanted with all her heart to believe Sumitra, Kausalya still hoped that it was the former. The alternative was chilling to contemplate and difficult to accept. She would know which one it was very soon.

'All right,' she said, moving to the door. 'I'll send for Captain Kumar and four quads and ask them to meet us in the south corridor. But we'll not go inside until the guards arrive, are we agreed on that?'

'Of course,' Sumitra said. She shuddered suddenly. 'You

think I want to go in there alone again? I'll have nightmares all my life about the moment she pushed me
through that wall! I thought I was falling into hell!'

Kausalya and Sumitra unbarred and unlatched the
doors. When they opened them, a female rakshak guard
was waiting outside. She was one of Sumitra's clans-
women. She saluted both maharanis smartly and addressed Sumitra.

'Maharani, as you requested, I've come to inform you
that Manthara-daiimaa has emerged from her chambers.'

9

Maharaja Janak reached the top stair of the tower and finished reciting the Gayatri mantra for the thousand and eighty-fourth time, one for each step. He stepped out into the centre of the large domed chamber named the Sage's Brow. Vishwamitra followed the king, with Rama and Lakshman close behind.

Rama experienced a moment of disorientation as he crossed the chamber. An image from his recurring nightmare flashed in his mind. Himself, standing in the identical Ayodhyan counterpart of this watchtower, there named the Seer's Eye. Leaning out of the large windowless portals running continuously around the circular chamber, watching with impotent rage as his beloved Ayodhya was ravaged by an enormous Asura horde.

He understood now that the nightmare had been implanted in his brain by the Lord of Lanka, Ravana himself. And that it was a vision of the future. Not the only future destined for him, but one of several possible futures that his own karma could lead him towards. A future that the Asura king was determined to make a reality.

Right now, as he walked grimly across the bright windswept stone floor of the Mithilan Sage's Brow, it felt like a very possible, even likely, future.

Already the sun was low in the western sky, its slanting

rays warming his right profile as he stood facing the southern side of the Sage's Brow. In less than two hours it would be dusk, and then night. The almost total darkness of a slender waning moon. Not a moonless night as his nightmare had depicted, but close enough. In the nightmare, he had assumed he was in Ayodhya, but now he knew that it was this very tower he had stood in during that awful vision. He had witnessed the rape of Mithila, not Ayodhya.

From the glimpse they had been given when Ravana had stepped through the supernatural portal in the assembly hall, the demon lord's threat appeared to be genuine. An Asura force was amassing on the north bank of the Ganga.

That would place the invaders within two yojanas' distance of Mithila. And that had been almost an hour ago. In another two hours or less, but certainly before sundown, the Asura armies would be at the city gates. Maharaja Janak had accepted this shattering news and its crushing implications with all the majesty and dignity of a true Arya sovereign. Ignoring his injuries at the hands of Ravana, the maharaja had ordered that the assembly hall be cleared at once, and had called for his council and Senapati Bharadwaj, the general in charge of Mithila's sadly diminished armed forces.

While the general had been given an immediate order to assemble his entire force, arming all volunteers and retired veterans, the maharaja and his council had debated their next course of action. The flurry of anxiety and dismay that had followed the council's acceptance of their predicament had been akin to an innocent man's reaction when told that he had been found guilty of an uncommitted crime and was to be sentenced to death within the hour. Why were the Asuras attacking? Why Mithila, now a holy city with almost no military power? Why had they not known of this earlier? How could such an enormous army have been raised by the Lord of Lanka and brought so swiftly and stealthily this far north without the Arya nations knowing?

Vishwamitra had intervened then, cutting short the panicked flurry of comments and queries. These questions were all irrelevant now, the sage had said sternly. They must put aside all discussions and move immediately to prepare themselves for the city's defence. The council's silence had been almost as heartrending as their earlier confusion.

Finally, the prime minister of Videha had appealed to the maharaja to in turn appeal to the brahmarishi for advice. Unlike Kosala, Videha had no guru of Vashishta's stature to guide their governance. This was partly because, unlike Kosala, which was a highly militarised state and required the constant supervision of a spiritual guru, Mithila was itself a spiritually enlightened city. There were more brahmins in Mithila alone than there were kshatriyas in all of the Videha nation. The ratio of brahmins to kshatriyas in Kosala and its capital Ayodhya was almost equal, but Videha had long since discarded its swords, bows and maces for prayer necklaces, red-ochre robes and wildwood staffs. A military crisis was something this once-martial nation no longer had the knowledge or the man-power to contend with, let alone confront.

Vishwamitra had said as much when appealed to by the maharaja. But the seer had seemed curiously calm and unruffled as he spelled out how poorly prepared the Videhan capital was to face the oncoming Asura forces. Even if it had been equipped with an army the size of, say, Ayodhya, Gandahar or Kaikeya, the three most martially powerful Arya cities, Mithila would not have been able to withstand such a massive surprise assault.

Even as they spoke, the outlying areas of the capital were being evacuated, all civilians and travellers brought into the city-fortress. Soon the gates would be shut and the walls manned. But despite its formidable defensive design – identical to that of its sister city Ayodhya – Mithila's defences were in no condition to face such an attack. It would take days, if not weeks, to rebuild the infrastructure needed to maintain a long siege, and that was only conditional on having an army large and well trained enough to undertake this mammoth task.

These reinforcements could possibly be had from the other Arya nations – most likely from Ayodhya, their closest neighbour. But that itself would take time. And their enemy was a few yojanas hence and approaching rapidly! Nay, the sage said decisively, they would have to face this onslaught on their own, with their existing resources.

After that harrowing session, Maharaja Janak, the seer-mage and the two rajkumars had made their way up to the top of this tower. From this vantage point, the sage said, they would be able to view the city entire as well as see the approach of the Asura armies.

Now, the brahmarishi pointed with his staff.

'They will come from the south. Look now and see the fury of their approach.'

Maharaja Janak and the two princes leaned forward, staring southwards. The city walls themselves extended outwards in concentric circles for a distance of a full yojana from the centrally located tower. The Sarayu river flowed beneath the tower and the palace complex itself, the architecture designed to vault over the gentle river without disturbing its natural course. The river flowed roughly north-west to south-east. As they peered out beyond the first city wall, they could see the golden thread

of the sun-kissed river winding its way into the distance.
At some point it crossed its sister river, the sacred Ganga,
before continuing its journey to the ocean.

The brooding darkness of a dense hilly forest, the
Mithilan equivalent of the Ayodhyan Southwoods,
loomed over the river's south bank. Several yojanas
further south, beyond the Shona river and the placid
groves of Siddh-ashrama, these menacing woods grew
in size and denseness to become the dreaded Dandaka-
van, the haunted forbidden woods that marked the southern border of Videha and all the Arya nations. Mithila was
the southernmost Arya city, designed to stand, like its
sister Ayodhya, as the first line of defence against any
attack from the south, the direction in which the distant
island of Lanka lay.

As Rama's eyes followed the brahmarishi's staff, he saw
what he was seeking. Shockingly close, just a little way
beyond the end of the Sarayu valley, was what seemed to
be a rising fog. It was clearly moving in a northward
direction, rolling steadily across the lush green Videhan
landscape. He knew that what seemed like fog was in fact
a cloud of dust raised by an enormous force marching at
considerable speed. The cloud's rolling swell trailed to a
plume that dwindled and rose in the far distance. He
wondered that nobody had noticed such a huge dustcloud.
It must have been visible for several hours after all. But
then he recalled that there were no other towers this tall in
Mithila, and that nobody kept watch for such things as
approaching dustclouds.

'Brahma be merciful,' Maharaja Janak said, his voice
still strained from the throttling he'd received at the hands
of the demon king. 'That front is well over a yojana wide!'

'Nay, raje,' Vishwamitra replied. 'It is closer to
three yojanas wide. The Asura hordes prefer to travel in

separate armies, but with all travelling laterally, so that each feels it is in the front line while keeping a prudent distance between individual species.'

'Three yojanas wide,' the maharaja said faintly. 'What size of army could cover a front that wide?'

'And six yojanas long,' Vishwamitra said calmly, as if estimating the size of a brahmin procession at a tirth-yatra. 'This is the main force of Ravana's vast army. The forces he sent to the other Arya capitals are less than a fifth of the size of this single horde. As I estimate it, his combined Asura armies number over ten million in all.'

'Ten million?' the maharaja said, leaning weakly against the stone overhang of the chamber.

'And four-fifths of that would make eight million,' the sage said. 'It is the second largest army ever assembled. The only force greater than this was raised by Ravana himself when he invaded Swarga-lok and sacked Indra-prastha, the capital city of the devas.'

Maharaja Janak's hands slid slowly down the stone pillar. He came to rest on the curved ledge of the window, sitting weakly as he contemplated the brahmarishi's words. Then he lowered his head to his hands, moaning softly, 'What have we done to deserve this fate, maha-dev? We are a good nation, deva-loving and pure of heart, deed and word. Our citizens follow the path of dharma and respect the laws of karma meticulously. I have devoted my life and resources to the pursuit of spiritual gain rather than the accumulation of material wealth. I have eschewed violence and embraced the creed of ahimsa, as have the majority of my people. We are known throughout the Arya nations as a brahmin nation. Why then are we being subjected to such devastation?'

He looked up at the brahmarishi, his eyes brimming with tears. 'Tell me, maha-dev. What have we done to

deserve this fate? Why do the devas seek to punish us thus?
What noble deed have we left undone, what mortal sin
have we committed? If it is my fault, then let me be blamed
and penalised. Why are my people to be subjected to this
karma? What is their error?'

Vishwamitra looked down sagely at the maharaja. The
chill wind sweeping through the open-walled chamber
billowed his robes and bent his long white hair and
streaming beard. The light of the setting sun caught his
proud regal features, making his ancient battle scars shine
red like freshly bleeding whiplashes.

'There is no error, Mithila-naresh. Neither your people
nor you are at fault here. This is simply the way the samay-
chakra turns. The great wheel of time does not differenti-
ate between good and evil.'

'But the devas do,' Janak said, his eyes flashing with angry
incomprehension now. He wiped his tears away roughly.
'They see and weigh our actions and our thoughts. It was
through his appeals to mighty Brahma and later the great
Shiva that Ravana himself obtained the shakti he now
wields. If a rakshasa with his unmatched history of countless
sins and crimes can be granted such power, why should a
holy and unblemished king such as I be treated so harshly?
Have the scales of celestial justice been broken and thrown
aside? Do the devas no longer respect dharma and karma?'

'It is dharma and karma that save you today, good
Janak. Your great and virtuous deeds and prayers have
earned you an enviable position among mortals. Few
individuals on this earth can claim as great a stake in
celestial admiration as yourself. Even we, the Seven Seers,
have watched and applauded your piousness and your
great achievements from afar.'

Janak shook his head, still lost in his miasma of shock
and grief.

Vishwamitra continued in a more gentle tone: 'In many ways, your eldest daughter Sita is a perfect symbol of the Videha nation. Pure, beautiful and honourable to the core. This great land deserves not to be wrested away as the lord of Asuras sought to do with beautiful Sita. It deserves instead a long, honourable and dignified existence, free from pain and strife, violence and humiliation.'

'And yet,' Janak cried out, his voice cracking with his anguish, 'who will grant Sita these things when Mithila herself is sure to fall tonight?'

'I shall protect Sita,' Rama said, stepping forward to show his face to his future father-in-law. 'I won her hand before the people of Mithila, and I shall honour and keep her as she deserves. No Asura, Ravana or any other, shall lay a hand on her as long as I stand.'

'Nor as long as I stand,' Lakshman said.

Janak looked at both of them.

Rama knew that his eyes and Lakshman's were glowing with the light of brahman. He could feel the shakti still coursing through his veins. It had not ceased to do so since the encounter in the assembly hall. Yet the voice that he spoke with was his own, uninfluenced by the power of the maha-mantras. He meant every word he said. After saving Sita from Ravana's attempt to win her at the swayamvara, Rama was honour-bound to wed her. And if the first stirrings of emotion in his breast were any indication, he would do so for a more compelling reason than to uphold honour.

Janak rose to his feet slowly. He put a hand on Rama's shoulder, then did the same to Lakshman as well. His hand felt cool to Rama's inflamed skin. 'I would hold you to that promise, young princes of Ayodhya, just as I would hold Rama to his well-won commitment.'

He looked to the south briefly, at the cloud of dust now

filling the view from side to side for as far as the eye could see, as if the horizon itself was burning and coming closer by the minute. 'Yet I fear that samay has decreed otherwise. Even I who believe in miracles do not see how we may survive this dreadful night, but if the devas were to see fit to allow us to do so, then on the morrow itself I would see Rama wed Sita with all due pomp and ceremony.'

The brahmarishi spoke quietly. 'And you would do well to consider taking Rajkumar Lakshman here as husband to your second daughter Urmila, raje. As well as joining the hands of their brothers Bharat and Shatrugan with those of your nieces and adopted daughters Mandavi and Shrutakirti. Even without consulting the rajkumars and rajkumaris on whether this meets their individual wishes, I would venture to propose this auspicious and excellent match. I am certain that Maharaja Dasaratha and the maharanis Kausalya, Kaikeyi and Sumitra would be more than pleased as well.'

Maharaja Janak stared at the sage. 'I would consider myself truly fortunate to see my daughters married into the House Suryavansha. And while I would need to make sure that each of them approves of the match, I can already tell you that my daughters are dearly fond of Rama's three brothers and think highly of them.'

He shook his head, continuing, 'But maha-dev, what is the use of discussing such matters when our very existence is in peril? By the time Surya completes tonight's circuit of the globe and returns to us tomorrow morning, neither Mithila nor the House Chandravansha will remain. What good does it do us to speak of the marriages of my daughters at such a time?'

Vishwamitra smiled. 'At such moments does history turn on its heel, just as our planet turns on its invisible axis, raje. There is no time more opportune to decide such matters than these cusps of history. If you indeed approve these matches, and I speak on behalf of the House Suryavansha by saying that they would not disapprove of them, then consider my earlier prediction fulfilled. Your life's desire will be granted, and on the morrow you shall see your four daughters wedded to four eminently suitable bridegrooms by their own consent. This I predict by the shakti given unto me by mighty Brahma himself.'

Janak's face was a conflicting battlefield of emotions. 'Maha-dev, your coming here was a result of my life's karma. May your words be true. I shall be blessed indeed if this were to come to pass as you describe it.' There was no need for him to add, 'although I cannot see how it possibly can'. His face spoke those words eloquently.

Vishwamitra placed a hand on the maharaja's shoulder in the same paternal gesture that the king had extended to the two rajkumars. 'Then let me make another auspicious prediction, Mithila-naresh. This one will gladden your heart as well.'

The seer pointed his staff south at the looming dust-cloud. 'I decree that this very night your great and virtuous city shall be given the fruit of its immense spiritual labours. You shall resist this approaching Asura horde and defend Mithila with great honour and valour.'

10

Captain Drishti Kumar led the way down the south corridor, his shortspear held in an aggressive attack stance. Four guards strode forward with him, two on either side, their speartips aligned perfectly with their captain's weapon. Kausalya and Sumitra followed close behind the captain and the quad. Twelve more guards enclosed the two maharanis in the defensive quadrangular formation for which the Kosalan army was famous.

The captain of the palace guard had arrived minutes after Kausalya and Sumitra reached the mouth of the south corridor, accompanied by sixteen of the ablest personal ang-rakshaks oathsworn to the royal family's protection. He had listened briefly to Kausalya's succinct explanation and had issued curt orders that were instantly passed down the line of back-up guards.

Even as they approached Manthara's residence, several dozen more guards were surrounding the wing of the palace where the daiimaa's apartment lay, blocking off every possible exit and entrance as well as evacuating all servants and other employees to a safe distance. Ayodhya had witnessed enough treachery to ensure that any new evidence of disloyalty would be met with ruthless discipline.

Sumitra had never seen the young captain of the palace

guard look as grim as he did now. She noticed that Drishti Kumar had begun to resemble his father, the illustrious Senapati Dheeraj Kumar, more closely than ever. Truly, this father and son were the backbone of Ayodhya's defence. As long as Kosala had Arya kshatriyas of the calibre of the House Kumar, Ayodhya would remain the Unconquerable.

They rounded a curve in the corridor, passing the portrait of the newly crowned young Maharaja Dasaratha that Sumitra had noticed the previous time she came this way. That had been last night, when her quest for the true culprit had led her to the daiimaa's chambers. Until then she had never visited this part of the palace before: maharanis didn't go to the residences of daiimaas; daiimaas were summoned to maharanis' chambers.

Sumitra was an exception in that she frequently visited her son's wet-nurse in her own residence. She and Sakuntala-daiimaa shared a relationship that was as warm and friendly as the one she had with Maharani Kausalya, and like most Kosalans she regarded the caste divisions as what they actually were – an economic system for more efficient organisation of labour rather than rigid class divisions. She wondered if Kaikeyi ever visited her daiimaa's quarters; she doubted it very much. Not only was Kaikeyi not the kind to befriend any other women – a restriction that didn't seem to apply to men, though – but had the Second Queen been coming here, Sumitra felt sure that Manthara's game would have been exposed a long time ago. Whatever Kaikeyi's faults – and her notoriety as a man's woman rather than a woman's was only one of a long list – treachery and treason were not among them. Manthara's long-lasting deception and betrayal had to have been outside the purview of Maharani Kaikeyi.

Which begged the other question: What hold, if any, did

Manthara exert over the Second Queen? How much of Kaikeyi's own sourness of disposition and bitterness of worldview stemmed from her wet-nurse's dark Asura leanings? Like most daiimaas, Manthara had been Kaikeyi's own wet-nurse before performing the same role for young Bharat, and daiimaas could wield a great deal of influence over their wards, even greater than the mothers of those children at times. In the case of the other rajkumars, this wasn't so, mainly because of Kausalya and Sumitra's close bonds with their sons. But Kaikeyi was notorious for her unmotherly ways and attitudes. Sumitra shuddered to think of little infant Bharat growing up in the care of a woman who secretly worshipped the lord of Asuras and sacrificed brahmin infants to that dark ungod. Later, when they had dealt with Manthara, they would have to look into the damage Manthara's secret evil side might have wrought on Kaikeyi's mind and Bharat's growth.

Right now, it was time to face the witch herself.

Captain Drishti Kumar spoke quickly to the four guards beside him. They strode forward in single file, with no pretence of being quiet or discreet. This was the heart of the royal palace. It was the enemy that would have to skulk around and hide if it chose to do so; they would march through its corridors like the proud ang-rakshaks they were, fearless and eager to give up their lives for their duty.

Sumitra and Kausalya waited with bated breath as the four soldiers marched around the curve of the corridor and disappeared from sight. After a moment or two, their fading footsteps stopped sharply. Sumitra knew they must have reached the doorway of the daiimaa's residence. After another moment, the marching footsteps resumed, this time growing louder and closer.

Two of the four guards reappeared and saluted their captain. They spoke to him briefly.

Captain Kumar turned and addressed the First Queen. 'Maharani, the guards posted outside the daiimaa's threshold say nothing worthy of alarm has transpired. They say the daiimaa is still cloistered within her apartment and has asked several times to be permitted to leave to visit her mistress Maharani Kaikeyi's chambers. What do you wish to do next?'

'I would like to go in and meet Manthara now,' Kausalya said. She glanced at Sumitra. 'Are you ready?'

'Yes,' Sumitra said.

The captain nodded.

'Follow me then, maharanis. And whatever happens, do not break out of the protection of the guards.'

Sumitra remembered the terrifying hours she had spent imprisoned in that stinking secret yagna chamber and shivered. She thought silently, Not for a million gold rupees! If the guards weren't there, she would never have gone back into the daiimaa's chambers.

As it was, she was very nervous at going back without Guru Vashishta. She hoped and prayed that soldiers and weapons would be sufficient to restrain the witch. Please, devi, you helped me escape that evil woman's clutches. Now help me expose and arrest her. From Kausalya's long thoughtful silences and dubious expressions during her explanation, Sumitra knew that the First Queen regarded this as a test of Sumitra's sanity itself. Not just the safety of the royal family and Ayodhya itself, but the Third Queen's reputation too was at stake here. If by some Asura trick, Manthara managed to deceive everyone again, Sumitra herself would be regarded as the villain of the piece. She was risking everything on this jaunt. And yet she had no choice.

What must be done must be done, she thought, setting her jaw grimly. In that instant, her resemblance to Lakshman was very striking.

Drishti Kumar turned back to the two waiting guards and snapped off a quick order. Then he and the guards began marching forward again.

Kausalya followed them, enclosed by the phalanx of spear-wielding rakshaks.

Her heart skipping in her suddenly ice-cold breast, Sumitra followed.

Manthara sat calmly on the mat, her prayer beads clutched in her right hand, chanting the mantra softly but just loud enough to be heard within a yard's distance, rocking herself to and fro in rhythm with the recitation. She continued to ignore the two guards standing to either side, their spears pointing directly at her.

The bead-curtain at the door shirred as someone entered. Without looking up or breaking rhythm, she knew it was Captain Drishti Kumar. He was followed by more guards, who formed a quad around her, spears pointing within the square, and then by the maharanis Kausalya and Sumitra. She knew that Sumitra's face blanched when she saw her on the floor, but the Third Queen remained silent, her jaws grinding hard together in a manner that was strongly reminiscent of her sons.

Manthara continued to recite her mantra with the self-absorbed air of a devotee lost in the ecstasy of prayer. After a brief consultation with the First Queen, Captain Drishti Kumar spoke in a curt but formal tone.

'Daiimaa, rise to your feet and greet your queens.'

Manthara continued to the end of the repetition of the mantra, then, as the captain was about to repeat his command in a harsher tone, raised the prayer beads to her lips, kissed them devoutly, and placed them on the book stand in front of her.

As she struggled to raise herself off the floor, she saw that Maharani Kausalya wanted to order the captain to help her up, but decided against it. It was one of the things she had never been able to understand about Kausalya. How could the queen be so ruthless and so humane at the same time? But then that was the Arya way. To go to war against your own kith and kin, yet obey the rules of warfare scrupulously. Madness, mortal madness!

Manthara gained her feet at last and peered up at the two queens, who were watching her as intently as a mongoose watched a cobra. She joined her hands in a respectful namaskar. 'Namaste, Maharani Kausalya. Namaste, Maharani Sumitra. You do me great honour by visiting my humble residence. To what do I owe this privilege?'

Kausalya's eyes narrowed. Evidently, nothing Manthara had done or said thus far was what she had expected. That made the First Queen suspicious. She was trying to decide if Manthara had genuinely meant her ritual response or if she was just being bitterly ironic. The latter was more her style, Manthara conceded, but she had been careful to keep the statements accentless and plain. They weren't going to catch her out on something as trivial as tone of voice!

'Daiimaa,' Kausalya said curtly, resorting to formal behaviour by the use of Manthara's work-title rather than her name, 'if you have anything to confess, do so now. The penalty for treason, conspiracy and attempted assassination is too harsh to commute. But if you show remorse and admit your guilt now it may bring some relief to your immortal aatma. When your judgement on Prithvi ends and you stand before that great celestial court in Swarga-lok, you may well be judged on the actions and words you now perform. Bear that in mind before you speak.'

Manthara allowed an expression of incredulity to appear on her wizened face. It was genuine, thanks to the First Queen's own words. 'Maharani,' she said, hearing the surprise in her voice. 'Treason? Conspiracy? Attempted assassination? Who has committed these crimes? If you are suggesting that I would be responsible for such heinous sins, then surely I would be judged not in Swargalok, but sent straight to Patal, the lowest level of Narak!'

Kausalya stepped forward. 'So then you deny these charges? Think before you reply. Captain Drishti Kumar here bears formal witness to everything you do or say and may well be called upon to testify against you if so required.'

'Deny? I cannot comprehend such allegations, my lady. How can I deny them then?'

Kausalya glanced at Sumitra. The Third Queen's eyes were glowing like embers now, their soft brown pupils fiery with growing anger. 'Sumitra? Do you want to say anything at this point?'

'Only that she should have been an actress, not a daiimaa. She would have earned a fortune performing on the stage! She's lying to save her skin.'

Manthara turned her distressed gaze to Sumitra. 'Maharani? Would I lie to my own liege-queens?'

'Yes, you would! You have lied. And killed, and conspired, and indulged in a hundred heinous deeds for the sake of your evil master. He's your liege, not Dasaratha. Go on, say his name, admit it! Ravana! Say it!'

Kausalya's hand caught Sumitra's and squeezed it lightly. 'Easy, Sumitra. Let me do the talking.' She looked at Manthara again. 'Daiimaa, by the authority of the maharaja himself, I am now ordering a search of your apartment. For the last time I ask you, do you wish to confess?'

Manthara joined her hands again, this time not in a namaskar but in an attitude of appeal. Her hands shook naturally enough of their arthritic ailing, and putting a tremble in her voice came even more easily. 'Mistress, I beseech you, whatever this misunderstanding is, I pray to the devas that it should be cleared away at once. I do not understand what it is I am accused of. Why do you torment an old lady thus?'

Kausalya's eyes flickered for a second. Got you, Manthara thought triumphantly, smiling inside if not on the surface. The words 'old lady' had struck home deeply, she knew. All Aryas bore great respect for the elderly, but some, like Kausalya, considered it their dharma to always treat them with respect. She admired the strength of will that made the First Queen take such strong action against an old and disabled employee of the royal family. Clearly the Third Queen had done a good job of convincing her senior queen.

Kausalya paused, then said quietly, 'If, by some chance, I am incorrect in my assumptions, then I shall ask your forgiveness for treating you thus. But at present, I must order Captain Drishti Kumar to conduct a full and thorough search of your apartment. Do you have anything further to say that could be of use to yourself?'

Manthara raised her hands skywards. 'May Almighty Sri have mercy on my ageing aatma,' she said shakily, knowing full well that the Mother-Creator was Kausalya's patron deity.

She was pleased by the touch of anguish in her voice.

Kausalya's voice, in contrast, sounded strained and worried as she said, 'Captain, ask your men to search the apartment thoroughly. Spare no effort. And I would

appreciate it if you would accompany me to the daiimaa's
pooja chamber. I wish to search that place personally.'

The captain issued orders to his men, ending with,
'Break the place apart if you have to.'

Palace guards filed into the apartment in a seemingly
endless flow, marching through the corridors and rooms.
Manthara shook her head mournfully, muttering softly to
herself in agitation. She felt Third Queen Sumitra's eyes
boring into her.

A guard called out from the north wall of the apartment,
addressing his captain.

Drishti Kumar turned to the maharanis. 'The pooja
room, maharani. Come with me.'

Manthara waited a few moments as the two queens and
the captain, accompanied by a double-quad of guards that
seemed to be linked to the maharanis by invisible rods, left
the room and entered the pooja room. She lurched after
them, ignoring the guards working everywhere, tearing
open mattresses, spearing pillows, smashing through the
rear walls of closets and cabinets, taking their captain's
last words very seriously.

She heard a shout of outrage from inside the pooja
room. It was the Third Queen.

As she reached the doorway of the pooja room, she
heard Sumitra say, 'It's sorcery! Kausalya, I told you the
woman's a witch! She did this with her black art somehow. You have to believe me!'

Manthara entered the pooja room and looked in to see
the main altar shifted carefully to one side to allow access
to the rear wall. Captain Drishti Kumar, the two maharanis and their eight guards were arranged in a tableau that
seemed quite hilarious to Manthara's eyes. They were
staring at the window that occupied a large part of the
rear wall. The evening sky was clearly visible through it.

The light of the setting sun filled the room indirectly, lighting everyone's faces in a soft reddish-orange glow.

Sumitra pointed accusingly at Manthara. 'She did this somehow, Kausalya. She changed this whole room. I tell you, when I was here earlier, there was no window at all. Just a wall. And behind that wall was the secret yagna chamber where she's been conducting her vile sacrifices!'

Kausalya was staring at the window. 'I understand that, Sumitra. But how could she have changed the room? Even sorcery can't alter the design of the palace itself. If she did wield such huge shakti – and, mind you, that's a very big if – then we would be able to tell at once just by seeing how the building's structure is changed.'

Sumitra nodded. 'You're absolutely right! She's changed the structure of the building! Ask Drishti Kumar to check. Go on!'

Kausalya looked at the captain. 'What do you think, Captain? Could you find out for us if this part of the palace could somehow have been altered through sorcery?'

Drishti Kumar hesitated, glancing at Maharani Sumitra.

'Go on, Captain,' Kausalya said. 'You can speak your mind freely.'

'Maharanis,' he said, 'I can vouch for this myself, since this section of the palace used to be the senapati quarters a long time ago. This was before the end of the Last Asura War and I was but a slip of a lad then. Yet I remember every wall and crevice of this apartment well, because it was my father's.'

'Of course,' Kausalya said, looking astonished. 'That was before the cantonment complex was built, wasn't it?' She looked at Sumitra. 'Before we came here as young brides, Sumitra. A long time ago.'

'Just so, maharani,' Drishti Kumar said. 'Yet not so long ago for those who remember.'

Kausalya nodded. The captain had lost three uncles and four brothers in the Last Asura War. This apartment must be filled with painful yet nostalgic memories for him. 'I understand, Captain. Tell me then, do you recall this room specifically?'

'I do, maharani. It was our pooja room then as well, since it's the only north-facing room.'

He pointed at the window with the haft of his spear. 'Our altar was located on that wall too, since it was the north wall.'

He paused and looked at Maharani Sumitra. 'And the window was always there.'

Sumitra cried out in shame and humiliation. She buried her face in her hands, unable to bear the disappointment. Manthara wanted to drop her old-hag act and leap up and down. But she was aware that although they weren't watching her directly, everybody was keenly aware of her presence, and the two guards who had first entered the apartment were still standing to either side of her, their spears pointing at her heart and her vitals.

She allowed herself a smile of triumph, concealing it with a cry of relief. Throwing her hands together, she raised them to her forehead, directing her words at the altar across the room. 'Truly, the devi watches over me and protects me!'

She resisted the urge to spit after saying the words. Just a little while longer and this charade would be over, and she could continue with her efforts on behalf of the Dark Lord. She needed to perform another yagna and summon Ravana soon. Shifting the corridors of the palace as well as her quarters from one end to the other had used up every last ounce of her shakti. And to have accomplished this feat of dark sorcery without anyone noticing . . . that was surely her crowning achievement. Now, drained as she was, she needed more power desperately, and only her master could provide that.

She also needed healing badly, and only Ravana could do that as well. The wounds that Sumitra had inflicted on her with the trident were concealed for the moment by a maya spell. Even if the Third Queen insisted on having her strip-searched here and now, they would find nary a blemish on her bony chest. But beneath the illusion, the wounds were still there, still bleeding, still shriekingly painful.

Sita gained the top of the Sage's Brow, Nakhudi close behind her.

She arrived just in time to hear the brahmarishi say to her father, 'You shall resist this approaching Asura horde and defend Mithila with great honour and valour.'

Maharaja Janak stared at the sage with a strange mixture of emotions. 'Maha-dev, you are infinite in your wisdom. May you not reveal to us what the outcome of this conflict will be?'

'Nay, Janak,' the sage replied. 'That is forbidden to me. Not because I do not wish to set your mind at ease, but because the samay chakra has infinite minute variations. Just as a compass may not point precisely to the north or the east, thus a future event may have an outcome that is not wholly good or bad. And this is a broad simplification. A compass needle may point not even north-east, but north-by-north-east, for example. In the case of geography, this will result in a definite direction.' The seer pointed his staff over the maharaja's shoulder. 'That way is north-by-north-east exactly, but in mortal events, too many factors and lives are interwoven in a constantly changing, enormously complex pattern. So your great and pious city may survive, yet if you were to lose someone dear to you in the conflict, would you count it as success or as failure?'

Janak joined his hands together. 'Maha-dev, when you first arrived this morning, I told you in my throne room that my life's only remaining selfish desire was to see my daughters wed happily. But what I ask now is not a selfish whim, it is for the greater good of the Videhan people in particular and the Arya nations at large. Tell me then, will Mithila survive this invasion or will we be overrun by the hordes?'

Vishwamitra was silent for a long moment before he replied. 'I have already given you my prediction, raje. Ask me no more. To reveal too much would be to tamper with the finer workings of the samay chakra itself. For by knowing a certain event, a person may seek to influence that event and change its predestined outcome.'

Sita stepped forward, bowing her head formally and performing a namaskar as she approached the sage. 'And is it possible to do so? To influence and change the outcome of an event?'

Vishwamitra turned his wise grey eyes on her. She felt them pierce through to her very soul, searching her consciousness the way a torch might illuminate a darkened cave.

'Rajkumari Sita, you share your father's curiosity for metaphysics and spirituality. Your question is a very wise one. It deserves a wise answer. You ask me whether, knowing the predestined outcome of an event, it is possible to influence and change that outcome. The answer then is this: It is not humanly possible to know the predestined outcome of any event. This is what I was just trying to explain to your good father. The variations in the samay chakra's movements are too complex, too minute, for any mortal mind to comprehend, understand, analyse and predict. Even astrology gives you only the broadest indications of what may transpire. Even if two persons are born at the same instant in the same place, they will not have the same life-history. This is a law of science, as you well know from your gurukul studies. Hence cold, hard, precise science determines the apparently mystical workings of the universe and metaphysics helps us understand those workings. But no mortal may master both science and spirituality equally and completely.'

'And if a mortal were to master both, Guru-dev?' Sita said.

Vishwamitra raised his eyebrows. 'Then that person would be a deva or devi, not a mortal. And to answer your first question again, yes, then he or she would be able to know the exact outcome of an event and could influence and change the outcome of that event.' He sighed and gestured at himself. 'I am unfortunately mortal. And at times like this, I am painfully reminded of it.'

Sita saw Rama looking at the southern side of the tower.

'Maha-dev.' Rama's voice was tight and tense.

Sita turned to look at what Rama had seen. Her eyes found it at once but it took her several seconds to come to terms with the evidence of her eyes and accept that she was really seeing it.

'Devi protect us!' she said hoarsely, clutching the hilt of her sword. She had changed into full battle armour after the swayamvara.

The entire southern horizon was a rolling mass of dust. The dustcloud rose a hundred yards in the air, she saw, and spanned the horizon from end to end. Like a fiendish freak of nature, it caught the light of the setting sun, burning bright shining red.

At that angle and in that light, it resembled a tidal wave of blood rolling towards Mithila.

*   *   *

Bejoo stared up at the southern sky with a feeling close to awe. Except that the Vajra captain was filled with too much dread and anger to be awed by the incredible sight. Just knowing what was producing that dustcloud was enough to taint any admiration he might feel for the epic proportions of the sight.

The Vajra captain was mounted on his horse once more. Sona Chital was beside him, and so was the rest of his Vajra. They had arrived in Mithila barely an hour before the order went out to bring in all citizens and bar the seven gates. The Siddh-ashrama procession had been delayed at the Ganga crossing; every last brahmin and brahmacharya had insisted on immersing himself and performing the full ritual before proceeding further. From the looks of it, Bejoo had commented, Sona Chital and the Vajra kshatriyas had spent a little time bathing in the sacred river as well.

The lieutenant had admitted that they had taken a dip. When asked why they hadn't done so at the River Shona, where they had spent the whole of the previous evening and night, Sona Chital had explained to his captain, 'Any other river is just water. It washes your body. The Ganga cleanses your soul.'

Bejoo's soul didn't feel very clean at the moment. As he sat on the fair ground and watched the Asura dustcloud approach, he felt very dirty and tainted. Not by his own misdeeds, but by the very sight of that approaching holocaust. He was old enough to have memories of the Last Asura War. Bad memories, all. And now here was the stormcloud risen again, rolling across the land like a juggernaut of hellish destruction.

He knew all the facts of the matter. Of how woefully inadequate Mithila's defences were, how underequipped the army was in numbers, training and weapons. There was nothing he could do about that. By an ironic twist of karma, his mission to protect the rajkumars had brought him here to this neighbouring land and dropped him bang into the middle of a situation where he and his Vajra were among the most able warriors available. True, there were a few other strong orders. The Mithila bowmen, renowned for their skill with the unwieldy double-curved longbow, were lined up on the walls of the city, ready to wreak havoc. But they were pitifully few in number to begin with, and compared to the odds, they faced an impossible task.

So this is what it comes down to, Bejoo thought sombrely. One last stand in a strange city, fighting unbeatable odds. No hope of survival, no chance of victory. Just certain death to face. A horrible, agonising, brutal end to a long and equally brutal life. There had been moments of great beauty, peace even. He had not fought any needless fights, nor taken life for pleasure as some warriors did when intoxicated by the power of their youth and strength. He had fulfilled his dharma, done all that was demanded of him, and had done it well.

He had loved a wonderful woman, and had lived a fine life with her. He would leave her secure in life and wanting for nothing. Except for the children they had both desired so much and had never been able to have. In his prayers to his patron deity, Shaneshwara, Bejoo had prayed every single day that he would die fighting with his fellows by his side and Ayodhya behind him. He was getting half his wish. And Mithila was as worthy of defence as Ayodhya. He would die a good, honourable death.

He reached his decision then. They would not wait within the innermost wall for the enemy to breach the gates. A last line of defence was hardly any use once the Asuras broke into the inner fortress and township. By that time, all the remaining kshatriyas in Mithila would be gathered here, making their last stand in these confined quarters, giving their lives to defend each inch of precious mother-soil. That was their duty, their dharma even.

But he was not Mithilan. He had leeway in choosing where to deploy his men and how to do so. Senapati Bharadwaj had said as much to him a short while ago. The veteran general knew that with these odds, no formation or strategy could even delay the inevitable. It was a hopeless, desperate, doomed last stand, and all they could do was make that stand bravely, taking as many of the enemy as they could before they died. Bejoo was free to do as he pleased.

He decided he would do what he would have done in Ayodhya. There, with the inner city manned thoroughly and every egress and ingress guarded heavily, the city's Vajra units would have been ordered to ride forth from the sally ports and inflict planned damage on particular parts of the besieging army before returning to await orders for the next sally. Of course, there they would be replenished with reinforcements and each sally would be carefully planned and ordered by senapatis observing from the Seer's Eye to achieve a strategic gain. Here, he had no back-up, no strategy, not even the guarantee that he would be able to return safely to the sally port he had left from. But it was what his men were trained to do in the event of a siege, and it was better than waiting here and listening and watching the horrors of the first waves, waiting for the monsters to kill all the lines of defence and come rolling in to wash over them.

This way, at least they would die as Vajra kshatriyas ought to die – striking with the speed and accuracy for which they were named. Like bolts of lightning flung by the hand of Indra himself, digging into the flanks of the

Asura invaders and leaving them a little bloodier and messier each time.

He rode a few yards forward, then turned his horse to face his men. They were drawn up in a straight line, unlike their usual spear formation, the cavalry, chariot, bigfoot all arrayed in one long row. At least it made it easier for him to speak to them.

'Vajra,' he said, speaking loud enough to be heard down the line. The lead elephant raised its trunk to half-mast in salute and trumpeted briefly to acknowledge the captain. 'We have but two choices here. To stay and wait within these walls. Or to go out and harry the enemy in the open. Each course will certainly lead to our ends. You already know that the odds are insurmountable. By staying here, we may hope that the beasts change their mind halfway through and decide to go scurrying back home.'

'Why would they do that, Captain?' Sona Chital asked curiously.

Bejoo shrugged, his eyes glinting mischievously. 'Deva knows. Maybe they might remember some forgotten chore. Or get terrified at the sight of so many brahmins.'

A wave of laughter broke out.

Bejoo smiled. 'Anyway, I'm in favour of sallying forth and biting the monster in the haunches as best we can before he slams us into the dirt. It's not going to be much fun with a host that size, but it's what we do. I for one would rather go down fighting in open country than wait cloistered here until those scum come to pick us off. But these are unusual circumstances. We are free to go as we please and fight as we will. So I leave it up to you to decide what you would do. Sally forth and nip the giant in the testicles—'

Another burst of laughter.

'Or stay here and wait for the giant to come and smash us.'

He spread his arms wide. 'The choice is yours. Decide quickly. Personally, I prefer the former. I'm waiting five minutes then riding out of the gates before it's too late. Those who wish to follow, do so. Those who wish to stay behind, do so. Either way, we'll all feed the carrion birds come dawn and will be remembered as the Vajra who fought like lightning bolts, and died just as quickly!'

He turned his horse around to avoid seeing the men's faces and influencing them unduly. When five minutes was up, he nudged his horse forward, whispering affectionately to her, 'Come on, old lady, let's go for one last ride together.'

She whinnied and trotted towards the side gate that had once been used as the route to the sally port. Because the layout of the city was identical to that of Ayodhya, that was one less hurdle to cross. The odds were huge enough as it was. The captains at the gates had been told to let his Vajra leave if they wished to do so at any time. They saluted him smartly as he rode past. He returned the salute just as respectfully. Mithila's small standing army might be limited in numbers, but their discipline and spirit weren't limited in any way. He felt a pang of regret for these brave outnumbered men and women who would die today without a ghost of a fighting chance.

The bowmen on the walls waved to him as he rode past, shouting slogans of encouragement. Mostly they yelled the Videhan war cry, 'Satyamev Jaitey!' Truth Always Triumphs. He wished that were the case: in his experience, more often than not, truth lost out to reality. Today was yet another instance.

He vowed not to look back until he was out of the sally port and riding across open land, headed south-east. He intended to circle the city and meet the foe as they made their first attack, staying far enough to the west to be out of range of the Mithila arrows.

He had no knowledge of how the Asura forces were arrayed but he prayed he wouldn't find pisacas before him. He couldn't stand any of the species, but at least rakshasas, gandharvas and vetaals walked on two legs, and nagas and uragas stood more or less upright as they slithered along.

Pisacas crawled like the giant carapaced insectile beasts they were, and they spouted that disgustingly foul ichor when you cut them, and if they got you, they laid their horrendous eggs within your belly, fusing the wound with their flame-throwing mouths. You lay there unconscious for hours on the battlefield until the eggs were ready to hatch, at which point the younglings ate their way out of you, killing you if you were lucky, or leaving you lying there half-eaten and half-alive until eventually you succumbed.

Please, Shani-deva, he prayed silently, give me anything but pisacas.

When he was a half-mile out from the city, he looked back at last.

Every last member of his Vajra was behind him, following in perfect attack formation, bigfoot in front, wheel and horse following. He studied them for a moment, then blinked rapidly and turned back to face forward.

'Looks like we're not alone after all, old girl,' he told the horse. She didn't reply. Maybe she was as moved as he was.

He was out of range of Mithila now, and riding directly toward the dustcloud. It loomed impossibly high above the landscape, dwarfing everything around, seeming to stretch like a wall reaching up to the sky itself. Now the sound of the Asura hordes was audible; he could hear the keening, wailing and howling of the species as they smelt the sweet blood and soft flesh of the mortals in their walled city. It was a sound that made babies stop crying in sheer fright. No human ear could hear it and be unmoved.

Bejoo glanced back one last time at his Vajra. Pride swelled in his chest like a gorge of fire. He raised his sword, urging them on, then pointed the sword forward, indicating a small hillock from which they could make a more effective downward rush. Strike like lightning, die like thunder.

'Jai Shree Shaneshwara,' he said softly. There was no need to shout it. In moments, when the army beneath that vaulting dustcloud arrived, the noise would be too great to hear anything. Even his own last prayers.

'Guru-dev,' Rama said softly, 'I ask your leave to go to the first gate and face the assault.'

'And I ask your leave to go with Rama and fight by his shoulder,' Lakshman said.

Sita looked at her father. His face was wan and pinched. His eyes were riveted to the looming dustcloud. It was now less than a yojana distant and closing fast. Already, the top of the cloud reached twice as high as the three-hundred-yard-high Sage's Brow, darkening the entire horizon from west to east. The slanting light of the setting sun, almost at its nadir now, continued to glow red and deep purple where it caught the countless dust motes of the approaching cloud, turning it into one enormous blood wave.

'Father,' she said, 'I too wish to fight. I will not sit in my chambers and wait until the demon hordes break through. I wish to use my last moments defending our city and our heritage. I beg of you, do not deny me this last honourable act.'

Janak gazed ahead with unfocused eyes. The maharaja seemed to have reached a place beyond anger, hate or fear. He had the preternatural slowness of a saint, oblivious to every worldly pain or pleasure. But when his eyes rested on Sita, life returned to them. He strode forward, enfolding her in his arms.

'My beloved child,' he said, his voice filled with the tears his dry eyes were not shedding. 'If this were a normal day, by this time you would be married and would be the wife of Rajkumar Rama Chandra. You would be embarking on a new life, a new hope, a new future.' He gestured at the approaching cloud. 'Instead, you face this. And now you ask my leave to go out into that monstrous . . . thing and fight to the death? What can I say, my lovely Sita? Do you think any father can tell his child yes, go out into that storm and let yourself be torn to shreds by creatures from the lowest levels of hell?'

Sita shook her head. 'If Rama and Lakshman can go, why can't I?'

'If your sisters can stay, why can't you?' Janak replied.

Vishwamitra held up a hand. 'Hush, Sita, Janak. Neither will you be required to sacrifice your lives defending Mithila, nor will the rajkumars of Ayodhya need to do so.'

All eyes turned to the sage. He pointed his staff at the cloud, now turning violet and indigo with the darkening light. The sun was sliced in half by the western sky, its southern side shimmering in the haze of the approaching dustcloud.

'This was all ordained and foreseen,' he said. 'The reassembling of the Asura armies, the building of the vast fleet, the crossing of the great ocean, the subterfuge and spying and deception to avoid the Arya nations learning about the invasion in time to prevent it, even Ravana's attendance at your swayamvara, Rajkumari Sita. Everything was foreseen and foretold by the omens and the astrologers. Right up to the siege of Mithila and beyond.'

'Siege, maha-dev?' Janak's voice was bitter but not angry. 'What siege? We will be overrun in moments by that host. This is a massacre, great one. It is no siege.'

'And yet a siege it is. For Mithila is only a symbol of the Arya nations as a whole. All of Arya is besieged by the Asura menace, in the same way that a noble person is constantly besieged by impure thoughts and desires. What else is mortal life if not one long siege against the weaknesses and temptations of the flesh? Today, this eternal conflict is played out in reality, with the body of Mithila being invaded by the Asura hordes. And as mortals individually combat their mortal desires, so also must Mithila defend itself against the invaders.'

'But how will we do so?' Janak asked, the desperation in his voice making Sita wince. 'Give us a way and we will do it, maha-dev. Show us a road and we shall take it.'

Vishwamitra nodded. 'That is my dharma. That is why the Seven Seers were ordained. To be The Ones Who Show The Way. I do indeed have a road to show you, my good Janak. But you must prepare yourself. For as often happens with such choices, the road that lies before you is almost as treacherous as the dilemma in which you now stand.'

Janak rubbed his forehead with his knuckles, a gesture he made when troubled. 'You speak in riddles, maha-dev. And yet I listen with all reverence. Show me the way.'

Vishwamitra nodded. 'Very well then. I shall show you.'

The brahmarishi reached into the folds of his robes and pulled something out. It was an object so small, it fitted into his closed fist. 'This was given to me this morning by the maharishi Gautama, when I restored his wife to him.'

Vishwamitra looked at Rama and Lakshman. 'The rajkumars assisted me in that mission, as did certain other brave companions.' He didn't look at Sita and Nakhudi, and he didn't name them. The maharaja still knew nothing of his daughter's escapade, and, Rama thought, this was no time to speak of the matter.

'The maharishi Gautama gave this to me willingly, for one seer may give it to another if he pleases. I made the trip to save Ahilya and restore her to her estranged husband for the express purpose of securing this favour. As you shall see, it is not a thing easily obtained, but once obtained, the owner desires to give it away as soon as possible. Yet it may not be given into the wrong hands. The maharishi Gautama actually thanked me for taking this immense burden from him, for very great power such as this object brings is a burden.'

Rama looked at the sage's closed fist, willing himself to see through the bunched fingers. All he could see was the fine tracery of scars around the back of the sage's hand, marking the many times he had stopped a blow with his sword pommel and had been cut on the hand.

'Maha-dev,' the maharaja said, staring with equally rapt intensity at the closed fist, 'will this object of power be able to help defend Mithila from this invasion? Will it perhaps enable us to hold the enemy at bay long enough to receive help from the other Arya nations? Turn this slaughter into a siege, as you put it yourself?'

Vishwamitra sighed softly. His face, caught by the fading light of the almost set sun, looked every bit its age. Five thousand years of living and abstinence and hard penance and guiding the lives and actions of his mortal fellows had taken its toll, Rama realised. And what a toll it was.

'Nay, raje,' the seer said sadly. 'What I received from Maharishi Gautama and which he in turn received from mighty Brahma himself will help in neither defence or delay. It will destroy the entire Asura force in one blow!'

He opened his hand and showed them the object in his palm. It was a tiny scroll, they saw now. A little piece of parchment weighed down by some mystic force – even the fierce wind buffeting them didn't stir it. There were words in Sanskrit written on the piece of parchment. A mantra. Like so many other great keys to brahman power.

'This is the Brahm-astra. The weapon of the Creator Brahma himself. It is the most potent and terrible weapon ever created. And it exists for one purpose only. To wipe out one's enemy. Not to conquer, defeat, or achieve victory over, but simply to decimate. It would be like slaughtering the entire force of Ravana in one flash of an eyeblink. More terrible and awesome than even the one-sided slaughter that the lord of Asuras seeks to inflict upon you. For at least you and your supporters can lift a sword and cut down an Asura or ten before they kill you. By using the Brahm-astra, you will massacre them without a chance of survival. The entire horde you see approaching now, less than five miles from the city gates, will cease to exist. They will in fact be uncreated through the cosmic power of Brahma's own weapon.'

He reached out the hand to Maharaja Janak. 'Here,' he said, 'I give you this Brahm-astra. You may use it but once. And by doing so, you damn your soul to an endless cycle of karmic rebirth. No more will you be able to redeem yourself through good words, good deeds, good thoughts or prayer. By using this most terrible of all weapons in creation, you give up your right to absolution for ever. You will never attain salvation, or nirvana, or enlightenment. And never will you attain oneness with brahman.'

Janak staggered back. Sita and Nakhudi both reached out and supported him. He remained on his feet but his face was drained of all colour. The last tip of the setting sun was all that remained above the western horizon. Its rays caught the maharaja's face and cast it in a deathly pallor.

'Maha-dev,' he said, his voice choked with emotion, 'you ask me, a man who has devoted his entire life to the attainment of spiritual salvation, to give up the chance of absolution, enlightenment and even nirvana? You ask me to damn my eternal soul irrevocably? To be lost in an endless cycle of karmic rebirth, forever suffering for my sins and crimes?'

'Not just you, Janak, but all Aryas living at this time. For it is in their interest that you seek to destroy this Asura menace. You will not be alone in your spiritual excommunication. Every living Arya will share in that eternal crime. This is the price you pay for using the Brahm-astra.'

The sage gestured with the staff in his other hand. 'You have but a little time to wield it, Janak. Use it now and save your people.'

The sun slipped below the edge of the horizon and the last rays of the sun god faded from the sky. From the south, the distant rumbling of the approaching Asura army grew into a roar of exultation. The long day had ended. Night had fallen on Mithila city, for perhaps the last time in its illustrious history.

Maharaja Janak turned his face away, sobbing. The tears that he could not release before now spilled freely down his lined face. 'I cannot do it,' he cried. 'I cannot commit such a sin. It would be like condemning all of mortalkind to eternal damnation. We would be no different from Asuras then, human in appearance but ungodly in our lost aatmas.'

Vishwamitra sighed. 'Then we are lost. For I cannot wield the weapon. As a seer ordained by Brahma himself, it is the one dev-astra forbidden to me. Were I to attempt it, I might destroy all of humankind. This is a precaution laid down by mighty Brahma in his infinite wisdom. For no one person should possess so much power.'

There was a long moment of silence then, as everyone assimilated the implications of the seer-mage's words.

Into that silence, Rama said, 'I will do it, Guru-dev. I shall wield the Brahm-astra.'

Bejoo waited on the top of the hillock, on the south bank of the Sarayu. His view of the southern horizon was limited by the rising cliff beyond which lay the beginings of the Southwoods that led eventually to Dandaka-van. The sunlight had faded as well, leaving a misty haze that illuminated everything with an ominous pinkish light. He could hear and feel the thundering approach of the invaders clearly now. The entire ground seemed to rattle and shiver with the impact of those pounding hoofs, claws, talons, pugs and whatever other terms described the nether limbs of Asuras. Loose soil fell in a ceaseless shower from the sides of the cliffs, adding to the particles of dust and haze in the air.

It was like being in the heart of a funeral pyre after a battle, surrounded by the smoke of a thousand burning corpses. The only thing missing right now was the awful sweet stench of roasting human flesh. Bejoo was glad of one thing: at least this time he wouldn't have to lug the bodies of fallen comrades to the pyres. This time it would be someone else's task to carry him. If there was enough left of him to carry, and if there was anyone left to carry it.

The dustcloud was a solid wall now, rising as high as the eye could see. As he watched, it seemed to slow visibly, the roiling reducing to a slow churning. After a moment, the thundering impact reduced as well. He understood at once what was happening: the Asura hordes were slowing as they came in sight of their destination.

He watched as the cloud hung suspended in the air, thick as a brick wall and as dense.

For a long moment, nothing happened. The rumbling died away completely and the valley fell silent as a stone. The wall of dust remained motionless and still, neither advancing forward nor dissipating, catching the residual light of the sun, sunken below the horizon but still throwing its rays high up into the sky over this part of the earth.

Then, like a dancer's face emerging from a diaphanous veil, the Asuras emerged from the wall of dust. They seethed and swarmed down the valley at a pace twice as fast as a mortal walk. They were almost at the end of their long march now, the march that had begun on the shores of a bayside town named Dhuj many hours earlier. Their alien jaws salivated in anticipation of their inevitable triumph.

Bejoo saw movement out of the periphery of his vision. He raised his eyes and saw the tops of the cliffs swarming with dark shapes. Asuras were climbing down the almost vertical sides, swarming like lizards descending a wall. He watched as the Asura armies covered the earth before him, approaching steadily. A mile, then half a mile, and finally, a quarter-mile away.

He raised his sword, preparing to give the order to charge. He wouldn't wait for those vermin to come at him. He would go to them and show them how Vajra kshatriyas fought.

And how they died.

All eyes turned to Rama. He stood resolute, addressing the brahmarishi. 'Grant me the Brahm-astra, maha-dev. Allow me to wield it and save Mithila.'

Vishwamitra's eyes were filled with an emotion that Lakshman hadn't thought the brahmarishi was capable of feeling; the seer's face showed actual pain as he looked at Rama.

'You do not know what you ask, Rama. This is not like the other dev-astras I gave unto you earlier. This is the Brahm-astra, the supreme weapon of all creation. Used correctly, it can certainly dispel the Asura armies before they overrun this city. But that is only a fraction of its boundless power. For by using the power of anti-brahman, the antithesis of the force that all matter is created from, it cancels out brahman itself.'

'Forgive me, Guru-dev,' Rama asked, 'but I do not comprehend your meaning. Are you saying I cannot wield the Brahm-astra?'

Vishwamitra shook his head sadly. 'Would that it were so. In fact, you are the perfect person to wield it. Infused with the maha-mantras Bala and Atibala, proven in your championship of brahman by your triumph over the Asuras of Bhayanak-van, endowed with the dev-astras I gifted unto you, you would be able to wield this weapon masterfully, destroying only the Asura hordes and no more. Few other kshatriyas would be able to do so as skilfully.'

The sage indicated the others, watching with rapt attention. 'Not even your brother Lakshman, nor the valiant kshatriya princess Sita, nor even her formidable guardian can claim to be as well versed in battling Asuras as you already are, young Rama. Even at your tender age, you have championed the cause of brahman more notably than a thousand thousand veterans of the Last Asura War ever did. For who amongst them can claim to have downed a rakshasi of Tataka's mighty stature, her hundreds of hybrid offspring, as well as her ferocious sons Mareech and Subahu. Nay, Rama Chandra, it is as if mighty Brahma himself has chosen to bring you here for this very task.'

Rama nodded. 'So this is the end for which I was brought here. Instead of going to Ayodhya.'

'Indeed, Rama. This was your dharma. And while I did not know precisely what the end would be, I knew that the road was correct. Hence it was given to me to ensure that you came on this journey. Not just to gain a perfect bride and dispel the rapacious lord of the Asuras, but to break the siege of Mithila with one single blow.'

'Then grant me your ashirwaad, Guru-dev. And let me use the Brahm-astra before it is too late.'

Vishwamitra held up his hand, his lined palm as creased with age as his weathered face. 'Wait a moment longer, Rama. There is one last thing I must tell you before you do this.'

'Speak then, master.'

Vishwamitra sighed and inclined his head, as if unable to speak the next words directly. 'There is a price to be paid for using the Brahm-astra. Because this is the ultimate weapon of brahman, and because it employs the universe-destroying force of anti-brahman, the wielder will lose all other brahman shakti. In short, Rama, if you use the Brahm-astra, you will save Mithila and all Arya certainly, but you will lose all the brahman power I have given unto you. You will become once more an ordinary mortal, stripped of all divine protection for your days on this mortal plane, and nothing you do or say will ever earn you even a mite of that power again. This is the toll demanded of the one who wields the Brahm-astra. Pray, answer me wisely now. Are you willing to pay this price?'

'So be it,' Rama said. As he spoke, his eyes flashed with the blue light of brahman and even his tongue flicked sparks of blue illumination in the gathering dusky light of twilight. 'If that is all it costs to save so many lives, it is naught. Give me the weapon, brahmarishi. Let me do what my dharma demands.'

Lakshman reached out, catching Rama's hand as he held it out to the sage. 'Brother. If you do this, you will earn the wrath of the Asuras for ever. And at your next encounter, you will be naked of all power. Without your brahmin shakti, how can you hope to fight against the forces of evil henceforth?'

Rama shook off Lakshman's hand. 'Hush, brother. The time for debate is past. The sands of samay have run through our fingers now. This step must be taken and taken at once. Give me the Brahm-astra, sage. Give it to me now!'

The sage stepped forward, holding out the parchment scroll. But even as Rama's hand closed over the tiny curl of precious papyrus, Lakshman's hand lunged out and caught Rama's fist. Rama stared at his brother, his eyes flashing blue sparks.

Lakshman's eyes shone back with equal intensity, lit by the shakti of his own power.

'Then let us share in this as well,' Lakshman cried. 'Let us wield the astra together.'

Rama was still for a moment. Then a smile opened his face from the mouth outwards, like an invisible blade unveiling his soul. It was a terrible smile to behold. 'So be it, brother. Together in this, as in all else!'

As the others watched in wordless stupefaction, Rama and Lakshman stepped forward to the southern windows of the tower. Rama opened his hand, holding up the parchment with the mantra written on it. The corner of the tiny chit fluttered in the wind. Lakshman caught the other side and held it firm and still.

With an invocation to the devas, speaking as if with a single voice, Rama and Lakshman began to read the Brahm-astra mantra.

Bejoo's horse charged forward with a loud neigh of protest. Even though the mare had given him years of good service and had served through any number of violent encounters, she had only carried him into battle against Asuras once before. And, on that occasion in the Bhayanak-van battle, she had faltered momentarily and had needed to be goaded on. Now she tried to turn her head aside, seeking to take a different path, anything to avoid charging headlong at that seething mass of alien predators.

The Asura force stank. The reek coming off them was unbearable and indescribable. It was like a thousand cesspools and a thousand corpse-laden battlefields all thrown together. It was like the stench of fluids exuded by insects in the deep forest. Or by bats in a subterranean cavern that had not had fresh air blow through it for a thousand years. It was like death itself, and Bejoo knew the smell of death, for he had faced it often before. It drew you towards it, despite the disgusting odour, drew you in like a kite on a length of twine, calling you with its horrible yet mesmerising stench.

Bejoo went to meet his death.

The Vajra rode behind him. He could feel the pounding impact of the bigfoot, hear their trumpeting, the rattling of the chariot wheels, the lusty cries of his men. Arrows fired by the chariot archers flew overhead, arcing through the smoky air to fall out of sight in the Asura ranks. They seemed like pitiful pebbles tossed against a thousand-yard-high waterfall.

A hundred yards ahead, the line of Asuras roared and howled and urged him on. As a war veteran, he understood why they weren't advancing any more. They were waiting for their leader to give the command. When that command came, they would smash through Mithila as easily as a fist through a paper wall. But for now they waited. And he rode towards them like an insane fool.

Now he could see individual Asuras in the dense black mass. The air was foggier here, the dustcloud raised by the enormous army still standing high in the sky. On the ground, the dust-filled air coupled with the gathering dusk made it difficult to see clearly more than a few dozen yards ahead. But he could make out the unmistakable shapes of nagas, their large hooded heads rising yards above the ground. They hissed and seethed at his approach. And beside the nagas were yaksas, shape-shifters. Bejoo's heart lurched. Yaksas were the only other species he hated almost as much as pisacas. The Elvish races could wreak havoc in his Vajra's ranks. Their ability to morph into different animal forms, or even half-forms, meant that they could confuse the most obedient bigfoot or horse. Without their mounts, even Vajra kshatriyas couldn't hope to last long against the towering nagas and the inevitable uragas which would come in their wake.

But it was too late for second thoughts now. Bejoo cried his battle call and forced his protesting mount directly at the front line of the Asuras. Ten yards now, then seven, then five . . . four . . . three . . .

And then he was amongst them, slashing into the top of the hood of the lead naga, a gleaming black-hooded beast stippled with red spots. The creature lunged at him, its yard-high fangs flashing, venom spilling from its eager sacs, its diamond-bright eyes glinting hatefully. Bejoo's sword drove through the top of its hood, dividing its head in two. The naga swayed for a moment, then fell back, blocking its companions to either side.

Bejoo cried out in exultation, caught in the heat of battle fever. He had drawn first blood. Or, to be more accurate, first venom.

A moment later, his Vajra crashed into the Asura ranks to either side, an elephant trumpeting as it smashed a naga hood beneath its massive feet, chariots carrying their lance-wielding riders over the coils of nagas, crushing the serpentine bodies, to drive their pointed lances into the hoods and eyes of other nagas.

As the princes of Ayodhya called out the words of the Brahm-astra, Sita felt the change in the floor beneath her feet. The Sage's Brow, like its corresponding tower in the capital cities of each of the seven Arya nations, was said to be built with the shakti of brahman, raised by the Seven Seers themselves. And the Seers were ordained by Brahma, creator of the universe, the foremost channel of brahman shakti. As if in recognition of this fact, the tower itself seemed to be coming alive as the recitation progressed. It vibrated and thrummed in response to the mantra's chanting. Below the sound of the shrieking wind, Sita could hear a faint ringing echo. Was that merely the voices of Rama and Lakshman reverberating off the stone walls? Or was it that the walls themselves, along with every single stone of which the tower was composed, had begun to echo the potent syllables?

She looked around and saw her father gripping the edge of a windowsill to avoid being knocked off his feet. Even hulking Nakhudi, squinting fiercely, was crouching to maintain her balance. Only Brahmarishi Vishwamitra seemed untouched by the wind; he seemed almost to relish the unleashing of power, his flowing beard and tresses flickering in the eddies and currents like a white banner in a battlefield.

The wind was growing stronger by the minute, as if Vayu, the wind god, was being called down to join in the battle himself. The sky outside the tower had turned deep blue, the blue of the shakti of brahman energy. Sita saw that this was not a result of refracted sunlight or the twilight; it was a supernatural light effected by the mantra itself. It was as if the forces of the universe were being called together to coalesce their powers in one mighty blow.

Somewhere through the sound of the wind and the chanting of the mantras, she also heard the sound of the Asura army massed below. They were howling to be unleashed. Awaiting the final order to fall on the mortal city and tear it to pieces.

The resonant voice of Rama-Lakshman – for they were as one being now, not two – rode the rising howl of the wind, reached a climax, and then fell silent.

The mantra was over.

The Brahm-astra had been unleashed.

*   *   *

Jatayu led its forces high above the hills, above the enormous dustcloud raised by the Asura armies, above even the clouds. From this height, it could see the cusp of the sun. Twilight had already fallen across the earth below, but where it flew, the sun still shone, catching its wings and warming them.

It cried its ululating hoarse cry, and its brethren answered, calling back. Their screeching cries filled the sky for miles around, terrifying birds flying to their nests for the night. Jatayu loved the sensation of power that came before an assault like this one. And the promise of food. It had chosen to remain hungry even after receiving the Lord of Lanka's orders, knowing that the edge its hunger gave it would make it that much more vicious in the battle.

It swooped down through a cloud and saw the landmarks that indicated it was reaching Mithila. It called to its companions and they passed the word along. It had close to a thousand bird-beasts with it, mostly jatayus like itself, man-vultures, but also a large clutch of garudas, man-eagles descended from the great Garuda himself, and several other subspecies.

A moment later, it saw the familiar concentric circles of Mithila, and the Asura armies massed on its south side, stretching for yojanas in both directions, and yojanas back almost to the banks of the Ganga. It wondered how Ravana had convinced his forces to cross the sacred river. Most Asuras feared the brahman-blessed water, believing it would melt them down to nothingness on contact.

Jatayu itself had lived long enough to know that this wasn't strictly true. It depended on the species of Asura really. For instance, vetaals would indeed melt like running hot wax if they came into contact with Ganga waters. But rakshasas were not affected usually – unless they were vetaal-rakshasa crossbreeds. Jatayu's kind wasn't affected either, but it would still take a very large whip to get it to touch even a wingtip to that sacred body of water. It was sheer folly to attempt such madness; like standing before Shiva and waiting witlessly for his third eye to open.

Jatayu called out the final order and began the spiralling descent that would take it quickest into the city. Now it could clearly see the flashes of white- and ochre-clad mortals assembled in large groups across the city.

Brahmins! They would hardly know what had hit them. In another few seconds, the sky would fall upon them, tearing their soft flesh with bone-hard beaks and sword-sharp claws. The streets of Mithila would run red with brahmin blood tonight.

It was only a few hundred yards from the ground when it felt the massive wave of brahman shakti unleashed. It had time to cry out one last time before being buffeted up, up, up, high above the clouds, higher than it had ever flown before in its five thousand years of existence. It felt its wings tear to shreds and was blanketed by agony.

Then the world vanished from existence.

Bejoo felt the wave hit before he saw it. In fact, he never actually saw it. All he knew was that some tremendous force, the likes of which he had never heard of nor seen before, was sweeping across the entire surface of the earth. It came from behind him, which meant its source was Mithila. But that was all he knew. Then the wave struck him and knocked him off his horse, flinging him to the ground and pressing him flat, like a thousand bigfoot standing on his back.

Ahead of him, the wave rolled on, tearing through the Asura ranks, shredding the nagas to bits so tiny that they were as powdered rang at a Holi festival. The Asura hordes behind the front ranks sensed some awesome force being unleashed and cried out in horror and rage.

Then the aftershock struck Bejoo, even as the wave itself was still rolling across the Asura armies, and he lost consciousness.

From the vantage of the Sage's Brow, the two princes of Ayodhya, Rajkumari Sita and her father, and the body-guard Nakhudi all watched. They saw the deep blue wave of brahman ripple outward from the tower itself, rolling harmlessly over humans and their animal friends and the city and its structures. But when it reached the Asura armies massed on the south bank of the Sarayu, the effect was numbing.

The dense black hordes of Asuras disintegrated as the wave touched them, turning into powder, like the dust-cloud their tramping hoofs and paws had raised on their northward march.

An instant later, as the aftershock hit, the powder itself disintegrated into nothingness. Here and there, particles of coloured light, red, purple-black, green, lingered in the air for a moment, then faded away as well.

In the sky, the Asura bird-host was falling to attack when the wave hit them. Sita saw the leader of the host, a man-vulture-shaped being, buffeted by the first ripples and thrown in an arcing sweep across the bowl of the sky. The rest of the host suffered the same fate as their ground-borne Asura brethren: powdered and then disintegrated.

A moment later, the last echoes of the wave faded away, leaving behind a silence as deafening as the wave itself.

The entire Asura army had vanished from the south bank, leaving no trace that they had ever been there.

Except for the dark hanging mass of the dustcloud that was still visible in the dusky twilight light. That was the

only sign that remained to mark that the great alien army
had ever existed.

Brahmarishi Vishwamitra had kept his face averted as
the wave struck.

Now, he turned and looked southwards, at the vanished
army. Then he raised his gaze to Rama and Lakshman,
who stood, staring together with identical expressions of
shocked numbness. The blue light of brahman was gone
entirely from their faces, making them appear oddly
naked.

'It is done,' said the brahmarishi.

To Sita's surprise, the seer-mage's eyes welled with
tears. He stepped forward and embraced both the princes
at once, his large bony arms encircling the two slender
young torsos easily. He hugged them tight, as tightly as a
father bidding his sons goodbye.

'You have done the impossible,' he said at last, tears
flowing freely down his lined, ancient face. 'You have rid
the world of almost all the evil of Ravana. Never again will
he be able to assemble such a vast army. Surely, he has a
large number of wretched Asuras still extant on his island-
fortress of Lanka, but he will never again be able to
assemble a force vast enough to invade the mortal realm.
Even his vast fleet, Asura-polluted as it was, is gone,
destroyed by the Brahm-astra.'

Rama's voice was hoarse, choked with his own emotion. 'Is it truly over then? The Asura threat to our people?
Is it finally ended?'

Vishwamitra released them both and turned away. Only
Sita saw the seer-mage's face clearly as it looked away
from Rama and Lakshman. The anguish on those ancient
features was unmistakable.

'The threat is ended,' the sage said. But there was no joy
on his face, or in his voice.

GLOSSARY

This 21st-century retelling of *The Ramayana* freely uses words and phrases from Sanskrit as well as other ethnic Indian languages. Many of these have widely varying meanings depending on the context in which they're used – and even depending on whether they were used in times ancient, medieval or present-day. This glossary explains their meanings according to their contextual usage in this book rather than their strict dictionary definitions. AKB.

aagya: permission.

aangan: entrance; courtyard.

aaram: rest.

aarti: prayer ceremony.

aatma: spirit; soul.

aatma-hatya: suicide.

acamana: ritual offering of water to Surya the sun-god at sunrise and sunset.

agar: black gummy stuff of which joss sticks are made.

agarbatti: incense prayer sticks made of agar; joss sticks.

agni: fire; fire-god.

agnihotra: fire-sacrifice; offering to the fire-god agni. Originally, in Vedic times, this meant an animal-sacrifice. Later, as the Vedic faith evolved into vegetarian-favouring Hinduism, it became any ritual fire-offering. The origin of the current-day Hindu practice of anointing a fire with ghee (clarified butter) and other ritual offerings.

Aja-putra: literally, son of Aja, in which Aja was the previous Surya-vansha king of Ayodhya; it was common to refer to Aryas as 'son of (father's name)'; e.g. Rama would be addressed as 'Dasaratha-putra'.

akasa-chamber: from the word 'akasa' meaning sky. A room with the ceiling open to the sky, used for relaxation.

akhada: wrestling square.

akshohini: a division of the army with representation from the four main forces – battle elephants, chariots with archers, armoured cavalry, and infantry.

amrit: nectar of the devas; the elixir of eternal life, one of many divine wonders produced by the churning of the oceans in ancient pre-Vedic times. The central cause of the original hostility between the devas and the Asuras, in which the Asuras sought the amrit in order to gain immortality like the devas but the devas refused them the amrit.

an-anga: bodiless.

anarth ashram: orphanage.

anashya: indestructible.

an-atmaa: soulless.

angoor: grape.

ang-vastra: length of cloth covering upper body – similar to the upper folds of a Roman toga; any bodily garment.

anjan: kohl; kajal.

apsara: any of countless beautiful danseuses in the celestial court of lord Indra, king of the devas.

arghya: the traditional washing of the feet, used to ceremonially welcome a visitor, literally by washing the dust of the road off his feet.

Arya: Literally, noble or pure. Commonly mispelled and mispronounced as 'Aryan.' A group of ancient Indian warrior tribes believed to have flourished for several millennia in the period before Christ. Controversially thought by some historians to have been descended from Teutonics who migrated to the Indian sub-continent and later returned – although current Indian historical scholars reject this view and maintain that the Aryas were completely indigenous to the region. Recent archaeological evidence seems to confirm that the Aryas migrated *from* India to Europe, rather than the other way around. Both views have their staunch supporters.

asana: a yogic posture, or series of postures similar to the kathas of martial arts – which are historically believed to have originated from South-Central India and have the same progenesis as yoga.

ashirwaad: blessings.

Ashok: a boy's given name.

ashubh: inauspicious.

ashwamedha: the horse ceremony. A declaration of supremacy issued by a king, tantamount to challenging one's neighbouring kingdoms to submit to one's superior strength.

astra: weapon.

Asura: anti-god: literally, a-Sura or anti-Sura, where Sura meant the clan of the gods and anyone who stood against them was referred to as an a-Sura. Loosely used to describe any demonic creature or evil being.

atee-sundar: very beautiful. Well done or well said.

atma-brahman: soul force; one's given or acquired spiritual energy.

atman: soul; spirit.

Awadhi: Ayodhyan commonspeak; the local language, a dialect of Hindi.

awamas: the moon's least visible phase.

awamas ki raat: moonless night.

Ayodhya: the capital city of Kosala.

Ayodhya-naresh: master of Ayodhya. King.

ayushmaanbhav: long life; generally used as a greeting from an elder to a younger, as in 'live long.'

baalu: bear (see also rksa).

badmash: rascal, scoundrel, mischievous one.

bagh: big cat, interchangeably used for lion, tiger and most other related species of large, predatory cat.

bagheera: panther or leopard.

baithak-sthan: rest-area; lounge.

balak: boy.

balidaan: sacrifice.

bandara: monkey; any simian species.

barkha: rainstorm.

bete: child.

bhaang: An intoxicating concoction made by mixing the leaf of the poppy plant with hand-churned buttermilk. Typically consumed at Holi celebrations by adult Hindus. Also smoked in hookahs or traditional bongs as pot.

bhaangra: robust and vigorous north Indian (punjabi) folk dance.

bhade bhaiya: older brother.

bhagyavan: blessed one; fortunate woman.

bhai: brother.

bhajan: a devotional chant.

bhakti: devotion.

bharat-varsha: the original name for India; literally, *land of bharata* after the ancient Arya king Bharata.

bhashan: lecture.

bhayanak: frightening, terrifying.

bhes-bhav: physical appearance.

bhojanshalya: dining hall.

bhor: extreme; as in *bhor suvah*: extreme (early) morning.

bhung: useless; negated.

bindi: a blood-red circular dot worn by Hindu women on their foreheads to indicate their married status. Now worn in a variety of colours and shapes as a fashion accessory.

brahmachari: see brahmacharya.

brahmacharya: a boy or man who devotes the first 25 years of his life to prayer, celibacy, and the study of the vedic sciences under the tutelage of a brahmin guru.

brahman: the substance of which all matter is created. Literally, the stuff of existence.

brahmarishi: an enlightened holy man who has attained the highest level of grace; literally, a rishi or holy man, whom Brahma, creator of all things, has blessed.

brahmin: the priestly caste. Highest in order.

buddhi: intellect; mind; intelligence.

chacha: uncle; father's younger brother.

chaddar: sheet.

Chaitra: the month of spring; roughly corresponds to the latter half of March and first half of April.

charas: opium.

chaturta: cleverness.

chaukat: a square. Most Indian houses were designed as a square, with an entrance on one wall and the house occupying the other three walls. In the centre was an open chaukat where visitors (or intruders) could be seen from any room in the house.

chaupat: an ancient Indian war strategy dice game, universally acknowledged to be the original inspiration for chess, played on a flat piece of cloth or board by rolling bone-dice to decide moves, involving pieces representing the four akshohini of the Arya army - elephants, chariot, foot-soldiers, knights.

chillum: toke; a smoking-pipe used to inhale charas (opium).

chini kulang: a variety of bird.

choli: breast-cloth; a garment used to cover a woman's upper body.

chotti: pig-tail.

chowkidari: the act of guarding a person or place like a sentry or chowkidar.

chudail: banshee; female ghost; witch.

chunna: lime-powder or a mixture of lime-powder and water; used to whitewash outer or inner walls; also eaten in edible form in paan or mixed directly with tobacco.

chunnri: a strip of cloth used by a woman to cover her breasts and cleavage, also used to cover the head before elders or during prayer.

chupp-a-chuppi: hide and seek.

crore: one hundred hundred thousand; one hundred lakhs; ten million.

daiimaa: brood-mother, clan-mother, wet nurse, governess. A woman serving first as midwife to the expecting mother, then later as wet-nurse, governess and au pair.

dakshina/guru-dakshina: ritual payment by a kshatriya to a brahmin on demand.

daku: dacoit; highway bandit; jungle thief.

danav: a species of Asura.

darbha: a variety of thick grass.

darshan: the Hindu act of gazing reverentially upon the face of a divine idol, an essential part of worship; literally, *viewing*.

dasya: slave; servant.

Deepavali: the predominant Indian Hindu festival, the festival of lights. Also known as Diwali.

desh: land; country; nation.

deva: god. Several Indian devas have their equivalents in Greek and Norse mythology.

dev-astra: weapon of the devas; divine weapon.

dev-daasi/devdasi: prostitute.

devi: goddess.

dhanush-baan: bow and arrows.

dharma: sacred duty. A morally binding code of behaviour. The cornerstone of the Vedic faith.

dhobi: washerman (of clothes).

dhol: drum.

dollee: palanquin; travelling chair.

dosa: a flat crisp rice-pancake, a staple of South Indian cuisine.

dhoti: a white cotton lower garment, worn usually by Indian men.

diya: clay oil lamp.

drishti: vision; view; sight.

gaddha: donkey.

gaddhi: seat; literally, a cushion.

gaja-gamini: elephant-footed.

gandharva: forest nymph; when malevolent, also a species of Asura.

ganga-jal: sacred Ganges water.

ganja: charas; opium.

garuda: eagle, after the mythic giant magical eagle Garuda, the first-of-his-name, a major demi-god believed to be the creator and patron deity of all birdkind.

gauthan: village; any rural settlement.

gayaka: singer.

Gayatri: a woman's given name; also the most potent mantra of Hindus, recited before beginning any venture, or even at the start of one's day to ensure strength and success.

gharial: a sub-species of reptilian predator unique to the Indian sub-continent, similar to crocodiles and alligators in body but with a sword-shaped mouth.

ghat: literally, low-lying hill. Burning ghat usually refers to the places in which Hindu bodies are traditionally cremated.

gotra: sub-caste.

govinda: goatherd.

gulmohur: a species of Asian tree that produces beautiful red flowers in winter.

guru/guruji: a teacher, generally associated with a sage. The 'ji' is a sign of respect; it literally means 'sir', and can be added after any male name or title: eg, Ramaji.

guru-dakshina: see dakshina.

guru-dev: guru who is as a god, or deva; divine teacher.

gurukul: A guru's hermitage for scholars; a forest ashram school where students resided, maintaining the ashram and its grounds while being taught through lectures in the open air.

gurung: a vareity of bird.

hai: ave; hail; woe. An exclamation.

halwai: maker of sweets.

hatya: murder.

havan: sacrificial offering.

hawaldar: constable.

Holi: a major Indian festival and feast day, celebrated to mark the end of winter and the first day of spring, the last rest day before the start of the harvest season; celebrated with the throwing of coloured powders and coloured waters symbolising the colours of spring, and the eating of sweetmeats (mithai) and the drinking of bhaang.

Ikshvaku: the original kshatriya ancestral clan from which the Suryavansha line sprang. After the founder, Ikshvaaku.

imli ka butta: tamarind.

Indra: god of thunder and war. Equivalent to the Norse god Thor or the Greek god Ares.

indra-dhanush: literally, Indra's bow; a rainbow.

ishta: religious offering.

jadugar: magician.

jagganath: relentless and unstoppable Hindu god of war; another name for Ganesha; juggernaut.

Jai: boy's given name; hail.

Jai Mata Ki: Praise be to the Mother-Goddess.

Jai Shree: Praise to be Sri (or Shree), Divine Creator.

jaise aagya: as you wish; your wish is my command.

jal murghi: a variety of Indian bird; literally, water-fowl.

jal-bartans: vessels for drinking water.

jaldi: quickly; in haste.

jalebi: Indian sweet, made by pouring dough into a tureen of boiling oil in spiralling shapes, removed, then drenched in sugar-syrup.

Jat: a proud, violently inclined, North Indian clan.

jatayu: vulture, after Jatayu, the first-of-its-name, the giant hybrid man-vulture, second only to Garuda in his leadership of birdkind.

jhadi-buti: literally, herbs and roots; herbal medicines.

jhadoo: Indian broom.

jhilli: a variety of Indian bird.

ji: yes (respectfully).

johar ka roti: a flat roasted pancake made from barley-flour.

johari: jeweller.

kaand: a section of a story; literally, a natural joint on a long stick of sugarcane or bamboo, used to mark off a count.

kabbadi: a game played by children and adults alike. India's official national sport.

kachua: tortoise.

kaho: speak.

kai-kai: harsh cawing sound.

kairee: a raw green mango, used to make pickle.

kajal: kohl.

kala: black.

kala jaadu: black magic.

kala kendra: art council.

kalakaar: artist.

kalarappa: ancient South Indian art of man-to-man combat, universally acknowledged to be the progenitor of Far Eastern martial arts – learned by visiting Chinese delegates and later adapted and evolved into the modern martial arts.

Kali: the goddess of vengeance. An avatar of the universal devi.

Kali-Yuga: the Age of Kali, prophesied to be the last and worst age of human civilisation.

Kama: god of love. The equivalent of the Greek Eros or sometimes Cupid.

kamasutra: the science of love.

karmic: pertaining to one's karma.

karya: deeds.

kasturi: deer-musk.

katha: story.

kathputhli: puppet.

kavee: poet.

kavya: poem.

kesar: saffron, extremely valuable then and now as an essential spice used in Indian cooking; traditionally given as a gift by kings to one another; worth several times more than its weight in gold.

khaas: special; unique.

khatiya: cot; bed.

khazana: treasure-trove; treasury.

khottey-sikkey: counterfeit coin/s.

khukhri: a kind of North Indian machete, favoured by the hilly gurkha tribes.

kintu: but; however.

kiran: ray (usually of light); a girl or boy's given name.

koel/koyal: Indian song-bird.

Kosala: a North-Central Indian kingdom believed to have flourished for several millennia before the start of the Christian era.

koyal: Indian song-bird.

krodh: wrath.

kshatriya: warrior caste. The highest of four castes in ancient India, the armed defenders of the tribe, skilled in martial combat and governance. Kings were always chosen from this caste. Later, with the Hindu shift towards pacifism and non-violence, the brahmin or priestly caste became predominant, with kshatriyas shifting into the second-highest position in contemporary India.

kumbha-rakshasa: dominant species of demons, lording over their fellow rakshasas as well as other Asura species because of their considerable size and strength; named after Kumbhakarna, the mammoth giant brother of Ravana, who grew to mountainous proportions owing to an ancient curse that condemned him to absorb the physical mass of any living thing he killed or ate. Unlike Kumbhakarna, the kumbhas (for short), do not grow larger with each kill or meal.

kumkum: red powder.

kundalee: horoscope.

kurta: an upper garment with a round neck, full sleeves. Like a shirt but slipped over the head like a tee shirt.

kusa or kusalavya: a lush variety of grass found in Northern and North-Central India, long-bladed and thick.

lakh: a hundred thousand.

langot: loin-cloth.

lingam: a simple unadorned representation of Lord Shiva, usually made of roughly carved black stone, shaped like an upward moulded pillar of stone with a blunt head that is traditionally anointed. Typically regarded by some Western scholars as a phallic object; a controversial view which has been repeatedly disproven by Indian scholars and study of ancient Vedic texts.

lohit: iron.

lota: a small metal pot with a handle, used to carry water.

lungi: a common lower-body garment; a sheet of cloth wrapped around the waist once or more times and tucked in or knotted, extending to the ankles; unisexual but more often worn by men.

maa: mother.

maang: the center point of the hairline on a person's forehead.

magarmach: Indian river crocodile.

maha: great. As in maha-mantra, maha-raja, maha-bharata, maha-guru, maha-dev, etc.

mahadev: great one.

mahal: palace; mansion; manse.

maharuk: a variety of Indian tree.

maha-mantra: supreme mantra or verse, such as the maha-mantra Gayatri. A potent catechism to ward off evil and ensure the success of one's efforts.

mahout: elephant-handler.

mahseer: a variety of Indian fish.

manch: literally, platform or dais; also, a gathering of elders or leaders of a community.

mandala: a purified proscribed circle.

mandap: a ceremonial dais on which prayer rituals and other ceremonies are conducted.

mandir: temple.

mangalsutra: a black thread necklace worn by a married woman as proof of her marital status.

mann: mind.

mantra: an invocation to the devas.

mantri: minister.

marg: road.

marg-darshak: guide, mentor, guru.

marg-saathi: fellow-traveller; companion on the road.

martya: human; all things pertaining to humankind.

mashaal: torch.

masthi: mischief.

matka: earthen pot.

maya: illusion.

mayini: witch, demoness.

melas: country fairs, carnivals.

mithaigalli: sweetmeat lane; a part of the market where the halwais (mithai-makers) line up their stalls.

mithun: Indian bison; a species of local buffalo.

mochee: cobbler.

mogra: a strongly scented white flower that blooms very briefly; worn by Indian women in their hair.

moksh: salvation.

mudra: gesture, especially during a dance performance; a symbolic action.

muhurat: an auspicious date to initiate an important undertaking. Even today in India, all important activities-marriages, coronations, the start of a a new venture-are always scheduled on a day and time found suitable according to the panchang (Hindu almanac) or muhurat calender.

mujra: a sensual dance.

naachwaali: dancing-girl or courtesan.

naashta: breakfast; also, an early evening refreshment (equivalent of the British 'tea').

naga: any species of snake; a species of Asura.

nagin: female cobra.

namak: salt.

namaskar/namaskaram: greetings. Usually said while joining one's palms together and bowing the head forward slightly. A mark of respect.

namaskara: see namaskar.

nanga: naked.

Narak: Hell.

naresh: lord, master. A royal title used to address a maharaja, the equivalent of 'your highness'.

natya: dance.

nautanki: song-and-dance melodrama, a cheap street play.

navami: an infant's naming day.

neem: an Indian tree whose leaves and bark are noted for their proven, highly efficacious medicinal properties.

nidra: an exalted, transcendental meditative state, a kind of yogic sleep.

odhini: woman's garment used specifically to cover the head, similar to pallo.

Om Hari Swaha: praised be to the Creator, Amen.

Om Namay: Praise be the Name of . . .

paan: the leaf of the betelnut plant, in which could be wrapped a variety of edible savouries, especially pieces of supari and chewing tobacco.

pahadi: a hill dweller or mountain man. Often used colloquially to connote a rude, ill-educated and ill-mannered person.

paisa: in the singular, a penny, the smallest individual unit of coinage, then and now. In the generic, money.

palas: a variety of Indian flowering tree.

pallo: the top fold of a woman's sari, used to conceal the breasts and cleavage of the wearer.

panchayat: a village committee usually of five (panch) persons.

parantu: but; however.

pari: angel; fairy.

patal: the lowermost level of narak, the lowest plane attainable in existence.

patang: kite.

payal: a delicately carved chain of tiny bells, usually of silver, worn as an anklet by women.

peda: a common, highly popular Indian sweet made of milk and sugar.

peepal: a species of tree with hanging roots and vines.

phanas: jackfruit.

phera: ritual circling of a sacred fire.

phool mala: flower-garland.

pisaca; a species of Asura.

pitashree: revered father.

pitchkarees: water-spouts; portable hand-pumps used by children in play.

pooja: prayer.

Pradhan-mantri: Prime Minister.

Prajapati: Creator; The One Who Made All Living Things; also used as term for butterflies, which are believed to represent the spirit of the Creator.

pranaam: a high form of namaste or greeting.

pranayam: a yogic method of breathing that enables biofeedback and control of the senses.

prarthana: intense, devout prayer.

prasadam: food blessed by the devas in the course of prayer; a sacramental offering.

prashna-uttar: question-answer.

pravachan: monologue or lecture, usually by a guru or mentor; to be imbibed in rapt silence.

Prithvi: Earth.

pundit: priest; master of religious ceremonies.

purnima: full moon; full moon night.

purohit: see pundit.

putra: son.

raat ki rani: colloquial name for a common Indian flower that blooms only at night; literally, 'queen of the night'.

rabadi: a popular Indian dessert of thickened sweetened milk, overboiled until the water drains and only thick layers of cream remain.

raja: king; liege; clan-chieftain.

raje: a more affectionate form of 'raja'. The 'e' suffix to a name ending in a vowel indicates intimacy and warmth.

raj-gaddhi: throne; seat of the king.

rajkumar: prince.

rajkumari: princess.

raj-marg: king's way; royally protected highway or road.

rajya sabha: king's council of ministers, a meeting of the same.

rakshak: protector.

rakshasas: a variety of Asura; roughly equivalent to the Western devil or demon. Singular/male: rakshas or rakshasa. Singular/feminine: rakshasi. Plural/both: rakshasas.

rang: colour; usually, coloured powder.

rang-birangi: colourful.

rangoli: the traditional Indian art of creating elaborate patterns on floors, usually at the entrances of domiciles, by carefully sprinkling coloured powder.

ras: juice.

rath/s: chariot/s.

rawa: a type of flour.

rishi: sadhu.

rksa: black mountain bear.

rudraksh: red beads, considered sacred by Hindus.

rupaiya: rupee. The main unit of currency in India even today.

rudraksh maala: a Hindu rosary or

prayer-bead necklace strung with rudraksh beads.

sabha: committee; parliament.

sadhu: literally, 'most holy' or 'most auspicious'; also used to denote a penitent hermit; holy man.

sadhuni: a female sadhu or woman whose life is dedicated to prayer and worship.

saivite: worshipper of Lord Shiva.

sakshi: a woman's close female friend.

samabhavimudra: celestial meditative stance.

samadhi: memorial.

samasya: problem, situation.

samay chakra: the chariot wheel of Time, turning relentlessly as god rides across the universe. A cornerstone of Hindu belief.

samjhe: 'understood?'

sandesh: message.

sandhyavandana: evening oblation; ritual offering of water and prayer to the sun at sunset; see also acamana.

Sanskriti; Arya culture and tradition.

saprem: supreme.

Satya-Yuga: Age of Truth.

sautan: husband's second wife; one's rival for a husband's affections.

savdhaan: caution.

senapati: commander of armed forces, a general.

sesa: rabbit.

shaasan: a type of low-lying couch with a backrest or armrest.

shagun: a variety of Indian tree; an auspicious event or occurrence.

shakti: strength, power, force. Used to describe divine power of a god, as in Kali-shakti or Goddess Kali's power.

shama: forgiveness. Colloquially, 'excuse me'.

Shani: god of weapons and destruction. Equivalent to the Greek god Saturn.

shantam: quiet, calm, serene; literally, 'be at peace'.

shanti: colloquialisation of shantam.

shastra: a science; an area of study.

shatru: enemy.

shikhsa: education; learning.

shishya/s: student/s of a guru.

shraap: curse; terrible invocation.

Shravan: a month in the Hindu calendar; usually the month of the rains; also, a boy's given name.

siddh: successful; blessed.

silbutta: grinding stone and board; pestle and mortar.

sindhoor: a blood-red powder used in marital rituals. Traditionally applied by a husband on his wife's hairline (maang) to indicate her status as a married woman. Hence, unmarried women and widows are not permitted to wear sindhoor. Although a bindi (dot) is now used as a modern equivalent and worn universally as a fashion accessory.

siphai: soldier; guard.

sitaphal: a variety of Indian fruit with sweet milky pods.

sloka: sacred verse.

smriti; hidden; secret

soma: wine made from the soma plant; a popular wine in ancient India.

sona: gold.

stree-hatya: murder of a woman.

sudra: the lowest caste, usually relegated to cleaning, hunting, tanning and other undesirable activities. The lowest in order.

suhaag raat: wedding night.

supari: betelnut.

Suryavansha: the Solar Dynasty, a line of kings that ruled over Kosala; literally, the clan of the sun-god, Surya.

sutaar: carpenter.

swaha: a term used to denote the auspicious and successful completion of a sloka or recitation; corresponds to the Latin "Amen".

swami: master; lord; naresh.

Swarga-lok/a: Heaven.

swayamvara: A ceremonial rite during which a woman of marriagable age was permitted to select a suitable husband. Eligible men wishing to apply would line up to be inspected by the bride-to-be. On finding a suitable mate, she would indicate her choice by placing the garland around his neck.

taal: rhythm; beat.

tabla: an Indian percussion instrument, a kind of drum sounded by striking the heel of the palm and the tips of the fingers.

tamasha: a show; performance; common street play.

tandav: the frenzied sexually charged celestial dance of Shiva the Destroyer by which he generates enough shakti to destroy the entire universe that Brahma the Creator may recreate it once again.

tandoor: an Indian barbecue.

tann: body.

tantrik: a worshipper of physical energy and sensual arts.

tapasvi: one who endures penance, usually with an aim to acquiring spritual prowess.

tapasya: penance.

teko: prostrate one's head, touching the forehead to the ground as a demonstration of devotion and obeisance.

thakur: lord; landowner.

thali: a round metal platter used for eating meals or for storing prayer items. The Indian equivalent of the Western 'dinnner plate'.

thrashbroom: a broom with harsh bristles, used for beating rugs and mattresses.

three worlds: Swarga-lok, Prithvi, Narak. Literally, Heaven, Earth, Hell.

tilak: ash or colour anointment on one's forehead, indicating that one has performed one's ritual prayers and sacrifices and is blessed with divine grace to perform one's duties.

tirth yatra: pilgrimage.

Treta-Yuga: Age of Reason.

trimurti: the holy Hindu trinity of Brahma, Vishnu and Shiva, respectively the Creator, Preserver and Destroyer.

trishul: trident.

tulsi: a variety of Indian plant known for its efficacious medicinal properties and regarded as a symbol of a happy and secure household; always grown in the courtyard of a house and prayed to daily by the woman of the house; also, a woman's given name.

upanisad: an ancient sacred Indian text.

uraga: a species of Asura.

vaid: physician trained in the art of Ayur-vaidya, the ancient Indian study of herbal medicine and healing.

vaisya: the trading or commercial caste. Third in order.

vajra: lightning bolt.

van: forest, jungle. Pronounced to rhyme with 'one'.

vanar: bandara; simian; any monkey species, but most commonly used to denote apes, especially the intelligent anthromorphic talking apes of this saga, forthcoming in Armies of Hanuman; Book Four of The Ramayana.

varna: caste; literally, occupational level or group.

varsha: rain; a woman's given name.

Veda: the sacred writings of the ancient Arya sages, comprising meditations, prayers, observations and scientific treatises on every conceivable human area of interest; the basis of Indian culture.

vetaal: a species of Asura; somewhat similar to the western concept of 'vampire' but not usually synonymous.

vidya: knowledge.

vinaashe: destruction; death.

yagna: religious fire-ritual.

yaksi: a female Yaksa; a species of Asura capable of shape-shifting; closely corresponding to (but not identical to) the western concept of Elves.

Yama: Yama-raj, lord of death and king of the underworld; literally Death personified as a large powerfully built dark-skinned man with woolly hair, who rides a black buffalo and carries a bag of souls.

yash: fame; adoration; admiration.

yoganidra: the supreme state of transcendence while meditating, usually indicated by the eyes being partly open yet seeing only the apparent nothingness of brahman; a divine near-sleep-like state.

yojana: a measurement of distance in ancient India, believed to have been equivalent to around nine miles.

yoni: female sexual organ; the 'yang' of 'yin and yang'.

yuga: age; historical period.